A String of Pearls

A String of Pearls

Ben Baglio

McKenna Publishing Group
San Luis Obispo, California

A String of Pearls

McKenna Publishing Group
San Luis Obispo, California, USA

First Edition 2002

Second Edition 2010

Printed in the United States of America

10 9 8 7 6 5 4 3 2

ISBN: 978-1-932172-34-8

LCCN: 2010921186

First Edition cover design by Patrick Space
Second Edition cover design by Leslie Parker
Interior design by Leslie Parker

Visit us on the Web at: www.mckennapubgrp.com

"Arma virumque cano"
  To Larry, for North Africa, Sicily, and Italy
    To Patsy, for Guadalcanal and Pelelieu
      To Sammy, for Utah Beach, The Bulge, and the Rhine

Thank You

Also by Ben Baglio

Kids Are The Easy Part

I'll Be Seeing You

American Patrol

It's Been A Long, Long Time

Prelude

The day dawned brilliantly. The vernal equinox was less than a week away, and the portents of spring were everywhere in New York. A walk through Central Park would detect forsythia buds prepared to burst, and crocus breaking through the warming earth. It was the season of renewal, of birth, and it was a fitting time to celebrate the conception of another of man's most magnificent structures. As Assistant Secretary of the Navy, thirty-two year old Franklin D. Roosevelt was the government dignitary designated to commemorate the laying of the keel of another super dreadnought battleship. It was the kind of task he relished. Roosevelt loved his job, the Navy, and the magnificent ships it was building to dominate the seas of the world.

Roosevelt braved the chill morning air dressed in a derby and woolen topcoat with hundreds of other similarly insulated guests as they gathered in the enormous building ways, one of the numerous wombs of the Brooklyn Navy Yard. Captain Albert Gleaves, commandant of the facility, smiled genuinely as the USS *Washington*, the receiving ship whose role was to announce this particular birth to the world, fired seventeen rounds from her saluting guns. Roosevelt's patented jutting-jaw smile was never broader as a crane lowered a fifty-foot long steel plate into position that would form the battleship's keel. It was followed by two smaller plates to the fore and rear.

Three-year-old Henry Williams, Jr., whose father was a naval architect employed by the yard, ran out on cue to put the ceremonial nickle-plated bolts through the pre-drilled holes in each of the plates, formally connecting them. These bolts were then removed, replaced by steel bolts, and given to the boy as a memento of the occasion. Then for some inexplicable reason, young Henry dashed directly for Mr. Roosevelt, and held the man's index finger for the longest time, wearing a smile as broad as the Assistant Secretary's. The genuinely amused Roosevelt, who gracefully posed for several scores of photographs taken with young Williams, bonded to him.

Roosevelt strode the ways with Gleaves as photographers and Mrs. Williams followed close by. Still smiling, he said to Gleaves, "So this is to be Battleship Number 39. From what I've read, she'll be enormous!"

"Yes, Mr. Secretary, indeed she will be. Her sister, the *Pennsylvania*, is

nearing completion in Newport News. We haven't received official word as
to what her name is to be, but we hear rumors that she'll be christened *North
Carolina*. The Secretary of Defense would be pleased for her to bear the name
of his home state."

"Those are just rumors, Captain. Mere titillations to keep the press busy
embellishing them. While old Joe Daniels would no doubt drip with pride by
naming BB-39 after his fair state, the president and I have decided on a different name."

"Are you at liberty to share it with me?"

"I can't tell you, Captain, because that will make you a member of our
conspiracy," Roosevelt laughed. "But I'll give you a hint," he said, playing to
the press. "She'll bear the name of one of our great states of the Union!" The
reporters bore ever nearer, pencils to pads, stumbling over each other for the
scoop.

"Begging your pardon, sir, but knowing that everyone of our BB's is named
after a state, that's like telling me ice is cold!"

"All right, all right," Roosevelt guffawed. "I'll give you another. This will
test your knowledge of American History. If you don't get it, I'll think none the
worse of you, as I assume that Naval Academy graduates can look things up."

"You assume well, sir. Now, the hint, please?"

Roosevelt cupped his hand, and whispered in Gleaves' ear, with little Henry
at full attention. "This state came into the Union in 1912. Just two years ago."

Gleaves bowed his head in thought. "That would be New Mexico or...I
think it's Oklahoma," he muttered, barely audibly. "No, it can't be Oklahoma.
We already have a battleship that will bear that name."

When he lifted his chin from his chest, Gleaves was momentarily surprised at Roosevelt's apparent disappearance. He looked to his right to see the
tall Assistant Secretary on a knee, whispering in the ear of Henry Williams,
Jr., whose precious child's smile widened as Roosevelt's breath tickled his ear.

"Now then, my good Captain Henry, tell Captain Gleaves what we will
call this great ship," Roosevelt said, sticking his chest out with pride. "Go on,
Captain," he said, gesturing with his index finger, which was still attached to
young Williams, in the direction of Gleaves.

Henry motioned Gleaves down to him, the newsmen pressing nearer. The
captain good-naturedly went along with the game, as the child was taking absolute delight in it. Henry took the opportunity to stroke Gleaves' beard once,
to the great amusement of the clean-shaven Roosevelt, then cupped his hand
to Gleaves' ear. When he noted members of the press corps still inching forward to hear this great secret, Henry became even more clandestine, and put

his other hand up to Gleaves' ear. Bringing his little face closer, he murmured, "Arisamona." Then, after accomplishing this great feat, he put both hands in his pocket, winked at Roosevelt, and rocked on the balls of his little feet. Even the press corps was forced to laugh.

At 608 feet long, almost a hundred feet wide, displacing 32,000 tons and mounting twelve fourteen-inch guns, the biggest afloat in four armored triple turrets, "Arisamona" would be one of the biggest battleships ever constructed when she was put into commission two years later. She was matched in size and firepower only by her sisters in the United States Navy.

Chapter 1

Yuri Popov hurried along beside his parents as they moved from the main street of their little village of Vitebsk onto the lake's broad shore. His hands were numb with cold, but the anxious look on his father's face told him he shouldn't release his grip. Yuri's heavy boots and shorter stride made it difficult to keep up trudging through the deep snow. He didn't complain: the fear pervading the crowd intuitively told him more was at stake than the discomfort of a little boy.

The scarf that had been meant to cover his fair face had long since slipped to his shoulders. The mucous from his runny nose froze on his upper lip, but he knew mother would clean it off when she could. It was impossible now because she was holding his infant sister, Nina.

Yuri looked up at the moon, and smiled at its stark beauty. Its full face made the snow and the surrounding hills and their forests blend in a tranquil glow with the frozen lake. The lake was so much fun. In summer, he caught eels with his father and swam all day. This winter he skated well enough to compete with the other boys in hockey. For some reason, though, the lake made him feel uneasy and vulnerable tonight.

Quite unexpectedly the crowd halted, and murmuring stilled.

Farther down the road, troops emerged from the forests—black shadows on horses whose breath vaporized into silvery steam. The nervous flock turned back to the village, only to face the horror of leaping flames and smoke billowing out of their homes and shops. Heavy hoof beats coming from the village turned their tense calm to mounting terror. Yuri looked to mother for a clue and saw tears streaming down her pretty face. Father pulled her close and lifted Yuri.

Yuri could clearly see the riders coming at them with raised sabers. Screaming people ran in all directions. A large man blind with panic knocked into his mother, who fell, leaving little Nina rolling from her arms. Father yelled at Yuri to run for the forest, and then ran to help mother and Nina.

Father had barely taken a step when he disappeared beneath a huge horse, whose rider was violently flaying his saber. Yuri felt his face splattered with something warm. At the sound of a gunshot the horse reared, dumping its rider into the snow. His pistol fell from its holster and the saber from his hand. Yuri hesitated only long enough to grab the fallen man's weapons.

The horsemen who had burned the village arrived to surround the crowd, preventing others from sheltering among the trees that now protected Yuri. He struggled to catch sight of his family, but no one was left standing. Most of the horsemen started down the road leading away from the village. Two stayed to complete the task of murdering the still-living wounded. Yuri dared not take a breath.

The two went to their dead comrade. They didn't know his weapons were now in the hands of eight-year-old Yuri Popov. A victim nearby stirred and called mother's name. One of the horsemen dismounted, walked casually to the groaning man, and shot him in the head. Yuri Popov's wide open eyes didn't flinch at the pistol's report. The horsemen laughed as they retrieved their fallen comrade's body and placed it across the rump of one of their horses.

Yuri aimed the pistol carefully. Rage made it difficult to steady the weapon, but he managed to site its barrel on the nearest horse and squeeze the trigger. The huge animal reared in agony, tossing its rider to the snow. Quickly, he cocked the pistol, and fired at the second horse, which crashed onto its rider. The man screamed as the animal's weight crushed his ribs. He again cocked the pistol as he walked cautiously to the first rider, struggling to get up. He fired a round directly into his chest from five feet away. He went to the second man crushed under the mortally wounded horse, whose death screams pierced the otherwise grim calm of the night. The man gasped for breath. Yuri placed the pistol at the horse's ear and fired. He stared at the rider, whose sparse breath raged epithets from a bloody, bearded mouth.

Yuri bent to kiss the cold face of mother, and covered Nina's crushed body with her blanket. He gazed at the disfigured face of father, whose blood oozed over the white snow.

Yuri took the saber from beneath his coat, and walked back to the man trapped under his horse. The horseman's eyes burned with fury at the sight of him, but the fury turned to terror when Yuri took the saber and swung it down with all his might. The razor-sharp blade sent the severed head rolling. Yuri returned the saber to its owner by burying it in his chest, but he pocketed the revolver. He wiped the frozen mucous from his lip on the man's coat.

Yuri returned to the first man and removed his gold-braided topcoat. Under it in a beautifully tooled holster was another pistol. It was like none he had ever seen. This one had no rotating cylinder to hold the bullets. It was sleek and black and looked quite menacing. He tried to manipulate it but thought better of forcing the issue. He tucked it his belt under the thick woolen sweater while trying to determine what the *COLT* engraved on its handle meant.

He spread the great coat on the snow beside the bodies of his family and sat on it, cradling the baby and singing their mother's favorite lullaby. Tears wouldn't come as much as he wished for them. He wretched, and his head was feverish, but the water didn't flow. Lying down with Nina next to him, he pulled the great coat over them and fell asleep with the moon as the only other mourner.

Voices awakened him. He peered into the dawn while his hand felt for the revolver. He found himself staring into eyes as blue as his own above a slender nose that sat atop a neatly trimmed brown mustache. This man, too, wore a topcoat, but it was brown, not the gray of the horsemen's, and his peaked cap had a red band around it.

"What's this?" the man asked.

Yuri couldn't understand a word he said.

"I say, are you quite all right?" The smiling face indicated he meant Yuri no harm, so he thought it best to give himself up. He thrust the revolver toward him barrel-first, but the man's expression quickly turned to alarm, and he jumped back to land with a thump squarely on his rear. He was about to reach for his own sidearm when he saw the child laugh. He joined him in his laughter as he carefully picked up the revolver the boy tossed to him.

Lieutenant Chad Eversole of British Army Intelligence had made a new friend. He helped the youngster to his feet and began walking him over to a small truck. Yuri pulled him back to the gray topcoat and uncovered the tiny bundle. "Nina," he said.

Eversole had fought throughout the World War, seeing sights and carnage to cause madness, but he never flinched from the task at hand. The death of this family had his chin quivering. He touched the boy's stony face, and shook his head.

The little boy took Eversole's hands from his face. He picked up the tiny body and carried it to mother. He pulled father's body closer, so all three were touching. He tenderly kissed each forehead, and turned to Eversole, his hand out.

"Yuri Popov," he said, almost defiantly.

"Chad," Eversole said, repeating the gesture. He looked away so the boy wouldn't see the tears on his cheeks.

"It isn't getting any easier, is it Chad?" his commanding officer said, waiting in the warmth of the truck's cab.

"No, Colonel, it's not. It's about time we went home. We're giving the bloody monarchists free reign by supporting them over Lenin's Bolshevik mob, and all their troops do is slaughter villagers. The Romanoffs are dead, and so is our argument."

"Ah, but Parliament disagrees. Churchill has made speech after speech about…"

"Damn Churchill! I'm surprised anyone still gives that windbag the time of day after what he did at Gallipoli! I was there! We didn't have a chance, just like we don't have a chance now. It's beyond us!" Eversole stroked Yuri's thick blond hair. The boy seemed alarmed at his outburst. "What makes us think we'll succeed in bowing the Russians?" he said in a softer voice. "They've repelled every invader, and they'll repel us as well, even though we're doing it sub rosa by supporting a dead monarchy. The World War has been over for three years, yet here we are still fighting, occupying a land where we have no business, all to keep the status quo."

"You ought to run for Parliament, Chad."

"I have a home—in the army. This poor little bloke doesn't, all thanks to the fat bottoms who sit in those hallowed seats," he said, watching Yuri munch on a honey-coated scone.

While Yuri couldn't follow his savior's remarks, he did understand that he was as alone in the world as anyone could get. It might make this Chad happier if he gave up the pistol in his belt, the barrel of which was pressing uncomfortably against his penis as he sat in the cramped cab. But he thought better of it. Others might come after him when there was no one to help. He would never be caught in that situation again.

Yuri drifted off to sleep as the truck headed westward. Eversole put his arm around the boy. He continued to stroke his hair and tried to make him as comfortable as he could. He found delight in taking care of this small, brave survivor. Though a bachelor, Eversole resolved to look after Yuri Popov's future.

"I say, Colonel, do you think there's room at Eton for a young Russian emigre?"

The colonel laughed. "There was room for you, Chad. There will be room for him."

Chapter 2

September 8, 1921
Campobello Island, Maine

"Eleanor, would you see to getting me a cup of tea?"

"Yes, Franklin. It will be right there," she called from the kitchen. The heavy cough that followed each of his utterances wasn't going away, despite numerous medications. He complained of severe pains in his joints, and now, peculiarly, in his thighs and calves. The cook poured boiling water into a mug that held an Earl Gray tea bag. Eleanor added honey and brought it to her husband, who sat covered with a blanket at a window watching his children frolic on the beach. He looked worse with each passing day.

Franklin Delano Roosevelt had been driving himself into this state of exhaustion for the past twelve months. In his thirty-ninth year of life, he had been nominated by his party to run on its ticket for vice-president with James Cox. Their message was ill-received by Americans, who especially wanted no part of the League of Nations the Democratic team supported. European problems should be solved by Europeans, and government was getting out of hand with all its regulations. That was the theme that carried the day for Harding's Republicans in 1920. Even with Roosevelt criss-crossing the country on a whistle-stop rampage, their team was defeated by seven million votes. He assured Eleanor that he didn't feel the least bit downhearted. His smile and jutting chin confirmed that statement.

Roosevelt even relaxed hard. Vacationing on Campobello Island was anything but a respite, what with his friends overrunning the estate and sailing from dawn to dusk. A week ago he had fallen overboard into the cold Maine water in a freakish accident. He made fun of his clumsiness, but he couldn't warm up, even late into the evening as he sat bundled in a blanket close to a roaring fire. The next day he was diagnosed with grippe, but Eleanor sensed something more ailed him. She had made plans to have him examined in Boston. He was never well again.

October 15, 1921
Boston

He tried to be buoyant and cheerful. The nurses laughed at his self-deprecating jokes and his hearty laughter, but deep in his heart Franklin D.

Roosevelt became a broken man when the doctor uttered the word *polio*. All his hopes and plans to build his country's future seemed to crash and burn. Yet, as the days lingered on and he wheeled himself around the hospital, he found himself face-to-face with the America he heretofore had known only remotely through some novel or policy statement. Here were crippled children, orphans, young and old rotting with every disease that afflicts the human condition, including loneliness, despair, and heartbreak. He talked to them, some of whom recognized him from the recent campaign, and he discovered that his resolve to improve their lot grew stronger each day. If withered legs prevented leading them in a march, he would carry them on his broad shoulders. His brilliant mind raced for ideas, accelerating the healing process of his body.

————

"Ah, Louis! So good of you to come! How are you, old chum?" Roosevelt extended his hand. Louis McHenry was Roosevelt's oldest political adviser and trusted friend. Eleanor thought him dour and severe, but he never failed to bring cheer to her husband, or challenge his argumentative spirit.

"Franklin, you can't run for president on the pity ticket. This polio thing was a bad choice."

"I thought you'd say something inappropriate, Louis, and you didn't let me down," Roosevelt laughed.

"Here," McHenry said tossing his friend the *New York Times*. "I brought it all the way from New York. I didn't want you to read any of the conservative Boston press and change your thinking."

"It would take more than that," Franklin replied. "This hospital taught me as much as my four years at Harvard about this thing we call America."

While Eleanor engaged McHenry in conversation, Roosevelt read the headline story in the November 14, 1921 edition. It reported the opening meeting of the Washington Naval Conference. Secretary of State Charles Evans Hughes hoped the session would limit the size and structure of each country's navy, assuming that war could be averted by slowing the race to build offensive firepower in the form of battleships.

"It's doomed to failure."

"What's that, dear?" Eleanor asked.

"This treaty. Will the proud naval tradition of Great Britain bow to limits? How can the Royal Navy preserve the Empire without its big stick? The Japanese are only held back from expansion into the Far East territories of Britain and France by a weak treaty. The British are building the Japanese battleships and training their crews. Then they use Japanese money to build their own battleships so they can keep the Japanese from doing what we all know they want to do—expand into Asia. All those Pacific islands the Japs got from Germany as the spoils of the World War would make great forward fleet bases."

"You're thinking like a president, my friend," McHenry said.

"You bet I am," Roosevelt stated, returning to the paper. "And another thing: how can the Japanese keep pace with us in constructing a fleet? They have only the resources in materiel we send them. We, and the British. It seems they will stand alone. The British have to do as we wish, as their only hope to hang on to their Empire is to have us support them against Japan. The Japanese hope to buy time by renewing their treaty with England."

"Sounds like a real corundrum," McHenry said, reading over Roosevelt's shoulder.

"No; it's change, pure and simple. Everyone is trying to keep as close to the status quo to avoid getting hurt, but there are always winners and losers."

"Who will lose?"

Roosevelt thought for a moment. "Initially, the Japanese; eventually, the whole world." He noted a small story on the bottom of the *Times* first page, involving the navy's efforts to turn a collier called the *Jupiter* into a ship designed to launch and retrieve airplanes at sea. Fascinated, he read on. A bright young officer, Captain Chester Nimitz, would work to incorporate the ship, to be renamed the *Langley*, into fleet operations. Roosevelt's mind raced with possibilities. He remembered reading about an army officer by the name of Billy Mitchell who had been sinking old battleships with planes all summer. He was giving the admirals fits.

"Now this fellah Nimitz wants to fly airplanes from ships. I don't think the battleships will stand a chance."

"Excuse me, Franklin?" Eleanor said.

"Airplane carriers! They will be the offensive weapons of future wars. My, I feel better!"

And to Eleanor, he looked better. At last he realized his brain wasn't paralyzed. She decided to talk him into running for the governorship of New York; so would all his friends, despite the protests of his doting mother. His vitality was again intoxicating.

Cambridge, Massachusetts

Another convivial individual was clowning in the living room of a Harvard classmate. Japan had sent Captain Isoroku Yamamoto to learn what he could as an academic, and to act as a military liaison with the negotiating team in Washington. He was one of the few who realized the Anglo countries would band together in their distrust of the yellow man, and that the treaty, no matter how genuinely fair it might seem in world opinion, would not serve the interests of his country. Yet he was totally enamored with America, and its unbelievable industrial capacity. He realized that Japan must follow a political course to gain dominance in the East while remaining as valuable a friend to America as the colonial Great Britain was. The means were puzzling, yet do it they must, for Japan would lose a long-term military engagement against the industrial capacity of the United States. For now, though, Yamamoto felt obliged to return the favor of his host's invitation by breaking the ice at this social gathering. He placed his head in the seat cushion of a chair and athletically hauled his body up in a headstand that would have made a gymnast proud. The guests roared.

Yamamoto carried a deck of cards, and a lucky piece of splintered decking contained in a silver amulet on his key chain. The piece of wood came from the leg wound he suffered in the Imperial Japanese Navy's great victory at Tsushima, where the Russian fleet was caught by a surprise attack in the opening salvos of the Russo-Japanese war. He considered it a charm because its entrance made him drop to the deck in pain a millisecond before the shrapnel that amputated two fingers of his left hand would have pierced his heart. As it was, it harmlessly embedded itself in the bulkhead just above where he lay sprawled on the deck. He fingered the deck of cards and asked, "Poker, anyone?"

December 10, 1924
Washington, D.C.

Roosevelt would have been astounded to know his predictions about the naval treaty were coming true, albeit with a little covert help. Lieutenant Jack Burns, a young pilot fresh out of Annapolis, was recuperating from injuries sustained from a horrific plane crash. A temporary assignment sent him to work in Naval Intelligence under the auspices of a civilian named Herbert O. Yardley. As Japan became westernized, its language had to be translated from ideographic symbols to *kama*, a sort of shorthand that was further translated into *romanji*, which could be telegraphed or cabled. Using his unique ability to translate three languages simultaneously, Yardley had managed the almost unbelievable feat of cracking the Japanese code.

Burns had grown up on the outskirts of a Japanese-dominated ghetto in San Francisco. His proficiency with the language was so good the Naval Academy offered him a teaching position upon his graduation from that institution just a year ago. However, naval aviation meant the excitement and admiration every young man craved.

This group, eventually to be titled OP-20-G, gave the American negotiating team knowledge of Japanese plans and proposals as they came over the international cable networks—before the Japanese negotiators did. It allowed them to set the agenda and stay one step ahead of the Japanese by putting forth proposals to limit their warship tonnage in return for security. For accepting a sharply curtailed shipbuilding program, the Japanese were guaranteed no British base north of Singapore or American bases west of Hawaii. The Japanese realized to deny these terms was to increase suspicion of their intentions. They knew they were being double-teamed by the Americans and the British. The agendas of the meetings seemed predetermined with proposals that set the tone to keep Japan a second-rate power. The loyalty demonstrated to the United States and Great Britain in the World War was not rewarded, let alone appreciated—she could have run amok in the Pacific while the Allies dealt with Germany. Diplomats assumed the naval treaty could promote the concept that power lay in security agreements; that is, if you were American or British. The Japanese knew well that the navy stood as the icon of a nation's destiny, and they were blatantly told that they were to remain second in power to the white nations. Japan knew this now better than ever. She reluctantly signed the treaty—to use the time it bought to lay the keels of giant warships, including aircraft carriers, which curiously seemed to be secondary in importance to battleships in British and American eyes.

This lesson was not lost on one British Major Chad Eversole, whom Burns had come to know and respect. The need to renew the Anglo-Japanese Pact was now moot. It allied the United States and Great Britain against the yellow expansionist threat, insuring Britain's Pacific colonial empire. Britain was free to pursue her interest in Europe and Africa, all of this due to the work of a man named Yardley, a British Army Major who genuinely enjoyed wearing the cloak and dagger, and a young twenty-two year-old American who couldn't wait to fly from the deck of the *Langley*.

Chapter 3

December 1, 1931
Pacific Ocean, 250 miles Northwest of Oahu

The huge, dull-gray warships heaved and rolled heavily as the angry north Pacific threw mountains of green water at them. Foaming spray partially obscured the murky early morning sky when the carriers' bows crashed into the trough of a wave. The smaller escort ships of the task force were at times completely obscured by the mountainous seas.

High-ranking officers conferred on the flagship's bridge. Normally, flight operations would be cancelled, but the element of surprise in attacking the base at Pearl Harbor would be lost if the mission was postponed. Their fleet always slept late on Sunday morning, and their long-range patrols might very well spot the oncoming task force, even at this extraordinary latitude, and launch a devastating counterstrike. Although none of their carrier planes would be involved, the American Navy and Army Air Force had hundreds of planes at Hickam Field and Ford Island. The admiral ordered the ships turned into the wind to launch their strike force.

Pilots downed remaining bites of breakfast. Some could not eat at all—anxiety filled their stomachs. They joked in the ready rooms, reviewed the latest intelligence estimates of the enemy's ship deployment and targets of opportunity. Mechanics made last-minute adjustments to the deadly dive bombers and torpedo planes that would "neutralize" the enemy fleet's battle line. Fighter pilots used their hands to describe pursuit tactics to each other. When the order to man their aircraft came, they hurried to the flight deck with their crewmen, strapped themselves into their birds of prey, and awaited their turn to leap from their carriers' bows.

The launch went without incident, and the pilots relaxed into their south-easterly course. It would be a flight of about ninety minutes. The planes homed in on Honolulu radio stations. Their weather reports indicated the sky above was clear, and the tide high. Excellent; their torpedoes would be less likely to sink into the harbor mud when released. The strike leader was jubilant.

He maintained radio silence until he saw the surf breaking on Oahu's beaches. After crossing some low mountains and widespread pineapple fields, he spotted the American fleet's magnificent battleships glinting in the rising

sun. They rested at their moorings, completely unaware of his looming presence. He radioed the flagship: "Surprise achieved."

"You all know what to do," the Admiral radioed to his force. "Select your
targets carefully—there's a lot riding on this."

The leader's section was assigned the USS *Arizona*. He dove directly at the
ship, centering his crosshairs on the smokestack amidships. Nothing moved
on-board as he tugged his bomb release and screamed upward.

The raiders were having a field day. The few fighters that rose to meet them
were quickly dispatched by their aggressive fighter escorts, who then made
strafing runs on the airfields to insure a counterattack couldn't be mounted on
their task force. A rout was under way.

Lieutenant Commander Jack Burns was elated at his strike force's success.
The mission he had originated and planned to the last detail would certainly
raise questions about the fleet's preparedness and operational theories. He
carefully controlled his emotions as he brought his Vindicator dive bomber
onto the flightdeck of the *Saratoga*. The old T4M torpedo planes were already
aboard.

The brand new Grumman FF-1's landed last. Flying in a Marine fighter
squadron on his first carrier deployment was a 2nd lieutenant who Burns had
come to know and respect. Andrew Seghesio, Annapolis class of '31, was as
close to perfection as a young man could be. Tall and muscular, Seghesio was
collegiate boxing champion whose bouts never went more than two rounds.
Third in his class at the Academy, he had been accepted at Stanford for doctoral work in theoretical physics. The Navy left the door open for him. His
thick, jet black hair, bright blue eyes, and skin given to tanning easily, turned
women's legs to rubber. His parents owned an Italian restaurant and bakery
that did a booming business in New York City. The few friends he allowed
near his sister, Lisa, decided on marriage the second they laid eyes on her. She
was even more beautiful than Andy was handsome. No one gawked at her for
very long though; the glare from Andy's electric blue eyes hurriedly brought
back the memory of Andy's abbreviated bouts. Well and good, but Burns was
taken with Seghesio because of his work ethic, his dedication to the team, and
the absolute brilliance with aerial weapons and tactics.

His commander listened intently whenever Andy spoke up, and his mates
always sought his counsel.

Master of the practical joke, his sense of humor was legendary. When the
pressure was on, Seghesio could be counted on to lighten things up, either
through leadership or his patented take on the hot foot.

"Commander Burns! We got 'em. Oh, God, did we get them!"

"We sure as hell did. Was that you tangling with that Boeing pursuit?"

"He didn't have a chance against my Grumman. Or me!"

"You're the perfect Marine Seghesio—a well-schooled braggart."

"Sir, you're confusing me."

"I'm so sorry—I overlooked your Marine handicap. Braggart means bullshitter, Seghesio."

"That's fine, sir. Thank you!"

"Lieutenant, it's time we debriefed."

The rest of Seghesio's squadron rallied around him as they made their way to the *Saratoga*'s ready room. "Yeah, I got him. No doubt about it. That Grumman and I are unbeatable," he said, as they rambled downstairs.

Burns looked over to the *Lexington*, about a mile to starboard. The two ships were twins, both converted to aircraft carriers from battle cruiser hulls as a result of the Washington Naval Treaty. Advertised at the treaty limit of 33,000 tons, the ships were closer to 36,000 tons and 900 feet long. *Lexington*'s signal light blinked out its Morse message:

WELL DONE. COMPLIMENTS TO BURNS AND ALL PILOTS.

ADMIRAL YARNELL

Although the two sisters were great competitors, their captains, Frank McCrary of *Saratoga* and Ernest J. King of *Lexington*, made a point of insisting on teamwork when a mission was at hand. Admiral Harry Yarnell was greatly impressed by the work of America's second and third carriers and how their squadrons and crews were changing the face of war at sea. The current exercise, carried out in the vicious sea the Pacific became in February, showed how far carrier aviation had come, and quickly. With powerful new planes on the drawing board, other missions like Grand Joint Exercise No. 4 would become the norm.

Aboard *Arizona*, the angry mood generated by the goddam carriers' "surprise attack" lifted considerably as she was getting underway. She had been asked to be President Hoover's official ship for a goodwill visit to the Caribbean. The president's men chose *Arizona* because she was in tiptop shape from a recent overhaul, but those in the know realized Hoover was pandering to the conservative West by sailing on a ship named for a Western state.

Petty Officer 3rd Class Gwyeth Jones had come aboard when she was in dry dock at the Norfolk Naval Shipyard being transformed into a more powerful warship. He had enlisted four years earlier to escape the Oklahoma dustbowls. An only child, he lived with an alcoholic mother who waited patiently for his Welsh-seaman father to return. At fourteen, he was orphaned by a locomotive that tore through a railroad crossing and a Model T with a drunk at the wheel and his mother naked beside him. Jones was now an all-Navy "lifer," a machinist by naval trade and involved with much of the work performed on the ship during her refit. He knew more about the battlewagon than her captain, and had become indispensable. It was evident to everyone that he was on the enlisted man's fast-track to a chief's rating. Tall and powerfully built, Jones' dark eyes, thinning hair, and well-trimmed beard made him a formidable presence. The only woman who held his heart was this steel ocean-going goliath.

Torpedo bulges were added to each of *Arizona*'s sides to protect her against the growing threat of submarines and the dastardly torpedo planes that buzzed her this morning. Not lost on the naval architects was the need to give her greater protection from plunging shellfire and aerial bombs. They also saw what Billy Mitchell's bombers did to the old World War battleships, so her second deck armor was increased to nearly eight inches, deemed enough to protect her from current and foreseeable future threats. Her total armor now exceeded 9500 tons. She also received the new boilers and turbines destined for a battleship that was cancelled to abide by the terms of the Washington Naval Treaty. The new propulsion system was lighter and more efficient, compensating for the extra weight in armor. Her old-fashioned cage-like masts were cut away, and tripod masts and new battle bridges were put in their places. Her offensive punch was enhanced by increasing the elevation of the fourteen-inch guns. Now those twelve awesome rifles could hurl a 1400 pound shell 34,000 yards, almost twice the distance of the original specification. Considered a vestige of past battle tactics, the torpedo tubes were also removed. They actually made her vulnerable to enemy torpedoes by breaking the line of the armored belt. In addition, the torpedo room ran from one side of the ship to the other. The former torpedo room was armored and compartmentalized, making the bow section stronger. In essence, *Arizona* was now as modern and formidable as any battleship afloat. In many eyes, BB-39 was prettier than the ship whose 1914 keel laying ceremony at the Brooklyn Navy Yard was presided over by now Governor of New York Franklin Delano Roosevelt.

December 5, 1931
Hiroshima Bay, Japan

The significance of a newspaper account of Grand Joint Exercise No.4 was not lost on one Rear Admiral Isoroku Yamamoto, as he sat reading it on the flag bridge of his beloved carrier *Akagi*, moored next to her sister *Kaga*. Both were also overweight "treaty babies," like *Lexington* and *Saratoga*. "Genda! Have you seen this?"

Minoru Genda was a bright young aviator who flew like Yamamoto would have if he were twenty years younger—as the admiral liked to say.

"Yes sir, I have. The possibilities are intriguing."

"So they are." Yamamoto's thoughts turned to the plans for two sister carriers *Hiryu* and *Soryu* he had recently reviewed.

Albany, New York

The honorable governor of New York State, the most populous in the Union, read the article in the *New York Herald Tribune* with a smile of amusement. Roosevelt thought those two carriers had really done a superbly evil deed, embarrassing the Army Air Corps, whose job was to defend the air space above the growing Hawaiian fortress of Pearl Harbor.

"Have you seen this, Averell?" he asked. Averell Harriman was both a close political confidant and best friend.

"Yes, I have. It seems the world is less safe with each passing day."

"I suppose you're right. We'll have a huge job to do in January."

"One step at a time. Just because Will Rogers proclaimed you president doesn't mean the nation has. 1932 is still a year away."

"We'll see about that," Roosevelt replied, with a characteristic jut of his chin. "The naval treaty is working to our disadvantage. Building warships will put people back to work, and we'll need a massive navy to counter the Japs. Their invasion of Manchuria leaves no doubt about their ultimate goal." He wheeled himself to the table where a servant was arranging his lunch, and crushed out the Camel attached to his cigarette holder. "That Hitler fellah scares me. Have you seen the numbers of people showing up at his rallies?" Roosevelt said, as he buttered a roll.

"He'll be history. The German people have had enough of uniforms and weapons. Look where it got them," Harriman replied.

"That's what scares me. I think they'll assume the only way to retrieve their national pride is to wear a uniform. They have nothing to lose. And they put people to work building warships, too."

"I see your point. Look at this picture of the shanties in Central Park. Do we have a choice? Anyway, the British and French will hold Hitler at bay. Their memories of the World War will make sure Germany is checked. But who will check the Japs? The British and French Pacific colonies are weak and vulnerable, and their loyalties become more of an issue each day."

London, England

Across the Atlantic, Chancellor of the Exchequer Winston Churchill was throwing a tantrum. He could not believe Baldwin, the conservative prime minister, was acquiescing to the whims of Indian insurgents. Independence? They didn't even know the meaning of the word, let alone work it out. The Japanese must be gloating. He wrote out his resignation from the Cabinet that would relegate him to a back seat in Parliament for an eternity.

"Winston," said Neville Chamberlain, a conservative-turned-liberal turned to whatever the current situation demanded. "The world is changing. We cannot hold back the hordes as easily as we used to."

"The longer one lives," Churchill replied, "the more one realizes that everything depends upon chance. It gets harder to believe that this omnipotent factor in human affairs arises simply from the blind interplay of events. Man's own contribution to his life story is continually dominated by an external superior power."

"Don't you think your views have something to do about your state of being? Do you see yourself as a victim of…of…fate?"

Churchill turned, his blue eyes gleaming with passion. "A victim? Hardly! Only a patient servant awaiting his time."

"Your time is dwindling, Winston. You've thrown your career away on issues that have far surpassed your viewpoints."

Churchill hated to waste a word in discussion with this worm of a man. He caught his temper just a degree below its boiling point. "You misunderstand. My beliefs remain steadfast. Situations change, not I."

"What will you do until that time, Churchill?" Chamberlain asked with a wry smile.

"Write. My views become more clarified when I write."

He sat for a minute in the empty House of Commons, and opened *The Daily Mail* to read with great curiosity the details of the recent United States Navy's exercise in the Pacific. If Britain were to keep her colonies, she needed to keep America as an ally. Japan was knocking at Asia's door, and if no one opened it with diplomacy, it seemed she was preparing to kick it in. America was in no mood to bolster any European war again. Indeed, if it hadn't been for his naval codebreakers serving him when he was First Lord of the Admiralty in 1917, England might have succumbed to Germany. It was their work that had intercepted and decoded the Zimmerman telegram that sought Mexico as an ally to Germany. Mexico was to get back all the lands it relinquished to the United States since The War of 1848 by attacking the United States if she entered the war against Germany. The sinking of the *Lusitainia* didn't have the effect of that stupid subterfuge known as the XYZ Affair in pushing the United States over the edge. Now, it would take more than that, as America gained nothing from the war.

Churchill returned home. In his study, he continued brooding over a whiskey and water. He took a Corona from a leather case and bit off the tip. As he lit it, his eyes settled on a book he kept on a shelf close to his desk. Entitled *Savrola*, he had written it in 1898 while a young officer serving in India with Her Majesty's Fourth Hussars. His gaze fixed upon the paragraph that read, "Under any circumstances, in any situation, Savrola knew himself to be a factor to be reckoned with; whatever the game, he would play it to his amusement, if not to his advantage." He remembered that the words were stimulated by reading of the sinking of the battleship *Maine* in Havana's harbor. How outlandishly stupid of the Spaniards, he thought. The suspicious destruction of that ship cost them the remnants of their empire. His own service in Cuba on the side of Spain's Royal Crown showed him the lengths to which the United States would go to rid its hemisphere of Europeans. One had to be careful as to how America was handled—or pushed. In the final outcome, it would be America that would decide the future of the world, and she was not to be taken lightly. It was so in 1917, and even more so today.

Churchill finished his whiskey and placed another log on the fire. He put the Corona in an ashtray just before he dozed off, dreaming great things.

———————

December 7, 1931
Washington, D.C.

A young United States Navy lieutenant named Joseph Rochefort had just returned from a two-year stay in Japan to his job at OP-20-G. They had just broken a new Orange code, the first that had been set by a cryptograph, or enciphering machine. Orange, the War Department's code name for Japan, had had every one of its naval codes broken since the early twenties. That it was happening concurrently in London at the Government Code and Cipher School (GCCS) under Major Chad Eversole would have been a real surprise for Rochefort, and everyone else at OP-20-G for that matter. OP-G-20 didn't share information with anyone, including its Army counterpart, let alone the British.

Chad Eversole had convinced the prime minister that eavesdropping on the Japanese was tantamount, and that code-breaking stations needed to be set up in Singapore and Hong Kong to monitor all Japanese radio traffic. Baldwin gave his approval, and Eversole began gathering resources the very next day.

Chapter 4

The brand new carrier USS *Enterprise* raced through the calm Caribbean waters at thirty-one knots. Her gestation represented five years of tender loving care in the birthing yards of Norfolk, Virginia. She and her twin sister *Yorktown* put a twinkle in President Franklin D. Roosevelt's eye. They were part of a ship building program designed to put Americans back to work during The Great Depression, and to counter the ships taking form in the birthing yards of Germany and Japan. Executive Order Number 6174 appropriated $238 million dollars for his beloved Navy and conceived the two carriers, along with thirty first-class warships. That the appropriations bill was passed so easily caused Roosevelt to remark to Secretary of the Navy Claude Swanson, "We got away with murder this time!" A third sister, *Hornet*, was well along in her gestation.

The SBD Dauntless dive bomber that Jack Burns was piloting had only a few hours of flying time entered in its log book. He was on a routine landing approach with visibility unlimited and not a burble of rough air. Two hundred yards from the *Enterprise*'s deck and flying at just under a hundred knots, he was watching the landing signal officer's paddles, when the engine's deep, throaty drone turned into a series of staccato popping noises. The rear gunner heard it too. "Sir, is everything okay up there?" asked a frightened John Zanetti. Vibrations rattled his body.

"I don't...Jesus Christ!" The engine suddenly burst into flames, spewing a trail of thick black smoke that immediately engulfed the cockpit. Burns struggled to maintain control, but as the dive bomber lost speed its left wing dipped in a stall. The plane pivoted on the depressed wingtip and spun into the sea.

Burns' head hit the instrument panel, gashing his forehead to the bone. Zanetti's back was slammed painfully into his seat. The aircraft's near-empty gas tanks provided temporary buoyancy, but this reprieve was short-lived. The SBD rapidly took on water. Semiconscious, Burns retained the presence of mind to unlatch his safety harness and crawl out onto the wing as the plane's nose dipped beneath the surface. He pulled the toggles of his Mae West and wiped away the curtain of blood from his eyes. Young Zanetti moaned. Though Burns managed to reach down to unhook his harness and inflate his vest, the world was turning black. He pitched into the sea, regaining consciousness just in time to see the plane's tail disappear. Tears turned to elation a few seconds later when his gunner's leather-helmeted head popped to the surface.

Captain Newton H. White ordered *Enterprise* to dead slow and watched apprehensively as the destroyer *Gwin* raced to the rescue. As she closed, four strong swimmers went overboard and stroked to the bobbing pair. Crewmen on the destroyer heaved the hapless pair to safety. Zanetti in a neck brace and Burns with a pressure bandage were rushed to the *Gwin*'s sickbay.

October 27, 1938
Rio de Janeiro

Every movement, even a deep breath, sent waves of pain through Burns' head.

"Go ahead, Doc," Jack Burns said. "You can leave me and get laid. I won't be going anywhere." He dared not laugh.

"Oh, I did that last night. You're the only one on the ship who hasn't sampled Rio's best, and you're not going to, either."

"My wife wouldn't have appreciated it anyway. Does she know what happened?"

"She only gets notified if you're dead. We don't want to bother her with trivia, or get her excited about your insurance," the doctor said as he began an examination.

"My neck aches."

"It would. Hitting the water at 100 knots has that effect. Some guys actually get killed that way."

"Doc, how long do you suppose before…"

"At least a year. Don't even think about climbing into a cockpit before then. You're grounded."

"I heal quickly, Doc. This is the second time I've…"

"Yes, I know. I've seen your medical records. This is much worse than a broken leg and a few cracked ribs. Are you having trouble focusing?" He shined a light in his patient's eyes, watching his pupils slowly dilate.

"Not a bit." Actually his vision was blurred, and the area behind his eyes throbbed with pain.

"You're full of shit. Here, take a look—if you can."

Jack Burns didn't recognize the person in the mirror. The eyes were purple, and the forehead, what wasn't covered by bandages, was a sickly, yellowish green.

"Sweet God above!"

"Don't call on Him again, Jack. He worked overtime to save you once... make that twice. I think He's trying to tell you to command a battleship and forget about flying. Now then, lie back and try to rest."

"What the hell am I going to do for a year?"

"Well, you had a stint in intelligence, and you know Japanese. The Navy will have plenty for you to do."

"How'd the *Big E* do so far?" Burns asked.

"She'll be the best ever. She's a special ship, Jack. You can almost feel she's blessed. I've served on a number of ships in my twenty years; but I dunno, this one has some kind of aura around her."

"I get that feeling, too," Burns remarked. There was very little shaking down to do on her shakedown cruise. The *Big E* just worked well, mechanically and spiritually.

July 30, 1939
New York City

Captain Andrew Seghesio felt like a child again as he strode through The New York World's Fair. The June day grew more beautiful as each hour passed, filling him with a sense of anticipation. He looked smashing. His job in the Marine Corps was unique, and those in the know said he was destined for major command responsibilities. He and three Navy pilots had been chosen to put Grumman's F4F Wildcat fighter through its acceptance trials. He had been living on Long Island near Grumman's Bethpage facility for almost a year, and particularly delighted in the area's magnificent beaches. He had a deep tan and the sparkling smile of a man who thoroughly enjoyed the physical and mental tasks life put before him. The more he flew the new Wildcat, the broader his smile became.

He was leaving the Democracity exposition in awe of industrial designer Henry Dreyfuss' idea of what a city would be like in the year 2039, and was on his way to his assignment at the Lagoon of Nations when he decided to visit GM's Futurama exhibit. He had time. Surprisingly, the line of patrons awaiting entrance was short. A conveyor delivered an upholstered chair and he took his turn to sit, only to find himself squeezed in by another. She almost fell out as their hips collided, but Seghesio's strong arms extended around her very trim waist, and held her in. He was embarrassed by finding his thumb on her breast. He did, however, note that the lace of her bra felt very nice indeed. He quickly let her go, and she bounded off his legs and onto the seat. The young woman was flushed with embarrassment.

"I'm terribly sorry," she stammered, in the most delightful English accent.

"No, please. It was my fault. I was so intent on getting on this ride, and I get a bit clumsy when I don't… concentrate," he said. The auburn-haired woman was the loveliest woman he had ever seen. His heart pounded and his forehead beaded with perspiration.

"Oh, dear, so do I." She gazed at him, taking in the deep blue eyes and charming smile. She also remembered how comforting his arms felt around her waist. She noticed his moist forehead. Good, she thought. My palms are soaked, his head could at least be a little dampened. "I suppose I should introduce myself. Mae Leland," she said, extending her hand.

"Andy Seghesio. Pleased to meet you." Did they make skin this soft and fair?

"That's Captain Seghesio, United States Marine Corps. Is that correct?"

"Why, yes, but it's unusual for a woman to spot that. I mean, you can tell I'm a Marine, but knowing my rank is something special."

"I also know you're a pilot," she said, pointing to the gold wings on his chest.

"Right again!"

"Don't be so amazed. My brother's a pilot in our RAF, and I work for Great Britain's military liaison at the consulate in New York."

"Oh, really? I thought you sounded like you were from Brooklyn." He laughed.

"No," she chuckled. "Kent. Anyway, I see lots of uniforms," she said, her eyes never leaving his face.

"For a minute there, I felt special."

"You are, Andy. You're the one I'm on this ride with." She didn't mean to say it, but it just came out; no matter how she tried, she couldn't wipe the grin off her face.

No one had ever said "Andy" like that. He sat gawking at her, not believing his incredible luck.

Futurama was the world's largest animated model, covering almost 36,000 square feet. The five hundred and fifty-two upholstered chairs carried spectators a full third of a mile to view fifty thousand miniature cars and trucks dotting a lilliputian landscape of farms, futuristic cities, and 100 mile-per-hour superhighways. It was billed as "a magic Aladdin-like flight through time and space."

Seghesio seemed occupied by the display, but the reality of it was he couldn't concentrate on it. As the ride came to its end, he reached for her hand to help her out.

"That was the highlight of my day," he said, placing his cap on his head.

"It was certainly an interesting exhibit," Mae replied.

"That, too." Oh, hell, what's there to lose? "Mae, I've got an official function I have to attend at the Lagoon of Nations. There's a luncheon after that, but..."

"Another coincidence! I'm supposed to be there, too, with my boss."

"Why don't we go together? Then I'd like to buy you dinner and get to know you better. I hope I'm not coming on too strong, Mae. It goes with the suit."

She laughed heartily. "That would be wonderful!"

Was it supposed to be this easy?

The Lagoon of Nations fielded a pavilion from almost every industrialized country in the world, except Germany. In hopes of promoting the concept of world peace, Grover Whalen, the fair's impresario, had asked each participant to send a few military representatives for a group photo and luncheon. He even invited the absent Germans, who politely but firmly refused. Hitler's speeches were inflammatory and darkly foreboding, and no staged photo would remove the Nazi Wehrmacht from Czechoslovakia, Austria, or the Rhineland. War was imminent, and everyone knew it.

The Japanese came, albeit reluctantly. Several members of the Japanese contingent felt uncomfortable lining up with men from England, Holland, Russia, Poland, and America. Roosevelt was tightening the screws on trade because of Japan's incursion into China, and the atmosphere between the two nations grew increasingly charged. The sinking of the gunboat *Panay* on the Yangtze River in December of 1937 had begun a series of punitive economic and diplomatic initiatives coupled with military posturing.

A Japanese naval aviator stared at Seghesio, who just as coldly and more menacingly stared back, introducing an unfortunate belligerence into the Lagoon's Court of Peace. The picture was taken, and as the groups headed for the outdoor luncheon, the two young men closed the distance between them. An American Navy captain and a Japanese admiral noted the hostility and moved to intervene. "That was a gesture of hope, don't you agree Captain Campbell?" said the Japanese commander in perfect English.

"Yes, Admiral Onishi, it was. Don't you think so, Captain...?"

"Seghesio, Andrew," he replied. "United States Marine Corps, sir."

"And you are...?" Onishi said to the other young man.

"Lieutenant Tomi Zai, Imperial Japanese Navy."

"Pleased, I'm sure," Seghesio said, taking his extended hand.

"Till we meet again, Captain," the Japanese said.

"I await that day with eager anticipation, Lieutenant Zai."

Tomi Zai bent at the waist, glaring as he rose. They took seats opposite each other at a table set with the finest of china and silver lent by the Waldorf Astoria specifically for the occasion. A centerpiece of roses adorned with a dove decorated each table.

"There's gloom in the air, my friend," Tom Campbell said.

"I hope our two countries can work out this difficulty," Saburo Onishi replied.

"I hope so, too. Funny, fifteen years ago, we were also on opposite sides— when my Princeton played your Harvard. That was good fun. You had your first hot dog with me, remember?"

"Ah, yes! Your Cloister Club represents a time of warmth and the optimism of youth. Too bad it's lost on those two," Onishi said, nodding toward the two aviators. "Let's remember the past, then, Tom. Perhaps its sunshine will drive the clouds away."

"Perhaps. Speaking of the future, how's your son doing?"

"Wonderfully. Juzo enters Eta Jima in the fall."

"More coincidence! My Michael is in his first year at Annapolis."

"Where did we go wrong, my friend?" Onishi said in laughter.

Campbell shook his head with amusement, but Onishi's innocent question struck a chord of despair. As much as he valued Onishi's long-time friendship, he couldn't excuse him or any Japanese from the slaughter, rape, and butchery of Nanking.

Andy finished his lunch, then went to Mae Leland. She never fully took her eyes off him, though she tried to anticipate his numerous glances, managing to look away just in time. She engaged Colonel Bader, her boss, in such vivacious chatter he wondered what had come over his usually reserved administrative aide.

"Do you like to dance, Mae?"

"Oh, yes! I especially love American jazz."

"I'm meeting a few friends tonight in a place in New Rochelle called Badalato's Glen Isle Casino. Glenn Miller's playing there and I've got reservations but no date. What do you say we run up there after dinner?"

"I say fine. Will you be needing me, Colonel?" she asked, more to be polite than for actual permission.

Bader now realized why she'd been acting so skittish.

"Not at all. Take care of her, Captain, she's irreplaceable," Bader said. As they walked away, he lit his pipe and shook his head.

Mae gave him a button she had just bought from one of the Fair's numerous vendors. "I HAVE SEEN THE FUTURE," it read. He thought it prophetic.

"Come on, Mae. There's lot's to do. Did you see Roosevelt on that television thing at the RCA pavilion?" Hand in hand they walked to the Fair's trademark Trylon and Perisphere. Seghesio noted the temperature rising, and it wasn't solely from the sun. Mae Leland noticed that her feet weren't bothered by her high heels—it seemed she'd become somewhat lighter the minute he touched her.

"May I ask you something?"

"Anything you want."

"Why didn't you and that Japanese fellow get along."

"Within a year, both of us will be trying very hard to kill each other."

She had heard it before. "What about Hitler? Don't you see him as more of a threat than the Japanese? I mean, they are somewhat backward, don't you agree?"

"Adolph and his boys are your problem, Mae. America isn't going to war again to save Europe from itself. We did that twenty-two years ago, and it left a very bad taste in our mouths. Don't underestimate the Japs. The Pacific is where the future economic power of the world lies. Your most productive colonies are Hong Kong and Singapore. I'd suggest you make peace with Hitler, leave the French to themselves, and concentrate on holding your empire. If you don't, the Japs will take it from you sooner than you can blink an eye. Their navy and the forward bases they're constructing are first-rate. From what we hear about China, so's the rest of their military. And from that combat experience, they're getting even better."

"What bases?" she asked, absorbing his every word.

"The Marianas, the Carolines. Their fleet anchorage at Truk rivals our Pearl Harbor. And they're building aircraft carriers; big, fast ones. You don't do all that without having an offensive strategy in mind."

She took it all in, making mental notes. It would be so much easier if this Marine weren't so good-looking, such a gentleman. And those strong arms; they were a topic of discussion themselves. Even that wayward thumb had its charm. She had to be friendly to get what she wanted. It was much too easy to forget her purpose.

The Chartwell Estate

"The story of the human race is war. Except for brief and precious interludes, there has never been peace in the world. I fear we are about to write another chapter in that story."

"Winston, you do go on and on," said Niles Chatham, putting down the newspaper with a slap. "Chamberlain bought the peace with that pompous

Bohemian corporal in Munich. In a few years the Germans will come to their senses and overthrow him." Chatham crossed his legs emphatically and tried to get back to his reading.

"Have you seen their magnificent army?" Churchill bellowed. Their air force is the most advanced in Europe. Their navy is filled with the most modern submarines and battleships. The lessons of the Spanish Civil War seem lost on everyone but me! Has anyone else read *Mein Kamph*? He spit on Versailles. That madman took Austria and Czechoslovakia without firing a shot, and we pandered to him with appeasement. Now he wants Poland. Chamberlain might as well have used the treaty he waved as toilet paper." He removed the Corona from his mouth long enough to smile at his daughter Mary and her friends at play in the garden of his estate. A surge of apprehension overtook him. "They parade at night, those Nazis, like Lucifer's demons. They carry torches and bear standards wrought from the belly of hell. Their evil is beyond definition."

"You're much an alarmist, Winston, and one who lives for the challenges of the past. War would be too destructive this time. It will not come to pass. There are too many memories of the debacle of a scant quarter century past."

"I fear you're wrong, my friend. That war is not over—it is on the verge of resuming with unbridled passion. The demise of the League of Nations and the Naval Treaty are testimony to that. War is rearing its ugly head, stirring within men the need to avenge the dishonor of the past, to quench their blood lust. And our sense of denial has given the forces of evil a quantum advantage."

"Right always wins over wrong. Always."

"True," Churchill replied, fixing a whiskey and water, "but the price of complacency is high. Herr Hitler is already exacting it. Have you heard the rumors of what he's doing with Jews?"

Chatham looked up; he hadn't a clue. "What's this about Jews?"

––––––––––

Hiroshima Bay

"So, Genda," Admiral Yamamoto said, "what tactical solutions have you devised?" Yamamoto liked his aggressive young air officer very much. He came to look upon him as a father would a son, and Genda knew it.

"Admiral, I think that developing a new bomb heavy enough to penetrate the deck armor of a battleship wouldn't be feasible in terms of cost, especially since one has already been invented."

"Explain yourself," Yamamoto said with a smile, "and understand that I realize you tease me just to see my eyebrows rise. It's been said you think I look rather foolish."

Minoru Genda caught the outburst of laughter as Yamamoto raised his eyebrows in the most ridiculous fashion. Yamamoto knew everything there was to know about anything, including how others portrayed him. Thank the gods for his sense of humor.

"Sir, our battleships carry projectiles approximately forty-one centimeters in diameter that weigh approximately 800 kilograms." He walked over to a meter-long model of a battleship, and held up a model of a Nakajima torpedo-bomber. "If a Type 97 aircraft accurately drops one of these projectiles from a height of 3000 meters, it should be able to penetrate through sixteen centimeters of armor, coincidentally close to the thickness of deck armor of this *Nevada*-class battleship. The projectile would have to be reshaped as a bomb by grinding down the rear, so we can add fins for stability. We also need to design a fuse to explode the device immediately after penetration."

"So, the bomb would have to be mostly steel to penetrate the battleship's armor." Yamamoto stroked his chin. "How much explosive could it carry? We have to take into account that it won't be as stable in flight as a shell that spins in a precise arc as it leaves the rifles of our battleships." He paused to organize his thoughts, sipping hot green tea. "Therefore, you would have to thicken the bomb casing to get to the desired degree of penetration, don't you agree? The shell would lose a tremendous amount of explosive capacity."

"We calculated we can carry only twenty kilograms of high explosive, enough to keep the ship from sailing for months if enough of the projectiles find their targets. But if the bombs are dropped from too high an altitude, they might pass right through the ship and explode on the harbor bottom; too low and they might bounce off. If they explode on contact, they would at least cause damage to the ship's superstructure and its command and control facilities." Genda hesitated and looked up at Yamamoto. "They would also kill many crew members with the shards of steel and splintered decking. But I don't envision even a direct hit causing a capital ship to sink."

"Interesting concept, Genda. I still think that we should also concentrate on the new torpedoes. Battleships' bellies are perfect targets. Ships of their *Nevada* class, old as they are, have been refitted with thicker deck armor. From what I understand, the *Arizona* and *Pennsylvania* class have also had an armor upgrade. Billy Mitchell's experiments haven't been lost on any navy."

"That is true, and their battleships were fitted with torpedo protection blisters, but I think they will collapse with enough hits. Torpedoes, too, might bury their noses in the mud if they are dropped at too great a height or too fast an approach. The confines of the area will require some excellent flying to cancel such disadvantages. Even with a perfect approach, we will still require that the modified torpedoes have an efficiency of 100 percent, considering the stakes."

"And so must the surprise factor," said Yamamoto. "Torpedo planes are sitting ducks to an alerted enemy. Togo's lessons about surprise against the Russians at Port Arthur demonstrate that."

"The thin-skinned carriers are another story. Our bombs and torpedoes would make easy work of them. The aviation gasoline they store makes them easy prey."

"No doubt, but the aircraft carrier is a new and untried weapon. A nation still identifies its strength by its battleships. Sink one, and you sink their morale." Yamamoto went to the porthole, and looked out across the massive fifteen-inch guns on his flagship, *Nagato*, and the city beyond Hiroshima Bay. His mind reviewed the estimates and calculations that had taken ownership of his being these last few months. Turning to Genda with a heavy look on his face he said, "If war with America comes in the next eighteen months, we will have a qualitative and quantitative advantage in weaponry," he said, "but for no more than a year. We must strike quickly and decisively and then seek peace with the United States that guarantees our interests yet saves them face." He bent to closely examine the very detailed battleship model, as if searching for tiny sailors making ready for sea. "Their British and French allies whose Pacific colonies we covet will try desperately to convince them our yellow race is bent on destroying them, so the task is further complicated. We cannot afford a long war. Already their shipyards are gearing up to produce the finest of giants in unheard of quantities."

"You're fond of them, aren't you?"

"They are a proud and just people who are quite satisfied with what the gods have given them," Yamamoto said, offering tea. "They have yet to explore their vast lands and exploit their resources." He smiled fondly when he said, "Do you know that you can drive in a straight line for hours in their western provinces?" He went to the world map hanging behind his desk. "However, their riches force them to play on the world stage," he said, sweeping an arm across the vast Pacific. "They tried desperately to stay out of the World War, yet they were figures drawn in an economic portrait painted with the pallet of German butchery on the high seas and diplomatic stupidity. Don't forget their historical links to the British. Their common language makes for common interests."

"The British betrayed us with the Naval Treaty, Admiral. We admired them so, and they turned their backs on us."

"That was simple economics. The British duped the United States into building its navy to protect their Pacific colonies. It saved the British the money they didn't have. They did it by convincing them that the Philippines are on our target list." He handed the teacup to Genda, and raised his own, sipping the hot liquid carefully. "And they are," he added, quite matter-of-factly. "Remember, we are not the color of the British; the Americans are."

"Don't you think the Germans will force them into war? Herr Hitler intends to dominate Europe, and that includes Great Britain. You know that."

"It won't be enough, not after their experience in the World War. But we need what the Europeans have taken out here," he said, pointing to the western Pacific rim, "and if America stands in the way, we'll necessarily have to push it aside. But they'll soon be building ships faster than we could sink them. If we attack them without a formal declaration of war, as Togo did to the Russians, they will want to see our race extinguished." He lit a cigarette with a Zippo lighter. "They are a generous and kind people until wronged or angered, those Americans," he said, fondling the lighter. "Then they become the worst killers in history. Their own Civil War is testament to what they were willing to do to each other, let alone yellow men who take advantage of them." He turned to Genda again. "Get those suckers you call card players. I'm in the mood for some poker," he said, fingering the lucky amulet in his pocket.

"With all due respect, Admiral, I cannot afford to be your air officer any longer."

Yamamoto gave him a bear hug.

San Pedro, California

Captain Isaac Kidd surveyed the freshly holystoned decks of his battleship with pride. Old as *Arizona* was, she still represented a force to be reckoned with. Her fourteen-inch rifles, all twelve of them, were as potent as any afloat, and while she might not be able to run with the fast carriers and cruisers, she could still hold her own against any battleship. Though surpassed by newer and faster types, she would still need to be neutralized, therefore giving the enemy something else to reckon with. Her big rifles presented a series of big problems, especially against shore installations. Even anchored here in San Pedro, she inspired awe. Kidd loved his ship and his crew and was proud to be standing on her bridge. In a few days she would be underway to maneuver with other battleships, then "swing around the hook" in San Francisco. Now that was a Navy town! The whole crew looked forward to that cruise.

"Begging your pardon, sir, but would you please review these readiness reports? The division chief needs them over on the *Maryland* as soon as possible."

"Sure thing. Are we set to make a good accounting of ourselves, Gwyeth?"

"I guarantee we will be the pride of the exercise, sir. Now, if we could only get those movie makers to leave us alone, we might be able to get some work done. I think my crew is going Hollywood on me."

"That's not the worst of it, Chief. You know those two comedians, Abbott and Costello?"

Jones laughed heartily. "The funniest men on the planet, sir. I can't help laughing hysterically when they take the screen. That movie *High Society* left me with a bellyache."

"They want *Arizona* as a set for their next picture. I hear it will be about a couple of misfits who join the Navy."

"Dear God! Just what we need." The chief's complexion reddened at the news. "Speaking of misfits, look at the three guys on that five-incher. Where the hell did those sons-a-bitches learn to clean a gun? Excuse me, sir."

Kidd watched as Jones scrambled down the ladders to the gun deck, and reamed out the poor seaman apprentices who were cleaning one of *his* guns incorrectly. The Navy would agree with the seamen that they were doing it the Navy way. The only error they made was not doing it Chief Petty Officer Gwyeth Jones' Navy way, which exacted a much higher standard as to what "clean" was all about on *his* ship. Kidd laughed heartily as he saw a young ensign straight out of Officer Candidate School coincidently exit a nearby hatch and happen upon the scene of Jones' tirade. The ensign quietly slipped back inside and gently closed the hatch.

Little Italy, New York City

Andrew Seghesio cut the cannoli as precisely as he could. The flaky pastry was difficult to separate neatly and the rich creamy filling speckled with citron difficult to contain. "Here you go, Mae," he said, putting the pastry on her plate. "You've got to taste this. I guarantee you when you go to heaven you'll find Jesus and Saint Peter sharing one of these."

"Andy! Shame on how you talk! Now I have to say more prayers for you tonight!" Lena Seghesio shook her head and pursed her lips.

"Honestly," Mae said, "I think I've gained ten pounds tonight. Do you always eat like this?"

"Only when I'm home. Ma tries to make up for my months at sea in one night. Since I've been stationed at Bethpage, Ma gets to stuff me two times a week. I've had to watch my weight, right ma?"

"Right. You come home too thin every time you go out on the boat."

"It's a ship, Ma."

"Boat, ship, what's the difference. Right Mae?"

"That's right Mother Seghesio," she said, as she smiled and hugged the delicately beautiful Italian woman.

"Andy, you want some more wine?" his father asked, slapping his son's back with his thick hand. Giovanni Seghesio was terribly proud of his son. His boy represented everything he came to America to achieve.

"No, Dad, thanks. Mae and I are going up to New Rochelle to do some dancing, and I have to drive."

"Lisa, Andy tells me you're a student."

"I'm finishing up my doctoral degree in education at Barnard this year."

"You should be married," Giovanni said with a wink at his son, knowing what was going to come.

"Oh, Papa! You don't like any of the men I bring around."

"They always have something else to do besides talk to me."

"They're Americans, Papa. Don't those Wall Street fellows who gorge themselves in here every day teach you anything?"

"You have a lovely place here, Mrs. Seghesio. And the food is wonderful. No wonder every table is occupied," said Mae.

"Ah, God, He smiles on us. We work hard, and He works hard in taking care of us. Especially Andy, with those *morte d'fama* airplanes he flies."

"I'll have to take you flying one day, Ma. I met Jesus up there yesterday and He said, 'Hey Andy! Nice to see you, *paisano*! By the way, thank your mother for all the candles she lights, but I'd rather have one of those cannolis.' That's what He said, honest." He stopped to finish the last bit of the cannoli he had cut for Mae. "You'd be surprised how much He looks like his pictures."

"I'm telling Father Rizzo about you. I can't pray enough to help you any more," she said, making the sign of the cross.

"Why do you tease your mother so?" Mae said in apparent dismay, more to please his mother than to scold him.

"He's a brat, Mae," Lisa chimed in. "He's always been a brat. He was constantly into mischief, but all that charm and that big brain of his always got him out of it. Even the nuns were taken with him, and he gave them a run for their money." She pushed at her brother's broad shoulder.

"Thanks, Lisa," he said, kissing her loudly on the cheek.

Lisa adored her big brother, who was more than kind to her. She had often gotten away with murder only because he was always there to protect her.

"What about the time he saved you from those wise guys who were grabbing you in the subway your first year at college?"

"They were harmless, Papa," Lisa said, looking away.

"Lifting up your dress? It's lucky Andy was home on leave and he heard you scream before I did, or I'd be in Sing Sing right now."

"Andy was lucky to get away before the police arrived. Don't you think you overreacted, Andy?"

"I was only trying to save them from Papa, and save Papa from Sing Sing."

"The *Daily News* said it took one of them three days to wake up. Another had both arms in casts and a broken nose. The lucky one had his jaw wired for three months," she said, turning to Mae, who stopped in mid-chew.

"They couldn't take a punch, Lisa. It was that simple. More cannoli, Mae?"

"I think Annapolis and the Marines weren't much of a challenge, were they Andy?" Mae said, a bit startled.

"Like Central Park in the spring. Stanford, though; that was another story. Those eggheads put me through hell when I did my Ph.D. in aeronautical engineering."

She couldn't believe her ears—or, for that matter, her heart. Mae Leland was flat out in love with a total paradox.

Pearl Harbor, Hawaii

Station Hypo, located in Building No. 1 at the Pearl Harbor Navy Yard hummed with activity. It had done an amazing amount of work in intercepting and deciphering Japanese transmissions along with Station Cast, located in the Cavite Navy Yard in the Philippines, all under the auspices of OP-20-G. Hypo's commander, Lieutenant Thomas Dyer, had pieced together the last bits of information required for breaking a new Japanese diplomatic cipher, under the name of Purple. The intercepted and transcribed messages would be distributed under the code name "Magic," which was what Dyer had christened the incredible machine he devised that cracked Purple.

Important as Magic was, it told nothing of the movements or intentions of the Imperial Japanese Navy, which was about to change its codes yet again. The Americans would have been startled to know that British codebreakers in Hong Kong were more proficient in this area, but the Purple code was giving them fits. But secrets are secrets, and are most valuable when the fewest know them, and that included allies. It was Chad Eversole's job to keep it that way. More startling to the Navy would have been the knowledge that the Army half of the OP-20-G operation had cracked the Japanese Navy's Blue cipher. However, with big changes afoot, Blue was about to become as dead as Latin.

Chapter 5

Andy Seghesio accelerated the 1938 Buick 46-C convertible onto Route 1. "What are you staring at?" he asked the girl beside him.

"Do you really have a Ph.D. from Stanford?"

"Of course. Doesn't everyone?"

He was terribly funny and witty and so full of life. Mae was finding it increasingly difficult to ask him the necessary questions as the intensity between them rose with each passing minute. It was a chance meeting of possibly great importance to England, but fate seemed to tell her there was more in store than military information. She was no Mata Hari, but her country was in grave danger, and she had to do her part—within moral bounds. Until now, it had been easy to flash those hazel eyes of hers at any American officer, leading him on to the point where he said more than he should have. This fellow, however, was different. Just one long passionate kiss might make her spill the beans.

"This is a gorgeous car, Andy. Is it new?"

"Only five months old. I bought it as a present to myself when I finished my last cruise on the *Lexington*."

"I guess big guys like big cars."

He turned to her wanting so very much to kiss her, but the time wasn't quite right, even though he sensed she would accept. However, the kiss he had in mind couldn't be delivered at forty miles per hour heading north on Route 1. Trying to change the mood to a more upbeat tempo, he said, "I'm glad you like to dance, Mae. Have you heard of Glenn Miller?"

"Hasn't everyone?" she said with a smirk.

Andy laughed. "Sorry, Mae. I don't mean to tease you. I just feel very comfortable being around you."

"Well, Andrew Seghesio, if it's of importance to you, I don't think I've ever spent a lovelier ten hours and fifteen minutes. But I bet you hear that a lot." She looked at him wanting an answer right then and there.

"It never mattered much until I heard it from you."

They arrived at the Glen Isle Casino just as the orchestra played *Moonlight Serenade,* its opening number. Andy couldn't wait to lead her onto the dance floor. The dreamy tune did wonders for young lovers, and it worked its magic again on this particular pair. She stood on the dance floor for the longest second waiting for him to take her in his arms. Her fingers touched the nape of his neck when he pressed her to him. Her forehead fit the turn of his chin, just below his lips. The world became a carefree, intimate little place filled with the strains of a clarinet-lead arrangement that might have well been playing at the steps of Paradise.

Glenn Miller well knew the magic of his theme. No matter where they played it, people came closer together. He played the tune longer than he usually did. He glanced at the Marine and his lady and saw it happen anew.

The crowd came here for jazz, and there was no better dance number than *In The Mood*. At the saxophones' first notes, people shrieked and squared off for the Lindy. Mae Leland surprised the hell out of Andrew Seghesio. She moved as if she had been brought up in Chicago instead of some little village in England.

They found Seghesio's two buddies, one a fellow Marine Corps flier, the other a Navy lieutenant who also wore wings of gold. Both escorted attractive blondes.

"I thought you didn't have a date, Andy. Have you been holding out on us?"

"Call it a stroke of luck. Tom Hamilton, meet Mae Leland, who's come all the way from Great Britain to dance with me. The guy wearing the pretty blue suit is John Munroe."

"I'm with the guy in the pretty blue suit," said Nancy Herbst, extending her hand. "Patty James doesn't know any better. She came with a Marine, too."

"What brings you to New York?" Patty asked.

"I work for the British Consulate."

"I shouldn't complain about fancy-suit assignments. I got my picture taken with her boss at that luncheon I got conned into going to today," Andy said. "We got to talking and the rest is history."

"So that's how you met the bulldog?" Nancy said.

"Well, not quite. Andrew dragged me onto a ride at Futurama," Mae said, stroking his chin with her index finger, looking helpless.

"Now that's the Andrew I know. Did he knock anybody out?" Munroe asked.

"Not then, but he almost had a run-in with this Japanese fellow at lunch."

"What are you trying to do, Andy, start a war before we're ready?" said Tom Hamilton.

"That gook was staring me down. I didn't like it, and I was about to tell him so when this Captain Campbell came over with a Jap admiral and broke it up."

"What do you mean you're not ready?" Mae asked. "We British assume you know of the Japanese threat, what with their invasion of China and all."

"It's just the way we are, Mae. We don't believe their capabilities or the intelligence we get on them because we have this preconceived notion that they're a bunch of near-sighted photographers who smile a lot and make crappy copycat products. Someone called it *cognitive dissonance*," Munroe said, taking a rum and coke from the tray offered by the waitress. "We fail to believe what we see because it doesn't match a preconceived notion. Even their German buddies think that way. Meanwhile, they've built a super navy, and their aircraft are superb. From what we can determine, you Brits aren't quite up to speed, either. That kraut with the funny haircut seems quite unimpressed with your military."

"I know a guy who's just back from China, and he says the Japs are field testing a new low-wing carrier fighter that's unbelievably fast and maneuverable," Hamilton said. "It's replacing their Type 97."

"When did you hear that?" Seghesio said, leaning forward.

"Just today. He came by Bethpage to look at the Wildcat."

"Now there's a new twist. Have you told anyone else?"

"What Wildcat?" Mae asked. "Are you turning animals into weapons?"

They all laughed. "No, Mae. That's the name of the new Grumman fighter we're throwing around," Hamilton said. "Anyway, I told the procurement officer. He said he'd pass it on."

"How nice of him." Seghesio made a mental note to call Jack Burns.

The conversation was getting unnerving. Suddenly hearing what she wanted to hear, Mae found it blasphemous. "Enough business!" she said. "I came here to dance, and so far I've only danced two numbers with you. Are you afraid of me or the Japs, Captain Seghesio?"

"I'm not afraid of anyone," he said, raising an eyebrow, "but right now, I'm intrigued with you." He reached for her hand. He held her close again all during *Sunrise Serenade.*

———————

0300 Hours, July 31, 1939
London

Yuri Popov blew on his gloves, as the damp chill of early morning air penetrated his bones. He raised his collar against the cold and pulled the woolen watch cap down over his ears. Even the Shetland turtleneck and thermal underwear couldn't keep him warm. London was still cold at 2:00 a.m. in July, and he'd been watching the dockside warehouse in Beckton for six hours, waiting for the two Germans to exit. He'd been following them all day. They had brought two whores from Soho with them and were having a grand time if the glimpses he got through the windows were any indication. Before they arrived, he'd gone through the warehouse and confirmed M1's suspicions. The shortwave radio, maps, and detailed notes indicated they were bomb-plotting the docks for the day the Luftwaffe would scream overhead. Papers swiped by a "pickpocket" identified them as Britishers who had died two years ago in a train wreck near Hamburg. It was time to give the Third Reich a warning message.

Popov had graduated from Eton and the Naval College at Dartmouth with honors. His mentor, Chad Eversole, became the father he'd lost so violently. When the headmaster at Eton called in a dither about the pistol he found hidden in the underwear drawer of Yuri's dresser, Eversole used his considerable clout to intervene on his behalf. He took the Colt .45 automatic and saw young Yuri's eyes tear. "I'm only holding it for you. You're safe here. You'll get it back when you need it. I promise you that." Yuri retained the barrel-chested body of his youth, but now it spread over a frame that exceeded six feet. He had thick blond hair, fair skin, and deep-set blue eyes the color of his mother's. His nose was almost a British classic, a fact not lost on Eversole, who teased him constantly about really being British and having been kidnapped by Russians while only days old. It wasn't at all displeasing to Popov, who had come to love his adopted country passionately.

He liked to drink ale, play rugby, and throw darts, which he did almost as well as he threw a commando knife. Technically, he was a lieutenant commander in His Majesty's Royal Navy, though he'd worked at the highest levels of British Intelligence for the past four years. He was able to think clearly and quickly under pressure. His first kill was a rebel during the Spanish Civil War who had discovered him about to blow up a bridge near Madrid. Even the Spaniard's bullet that tore through his arm didn't stop Popov from chasing the man down, and breaking his neck. The bridge blew a minute later.

A taxi stopped outside the warehouse. Popov immediately saw a way to make his mission even more efficient and effective. Pulling his turtleneck over his nose and donning dark glasses, he yanked open the driver's side door and pointed the silencer-equipped .45 at the man's head. "Run as fast as you can and as far as you can. Don't scream and don't look back, and you'll be fine. You'll be compensated. I promise."

Popov got behind the wheel and holstered the Colt. The Germans and their whores duly exited, and climbed into the cab. "Soho, please," said one. He almost sounded British. Popov smiled, and started the meter. He kept an eye on them with the rear view mirror. The women picked their pockets while the Germans were busy probing between their legs. It would be easier than he thought.

As soon as the whores left the cab, one of the Germans slurred, "White-hall, please." Popov instead took off for the Thames Surrey docks, with the Germans not having the faintest idea as to where they were heading. Five minutes later, he stopped abruptly by the wharf at the end of a deserted street. He pulled the keys from the ignition, jumped out, and ran down the street.

The Germans stared at each other, not knowing what to make of the crazy cabdriver. Fear took hold, abruptly sobering them. Each pulled a Luger from a holster strapped to their calfs, and scrambled from the cab, hunkering down near the rear wheels. Now it was a waiting game.

As one of them slightly exposed his head to check a shadow, a dull snap coincided with the shattering of his skull. He fell clumsily to the cobblestones. The other had no choice but to run for the river, but even as leapt, pain stabbed through his back. A second .45 slug shattered his heart. He never felt the third slug that passed clean through his neck.

Yuri Popov went to his kills and examined them for documents, but the whores had taken everything. The thought made him smile. He dragged the bodies to the wharf's edge and heaved them into the Thames. He picked up the Lugers and put on their safeties, then stuffed them in his waist, exactly as he had done with the .45 all those years ago.

He returned to the taxi, and checked the driver's documents. When he arrived at the noted address in a working class neighborhood he locked the cab, then wrapped the keys in a fifty-pound note. He went to the designated row house and slipped the package through the mail slot.

"Harry, is that you?" he heard a woman call.

Popov disappeared into the London night, just as the house lights went on, and a ragged Harry Watkins arrived with a policeman to find his cab safe and sound, and his night's earnings increased by fifty pounds.

The German embassy received a large, plain brown envelope that contained a clipping from the afternoon edition of the *London Daily Mail*. It described the "horrible murder" of Harvey Foxboro and James Cromwell, found floating in the Thames. The police promised to find the culprits "with all due expediency." In the same envelope was a microphone that would work nicely with a short-wave radio of German design.

––––––––––

0100 Hours, July 31, 1939
New York City

It was nearly one in the morning, but Andy and Mae danced on with electric energy.

"I like this song best, Andy. The harmonies of the instruments are beautiful. What's it called?" Mae asked.

"It's called *A String of Pearls*. Glenn wrote it for his wife to accompany a birthday gift," Andy said, nodding to the bandleader.

"Even the title is beautiful."

They returned to Manhattan slowly, with the convertible's top down to let in the full moon on that warm July evening. He didn't want the most perfect night of his life to end. From the way Mae rested her head of beautiful auburn hair on his shoulder, he felt confident the feeling was mutual. She suddenly quietly hummed *A String of Pearls* and he tried his best to keep harmony.

They walked to the consulate's door, neither saying a word. A nearby streetlight modeled her delicate features and put a sparkle in her eyes. He kissed her softly. They held each other as close as two human beings could and kissed again.

"May I call you tomorrow, Mae? Or is that 'can I call you tomorrow, Mae?' Or is that 'may I call you tomorrow, can?'"

"Oh, you are the worst! It's already tomorrow, and you had better call me, Captain. I'd like to spend the weekend with you."

"Count on it."

"My brother is arriving tomorrow evening, and I'd love for you to meet him."

"Great. I like RAF guys."

"I think you have quite a bit in common."

"I'm sure we do. Good night, Mae."

"Thank you for the loveliest day of my life."

"Wait until tomorrow...er, later today, that is!"

Colonel Bader stood in the consulate's foyer, puffing on his pipe. "Well?"

"He's testing a plane known as the Wildcat. They've gotten word from China that the Japs are field-testing a new fighter. He thinks the Japs are going to plaster us, because they're building aircraft carriers and have forward bases in the islands they obtained as war prizes from Germany after the World War. His friends think the same thing. They also know how unprepared we are to fight the Fuhrer's hoards. He's bright, a gentleman, a bruiser no sane person would confront, incredibly handsome, a great kisser, and has the greatest sense of humor I've known. I love him." She leaned against the door, weak in the knees.

"All that stuff about the Japs and the Nazis, Mae. It's old news. As for the rest, I wouldn't know. Be careful though; it's a dangerous time to fall in love."

"If you want my advice, Colonel, we ought to make friends with the Yanks.

There's a lot they can teach us. Pumping them for information will backfire on us, and, I can't do it any more. I'm a secretary, and that's what I'll be from here on. I intend to make Captain Andrew Seghesio my husband. Good night." She turned up the stairs.

"Mae, thank you," Bader called after her, "and good luck."

0400 Hours, August 1, 1939
San Francisco, California

Chief Petty Officer Gwyeth Jones was on his way to the launch that would return him to his mistress waiting offshore, fully lit from bow to stern. *Arizona* was always beautiful, but dressed for an evening on the town, she became a seductress. The shoreline was crowded by citizens who came out to see the show their Navy was putting on for them.

Jones' right arm smarted from the tattoo newly implanted on his biceps, the result of a bad poker hand. To prevent its chafing, he had rolled his short-sleeve shirt above the shoulder, thus exposing an ornately lettered *"BB-39"* above the words "USS *Arizona*." Ah, well. It was a deserved consequence for a stupid bluff with lousy cards. Thinking it vulgar, he had resisted the tattoo tradition common among the Navy's non-commissioned officer fraternity. That he now bore a three-color beauty would increase the winner's glee. Ah, what the hell do jelly-brained gunner's mates know anyway? He chuckled to himself at that thought, and reminded himself to use it the next time Zachariah Foster guffawed at the story behind his decoration. Actually, when he examined it yet again, the artwork wasn't all that bad.

His face sobered when he heard the thump of fists on flesh coming from the alley just ahead. Two men were pummeling another with obvious enjoyment. The victim was taking a ferocious beating, and blood spotted the pavement where Jones stood, about fifteen feet from the action. The man's trousers and underwear were down around his ankles. Action became mandatory when saw that he wore a Navy white uniform.

"Hey! What's going on?" Jones yelled.

"Look what we have here. Another sailor boy!" one of the men said.

"Yeah, but this one's more important. Look at the fancy suit," the other replied.

"This here nigger says he's in the Navy. We think the sumbitch stole the suit to disguise himself so's he could get some white women. Ain't that right, nigger?" He was shoving the man against a brick wall holding him by his throat.

"We caught this boy in our favorite fucking parlor, cozing up to our favorite bitches. We told him he didn't belong there, but he didn't move out fast enough, right nigger?" He slapped the man across his face.

"Fun's over, fellas. Let him alone and get lost. I'll make sure all is forgotten," Jones said, wishing to make peace to see to the injured man. The only color that mattered to him was Navy summer white. The fact that it was smeared with red heightened his concern.

"You're all wrong, sailor boy. We're gonna take care of him. He'll never do another white woman. No sirree," one of them said, as he was drawing a straight razor from his pocket.

"The hell you will, friend. Drop it—now."

"You plannin' to help him?" the one with the razor said.

"I'm planning on getting him back to his ship in one piece. Now, then. Please drop the razor, or put it in your pocket if you like. You've had your revenge, for what it's worth. Just get on with the night, okay?" Jones replied. His muscles tensed, and his senses becoming more acute. There would be no peaceful ending.

"We'll just see who's giving the orders." The second man pulled a night stick from his jacket and rushed Jones. The chief kicked the man in the knee and grabbed the arm wielding the weapon, slamming the attacker face first into the brick wall. Blood and teeth hit the pavement before his head did.

"Now there's only me and you," Jones said, picking up the night stick.

"And I still have this razor," the other man said, bringing the weapon down to the groin of the black man who still was immobile.

"You may get in a cut, but I guarantee you I'll beat your brains out of your nostrils. I promise."

The goon's eyes bulged wide with fear. The sight of his friend's blood oozing across the cement was discomforting. He backed against the wall still brandishing the razor, but now only to cover his escape from the man with the big stick. He reached the alley entrance and ran.

Jones went over to the fallen sailor. His lips were split and lacerations above both eyes gushed blood over swollen cheeks. "Hey, friend, can you hear me?" Jones asked.

"I can hear ya. Dear Lord, thank you for comin'," he said, trying to focus his savior's military dress cap, and the Chief Petty Officer insignia it carried. "I can hardly breathe."

"They worked over your ribs pretty good. Can you see all right?"

"Yeah, but my head's bangin' pretty bad."

"What's your ship, sailor?" Jones asked.

"The *Arizona*, Chief. I'm supposed to report tomorrow morning as the captain's steward. I was just lookin' for a little lovin' before I left. I ain't had no trouble in that place before."

"Save it. What's your name?"

"Joshua. Seaman Joshua K. Friar."

"Well, Seaman Friar, you're in luck. The *Arizona*'s my ship, too. Let's get you aboard her and have you looked at."

"Aye aye, Chief," Josh Friar said.

Jones took his handkerchief and Friar's tee shirt, and bandaged the wounds above his eyes as best he could. He then pulled Friar's underwear and trousers up. Friar was short and slightly built, and Jones decided he'd do better carrying him piggy back. He noted the thug lying in the alley groaned and began to stir.

"Hey, Chief. Nice tattoo!" Friar said in a most complimentary way.

"Friar. Don't push your luck."

As they approached a busy intersection to flag down a cab, the man with the razor reappeared, accompanied by a miscreant wielding a stiletto.

"Hey, sailor boys. The lesson isn't over!" Stiletto man tried very hard to look vicious, but a glare from Jones indicated he didn't have the heart for this.

Jones had enough—he'd lost at cards, his arm throbbed, his best dress khakis were stained with blood, and he was totally incensed that someone had dared to do harm to anyone wearing the uniform of the United States Navy—and a shipmate at that. If there were lessons to be learned here, Jones was going to do the teaching.

"I'm putting you down for a moment, Josh," he said, and gently laid him across the hood of a cab that had stopped at the corner in response to his wave. The driver jumped out in protest, but Jones' upraised hand forestalled him. "This'll only take a minute. Start the meter."

The man with the razor charged. At precisely the right moment, Jones grabbed the man's arm and twisted it by the wrist, using his momentum to slam him into the taxi's windshield pillar. His collarbone emitted a muted crack as his shoulder socket shattered. The blade fell to the ground. Jones gripped the dangling arm by the elbow and wrist, and broke it loudly over his knee. The man screamed once just before Jones' massive fist broke his nose. The whole affair took only five seconds.

The stiletto man dropped his blade in flight, but Jones caught him within a few steps. He slapped his face repeatedly, the insult delivering greater pain. The man fell to the ground, and found the chief's big index finger an inch from his nose. "Find nicer friends." Jones returned to help Friar into the cab. "The Wharf, please," he told the incredulous driver.

Gwyeth Jones helped Joshua Friar into the launch, ignoring the crowds still under the spell of the glowing temptress.

"You'll love the *Arizona*, Josh. And Captain Kidd is a helluva skipper. You'll like working for him."

"Chief, if you say so, I promise I'll like him. Thanks."

"No need for thanks. We're shipmates on the best ship in the Navy. We look out for each other. That's what we do best."

The captain saw Jones' blood-splattered uniform and the sailor being carried off to sickbay.

"Explain, Chief."

"What happened to the civilians?" Kidd asked when Jones had finished.

"Resting comfortably, sir."

"Anything else I should know?"

"No sir. That's it. By the way, it turns out Friar's your new steward. Nice kid, sir."

"Nice tattoo. Wait till Chief Foster sees it."

"His brain's turned to jelly. It's from being around those big booming guns too long, sir."

"Those guns are what this ship exists for."

"That's what those gunnery guys like to say, sir."

Kidd laughed. "You don't agree?"

"Sir, I just hate to admit she's such a formidable broad. She's too beautiful to be so tough."

1300 Hours, August 1, 1939
New York City

Andy and Mae strolled hand in hand down Manhattan's Fifth Avenue. New York on Saturday seemed to change from metropolis to small town. The weekday hustle-bustle became a slow-motion stroll. The setting remained the same, but the characters assumed a leisurely approach to the business of life.

"You don't look nearly as menacing in street clothes as you do in your uniform, Captain Seghesio."

"Actually, I'm wearing my special Marine uniform underneath. It's blue with red shorts, and the shirt has a red 'S' on it. The damned cape, though, keeps getting caught in my underwear."

"Ha! I should've just kept walking, and not said a word."

"Hey, do you know this place?"

"My goodness, no, but it certainly looks interesting. The famous Tiffany's!" She gazed at the precious metals and stones glittering in the sunlight.

"Let's go in, shall we?"

They wandered up and down the counters, Mae gasping at the selection. She stopped for a longer look at a showcase of pearls.

"You like them?" Andy said.

"I love them. My mother has a set my father brought back from China. She wears them on the holidays. I've always loved their shimmer. Look how the light plays on them with such lovely colors."

"What was your dad doing in China?"

"He was a diplomat in Peking. Oh, they're so beautiful!"

Time to be a hero. "Excuse me, sir. May we see those?"

"Surely." The nattily dressed salesman brought out the string of lovely jewels.

"Oh, I couldn't," Mae said.

"Why not?" Andy replied, clasping them around her graceful neck. "They look wonderful."

"Oh, my!" she said, upon seeing her reflection in the mirror on the counter. "They are smashing!" She turned a bit to take in the full effect of their lustrous sheen. "Oh, well. Enough of this," she said as she turned to let the salesman undo the clasp. "I've had my..."

"How much?" Andy asked.

"Three hundred dollars, sir, on our spring sale."

"Okay, then." Andy reached for his wallet.

Mae turned to him. "Andy! You can't!" Mae said, in disbelief.

"I'm a Marine. I can do anything I want. And we can't pass up a bargain like this. It would be un-American."

"But they're so expensive! We barely know..."

"What do we barely know, Miss Leland?"

She hugged him tightly when she felt her eyes begin to well. "Come on, Mae! I can't get to my wallet, and the man's waiting."

She didn't let go. He held her with one arm, and fumbled for his wallet with his other hand in the inside vest pocket of his sport coat.

"Jeez, Mae!" He shrugged at the salesman, who winked back. Everyone in the store wore a warm grin.

"Mae, you've got the whole place going nuts!" Her tears dampened his neck. "Come on, you're gonna stain my sport coat. It's brand new. Lisa gave it to me last Christmas, and if I ruin it she'll kill me."

"Thank you, sir. Here's your receipt. Should you wish to return the merchandise..."

"Let me ask you something, friend. Do you think that's even a remote possibility?"

"I can't believe how happy you make me," Mae said.

"Aren't I something?" he said with a laugh. "Now you have a string of pearls to go with your favorite song, Mae."

"In the mood, Andy?" she said with a laugh.

"From the moment we bumped butts on Futurama," he replied, holding her close.

"I'm not going near any other stores. You make my head spin, Seghesio, not to mention what you're doing to my heart."

"They call it love, Miss Leland."

Chapter 6

The summer months were flying. By July's end Jack Burns was released from Bethesda Naval Hospital, still unsteady on his feet and suffering from recurring blurred vision and an annoying ringing in his ears. The purple and yellow color was fading from his forehead, but a clearly visible one-inch scar remained above his left eye. His wife, Julie, fussed over him, and his two children were the constant craftsmen of all kinds of presents to cheer their father. What was really aggravating Burns as he "spent time in dry dock," as Julie liked to say, was that he would not now be the *Enterprise*'s first commander-air-group (CAG). He had spent countless hours advising in the carrier's construction dealing with her ability to launch, recover, and relaunch her air group with devastating efficiency; and he had been instrumental in the *Big E*'s shakedown. CAG was something he'd dreamed about his whole career. The visit by his long-time friend Joe Rochefort did little to console him.

"C'mon, Jack. Get over it. It's only for a little while. It'll be fun working together, and now you get to come to Hawaii. I tell you it's a slice of heaven. Just think how nice it will be for the family."

"The *Big E*'s going to Hawaii, too. I just know she is. You know how much it meant for me to CAG her?" Burns lamented. "I'll tell you. Everything. Now I'm back to being a spook."

"There's nobility in spookdom," Rochefort said, sounding more hurt than he was. He could only imagine Burns's anguish. CAG was a career move that might in the near future put Jack in the captain's cabin of the *Enterprise*, or one of the new *Essex*-class carriers just beginning gestation in Norfolk. His knowledge of carrier operations was second to none in the United States Navy. Even the Japanese considered him an expert. That Genda fellow they'd met in London just prior to Burns' departure to catch the *Enterprise* for her shakedown was a good example. He never let Burns out of his sight at any reception the naval attachés attended.

"Aw, Joe, I'm not demeaning your work. It's just not my first choice. You understand that, don't you? It's just that…Hey, stop that!" he yelled to Rochefort, who was feigning tears and blowing his nose on Jack's bathrobe.

"Judging solely from your history, I don't agree with what you think your first-choice is," he laughed. "Shit, Jack, you smack up a lot of expensive equipment. Those Speedy-Three's cost the Navy $30,000 each. How many of them do you think they're going to let you dent?" Rochefort said with a laugh.

"Very funny." Burns crossed his arms, trying not to smile. It didn't work. Joe Rochefort was just too damned funny. "Ah, well. So what are you working on, or should I say, how are you frittering away the government's money?"

Rochefort turned serious and leaned forward. "We broke the Japanese diplomatic code. We can read all their stuff faster than they can. We built a machine that reads Purple like we wrote it. We call the intercepts *Magic.*"

"Whoa! We've come a long way. What about their naval code?"

"That's where we hope you can help us. We can't crack it, even though it seems to be based on an older code we call Blue. We've got the dictionary down pretty well, but the additive tables are driving us nuts, and the sonsabitches are changing it every six months. We hope your knowledge of Japanese will make the difference. As upset as you are, it equals how happy I am you're with me."

Jack Burns found himself smiling. Joe Rochefort was one hell of a guy.

1200 Hours, August 24, 1939
Montauk Point, Long Island.

Cedric Leland was a blue-blooded cloud-buster of a flyboy, no doubt about it. A wiry six feet, with a shock of long blond hair, his ice-blue eyes rivaled those of his sister's lover. Andrew Seghesio and he hit it off like fraternity brothers on a panty raid. Aviation was always the topic of discussion whenever they were together, their hands performing an intricate ballet of aerial maneuvers as they talked. Once, Mae left the Seghesio's restaurant to go shopping with Lisa. They kissed both flyers goodbye, neither of whom realized they were gone until Andy's mother came to ask where they were. Neither could recall their departure. After all, they had been discussing how to recover the new twin-engined P-38 Lightening fighter from a flat spin, something Lockheed was having a hell of a time figuring out on its own.

Andy had taken Ced up in an SBD and showed him the divebombing techniques the Navy had developed. Even though fighters were his first love, Seghesio was qualified to fly every plane in the Navy's inventory. Cedric gained a whole new appreciation for his courage when he made a landing with the SBD on the *Yorktown* when she was inbound to the Brooklyn Navy Yard for a hull inspection, just to show Ced how it was done. Today found the pair strolling along the beaches of Montauk, Long Island, while Lisa and Mae tried to absorb the last few rays of the late August sun.

"Andy, look at that! Is that the *Queen Mary?*"

Seghesio raised his binoculars. "No, its not. *Mary's* got three stacks—but I think it's the *Normandie!* Her superstructure isn't as block-like as *Mary's*. Beautiful, isn't she?"

"Frankly, I think the *Queen's* a prettier lady," Cedric replied with a chuckle.

"You would. Speaking of pretty, is the Spitfire up to the Me-109?" Andy asked. "From what we hear, the Messerschmitt's a beauty."

"Our data tell us it's in a class by itself; but I think the Mark 3 Spit will have an edge in rate-of-climb, firepower, and dive speed. I don't expect the 109 is all that superior to the present Mark 2 Spit, but unless we get into a tangle, we won't know."

"Oh, you'll know soon enough. Count on it."

"You're at odds with your countrymen, Andy. You really think we're going at it again?"

"No doubt about it. It's just a matter of when, and I don't think you'll have all that long to wait. The treaty the Nazis just signed with the Russians guarantees it. They've protected their rear, and Western Europe is the front again. Poland will be first. That little bastard with the bad haircut has been pushing them for land concessions. They're weak and vulnerable, especially now since they can't count on the Russians for help. You and France are it, Ced. You should have smacked Hitler the minute he reoccupied the Rhineland."

"Doesn't America feel threatened?"

"Not by the Germans. The Japs are troubling us more. There's not much of a feeling for going to war in Europe again. Many still think the first time was a grand mistake. We're more concerned about the Philippines and Hawaii and what the Japanese are doing in China. When you have heroes like Charlie Lindbergh extolling the virtues of neutrality, getting public opinion aroused to battling across the Atlantic again is a tough nut to crack."

"If the Japs attack Singapore and Hong Kong, don't you think you'll be drawn in? Our possessions in the Pacific are everyone's concern. Not that the Japanese are such great warriors. Our colonial armies…"

Seghesio turned around so fast his neck muscles strained. "Your colonial armies will get creamed," he said. "Don't underestimate those sons-of-bitches. Right now they have an advantage in numbers and weapons technology. We never thought they'd take China, but they've gobbled up a chunk of it already. The Imperial Japanese Navy is first-rate. Their *Kaga* was the first carrier to launch an air group in combat. Rumor has it that they're building two monster battleships, and two more big fleet carriers are almost completed. If you ask me, they'll be able to do whatever they like in a year or so while we're still catching up. If they do it right, we'll be forced to sue for peace in six months, or give up the Pacific to the West Coast until we're ready for a comeback."

"Oh, come now, Andy!" Cedric Leland was incredulous. "Are you drinking more of your father's homemade wine? What about fuel for their fleet, or resources for replacing their ships when they're sunk? What about…"

"Hold on." Andy put his hand on Leland's shoulder. "I said they only have a six-month window to get it done. They'll have the military capability by mid-1941. Our stuff will still be in the pipeline, because they have a head start. Can you stop them from taking Malaya? What if Singapore falls? If you're in the clinches with the Germans, who's going to watch the store in the Pacific? Us? I just told you they're better than we are right now. Six months can be an eternity."

"Singapore is the strongest…"

"Singapore will fall in no time. How will you defend it when you can't resupply and reenforce it? The Germans will give you all the grief you can handle. You won't be able to spare your Navy. They'll be tied up keeping the Atlantic and the Mediterranean open."

"Then what about your Philippines? What chance do they have if the sons of Nippon are so strong?" Ced Leland said, bemused at the wit of his comment.

Seghesio looked at him deadpan. "Not an ice cube's chance in hell." They walked along in silence watching the gulls sweep over the dunes.

"What about the Wildcat? Is it up to the latest Japanese or German fighter types?"

"It's a toss-up. We build planes for the long haul, the Japanese for the short haul. Their range is greater, but they had to give up something—our boys in China say it's armor protection for the pilot and fuel tanks. The planes become torches or meat wagons with a few well-placed rounds, but you don't worry about losing airplanes and pilots if you don't plan on losing them for long. Our torpedo planes are pitiful. They're flying crematoriums. I think you'll agree that Dauntless we flew in is a sweetheart."

"Indeed! The Royal Navy's Swordfish torpedo planes are biplanes, Andy. What chance do you think those will have?" Leland said with a shake of his head.

"A good one if they attack in surprise. If not…well, there will be plenty of broken hearts." He picked up a flat rock and skimmed it along the waves. "Four skips. Pretty good, huh?"

"Excellent." Ced searched for the perfect stone. "Speaking of hearts, Andy, where do you and my sister stand? I don't mean to pry, but Mae is very dear to me. Even our parents are excited to know you, if only through letters. That string of pearls never leaves her neck."

"Then, Ced, I hope this never leaves her finger." Seghesio pulled a ring box from his pocket. The sun danced within the two-carat diamond, releasing a rainbow from each facet of the oval stone. "I'm going to give it to her next week at my parents' place for her birthday. What do you think?" A smile tweaked the corner of his mouth. "I mean, I would've asked your mom and dad, but I can't get over to England just now."

Cedric Leland pumped Andy's hand. "Welcome to the family! I've always wanted a brother just like you." He didn't mention that he and Lisa had progressed beyond the "just friends" stage. He threw his stone. "Ha, Seghesio! That was five skips!"

1300 Hours, September 1, 1939
Little Italy, New York City

Mae Leland cried non-stop for an hour. All it took to start her up again was another glance at the ring on her left hand. Lisa cried, too, all in the spirit of sisterhood, Andy said, as did Patty James and Carol Herbst. Mama Seghesio did what she always did when she cried, either for joy or despair—she made a lasagna. Andy, Tom Hamilton, John Munroe, and Cedric Leland drank scotch and beer. Papa Seghesio bought dinner for his favorite customers who happened to be in the restaurant, and drank wine.

"If I had known the whole world was going to turn upside down today, I wouldn't have done this," Andy slurred. "All I wanted to do was make Mae happy. This is getting out of hand. Was she always so emotional?"

"Always. When Father gave her a charm she had wanted for the longest time for her birthday, she cried all morning. When our spaniel Potts died, she cried for a week. I haven't a clue as to how long this will last."

"Forever, I hope," Tom Hamilton said. "A toast to a lifetime of love!" he said, as he stood holding a shot glass brimming with Johnny Walker Red.

A stone-faced Colonel Bader entered the restaurant quickly from the street, his eyes searching the room.

"Colonel, you're late!" Cedric exclaimed.

Bader's face didn't crack a smile when his eyes met Cedric's. "I've some bad news. We just received a cable from London. The Nazis invaded Poland this morning. The Polish army is reeling. Armor is pouring over the borders, and the Luftwaffe is bombing their rail links and roadways. They've struck like lightening and have made unbelievable progress."

The restaurant stilled. Everyone looked at Bader as if he had announced the Apocalypse. Most knew it to be literally so.

"I'm terribly sorry, everyone. I didn't mean to throw a wet blanket on the festivities."

"It's not your fault, Colonel Bader. That *figlio di putan* Tedeschi. It's his fault!" Papa Seghesio sat in despair.

Mae looked up at Andy, the corners of her mouth turning downward. "Oh, Andy! This ruins everything!" She began to cry, but this time the tears were bitter. She missed the glance of despair her brother shared with Lisa Seghesio.

"Hold on, Mae. It's only a setback, not the end. Colonel, have England and France declared war?"

"We expect that Prime Minister Chamberlain is discussing it as we speak. All military personnel have been called back to their units, if that's any indication. Cedric, I wouldn't venture too far from a telephone."

Leland's face seemed to glow, and his expression was not lost on Seghesio, Hamilton, or Munroe, whose faces showed a proud defiance.

"Okay, everyone. Let's remember what we're here for. My son and this lovely lady are gonna be one," Papa Seghesio said, as he brought another pitcher of beer.

"The first Jerry I shoot down will be for you, Andy," Leland said.

"And when you're up there, Ced, remember we're with you, too," Tommy Hamilton said as John Munroe nodded in agreement. "To the Royal Air Force!" Hamilton toasted. "God bless them!" It was far from bravado or cheerleading. Pilots loved each other, no matter what uniform they wore. That half were the enemy was a consequence of Destiny. Fighter pilots especially seemed to hear a higher calling. They could hate, but only after the respect for the man was supplanted by the need to destroy his uniform and the aircraft he flew in the pursuance of war. Theirs was a deadly craft that hinged on never taking the other man for granted.

No warrior was as fragile as the man flying the incredible machine that imparted superhuman abilities to its master. That they ventured upwards to the thin air above the good earth already made the death of the man a more honorable one than that of those who never left its surface. Dying alone, face unseen by his executioner, being torn apart in an explosion of volatile liquids, or perhaps trapped, wounded, and being burned alive, and aware of an imminently gruesome demise almost forced pilots to love each other. No sane man could send another to such a death, or accept it, without having the utmost respect for his victim.

Mae went to hug her big brother only to find Lisa already in his arms, her face buried in his shirt. Andy saw that Lisa and Cedric were closer than friends. Mae had known practically since their affair began. She turned to her fiance with a smile that made him lust for her.

_____

2100 Hours, September 1, 1939
10 Downing Street, London

"I need you here, Winston. The public demands your inclusion in the war cabinet. I guess you were right. He couldn't be trusted an iota," Chamberlain said.

"That argument was rendered academic the second the Germans crossed over the Polish border. What do you need me to do, Neville?" Churchill replied, chomping the end of a fresh Corona as he leaned forward to accept whatever assignment the prime minister was about to make. He knew it was only a matter of time before he sat in Chamberlain's place.

"What about your old post, First Lord of the Admiralty?"

The battlecruiser HMS *Hood* was steaming through the Atlantic that evening just south of the tip of Ireland, very close to where the *Lusitania* met her doom. On full submarine alert, she was heading a force of six other warships when Lieutenant William Shears' earphones came alive with a coded message he quickly deciphered. He ran to the officer of the deck and handed it to him with a broad smile. The OD let out a loud whoop and slapped him on the back. He then ordered the *Hood*'s signalman to flash the message to the other ships in the force.

WINSTON IS BACK

The fog horns blaring on his majesty's warships pierced the night in delirious acknowledgment for a full five minutes.

_____

2100 Hours, September 1, 1939
The White House

"What about the Japanese? Have they declared war?" Franklin D. Roosevelt asked his secretary of state. The cabinet had gathered that first evening to discuss the events they had anticipated for months.

"No, Mr. President, we don't expect a declaration from them as yet, despite their fondness for Hitler. They're not ready for war with us. They know we wouldn't tolerate a march on the British or French colonies in the Pacific."

"I don't think our toleration counts for much, Cordell," the Secretary of the Interior said. "What would stop them, their fear of Russia?"

"Right now, Mr. Ickes, it's their unpreparedness. Their fleet is growing and constantly training. If Japan were ready, she would have attacked without a declaration. They've done it before, and you can count on their doing it again," Harry Hopkins stated.

"It seems we're back to 1914," Roosevelt said. "Sooner or later, we'll be in this up to our necks."

"Let's take our time," Cordell Hull replied. "There's no need for us to take any action now. An expression of regret will do just fine for the present."

Harry Hopkins, Roosevelt's trusted advisor concurred. "That's correct. In the meantime, let's put our forces on alert and insure that our ships maintain the right of safe passage in open water. All ships, especially those of England and France, must be guaranteed safe passage while inside our territorial limits."

"Yup. This sounds like 1914 all over again." Roosevelt stifled a yawn. "Has anybody got a cigarette?" he asked, his jutting chin uplifted in confidence. "This time, we mustn't be caught up in events. We need to control them."

Chapter 7

First Lord of the Admiralty Winston Churchill didn't wait for the chauffeur to open the door of the Rolls Royce. He was anxious to get inside the extravagant mansion that now housed the Government Code and Cipher School and to speak with Chad Eversole about the "incredible breakthrough" his team had made. He quickened his steps and tipped his hat to the Royal Marine guards as the English oak door swung open. He handed his bowler, gloves, and cane to the valet, and as he took off his coat he looked up to see Chad Eversole walking into the foyer, his hand extended in greeting.

"You've done quite well to have landed this mansion as your headquarters," Churchill said, turning slowly to survey the vast magnificence of the place. "Bletchley Park is just far enough away from London to avoid the government's noses in your work yet near enough for your social life not to suffer."

"Well put, sir. I must admit both endeavors are going well." He directed Churchill into a wood-paneled study, where a roaring fire defied the winter chill. "Whiskey?" he offered, as Churchill settled into a well-stuffed leather-upholstered chair.

"Please, with lots of water. It will be a long day, I'm afraid. So, Chad," Churchill said crossing his legs and settling back comfortably, "what is this all about? Why all this intrigue? What's the urgency?"

"We've made a profound discovery about our greedy friends in the Far East." Eversole sat in a well-worn leather couch opposite Churchill, and leaned forward, his eyes reflecting the dancing fire a few meters away. "We've broken JN-25."

"That would be their fleet cipher."

"Absolutely. We know their every move as it's made. We're at the point where we can identify their individual ships. We've already got Yamamoto pegged down. I can almost predict his daily schedule on his flagship."

"Astounding!" Churchill replied, his face still reflecting surprise and delight.

"I thought you might want to know immediately. The consequences for our Far Eastern colonies will be enormous. It gives our forces an unseen and unheard weapon. If you know your enemy's plans, it's far easier to devise a defense."

"To say the least. What a windfall! It's as if we've been given an entire fleet!" Churchill exclaimed, walking to the fire, and taking a sip of his drink.

"Well, sir, in a realistic sense, we have," he said, producing a pack of Lucky Strikes. "When we share this with the Americans, they can deploy their Navy to..."

Churchill turned from the fire and cut him off sharply. "You will do nothing of the sort!"

His countenance changed dramatically, almost frightening Eversole. "Sir?" he replied, taking an unlit cigarette from his lips, "I have trouble with that. The yellow bastards have already seized the Spratley Islands, only seven hundred miles from Singapore. For what purpose, if not as a staging area for an assault on Malaya? Our Pacific colonies' safety depends on the American Navy defending them. Damn it! Why are you so dead set against their knowing this?"

Churchill's jaw clenched, and his eyes burned with fury at Eversole's insubordinate response. But Eversole was a bright and dedicated officer whose career was a model of exemplary service to the Crown. That he had been invited here told of his respect for the chain of command; he could have gone directly to Chamberlain. He took a deep breath and turned to the fire.

"Chad," he began, speaking slowly and passionately, "we are in a desperate situation. The Americans will be slower coming to our aid than they were in the First World War. Their country is more divided now than at any time in their short but proud history, because they sent their sons to die here twenty-three years ago, only to have us make a terrible mess of things again." He paused and reached into his breast pocket for a cigar. He bit off the end, and searched for a match in his vest. "A German U-boat torpedoed and sank the liner *Athenia* not a day after war was declared. Eight Americans drowned, but Roosevelt adamantly stuck to neutrality. They were far more outraged over the *Lusitania*. They are not at all willing to shed their sons' blood again on European soil. We mustn't be so quick to share such a profoundly important discovery with those whose reluctance to assist us might be encouraged by the false security of knowing what the Japs are up to. We must use this to our advantage in getting America fully engaged in the war."

"What if America is attacked by the Japanese? If we sit idly by, knowing full well..."

"That's precisely my point!" Churchill said, turning quickly to face Eversole. "I don't believe in the Japs' vaunted military capability. They haven't yet solidified their gains in feudal China. But what if the Japanese seize our possessions in the Pacific and America stands by, still proclaiming neutrality? Suppose the sons-of-bitches decide to attack American possessions in the Pacific. What if the United States is fully aware of the impending attack because we've give them JN-25? They could use their new Flying Fortress bombers to attack the Japanese fleet far to sea. They demonstrated that capability by playfully intercepting ocean liners seven hundred miles from New York. If they annihilate the Imperial Japanese Navy in a matter of weeks and the Japs sue for peace, we'll be left to face the Nazi hordes alone. Hitler might then make a pact with the Americans, whose minds still haven't changed about fighting in Europe again. Then they might take over our Far Eastern Empire as we're forced to capitulate to the Huns. We're so weak compared to the Germans. We need American help. If America isn't directly and successfully attacked in force we're on our own."

"Why see things so bleakly, sir? The French Army..."

"Colonel Eversole," Churchill replied, letting his shoulders slump, "you're the head of intelligence. Do you really have that much faith in the French Army?" he said, pointing his cigar hand at Eversole's heart.

Eversole's stare dropped to the Persian carpet.

"I thought so," Churchill said, finding matches on the fireplace to light the Corona. "We can only hope they last long enough and die nobly, to cause more outrage in America. I think that..." Churchill stopped in mid-sentence, suddenly becoming so flushed that Eversole thought the sixty-six-year-old facing him was about to have a stroke.

"Sir Winston? Are you quite all right?" Eversole said.

"Never better! This code we've come to know might be a double-edged sword. Not since Excalibur has there been such a mighty weapon!" He walked over to the huge world map hanging on one of the polished walnut panels, finishing his whiskey and water as he walked. "Chad, if you were the Jap, where would you first attack the Americans?"

"Right here, Sir Winston," Eversole replied, not wasting a moment in deliberation, pointing to a speck in the Pacific Ocean. "It's their most powerful forward base. The Philippines are closer to Japan, but not nearly as important to the direct defense of the United States, nor as easily re-supplied, that windbag MacArthur aside. If you neutralize this base," he continued, again pointing to the speck labeled Hawaii, "the isolation of the Philippines and the Western Pacific would be even more profound. The best thing from then on would be to keep the lifeline to Australia open. It would be difficult for the Japanese to take it. It would overwhelm their capabilities, at least until they were able to make full use of the resources of their newly captured possessions." He bit his lip when he found his finger pointing at Singapore, and eyeing Hong Kong.

"If things progress in Europe as I think they will, we must assure the Japanese succeed."

"Sir? I've lost you."

"Of course you have." Churchill laughed. He turned back to the map. "I'm getting ahead of myself. Or, should I say, behind." Churchill's eyes glazed over as he stared off into space. "I was drifting far back to my time in India and a conversation I had with a friend as we watched a magnificent sunset. We were discussing how the Spaniards would lose their empire over the sinking of the *Maine*, and…" His gaze shifted back to Eversole, and his eyes lost their dreamy veil. "Who's your best agent?" he asked, beaming like a little boy who just got away with mischief. "I have an idea that might ensure the Rising Sun doesn't set on us just yet. In fact, it might ultimately cause dusk to fall on the Germans."

Churchill's eyes focused again on that speck in the Pacific. *What was he up to?* Eversole wondered. His whole career had been dedicated to antagonizing his opposition at every turn while formulating the grandest of clandestine schemes to keep his adversaries off balance. Eversole's time in Russia was evidence of what the force called Winston Churchill could muster. Being in his presence as he eyed Hawaii like a wolf eyes a lamb gave Eversole a chill, despite standing so close to the roaring fire. He couldn't even guess what the First Lord was thinking, but he hadn't read *Savrola*.

***

March 1, 1940
London

Andrew and Mae were married on Christmas Day, 1939. The outbreak of war in Europe shortened their engagement because Andy thought the United States would soon be in the mix. He wanted Mae as his wife before he went off to do what he was trained for. It was a large wedding. Mae's parents flew the Atlantic, courtesy of the Royal Navy and Pan American Airways. A Royal Navy clipper flew them to Iceland, and a Pan Am Boeing 314 took them to the Marine Air Terminal at LaGuardia Airport. Tommy Hamilton was best man, and Lisa Seghesio was maid of honor. Jack and Julie Burns came, and Jack lost no opportunity to harass Andy unmercifully about his new rank of "plebe husband." His advice about bed chamber activity earned him an ear twist from Julie. John Munroe sent his apologies. The Navy had ordered him immediately to Oceana Naval Air Station to carrier-qualify the Grumman Wildcat, but his fiancé Nancy Herbst, attended. They held the reception in the ballroom of the Plaza Hotel, courtesy of a friend of Papa Seghesio, who had a few very solid connections in the hotel business.

Mae's wish to show off the handsome American souvenir she acquired at the World's Fair came true when Andy and Tommy Hamilton were given temporary duty in the United Kingdom as military attaches on March first. Their job was to report on the British war effort, their materiel requirements, and how their weapons and tactics matched those of the Germans. They were also to help RAF and American Army Air Force officers reconnoiter areas in the southern countryside that would make suitable bomber airfields.

Cedric Leland couldn't have been happier. "Just remember, Andy, she'll roll a bit faster than your Wildcat, and turn a bit quicker, too, because her wing loading is somewhat reduced."

"What about stall speed? I assume it's higher than the Wildcat's," Tommy Hamilton said.

"Correct. Just keep her nose up a bit. You'll get plenty of warning when it's about to happen. Ready to go?"

"You betcha!"

With that, the three of them mounted the left wings of their factory-new Supermarine Mark 3 Spitfires, fired up their Merlin Rolls-Royce engines, taxied into the wind, and soared into the springtime ether of King Arthur's beautiful, morning mist-covered countryside. Andy pressed the left rudder pedal, engaged more throttle, and gentled the joystick with its circular grip to the left. The mighty Merlin throbbed in perfect rhythm as his fighter kept formation with his two brother eagles. The landing gear retracted hydraulically with the pull of a handle, unlike the Wildcat's, whose gear was mechanically operated by turning a crank almost twenty times. It saved weight for the carrier-based fighter but was damned annoying to do. Ced was right; there was nothing quite like the Spit.

As they climbed to the south, the English Channel appeared on the horizon. Soon the chalk cliffs of Dover passed beneath their wings, and they were over water, with the Normandy shoreline soon rolling in where the sky met the earth. There, very soon, Tommy Hamilton realized, the fate of the European continent would be decided. The war had reached a lull. Something was up, all right, and speculation about what that might be was running wild. Some were suggesting that Hitler was conspiring with Stalin so Hitler could turn his legions on France with impunity to his rear. "Poppycock," one Frenchman called it. "Stalin must realize that Russia was the true target of history's latest corporal."

The aircraft turned back north after crossing the coastline at Pont du Hoc. Seghesio and Hamilton heard Leland respond to a message confirming their distance, altitude, and speed to an unknown caller, who merely identified himself as Omega.

"Blue one, this is three. Do you read, over?"

"Roger that," Leland replied.

"Who's Omega?"

"You are one smart American—follow me, and I'll show you."

They made landfall about twenty miles from their original encounter with the channel. Below them were rows of towers with odd-shaped cross members and a series of bunkers. Leland pointed down to the strange complex, and hand-signaled "O-M-E-G-A." He put his index finger to his mouth if to silence a child, and smiled wickedly.

"I still don't know what I saw," Tommy Hamilton said, as he exited the Spitfire's cockpit.

"You saw what we call RADAR. Your military has it, too, but it's something no one talks about."

"I've only read about it. You confirmed what they were reading, didn't you?" Andy said. Hamilton caught on.

"Exactly. They've just erected that particular station, and they're calibrating their equipment."

"I see it's facing the channel. Expecting trouble, Ced?" Tommy Hamilton said, with a smile.

"It's already here, Tommy. It's just a matter of time as to when it wants us for dinner." Cedric looked at his watch. "How about a pint before we go home? There's a grand pub a few minutes from here all the chaps frequent."

"I'd like to drink to the Spitfire. I've never enjoyed a flight so much as that one," Andy said.

"Make that two pints," Tommy agreed.

"She's beautiful, all right," Ced agreed. "I'd like to name mine Lisa. What do you think, Andy."

"I'd be honored; so would sis." Andy didn't tell him that Lisa would be arriving just in time for dinner.

1400 Hours, March 1, 1940
South Wales

Yuri Popov attached the two tanks of liquid, connected by coiled copper tubing that terminated at an explosive timer, to the nose of the five-inch artillery shell common to the United States Navy. He set the timer and dashed the fifty meters from the pit the shell sat in, to the protection of a sand-bagged bunker. "Here we go," he said to Chad Eversole, who watched intently. Thirty seconds later the pit erupted in flame, smoke, and flying dirt.

"I think we've got something here," Popov smiled.

"At the least. Tomorrow we'll try the new explosives with gunpowder. They should be just as foolproof. Ah, the wonders of science!" Eversole exclaimed.

"What did you call this nasty new stuff?" Yuri asked.

"Hypergolics. Liquids that explode on contact with each other. The timer merely allows them to connect through the copper tubing. When they're in the exact proportion…"

"I guess that means I stay out of France, then."

"Believe me, Yuri, there is plenty to do right here. I have something to keep you from getting bored just blowing things up. It involves an American diplomat who might think his duty is to make up the president's mind for him."

"I read the file today. The woman—can she be trusted? I've seen what women do to spies." He snickered.

"So you have, but you needn't worry about this one."

"Why am I blowing up artillery shells with this stuff?"

"I truly don't know. I'm just following orders from Royal Navy Ordnance. Admiral Shears gave me the specifics. I'm to report back to him on our little venture tomorrow morning."

"I'd bet on a commando raid on the U-boat pens at Wilhelmshaven. The goddamn things are impregnable to air attack and surface action."

"You're guess is as good as mine."

Yuri Popov trusted Chad Eversole. If he knew, Chad would have told him. What concerned him was the Russian question. Yuri knew men working out of Moscow who told him how weak the Red Army was and that Stalin needed time. Ever since war erupted, he had dreamed of that night on the lake, and in his sleep heard little Nina cry. It had never happened before.

2000 Hours, March 2, 1940
The White House

"So you think that the Russians will sign a pact with the Germans? What purpose does that serve?" Roosevelt asked Hopkins, setting the report on his crowded desk.

"Cordell agrees with me," Hopkins answered.

"It makes sense; our intelligence says the Red Army isn't up to stopping Hitler. Stalin killed all its leaders in the purges," Hull added.

"What about the Japanese?" Roosevelt said, looking at General George C. Marshall, the nation's top soldier.

"Their diplomats seem to think the linkage is a good idea. They figure the Russians won't attack them on their western flank because they're the Nazis' allies. It gives them a free hand in the Far East against the Brits and French. Bear in mind, Mr. President, that this is just an assessment made from bits and pieces of their Purple transmissions."

"What about the British? Has Averell got any feelings about this?"

"They're getting desperate," Hull replied.

Roosevelt reached across his desk and fumbled with a few papers before retrieving an envelope. "By the way, Joe Grew in Tokyo sent me this along with a translation of the newspaper clippings attached there," he said, pointing to the documents with his cigarette holder. "What do you and George think about this?"

Hull smiled as he finished the note and handed it to General Marshall, who openly chuckled. "It's preposterous, Mr. President. This kind of attack is a Japanese dreamscape," Hull replied.

"If they attack us anywhere, it would be the Philippines. That's why we're reenforcing MacArthur. They want Singapore and Hong Kong. Pearl Harbor is a long way from Tokyo," Marshall added.

Roosevelt's face bore an expression of angst that was becoming more common. He removed his glasses and rubbed his eyes before he looked up to the men across his desk. "I want to be perfectly sure we leave every avenue open for peace. I don't want us in this war because we bumbled an opportunity. Our military buildup shows our resolve to save the democracies of the world from this demonic terror that seems to have possessed the Japs and Germans. I don't want to be anybody's saps, but I must be assured that each of you will leave every opportunity open for negotiation. The American people deserve that, at the least. I don't want to take their sons because we sunk to the level of our adversaries, or, for that matter, our allies."

0800 Hours, March 3, 1940
The Sea of Japan

The practice torpedoes thudded into the battleship's sides with unerring accuracy. Ten planes, ten thuds. Next, the dive bombers screamed down on the battleship force. Using his binoculars, Genda could see the practice bombs spray their flour-like powder all over the *Kurishima*'s forecastle and forward turrets, as *Nagato* herself was struck again and again. The horizontal bombers, though, were not so effective. Of the twelve practice bombs dropped, only one met its end on the bow of *Nagato*. Genda frowned.

"Perhaps we should arm them with torpedoes instead. Ships underway are too difficult a target for aircraft bombing from high altitude," he said, turning to Yamamoto.

"Genda, you are too easily disappointed. This is only the first time they've tried. Besides, we plan to attack the ships at their moorings, and the only way we can attack the ships lying between their exposed sisters to port side and the island to starboard is to hit them with bombs. That's why we're developing those projectiles."

"But they will only cause moderate damage because they carry so little explosive. And what if we don't achieve surprise and their fleet gets underway just before our attacking planes arrive? What will we…"

"We will surprise them. We wish them out of action for six months. That's all the time we'll have, no matter how much destruction we cause with one attack. Their battleships don't have to sink, just be rendered impotent. Besides, think of the carriers! What will those special bombs do to them, moored help-lessly, filled with aviation gasoline? What if most of the ships are damaged when the second wave attacks? Then we can attack their land-based fortifica-tions. I know you're the aerial specialist, Genda, but it's difficult to blow up a hangar with a torpedo, is it not?"

Genda laughed heartily. Yamamoto had a way of putting things in perspec-tive. His warm smile implanted confidence. He looked up to see a flight of five of the new Zero fighters flash overhead in an arrowhead formation, its leader barrel-rolling in salute.

Yamamoto pointed upwards with tears in his eyes. "Genda, your Wild Eagles will not let you down. Look how magnificent they are!"

0900 Hours, March 3, 1940
"Wolf's Lair"

Adolph Hitler reviewed the notes of the meeting with the Japanese emis-sary Kurusu in the company of his foreign minister, Von Ribbentrop.

"Do you see the pact as keeping the Russians in the dark about our plans?" the Fuhrer asked.

"Yes, but it also forces the United States into the untenable situation of fighting to the east and west should she decide to enter the war. I still think they will not declare war on us, even if Japan carries out this attack on the Philippines they've proposed. Nevertheless, if our timetable holds true, the European continent will be ours and England neutralized. We will be rais-ing our flag in Moscow. Then the Japanese can attack the Pacific rim with impunity. The Italians can hold the Mediterranean with their fleet. If America doesn't reach an understanding with us by then, we declare war on her as well, and fulfill our treaty obligation."

"But why the Philippines?" Hitler asked. He walked to the world map and paused a moment to look out to the Bavarian Alps from one of Wolf's Lair's many windows. "I see Hawaii as the target of choice—it's where their fleet re-supplies."

"The Japanese want their Greater East Asia Co-Prosperity Sphere more than they want to subdue the United States. They are angrier at the French, Dutch, and British for their Asian colonialism than they are at America for supporting it. Hawaii means nothing."

"Horseshit!" Hitler shouted. "The bastards need to neutralize Hawaii!" He pounded the map with his fist. "Otherwise the United States Navy will rip off their heads and crap down their necks in no time! They lie to us! Any fool can see that! Who do they think they..."

"Fuhrer, if I may," Ribbentrop cut in, risking the wrath he had seen demonstrated time and again. He hurriedly continued when he saw that Hitler was taken aback by the interruption. "What does it matter where they attack? The result is the same. We will have maneuvered the United States out of the European war. They'll have to reach an accommodation with us to save England from invasion."

Hitler breathed deeply. "Very well," he said. "You will, however, do two things. First, the pact must be kept secret until the fall. Second, make sure nothing interferes with our preparations to cross the English Channel as soon as France capitulates. No peace initiatives are to be entertained, no matter who offers them."

"Yes, Fuhrer." Ribbentrop looked into Hitler's hypnotizing blue eyes. "May I offer one word of caution?" he said meekly.

"That's your job," he said, a false smile at the corners of his mouth.

"Reconsider the Channel crossing, should it come to that. History has proven it cannot be done since William the Conqueror."

"Ha!" Hitler exclaimed. "Neither has it proven Russia can't be conquered!" he said, slapping his leg, "but we will do that, too! No one has ever held the power I have in my hands!" Hitler said, clenching his fists. "Look at the mountains, Ribbentrop. Not ten years ago the French thought they were their own because they subdued us in the World War. Now they cower like moles in their Maginot Line pillboxes. Who else in history has built the state I have in ten years? The allies will fall to their knees! Our soldiers will spit on their bloated corpses as they march by in victory!"

"Yes, Fuhrer! Is there anything else?" Ribbentrop said, forcing a proud smile to his face. He had plenty of work to do, and he wanted to leave on good terms.

"Send in Jodl and Goering. Time is running short."

"Yes, Fuhrer."

"And Ribbentrop? What would you like to wager that the Japanese attack Pearl Harbor?"

"How about a case of Bavarian ale?" he responded. The Fuhrer's eyes had a friendly twinkle to them.

"So be it. And when I win it, none before will have ever tasted sweeter." He began to laugh.

"We shall see, Herr Hitler, we shall see." Ribbentrop laughed along with the man he regarded as the greatest on earth.

0800 Hours, March 3, 1940
London

Andy surveyed the *New York Daily News* that Lisa had brought over the Atlantic. Ever the sports enthusiast, he was pleased to see that the Rangers had at last won a Stanley Cup. He listened to the new Frank Sinatra recording of *I'll Never Smile Again,* with Mae's head on his shoulder.

"James Stewart was absolutely wonderful in the *Philadelphia Story* Andy. It was absolutely the best movie I've ever seen."

"Yeah, that Stewart is pretty good for a Princeton man. How's Mom and Dad?"

"They miss you, Andy. Having you so close for so long really spoiled Mama. They worry about you."

"They should worry about old Ced, Lisa," he said, pointing to his brother-in-law. "There's an ill wind blowing across the Channel."

"Plenty of people back home think it best for England to make peace with the Germans. Even Joe Kennedy says so, and he's our ambassador. Maybe the Germans are happy now that they have Poland," Lisa said, anxiously searching her big brother's eyes for a sign that she might be right.

"Hitler's appetite for conquest won't be satisfied anytime soon. Count on it. And there's the Japanese maw. It's all coming to a head soon."

"Congress is debating the draft bill. They say that it will force us into war."

"Lisa, draft bill or not, war will come."

"Andy, tell them about your fantastic airplane ride," Cedric said.

"Yes, Andy. Tell us how you flew a real fighter," Mae said, teasing her husband.

"Ced here got Tommy Hamilton and me set up with the Spitfire. It's an absolute delight of an airplane."

0900 Hours, March 3, 1940
San Pedro, California

"You take good of her, Jones. She's special to me. Something about her makes her seem…spiritual."

"She almost has a soul of her own, hasn't she, sir?" Jones helped Kidd find the right words.

"More than that. She senses things as if she knows more than we do. Remember how she wouldn't answer the helm in the fog? We were scared out of our wits that we'd collide with another ship, and if she had turned, we would have hit *Oklahoma* broadside."

"I've spent almost my entire career with her, sir. I know what you're saying."

Kidd looked his ship over from stem to stern, focusing briefly on her fourteen-inch rifles, then on the bridge from which he had given a thousand commands. He turned to rest his eyes on the two Kingfisher aircraft on her stern and atop turret three. He sighed heavily as men do when they fight back tears.

"In any event, Chief, Captain Train will count on you as much as I have. I've told him about your excellent work. He was well aware of your reputation before I finished uttering your name. He'll take *Arizona* to Pearl Harbor."

"Sir, if I may. I've never served under a finer officer. *Arizona* asked me to tell you she's just as impressed with you as well, and she looks forward to seeing you on her bridge again, with your new star on your collar and your ensign flying from her mast."

"I'd like to spend eternity there, Mister Jones, as long as I could have my family along. I've never had a better command, nor will I."

Jones froze at the captain's words, but dismissed them as the result of the emotion of the moment. *Arizona* stirred beneath them, an ever-so slight vibration crept into the soles of their feet.

"What was that?" Kidd asked.

"They're probably getting steam up for a boiler check, sir."

"Well, then, goodbye and good luck, Chief," Kidd said, shaking Jones' hand vigorously.

"Sir, good luck to you as well." Jones did a smart about-face and ordered "Attention on deck!" A commissioned officer usually served as the Officer of the Deck post, but Kidd asked Jones if he would fill in for this ceremony. The bosun's mate piped Kidd ashore, and the ship's company saluted their departing captain. The band played *For He's A Jolly Good Fellow* followed by *Anchor's Aweigh* as Rear Admiral Kidd's launch left for the San Pedro shore. *Arizona*'s foghorn sounded off for a full five seconds. Jones looked to the bridge to find the culprit, but saw no one. Nor did anyone else, including an equally bewildered officer not twenty feet from the horn's pull chain.

0800 Hours, March 7, 1940
New York Harbor

Halfway across the world, another foghorn sounded. A brand new ship had made her way down Scotland's River Clyde in the company of ten hardworking midwife tugboats four days before. She wore dull battleship gray rather than the striking black hull, white superstructure and red funnels that marked a Cunard liner. She was the greatest liner ever built, but the coming of war left her quite unfinished, not boasting the luxurious accouterments the rich and rising middle class she was built to serve might expect. She came into the world prematurely, so her birthing yard could be used by the much needed battleship, *Duke of York*.

Queen Elizabeth had to leave at once, as the tide that provided enough water under her keel would not come again for six long months. Rather than break her up, as had been suggested, the First Lord of the Admiralty decided to have her join her sister, the *Queen Mary*, in New York, a foster home where she would be safe from the Luftwaffe's probing bombers. Churchill figured the huge ships could carry 16,000 troops across the Atlantic—when the time came, of course. They would be vital to the war effort. Despite the secrecy, no doubt awaiting her crossing were the vicious U-Boats, sharks anxious to rip out her keel and put her on the bottom. That's why she sailed at night, zigzagging her way to New York at twenty-five knots. She was faster than that, but her brand new engines needed to be broken in before they could accommodate all her power.

She sailed into New York Harbor on March 7, blowing her foghorn in salute to the lady who blessed all newcomers. Thousands of well-wishers were on hand to greet her when she tied up at Pier 90. Besides her sisters *Mary* and *Aquitania*, her French cousins *Normandie* and *Ile de France* were on hand to greet her. Even the men on the sleek Italian siren *Rex* cheered her arrival.

Papa and Mama Seghesio treated her Captain Townley and his officers to dinner that evening. They all toasted Andy, Mae, Tommy, Lisa and Cedric most heartily. The enormity of the *Queen Elizabeth*'s gallant passage made everything seem righteous and possible. The First Lord of the Admiralty couldn't have been happier with the welcome the ship received in the New World. He couldn't have planned it any better than this. Perhaps there would bring an early, warm spring for England after all.

Chapter 8

1000 Hours, March 15, 1940
Pacific Ocean

The USS *Arizona*'s bow smashed through the fifteen-foot swells, throwing up plumes of spray that rainbowed in the bright Pacific sun. The sea foamed at her stern, torn by her four propellers that pushed her west to Hawaii. The younger crewmen were excited in spite of their circumstances. Hula girls, bleached white sand, warmth, and all the pleasures of a tropical paradise they may have only read about in *Treasure Island* would be theirs for the taking in a few short days.

Chief Jones smiled proudly as his ship heaved and rolled with the ocean's fury, whipped up by a thirty-five knot wind. She pulsed with the power of life. The crew, however, would pay a heavy price; her topsides needed to be cleaned of the salt spray, and her teak decks holystoned. He was always amused when sailors on their first cruise found out just how hard it was to keep the old girl ship-shape. *Arizona*'s quarterdeck was especially difficult to maintain. Battle-ships are necessarily built with low-slung hulls to keep their vital organs below the waterline and protected against shellfire. *Arizona*'s quarterdeck was cut ten feet below the foredeck, which further complicated matters. It was always awash in heavy seas and, as a result, was near impossible to keep shipshape. What exacerbated matters was the fact that her two stern turrets sat there, as did the one of the two catapults and its Kingfisher aircraft. Jones would find the crew's biggest smart-alecks and malcontents to swab and holystone that quarterdeck. So far none had emerged, but *Arizona* was only a day out of San Pedro.

As long as her bow was cleaving the ocean's mountainous waves, Jones was happy. Joshua Friar, on the other hand, wished for a visit from the Angel of Death. For the first time since coming aboard he was as seasick as anyone had ever been. His job of preparing the captain's mess was always an arduous one, but the mere sight of food caused his empty stomach to heave. The ship's surgeon had given him some Dramamine, but it was of little help.

"Hey Josh, how're you doing!" Chief Jones said, upon seeing one of his favorites as he made his daily rounds.

"I'm dying. Oh, God, can't you make this ship stop tossin' and turnin' so?"

Most seasick men had an ashen complexion. Friar's ethnicity made this impossible to detect. There was no mistaking his retching. "Shit, Josh, have you seen the doc? You can't..."

"He might just as well have pronounced me dead! He gave me some pills but..."

"Let's go," he said in the gruff style of a Chief Petty Officer.

Friar stiffened. "Outside? Lordy, you're not gonna throw me over the side, are ya? I'll get better, Chief! I promise!"

"Goddammit, Friar! I saved your ass awhile back, remember? Do you think I'd kill you and let the captain go hungry? C'mon. I promise you'll feel better."

The worst treatment for seasickness was not having a horizon to look at. Laying down exacerbated the symptoms. Though it was windy and the seas were heavy, the temperature was a crisp fifty-five degrees and the sky was brilliantly blue. Jones helped Friar through the hatch and put his hand on the rail of the bridge, while Captain Train looked on in amusement. Jones was forever living up to his advanced notices.

"There now. Look right past the bow. Concentrate on the horizon and breathe deeply. Keep this on in case you fall," Jones said, tightening a safety line around Josh's waist. "You'll be okay."

"I owe you again, Chief. Someday, I'll..."

"Save it, Friar. Like I said, shipmates look out for each other," Jones answered, pulling Josh's woolen watch cap down and his pea coat collar up. "Just stay warm, enjoy the day, and the ship," he said, giving him a reassuring slap on the shoulder. "She loves this stuff!"

The heavy seas diminished by mid-afternoon, and the Dramamine had a chance to work. The fresh air cleared Friar's head and eased his stomach. Captain Train and his staff had a gourmet meal at 2100 hours that night. He asked Jones to join the officers' mess as a thank-you "for a job well done."

1400 Hours, March 15, 1940
Oxford, England

"I don't want to go back, Cedric. I need to be with you," Lisa said, sitting up on the picnic blanket. The rolling hills just north of Oxford provided a romantic background for the young lovers whose heads were light with the advance of spring.

"But what about your studies? The interruption would do your work no good. Besides, England won't be a safe place for long."

"I don't think anywhere in the world will. I love you."

He looked into her beautiful blue eyes. The tear rolling down her cheek interfered with his determination. War or no war, it would be stupid to deny himself the woman who thought he walked on water. "I love you, too, Lisa," he said, as he gently kissed her.

"I know you're worried, but it seems all our futures have been put on hold," Lisa said, sniffling.

He handed her a handkerchief. "I guess we need to live for today, but Lisa, I'll not have you unless we're married. I don't know anything about any previous arrangements you've had with boyfriends, but you must know..."

"Cedric," she laughed, "I'm Italian. My brother beat up anyone who even glanced at me with a flirtatious eye."

"How about mid-June? That gives us a few months to prepare. What do you say?"

"Fine. I'll have Mother and Father come out, and...how about we honeymoon in Paris? I've never seen it, but my friends say it's absolutely lovely."

"And it is, especially when summer rolls in. The city literally blossoms. You'll love it at night—all those beautiful, warm lights transform it into a heaven on earth."

She looked up to him and she kissed him. Her lips had never before felt so warm and full.

"I hope Andy's pleased," he said, holding her close, his hand playing with her thick black hair.

"You're one of the few men he's ever liked, as far as I'm concerned. It must have to do with this pilot stuff," she said, her index finger skimming his Royal Air Force wings.

0900 Hours, March 15, 1940
London

Yuri Popov eyed the slender blonde as she exited the underground. She was wearing a black coat and hat and high heels, and carried a copy of the *London Times* under her right arm. He flashed the headlights on the Bentley twice, and got out to open the passenger door for her. He noticed her shapely legs as she brought them up over the rocker panel and into the car.

"Yvette Montage," she said. "And you?"

"Yuri Popov. I feel as if we've met before."

"We have, but I was a brunette then. I and another so-called 'whore' from Soho were in the company of two gentlemen who spoke excellent German. You dropped us off before the two gentlemen met an untimely death. Perhaps you read about it in the papers?" she said, a sly smile crossing her face.

"You're not...impossible!" he blurted.

"Dear Yuri! Come now! Do you think you could have done it all by your-self? Someone got them drunk and someone made them vulnerable. Someone asked to go home after giving those two bastards the send-off of a lifetime. Did you think you'd done it all by yourself?"

"I was told another agent would be involved, but I didn't think it in-volved…well, you know…ah…"

"It's been used to set up men throughout history." She took great pleasure in the astonished look on Popov's face. "I should damned near be fucked inside out by the time this latest chapter is written," she added, looking at the barrage balloons floating overhead.

"I'm sure the Queen herself will thank you for your efforts," he said tersely.

"If her Majesty wanted to help the war effort, I probably could get her some work." She started to wind her watch. "Shit, it's stopped. What time have you got, Yuri?" She brushed his shoulder as she leaned over to get a look at the clock on the Bentley's dash. Her touch caused him to stir. This woman was in a class by herself. The smell of her perfume, her carefully applied makeup, and her long blonde tresses made it difficult to concentrate. Her legs alone would be worth a portion of the crown jewels to some men.

"How did you get into the business?" he asked.

"Which business, whoring or intelligence? I was in the first before I tried the second. The money is better, and killing some lad who wants to play rough won't wind me up in Scotland Yard again."

"Again?" he said, stealing a glance at her ample bosom.

"That's where I was recruited. It was to do a few jobs now and then for M 1, or the gallows for stabbing the son of a bitch who started slapping me around when I asked to be paid."

"Do you know what this is all about, Yvette?"

"I haven't a clue. All I was told was to meet the man in the black Bentley. Nice auto, by the way, Yuri. Is it yours?"

"Yes, it is. I guess we'll find out when we see Admiral Shears."

"I'm sure the First Lord might have a few notions, don't you think, Yuri?" She gave a suggestive chuckle.

"You sound like you know him."

"Let's just say we've done business."

"Then business will be booming. He'll be prime minister as soon as the Jerrys cross into France or Belgium. I'm sure he'll provide you with plenty of work."

"Whatever; I'm always on the lookout for new friends."

Popov couldn't make heads or tails out of the situation. He'd never worked with a woman, let alone this kind. But he already had, hadn't he? Though the thought intrigued him, his cautious nature held his comments in check.

"Your name is French. I bet we find ourselves in France."

"My parents were, and I speak it, but I'm English. I don't do cross-Channel work," Yvette said.

"Even if the reward makes it worth while?"

"I don't want to fuck you, if that's what you mean. You might make it too easy to mix business with pleasure, Mr. Popov," Yvette said, her face bearing the sexiest expression he had ever seen.

"I meant money," Yuri said sheepishly.

"I'd rather work here. Let's leave it at that."

She reached in her bag to retrieve a lipstick tube. Yuri liked to watch women put on makeup, almost as much as he enjoyed watching them put on their stockings. He thought it most alluring, so very feminine. Yvette must have written the script for his pleasure, judging from the pulse in his loins.

"You're Russian, right?" she said.

"I was brought here after the World War. My parents were killed by Czarists."

"Oh?" She said that simple word more in empathy than surprise. "Mine were killed by the retreating Germans. I grew up in orphanages and foster homes. I discovered I had a gift for alluring men. I was told so by a foster father when I was thirteen. Some pair we are, hey Popov?" She winked at him, and gave him a playful poke. The feel of his well-muscled arm caused her pulse to quicken ever so slightly.

The two agents made their way to Admiral Shears' office, showing their passes at each door, stairwell, and elevator stand. The tension in the building was readily apparent, undoubtedly induced by the sandbags and Royal Marine guards at the entrance. No one smiled, and everyone seemed to be hurrying, even to the water cooler. The more gold braid on the uniformed sleeve or epaulet, the more dour the expression and the quicker the pace. Popov determined that Herr Hitler had already won a major battle, and no one in this building had bled a drop.

Chad Eversole greeted them in a hallway guarded by two Royal Marines with Sten guns.

"It's nice to see you," Eversole said, extending his hand.

"And good to see you, sir." He watched as Eversole cast his eyes on Yvette, waiting for him to say something; but he just smiled. "Oh, excuse me, sir! This is Yvette Montage. She's the agent you said Admiral Shears recommended."

Eversole took her hand and shook it gently, and smiled warmly, but he was still seething inside. No one had told him of her participation, nor asked his advice. As far as he knew, her only role was to seduce an American diplomat. From what he understood, this meeting was to initiate something grander. But he was a professional; he'd see how it played out.

"Well, now. Everyone's here. Let's go in and have some tea," Shears said, opening his office door, his broad face with its ruddy cheeks aglow. Shears had a full head of gray hair, pleasant gray eyes, and a square jaw. He stood at 5'10" and was slightly overweight as might be expected for a man of fifty-five years. He held a large briar pipe in one small, thick-fingered hand that seeped a pleasant aroma. His other hand was placed in his jacket pocket up to the thumb. "It's good to see you again, Yvette," he said, taking the young woman's hand.

"How's young William doing?" she asked.

"Just fine. He's on the *Hood*, you know. Communications officer."

"That's wonderful. Have you met Yuri Popov?"

"Only through reputation," Shears said, turning to meet the tight-jawed young man appraising him. "Commander, it's good to make your acquaintance."

"Thank you, sir." Yuri noted Yvette's surprise at his heretofore unknown standing in the Royal Navy.

"How are you doing, Eversole?" Shears asked, again rather jolly at Eversole's presence.

Eversole maintained his pleasant facade. "Very fine, sir," he responded.

The four of them gathered around a table holding a steaming kettle, scones, and cups and saucers in the corner of the large office that was studded by models of sailing ships, dreadnoughts, seascapes, and all sorts of nautical memorabilia.

"That cutlass is an interesting piece, Admiral," Yuri said.

Shears retrieved it and had just started relating its history when they heard a voice clearing itself.

"Good morning, everyone. Thank you for coming. Is that tea nice and hot? It's frightfully chilly for March, don't you agree?" Churchill's eyes twinkled at their surprised recognition.

"Good morning, Sir Winston. Let's be seated and proceed, shall we?" Shears said, resting the cutlass on the table and then lifting the kettle. "The First Lord is going to have a busy day, I'm sure," Shears said.

"Are the Huns at the gate, Sir Winston?" Eversole asked in jest.

"Not quite, but they're on their way. They invaded Belgium, Holland, and Luxembourg this morning. It seals off their northern flank, with Norway and

Denmark already under their obnoxious flag," Churchill replied, lighting a Corona. "Thank you, Admiral," he said as Shears handed him a teacup. Shears' face showed no surprise; Eversole concluded he must have already known.

"Your estimate on their strategy was totally accurate, Chad."

"So it was. They're going to flank the Maginot Line, just as we told the French. They'll be in Paris by July." He suddenly realized he was speaking to the de facto prime minister. He mused that King George must be considering that very issue now.

Yvette turned to Yuri, shaking her head and grinning. Her message was clear: France wasn't their target. Why waste time on a lost cause?

"We have certain contingency plans worked out that involve the people in this room. If…rather when, France falls, we are alone against the Nazis."

"Mr. Churchill, I am Commander Yuri Popov, of His Majesty's Royal Navy."

"I know of you, Commander. Your reputation precedes you."

"Thank you, sir. If I may, sir, Russia will stand with us. She…"

"I know of your blood ties to Mother Russia, Yuri. Remember, though, that Stalin signed a pact of non-aggression with Hitler this past August. Stalin is trying to buy time to prepare for the inevitable."

"Which is?" Popov asked.

"Eventual attack. And it will come, no doubt about it," Churchill said. "The little corporal wants to do two things never before accomplished in history: conquer Russia and cross the English Channel. Very shortly, he will have the capacity to do both."

"Our expeditionary force in France will hold…"

Shears cut the pugilistic Popov off. "We relied on the French to be full-fledged participants in their own defense, Commander. It never happened. They put too much emphasis on that stupid static defense line. It represents World War thinking that the German Blitz will render useless. More men died in accidents building it than will be lost defending it."

"But what of the expeditionary force, then?" Popov asked.

"They will buy us only time. We'll somehow extract them and their equipment in due course," Eversole replied.

"And time is the critical factor. If we use it wisely, it will offset our lack of materiel. It will also allow that stupid goose-stepping bastard to make a few monumental mistakes as he becomes restless for major victories and for the Japanese to become bolder," Churchill said, getting up and returning his teacup to the table, where he picked the cutlass up and examined it, hefting its weight with a smile on his face. "Time will also allow circumstance to evolve so the United States is fully engaged in the war on our side," he said, turning and swinging the cutlass with a flourish.

"Sir, I think that's too optimistic. Isolationists gain new members in their Congress every day!" Eversole cautioned.

"The United States will enter, either willingly or by my dragging her in by her heels, and this group will stand ready and plan to promote that occurrence. If we fail, England dies. Let that thought temper your feelings. Shears will inform you of your responsibilities. Consider yourself at the front; do what you must to survive. Even more so, do what you must to insure England survives. It might not require very much, or it might prove unbelievably treacherous."

"As of yesterday President Roosevelt has indefinitely extended the Pacific Fleet's stay at Pearl Harbor," Shears said.

"Is that so?" Churchill said with a broad smile crossing his face. "As I said, time must be treated as the most precious of jewels." Churchill placed the cutlass back on the table and said, "I must go. Time is of the essence, even for me."

Churchill took his coat and hat and left in the company of the Royal Marines, convinced that keeping Eversole in the dark about certain aspects of the graduated plan he was hatching was the right thing to do. He wasn't sure the depth of Eversole's guts matched the depth of his character and honor. Being so honorable was a problem these days. England's honor would have to transcend the honor of all others.

Eversole picked up the cutlass and went to remount it on the wall. It was then he saw the inscription on its handle, engraved in the writing style common in the 1700's. It read, *To Captain John Paul Jones, United States Navy, for your service to our Country. B. Franklin.*

0800 Hours, March 17, 1940
Hiroshima Bay

Minoru Genda climbed his way to *Nagato*'s bridge for his appointment with Admiral Yamamoto. His excitement was so high that he tripped several times on the narrow ladders. Yamamoto sat on a stool surveying Hiroshima Bay with his binoculars. At the sound of Genda's voice, he got up and hugged the commander affectionately.

"You look well! How did your Wild Eagles do this time?"

"I'm very pleased with their performance, Admiral. The performance of our horizontal bombers becomes better each sortie. I feel more confident than I did six months ago."

"See? I told you so."

"The American Pacific Fleet has been ordered to remain at Pearl

Harbor indefinitely."

"It seems that they are doing what we expected. I think we might very well succeed, Genda. I, too, am growing in certainty with each day."

"Admiral, for the strategy of surprise to succeed, we will require the most up-to-date intelligence gathering we've ever attempted. We will need to know the routine of the American fleet, when they train, when they rest. We will need to know the exact anchorage location of each ship, and whether they are protected by torpedo nets. All that will determine how we assign targets to our squadrons, even to individual planes. We mustn't squander a bomb or torpedo."

Yamamoto had not thought about this nearly as much as Genda had. He was more pleased than surprised that the command structure was working perfectly. As admiral, he had devised the strategy. As commander in charge of the attack, Genda's management of tactical detail was perfection itself.

"What do you recommend?"

"A Navy man should be assigned to the staff of our consulate in Hawaii. We cannot tell him the obvious, but anyone with the brains to be the kind of spy we are looking for will deduce the details for himself. If he is detained, he cannot know the intricacies of the plan itself."

"Agreed. See to it."

That evening Yamamoto read the American newspapers the embassy in Washington sent along at his request. He noted with consternation a story describing the conception and gestation of the first American battleship to be conceived since 1921. She would be called the *Washington*. He realized again how small a window for victory remained opened to him. If he sunk every ship in Pearl Harbor, in a year they would be replaced. Among them would be this new monster, dwarfing any presently deployed battleship of their Pacific fleet. *Washington* surely had sisters and cousins who also were about to feel the first stirrings of life in those countless American shipyard wombs. He put the *Post* down and ventured out to the bridge. A storm was brewing to the east, but the lights of Hiroshima remained bright. How prophetic.

1000 Hours, March 18, 1940
The White House

President Roosevelt was visibly shaken when he learned of the German spearhead into the Low Countries. "Surely, there will be a decisive battle. The Germans can't be that strong. How would they hold Denmark and Norway and still invade Belgium?"

"Mr. President, the German Wehrmacht and Luftwaffe are the most modern in the world. They are making brilliant use of armor and close air support.

Before the French or English know where they're being attacked in strength, the battle's over, the gains consolidated, and the next attack taking place. The French will fall quickly and England will be alone very shortly," General Marshall explained.

"I think it's time to lend a modicum of support to the cause of Great Britain," Cordell Hull said. "We cannot allow Herr Hitler to think she stands alone."

"What would you have me do? You've heard the rumblings in Congress about the draft bill. I don't think the country's been so divided since the Civil War."

"Churchill has requested information of a scientific and technical nature in return for giving us some. I think we should comply. The British have developed a device called the *magnitron* that is the core of their radar system. They've also developed a proximity fuse for antiaircraft shells that makes it likely that a near-miss will be as fatal as a hit."

"What do they want?" Roosevelt asked.

"They've not made a specific request, Mr. President, but I think we should share our Purple code machines with them," Marshall responded.

"Purple gives us Magic, correct?" Roosevelt asked, "and, Magic ciphers the Japanese diplomatic messages, correct?"

"Yes, sir."

"Well, the last I've heard, the Nazis are giving the British fits. How the hell would giving them a Japanese code machine help them? It's like having an English-Japanese dictionary when you're stuck in Berlin!" Roosevelt guffawed. Harry Hopkins was laughing with him. Then he noted that Hull looked at Marshall with an upturned eyebrow. Marshall smiled broadly. "What don't I know that's making you two look like the cat that ate the canary?"

"We have it on good account that the British have broken the German diplomatic and military code. They call the machine *Enigma*." The Oval Office fell silent as Hopkins moved closer to the president.

"If the British have a clear idea of what the Japanese are planning to do, it would help them in the defense of Hong Kong and Singapore, should the Japanese decide to attack. That would limit our involvement and keep us out of harm's way, at least until we're ready to take the Japs on. If we had an *Enigma* machine, we might be better able to aid Britain when the time comes. We would also have a better defense against their U-Boats. We're seeing them right off New York harbor," Hull added.

Roosevelt looked out the window, taking time to note that life was blooming in the gardens. Soon summer would be upon the capital, and with it the battle for the Selective Training and Service Act, which would raise the temperature considerably on Capitol Hill. If America was caught unprepared by the forces of evil to her east and west, and if he allowed an opportunity to slide by that might have saved an American boy's life, he would be vilified. He really had no choice.

"Let's see if we can do business," he said, putting a Camel directly to his lips. "Trade a Purple for an Enigma. We'll both benefit. I want that other stuff you mentioned, too. We'll be good neighbors if we cannot be family."

"General, can we read the Japs' naval code yet?" Hopkins asked.

"We make progress, but they change it too frequently. It's almost as if they're not happy with it, either," said Marshall.

"If we could read it, we'd be far ahead of the game."

"Why? Their diplomatic code tells us what they're up to. We'll know their moves almost before they do."

"I guarantee you, General Marshall, that when war comes, their diplomats will be the last to know," Roosevelt replied, wheeling his chair from behind his desk. "It will start with a surprise attack, the way they've opened every other war in their history. And, they'll lead with their Navy." Roosevelt turned his chair to the window again. "I'd give a king's ransom to break their Naval code. It holds all their secrets."

"We'll be ready."

"We'll try to be, but they have an excellent chance to succeed because we'll always be half-ready. Our country will not come to closure on the issue of risking war. We can be only so preemptive. We'll fall victim because of it."

"The Japanese aren't as strong as we are, Mr. President. Keeping the fleet at Pearl Harbor made a powerful statement as to the limits of our patience," Hull replied.

"I had no choice, but all it accomplished was to force them to confirm their suspicions that attacking Singapore and Hong Kong meant war with us," Roosevelt said, opening the door for his guests, "and, I gave them a dare."

"Which was?" Hull asked, putting on his coat and hat.

"Pearl Harbor." He looked to Marshall and said, "Doug MacArthur in the Philippines thinks the Japs will attack him first. You'd better see he's pacified before he yaps his big mouth to all the newspapers."

"That will mean taking stuff in the pipeline to Pearl and giving it to him."

"See to it. I don't need more of a ruckus in Congress about how poor Douglas is being short-changed and how fast the Philippines will fall."

"But they will, sir. Our Orange War Plan counts on the fleet to keep open the supply lines with our forward defense in Hawaii. We want to evacuate

Douglas' army to Australia, not reenforce it."

"I know that; just make sure that pain in the ass does."

0800 Hours, June 6, 1940
Dunkirk, France

Cedric Leland pulled up hard after the Stuka dive bomber had just made a bombing run on the troop transport below. He wanted to make sure this particular Stuka wouldn't live to drop another bomb. He banked after the gyrating plane and aimed through his electric gunsight. The Stuka's rear gunner opened up and streaks of tracer rounds and unseen solid shot reached for the vital organs of his Spitfire or his body.

It was for naught. A burst from the eight machine guns in the Spitfire's wings sent tracers into the enemy's cockpit, sending shattered plexiglas and metal flying. The mottled gray and black Stuka stopped its panicked maneuvers, and was suddenly flying straight and level. Cedric pulled up to examine it.

The gunner lay slumped in a bloody heap over his weapon. What remained of the cockpit was splattered with blood. The pilot looked over at him, raising his head up with difficulty. One crimson-coated arm reached up to pull the cockpit back, but it would not open. The expression of hopelessness and pain that filled his goggled face stung Cedric Leland to the core.

The German must have realized it was the end. He seemed to focus on Ced's face and half-smiled. Straightening up, he nodded and rolled the Stuka away in a shallow dive.

Leland followed, but hesitated just before bringing his guns to life again. He thought of the pilot's family who knew their loved one was playing a dangerous game, but they couldn't know he was about to lose his life above the coast of France on this fine June morning. Leland knew this very pilot might have been the instrument of death to some exhausted British Tommy or a child in Warsaw. He pushed the firing button.

Cedric Leland shot down another Stuka not ten minutes later, and sufficiently holed an Me-109 that its pilot thought better of continuing the dogfight. Ced himself was dangerously low on fuel and returned to Biggin Hill.

The ground crew shouted and cheered when he pulled the Spitfire into its revetment. He acknowledged their accolades then walked to the debriefing room. He'd be flying again in an hour, as soon as the Spit was refueled and rearmed. Wearily he described to the debriefing officer the scene over Dunkirk—a beach in shambles holding the core of the British Army, reeling from an attack that would wipe them from France, and raise the Swastika over the Continent. He went to the mess hall, but finding himself unable to eat, he just poured himself a mug of hot tea. Pilots in his flight were already reassembling for another sortie in support of the British Army's evacuation. As he gathered up his gear, Andy Seghesio came in.

"Is it as bad as we hear?" Andy asked him, offering him a cigarette.

"It's havoc. Even if we get the men out, all their equipment's lost. It'll be a miracle if we survive the year. The German Army and Air Force are magnificent," he said, running his hand through his thick blond hair.

Andy smiled and put his arm around Cedric's shoulders. "I heard you've got six kills so far."

Cedric nodded. He shook Andy's hand and headed for his fighter. Just before he walked out the mess hall door, he turned to Andy and said, "It's not nearly as glamorous as we thought it would be, Andy. They have faces, too."

Andy said nothing. He didn't have to. Fighter pilots didn't want to acknowledge the obvious, but Ced had seen past the plane and the uniform. Indeed, a human being was in that other plane.

"You're an ace now, Cedric," Andy said, trying to be buoyant. A fighter pilot should never take to the sky unless his ego was already up there.

Cedric turned to him, and a pained smile crossed his face. "So I am. Well then, when I get back, we'll have to celebrate."

"Be careful up there, Ced."

It sounded trite, but Cedric got the real message. "What choice do I have?"

Andy watched the flight of four Spitfires vanish, heading due south, followed by two flights of Hurricane fighters. It was hard to stay behind. He secretly wished for some whim of diplomacy that would allow him to fly Cedric's wing. It wasn't to be, at least for awhile. He looked at his watch, remembering he had promised Mae a trip to London to see a show called *Me and My Girl.* She was doing a crazy dance called the Lambert Walk around their flat all day, and mentioned repeatedly that it was from the show. He took the hint, and also got tickets for Lisa and Ced. It was unlikely he'd be able to make it and Lisa probably wouldn't go without him. He hated to waste the two tickets. Perhaps he'd offer them to the embassy's new British naval liaison officer and his wife. They were a lovely couple, and Mae was particularly taken with Yvette.

Dunkirk was evacuated successfully, but Paris fell to the Nazis on 14 June 1940, the same day Lisa and Cedric were married in a hastily assembled ceremony, with Mae and Andy serving as matron of honor and best man.

Winston Churchill took great delight in Roosevelt's declaration of a national emergency on 27 June 1940. He also had learned that the enormously popular president would seek a third term. "This is sent by God himself," he remarked to Shears. "We now won't have to restart our efforts with someone new and perhaps hostile."

Chapter 9

1700 Hours, July 4, 1940
London

Andy opened the letter from the diplomatic pouch and grinned in amusement. Hearing from Jack Burns was always a treat. He routinely castigated the Marine Corps, seasoning it with just the right amount of expletives to produce laughter rather than anger. "You'd think the Marines would learn from their mistakes," he wrote, "but then I hear they promoted you again. I'll offer my congratulations in person when I see you in a few weeks. Then again, I may choose to forget. By the way, Andy, do you still have a hard time getting it up with women? Perhaps you should ask your wife to wear your uniform to bed, MAJOR Seghesio!"

Burns went on to mention his upcoming special assignment in London. Andy was thrilled at the prospect. "As much as I look forward to seeing you and Mae again, I can't help thinking I'm literally missing the boat here. Hawaii is beautiful, but every time the *Enterprise* leaves Pearl she sails right past my window, and I start feeling sorry for myself all over again. I still get dizzy spells and headaches, and my vision isn't back to where it was before Zanetti and I spun in. I fear I'll never fly again; it tears me up. Joe Rochefort is no comfort. Whenever I start looking wistful, that queer son of a bitch makes a paper airplane, writes 'Nevermore' on it, and throws it at my desk. Then he laughs like hell. I think I'll kill him."

1400 Hours, July 4, 1940
Pearl Harbor, Hawaii

Arizona was moored off Ford Island, astern of her sisters *Tennessee* and *West Virginia*. Ahead of them were *California*, *Maryland*, *Oklahoma*, and *Pennsylvania*. *Nevada* occupied the berth just astern of her. Those magnificent ships would make anyone wonder how an enemy might dare threaten the United States. The configuration of ships on the south shore of Ford Island became known as Battleship Row soon after the Pacific Fleet settled into its new home. Chief Jones looked proudly at the battle line and felt tremendously privileged to be a part of it. Even Joshua Friar took great delight in it. He had become a real seafaring man as far as Jones was concerned, and his good humor, kindness, and willingness always to lend a hand got him a measure of respect accorded few other Negroes. Jones took no credit for it; it was the *Arizona*'s doing. She wouldn't have her men judged on the color of their skin. They all had America's blood coursing through their veins.

"Chief, we need to talk," Captain Train said, looking over his reading glasses at the erect figure before him.

"Yes, sir?" Jones asked inquisitively. He sensed something was about to go sour.

Train took a deep breath, removed his glasses, and leaned back in his chair. This wasn't going to be easy. "Chief, have a seat," he said. "The new battleships *South Dakota, North Carolina,* and *Washington* are to come off the ways in the next twelve months, and they're starting to assemble crews."

Jones stiffened. He knew what that meant. Someone in the Bureau of Personnel found out where he had been hiding all these years.

"I'll do what the Navy wants me to, sir."

"I can try to dissuade them from taking you right away. They want to build their cadres to become efficient quickly while the ships are fitting out. Before their keels touch the sea, their men will know the ships intimately, so they'll be effective units of the fleet all the more quickly. I can say I need you for the time being, but the message seems clear. Your name headed the personnel inquiry list. I guess the Navy thinks as highly of you as I do. They want the best men to build the new ships' hearts and souls, just like you've done here."

"My preference is to stay with the *Arizona*, sir. I'll leave it at that."

"Okay. I'll see what I can do."

It was the first time in all his years in the navy that Jones felt so helpless. The larger body had no concern for the individual cell. He was one with the *Arizona,* her interpreter when she spoke to her masters. Perhaps that was considered so much drivel by the powers that be, but a chief's job is to merge living flesh with cold metal. Crew members came and went; captains did too, but the ship would go on. Why would a CPO be more important? Jones shook his head. The Navy would do what it wanted, reasonable or not.

A slight shudder beneath his feet interrupted his musing. He looked back, astonished to see that the *Arizona* had snapped her stern mooring line. One end of the thick hawser was floating away, the other dragged along the surface with the *Arizona*'s swaying ass end. The amidships line then came undone, as if invisible hands had conspired to loosen it, and the ship began pivoting on her remaining bow line, swinging out into the channel with the tide.

Jones raced for the stern, his heart pounding harder when he noticed the cruiser *Raleigh* bearing down the channel that *Arizona* was to block. He picked up the combat phone attached to the sternmost gun turret, and yelled to the bridge, "Sound the collision alarm!" The startled officer of the deck hadn't realized what was happening; he was very involved with meticulously maintaining the ship's log. After all, she was safely moored in her berth. What could happen?

The bellowing horn brought a harbor tug racing up the channel, signaling *Raleigh* to reverse her engines and swing her rudder to port. She slowed and turned enough to allow *Arizona*'s stern to swing harmlessly off her starboard bow.

Jones corralled sailors roused to action by the ship's mournful horn, and had them break out another hawser. Men on Ford Island gathered to receive the new mooring line, while Captain Train sent volunteers over the starboard side to bring two smaller guide lines attached to the hawser through the mooring buoy, and then on to shore.

The tug came to nuzzle *Arizona*'s stern, gently nudging her out of the channel and aligning her with her berth. Jones helped the two sailors back aboard and hugged them. One of them was a Negro he knew by the name of Friar.

"Well done, Josh!" he exclaimed.

"My pleasure, Chief. I'd better get below and dried up. The captain's roast has to come out of the oven. I want to keep that man happy."

"He wouldn't have been happy if his ship had the *Raleigh* sticking out of her ass in the middle of Pearl Harbor!" Jones gave him a slap on the back.

"I certainly wouldn't have been!" Train added. "Nice job, Josh. You too, Cleary," he said, shaking their hands. As the men dispersed to their normal routines, Train brought Jones into the rearmost fourteen inch turret and closed the door behind them.

"What the hell is up with this ship?" he asked in frustration.

"Sir?"

"She's spooked, dammit! Last week she dropped her anchor just before we tied up. No one could figure out why. When we returned from gunnery exercises three days ago, she wouldn't respond to her port engines as if she didn't want to tie up here. And now this. How many goddamn coincidences can there be?" Train removed his cap and wiped his sweating brow. "It's as if she hates Pearl Harbor."

Jones looked at his captain quizzically, and said, "Sir, she does hate it here. I thought you knew that."

0700 Hours, July 30, 1940
The English Channel

Andy Seghesio was at 10,000 feet, ten miles due south of Dover. Jack Burns was in the radar control bunker, amazed at the new secret weapon. He put on a microphone and headset, and the radar operator pointed to the blob of light on the screen.

"That's your boy," Simon McVee said to Burns. "He's at angels ten, course 90, speed 250 knots. Go ahead, commander, ask him." He beamed with pride.

Burns smiled back, knowing what he would hear. "Yankee One, this is Yorktown. Report altitude, heading, and speed. Over."

"Yorktown, this is Yankee One. I'm at angels ten, course 90, speed 265. Over," Seghesio responded.

"What garbage!" Burns bellowed, suppressing a laugh. "That piece of crap got the speed wrong!" McVee laughed and looked back at his screen. He gasped at the sight of a large white blip converging at 200 knots on the little one that was Seghesio's lone Spitfire.

"What's that?" Burns asked, suddenly apprehensive at the frightened look on McVee's pale face.

"It's all hell breaking loose!" he replied, fumbling a phone, and trying to talk calmly when he finally positioned it to his ear. "Alert! This is no drill! Many bandits heading north, bearing ten degrees north northwest! Repeat! This is no drill!"

"Seghesio's still out there!" Burns yelped, pointing to the dot that represented the flesh and blood of his friend.

"Shit! Yankee One! Return to base immediately! Confirm!"

No response, but the blip turned south.

"He's climbing!" McVee shouted.

"Seghesio! Get back here!" Burns screamed. "Andy, do you read me? Get back here!"

Seghesio's eagle eyes spotted the German formation when it was just a speck due south of him. He reacted as he was trained to do. That he was a neutral flying a fighter with British markings hadn't crossed his mind; that Germany was his enemy had.

"He's going to 300 knots! Make that 320, Commander Burns," McVee said.

"Seghesio! Listen to me, dammit! What the hell are you doing?" Burns yelled.

"I'm moving to identify what initially appears to be a flight of twenty hostile aircraft. Send some help. I think I've got the bastards cornered!"

Seghesio leveled off at 30,000 feet. He was slightly ahead and 10,000 feet above the Heinkel bombers escorted by Messerschmitt fighters. He rolled the Spitfire onto its back and dove at the head of the German formation without being spotted. He charged his guns.

The Luftwaffe had turned its attention from England's cities to the RAF airfields; neutralizing them meant air superiority, and that paved the way for invasion. The RAF swore it wouldn't happen. Andy Seghesio had seen what those German aircraft had done at Dunkirk. If the shit hit the fan when he got back…if he got back…so be it. They weren't about to throw him out of the Marines.

The Germans were flying a staggered altitude formation, designed to allow maneuvering room and the concentration of defensive fire should they be intercepted. Andy picked out the highest Heinkel and opened fire one thousand feet above it. Tracers tore into the German's right wing. No smoke or fire. The plane just blew up.

He rolled slightly in his dive, switching targets to the next bomber, and again pressed the trigger. Its belly emitted a thin trail of smoke as it staggered out of formation and headed to the Channel below.

A Messerschmitt 109 pulled up and over to engage the diving Spitfire, flying right into Andy's gunsight. Another enemy plane blew apart.

Three down in the forty-five seconds elapsed since he first pressed the firing button.

An Me-109 followed him down after he dove past the formation. Andy split-essed the Spitfire, recovering only a thousand feet above the water. The German tried to follow, but on the verge of a stall applied power in an attempt to bank away. Andy rapidly closed with the German. He fired again, and the Me-109 just rolled over on its back and flew into the sea.

Burns never stopped yelling for him to disengage. He realized what was happening, but in the melee of the blips, he lost track of which one represented Seghesio's Spitfire. Then from the north came other blips merging with the German formation. The German blip shrank, with little blips separating from it and disappearing. The Germans had been thwarted.

"Seghesio! If you're alive…" Burns shouted.

"This is Yankee One, over. What the hell are you yelling about? You're scaring the hell out of everyone!"

"Who told you to attack that formation? You are not authorized…"

"What attack? Begging your pardon, sir, but are you talking to me? I merely sought to identify the formation."

Burns was had. How could he accuse Seghesio of action he hadn't eye-witnessed? Seghesio's word was as good as his.

"I saw what you did, Andy. I saw it right here!" Burns said, trying to seize the upper hand.

"Sir, I climbed to avoid a formation of what I identified as hostile aircraft. I dove through them to confuse them when I thought I was about to be attacked, sir. The RAF Spitfires did all the shooting."

"What if I check and see if your guns were fired, wise-ass?" Burns countered.

"Oh, I fired my guns, but only to lighten the aircraft so I could run for it, sir."

Burns was silent; he had been beaten. "Seghesio, you're a cocksucking Marine liar! And I'll leave it at that."

"Aye, aye, sir."

"He'll be passing overhead in a minute, sir. Want to go out and wave to him?" McVee offered, unable to contain his glee.

The Spit flew by, barely five hundred feet above the radar station, performing a perfectly executed series of four victory rolls.

At Biggin Hill, a jubilant Cedric Leland and his squadron mates greeted Seghesio as he taxied to a halt.

"You got four of the bastards!" Tommy Hamilton yelled.

"I'm also gonna catch hell if Commander Burns finds his way over here!"

Ced shook his brother-in-law's hand with fervor. He looked over Andy's shoulder, casually giving the Spitfire a quick visual check. His eyes caught something. "Andy," he said, "I think there is something you need to know."

"What's that?" Seghesio said, still shaking hands.

"They shoot back." He pointed to five bullet holes less than a foot behind the glass of the cockpit. He watched the smile ebb from Seghesio's face, and felt another coughing spell coming on.

"Have you seen a doctor for that?" Andy asked him.

"It's bronchitis, Andy. We all have it—too much flying at high altitude, too much pure oxygen, not enough sleep. It's part of the game," Cedric said, taking out a handkerchief.

Two hours later Andy returned to examine the Spitfire's guns and saw several other men in casual civilian clothes and leather jackets inspecting the plane. The ground crew hadn't wasted any time in canonizing the aircraft; its nose was adorned with four painted Iron Crosses. "Are you Seghesio?" one of the men who came forward asked.

Andy looked at him, a bit startled. His speech was American. Were they military, about to come down on him for his brash action? "Yes, I am. And you?" he said, trying to hide his trepidation.

"Major Robert Adorneo. Nice to meet you, paisano. You're a Marine, aren't you?"

"Yes. I'm attached to the embassy. I was flying a radar calibration flight when…"

"Save it. You don't owe me an explanation. I'm temporarily detached, shall we say, from the Army Air Corps. We're here to learn fighter tactics from the RAF. Seems you've been learning real well, Andy."

"So, are you supposed to be the European version of the Flying Tigers?" Andy said, feeling much safer now.

"Good analogy. Want to join up?" Adorneo said.

"He's already spoken for," came a voice from behind. It was Jack Burns. "May I see you a minute, Major?" Burns was smiling from ear to ear. If anything, he was envious of the young lion's four kills.

One thing, however, struck Seghesio—America might not be at at war with Germany, but Americans were.

1800 Hours, August 15, 1940
Carrier *Akagi*

"Genda, I have news for you," Yamamoto said. The tired commander had been flying all day, driving his squadrons mercilessly. Yamamoto's cheerful face served as an elixir to banish weariness.

"Yes, sir. What might that be?"

"A British ship called the *Automedon* was seized by the German raider *Atlantis* two weeks ago. It contained a treasure trove of documents. Our allies passed it along when they docked in Yokohama with British prisoners. Here, take a look."

In the original English, Genda read through a document that caused his eyes to widen. "They've admitted they cannot defend Singapore!"

"So the American Navy is all that stands in our way!"

"Could this information have been planted? It sounds far too good to be genuine." Caution crossed Genda's face.

"That's what Admiral Kondo said, but the ship was taken by surprise. British lives were lost. I don't think they would have given so much to protect a lie."

Genda paused to reread the information. "Admiral, we must increase our training of the air groups, and get *Shokaku* and *Zuikaku* into the fleet exercises as soon as possible. This opportunity is golden."

"Yes. Our attack must be perfect to give us that six months."

"We must get our new diplomat to Hawaii as soon as possible. His intelligence will be invaluable."

"Have you chosen someone?" Yamamoto asked.

"I have his file in my quarters, sir. Would you care to review it?"

0900 Hours, September 1, 1940
London

A young boy of no more than eight had lost his parents and two sisters to a 250-kilogram Nazi bomb during last night's raid. Churchill talked with the youngster awhile, out of earshot from the ever-present press, and managed to get the youngster to smile. He then rose, shook the lad's hand, and walked him to relatives who would become his family. He turned away in tears. Not even Winston Churchill was immune to heartache. Fifty old destroyers and the letters of support he received from Roosevelt didn't stop the bombs raining down on Britain's cities. He found himself thinking more desperately. Those ideas he considered daring two months ago were fast becoming more a reasonable course of action.

1200 Hours, November 2, 1940
Honolulu

The liner *Taiho Maru* docked at the Japan Lines pier in the port of Honolulu. Soon after, a short, wiry young man disembarked and presented his passport and diplomatic credentials at the customs office.

"Jaburo Oka?" the customs official asked, peering over his reading glasses with a suspicious expression that unnerved Oka.

"Do you have anything to declare?"

The Japanese spilled the contents of his suitcase accidently as he tried to open a stubborn latch.

"There is nothing to be nervous about. You will soon be on your way. This is routine."

"Thank you. I apologize for my sloppiness. It's my first time out of Japan. I'm very sorry."

"Everything seems to be in order. You may go," the agent said, handing Oka's paperwork back to him. "Enjoy your stay in Hawaii. Aloha!"

"Yes. Aloha to you as well!" Oka replied with the biggest smile he could manage, and several deep bows.

"Take me to Pearl Harbor," he instructed the chauffeur of the embassy's Chevrolet sedan.

"Sir? My instructions are to…"

"Never mind your instructions," Oka said, lighting a cigarette and unfolding a map he took from his vest pocket. "Go no faster than thirty miles per hour. Understood?"

"Yes sir!" the driver answered politely. Looking at him in the rear view mirror, he was shocked at the man's change of personality.

Oka studied the map, noting the landmarks he was told to look for and watching the time elapsed and the speed of the sedan. "Stop here," Oka ordered a few minutes later. "I want to get out for a moment. If anyone asks why you stopped, tell them your passenger needed to empty his bladder, and you're awaiting his return."

Oka walked down the road fifty paces and turned into the underbrush. He proceeded slowly, clearing the palm fronds from his path. What he sought appeared so unexpectedly that he gasped. There before him lay the battle line of the United States Navy's Pacific Fleet. Identifying some of the ships was more difficult than he thought, but there were two about which he was certain. The aircraft carrier *Enterprise* had a bold number six painted on her island structure, and he would recognize *Arizona*'s tripod masts in the dead of night.

He had been furious at Genda when he was called to the flag bridge of *Akagi* and informed of the mission. He knew his presence in Hawaii meant he would not be included in the attack every pilot knew was coming, though Genda continued to be evasive as to the target.

"Don't you think I know what we're up to?" he screamed.

"I don't even know yet. If you knew all of what we're up to, your mission is already compromised! I'm asking you to be spy, Lieutenant Zai."

"Stop playing me as a fool! Commander Genda, I've trained all my life for this mission! Now I'll literally be a bystander!" Zai continued to rail, his chin aquiver. "I'm disgraced!"

Genda took a deep breath and looked into Zai's welling eyes. What a great disservice it must seem to the proud pilot.

"Tomi, you must believe me. Your excellence and dedication make you the perfect choice. If we come to it, those who fly the strike will succeed because of your brave work."

Zai had no choice. He was too much the warrior to admit that the new assignment was the most important of his life. Pride forced him into one last threat. "I will appeal to the commander of combined fleet if I have to!"

"There is no need. He is the one who chose you. I hope you accept this duty and complete it with the same fervor you've displayed in all your undertakings since we admitted you to Eta Jima," said a voice behind him. Zai whirled around to see Admiral Yamamoto standing in the hatchway behind him, a smile crossing his broad face. Zai's tears flowed freely as his chest heaved.

"It's quite all right, Lieutenant. I understand your bitterness, but the only others I would rather put in Hawaii are myself and Genda. Unfortunately, both of us would be recognized faster than a pimp in Chicago."

Zai laughed along with his two commanders. It wouldn't be as satisfying as flying a Zero to glory, but…here he was, in the nest of America's policy enforcers, closer than any Japanese naval officer had been in years.

1500 Hours, November 6, 1940
Biggin Hill

Winston Churchill watched the fighters scramble aloft, heading to the spot where the coast watchers and radar operators said the Germans would be, perhaps on their way to this very fighter base. He had been with the pilots that whole November morning, lunching with them after presenting the DSO to several outstanding aviators. The one who really impressed him was Cedric Leland—so pale and gaunt, ravaged by flu, and very tired. Yet he managed to joke with the prime minister, telling him the tide would soon turn and not to lose hope.

"Young man, hope is my job, and my job becomes easier because of men like you," Churchill responded. The siren wailed, and he and his mates were off. He noted four Iron Crosses painted on the nose of the Spitfire Leland was flying. There was a curious metal patchwork behind the canopy, so hastily applied that its camouflage did not match the rest of the fighter. Churchill counted ten Spitfires taking off and heading south to defend the homeland. A jeep equipped with a radio pulled up for his benefit, and its operator set the volume up so the prime minister could hear what was taking place ten miles away at ten thousand feet. The screams were terrifying, the shouts of joy invigorating.

In a matter of ten minutes, the battle was over. Seven Spitfires returned, one of them smoking badly, with pieces of its tailfin and parts of its left wing missing. The canopy glass was gone, and the cockpit was riddled with holes. Two planes flew on either wing, as if to coach their wounded nest mate back to safety. Its pilot made a perfect landing, rolling out to a halt on the revetment. Churchill got in the jeep and told its driver to head for the plane.

Cedric Leland was being hauled from the blood-splattered cockpit just as Churchill's jeep arrived. The young man's face streamed blood from numerous cuts, and the leg of his flying suit was crimson.

"Why didn't you bail out when we told you to? My God, man, you were free and clear," a fellow pilot asked, his face streaming tears, as he held Cedric's shoulders.

"We need the ship, Billy. She was in control, wasn't afire. I just didn't expect that Jerry to swing around on me. It was a mistake, just a mistake. Don't think badly of me." He coughed. His face was ashen, his eyes glazed, and his lips blue.

"He's lost a lot of blood. Let's get him to..." The doctor didn't finish the sentence. He saw Cedric's chest stop heaving and looked up at Andy Seghesio, who had just arrived in a sprint. He knew their relationship. All he could say was, "I'm sorry, Major."

Churchill observed the drama from twenty feet way. He found himself on the point of tears. The American Marine walked past him, his face buried in his hands.

What would that young fellow have become, given the chance? Churchill stopped that line of thought, angry at himself for giving in to it. The man was a warrior, the best the British had to offer. To think of what he might have been only cheapened what he was and trivialized his death. So others could go on to do great things someday was what his valor was all about. "Never have so many owed so much to so few," he muttered.

Andy Seghesio arrived home with Tommy Hamilton to find Mae and Lisa together in the kitchen, cheerfully doing that Lambert Walk dance. The expression on his face said it all. He and Tommy held them close, not knowing what else to do.

Chapter 10

"Where do you think we're going?" Seghesio asked Burns.

"Popov said we'd be in for a real treat, a Navy flyer's dream, not that you could believe any of these lying Limey bastards."

"Hey, I'm married to one of them," Seghesio said with a smile.

"Excluding her," Burns laughed.

Seven hours later the Lancaster bomber landed on Malta, the British fortress that stood between the Axis and its domination of the Mediterranean. Burns and Seghesio saw two Royal Navy Swordfish carrier-based torpedo planes on the runway. As soon as they left the bomber, two Royal Navy pilots came over to introduce themselves.

"You chaps must be Seghesio and Burns. Glad to meet you!" they said, shaking hands vigorously. "I'm Captain Miles Brown and this is Captain Hugh Douglas. Come along, we've much to do."

The Brits were happier than anyone in their position had a right to be. The Swordfish was an old canvas, wood, and metal relic of a biplane that would be more comfortable in a World War I museum than flying against the forces of the Third Reich. Even though it looked like a well-placed match would set it off, it had tremendous lifting capacity, able to carry a 1500 pound torpedo, or an equal weight in bombs. Their apparent fragility was of no concern to Burns or Seghesio, whose initial flight training was in the SNJ, an aircraft much like them. Their now-obvious destination excited them.

"On to the HMS *Illustrious*, gentlemen. We're about to give our Italian friends a big surprise," Brown said with an ear-to-ear grin. He gave each of them a fleece-lined flight suit. "Don't forget the parachute. You never know with these old birds." He laughed.

Two hours later, the Swordfish were on landing approach. Each made a perfect trap. Nearly deaf from the engine's moan and chilled to the bone, Burns was happy to be out of the open cockpit; Mediterranean Sea or not, it was still November. Brown and Douglas took their colleagues to the squadron ready room, and introduced them around.

Lieutenant Commander Kenneth Williamson laughed with a typical British guffaw, as Burns asked them to pardon having a Marine on their ship. "I see things haven't changed much since my time in Oceana. I was a liaison officer there for two years. Great duty! I flew your Devastator torpedo plane right after its introduction. Nice machine!"

"Not anymore," Burns responded. "It's totally outclassed."

"Well then, you must think the Swordfish is a flying coffin."

"How do you guys manage it?" Seghesio asked. "I mean no disrespect, Commander, but the airplane has seen better days."

"Call me Ken, Andy. It has, but just like your Congress, we had a Parliament that thought the world was all peaches and cream until that Nazi bastard started this ruckus. The military pays for the mistakes of its leaders with blood. It's just our lot," Williamson said with a shrug of his shoulders. "We have to make do with what's available."

"Why are we out here in the middle of the Mediterranean?" Burns asked.

"Go ahead, Miles. Tell them," Williamson said as he lit his pipe.

"Il Duce is about to get the surprise of his life. We're to raid Taranto where they have major elements of their battle line at anchor."

"You'd better go with your prayer beads in your pockets, gentlemen," Andy said. "That base is well-fortified, at least according to the intelligence guys. I don't want to upset your morale, or anything, but..."

"It's well thought out, Andy. We're attacking them at night. We took a lot of our operational data and philosophy from the mock attack we understand you two made on Pearl Harbor some years ago." Their surprised looks delighted Williamson.

"Is your intelligence up to the task?" Burns asked.

"It is. We've had a submarine reconnoitering just outside the harbor entrance, counting the ships coming in and out."

"Brave men in that sub," Andy muttered.

"The bravest. We owe them this one," Hugh Douglas said.

"Come. Let me show you the *Illustrious*. Tell me how it compares to your *Enterprise*," Williamson said.

"That's a sore point with him," Seghesio said.

"Why's that?"

"I was to command her air group until I crashed on a normal approach. Engine failure. I'm still seeing stars," Burns said.

"That's too bad, Jack. Something else will come along; you watch and see." Williamson took Burns by the shoulder.

Burns was starting to like the man, despite his determination to hate everything British. Andy got along with everyone. *What could you expect,* Burns mused. He was a Marine.

"What's your tactical basis?" Andy asked.

"Well, it certainly isn't the strength of our aircraft!" Miles said.

"Surprise. Plain and simple. They'd never expect us to attack their lair. They are in for a shock! I think this will be the easiest mission we'll ever fly. The cocky bastards are in for a real thrashing!" Hugh said.

Illustrious couldn't carry as many aircraft as *Enterprise*, but her flight deck consisted of three inches of armor plate, which made her much less vulnerable to bomb damage than her American sisters, whose decks were light metal covered with teak. The ship seemed ponderous as she sliced through the waves, but by the same token, she also exuded a battleship-like sturdiness uncommon in the fleet-footed American types. It was hoped that *Enterprise* could outmaneuver most of her attackers, and still be able to absorb a few hammer blows because of her advanced design. *Illustrious,* on the other hand, would just absorb the blows and didn't put much emphasis about escaping. *Illustrious* was designed for operations in European waters within easy range of land-based enemy aircraft, and her range was short, where *Enterprise* was built to sail the huge expanse of the Pacific, so her legs were much longer. Each ship, however, was manned by men with high morale, high expectations, and a keen sense of getting the job done. Though *Enterprise* had yet to fire a shot in anger, her men would have no problem when the time came, just like *Illustrious*'s crew had risen to the challenge.

Shortly after dusk Williamson briefed his eleven other pilots. "Now remember. Don't get caught up in doing something brave. We've got the night and surprise on our side. Wills and McCartney will fly the two kites with the flares. Don't attack until the targets are illuminated. Take your time in choosing your targets. I want everyone back here for breakfast tomorrow," he said, a sad smile crossing his face.

"All right. Let's get on with it. Let's see if we can catch our Italian friends with a forkful of spaghetti in their hands!"

The pilots left, arms around each other and shaking hands all around. Their gunners were already in the aircraft warming up on the flight deck.

"See you in several hours, if the Lord smiles upon me," Williamson said, shaking the American's hands. He climbed into his cockpit and positioned the Swordfish for takeoff. When the launch officer's arm moved downward, Williamson released the brakes, gunned the engine, raced down the deck, and was gone into the night.

"You know, Jack, we couldn't pull off something like this. We have no night attack capability."

"You're reading my mind, Andy. Maybe we can learn something from these

Limey bastards after all. These guys are superb. Dear Lord, bring them back," Burns murmured, with a tear running down his cheek. Andy put his arm around Burns' shoulder, the tears coming to his own eyes as the drone of the Swordfish faded in the cloudless Mediterranean sky. As always, the fraternity uniting pilots superseded rank and national insignia.

Burns lit one cigarette after another awaiting word on the strike. At last the combat information center's radio crackled to life. The strike had arrived over the target.

"Steady now, boys. Steady. There they are! Look! Their BBs are here, just as we expected! Okay, let's go, and no mistakes!"

"I got a hit! Did you see the torpedo hit her? Look! She's starting to burn! Ha!"

"Jimmy, pull up! Up Jimmy!

"No use, commander. I got my torpedo in her side, though. See you."

"Jimmy! Oh my God!"

"That cruiser's burning. She's lighting up the whole harbor. There's another BB over to the north."

"Attack her! That's it. Yes!"

"Il Duce is going to need his bromide tomorrow. Ha!"

The talk brought smiles to the faces of those on the bridge, even though they realized Jimmy Wellington and his gunner would not be returning. The moment was not lost on Seghesio and Burns. A great victory was in the making, but few who would learn of it tomorrow would feel their pain of the death of Jimmy Wellington's and his gunner. And no one could account for what happened to Douglas Yates. He and his gunner simply disappeared.

0600 Hours, December 7, 1940
Bremerton Naval Shipyard, Washington

Arizona seemed at ease in the dry dock, even though the weather had been dreary as weather usually was in December. She had arrived a few days prior for an overhaul and a hull inspection. Her men were scattered across the United States, on leave or reporting to her new sisters in the birthing yards in Philadelphia, Newport News, or New York. Only a skeleton crew remained aboard, one of whom who managed to avoid transfer. CPO Gwyeth Jones had made himself irreplaceable again, at least for a while. The construction and repair, minor as it was, plus the new equipment being installed needed the keen eye of one who knew the ship best.

There was talk about another class of battleship that was to make all others pale in comparison. The *Iowa* class would be the most modern and deadliest battleships ever constructed. Jones was told by an admiral himself in no uncertain terms that as of January, 1942, when *Arizona* would again visit Bremerton for the installation of a new-fangled device called radar, he would walk down her gangway for the last time, no ifs, ands, or buts.

"That's a year from now," Jones said to Joshua Friar.

"A lot of shit can happen in a year, Chief. How about some more chicken soup?"

"Don't mind if I do, Josh. It warms you right to the soul."

Friar's face could light up a dungeon whenever the chief complimented him.

0900 Hours, March 20, 1941
The White House

"Don't you think the British feel a bit better about our commitment to them now that we've signed on with Lend-Lease?" Roosevelt said as he cut the roast beef on his plate.

"I think they want a declaration of war, sir," Harry Hopkins replied.

"Well, they won't get it anytime soon. Does Churchill think I'm a despot?" Roosevelt said angrily.

"His war cabinet's thinking is philosophically based on preventative strategy," Cordell Hull replied.

"Meaning?"

"The sooner we enter the war, the less our casualties will be, and the less likely the Japanese will be to attack us in the Philippines," Secretary of War Henry Stimson added.

Roosevelt's utensils dropped heavily on his plate. "Has anyone told Churchill that's why we passed the draft bill, for God's sake! Here," Roosevelt said, pushing away his plate and shuffling through the papers on his desk. "Send him this. 'You will slit the throat of the last democracy still living, you accord to Hitler his greatest triumph'. On the headstone of American democracy he will inscribe 'here lies the foremost victim of the war of nerves.' It's what Burton Wheeler, the senator from the great state of Montana, said when we passed the draft bill in September. Being able to get Lend-Lease through that bunch still has me confounded."

"Mr. President, this just came through. It's from Reuters," his secretary said.

Roosevelt opened the package and read the sheaf of papers within. A smile of realized expectation crossed his face. "Well, gentlemen, all of this is rendered academic. The Japs, the Nazis, and the Italians have signed a tripartite pact. I'll bet my last dollar that in three or so months, Hitler will turn his forces on Joe Stalin."

"Outrageous! How can they be so bold as to…"

"Come now, Cordell. It makes perfect sense. England is to be neutralized in a few months. The Italians get their *mare nostrum* Mediterranean, the Japs get the Far Eastern empires of France and Britain, and probably Holland too!" Roosevelt responded.

"This is an act that cannot go unchallenged! What if…Hitler decides to invade Great Britain?" Hull stammered, shaking with anger.

"What does he want with a resource-deficient island that is already surrounded? He won't waste casualties on the British. Personally, I maintain he has a special affinity for them. Hell, he could have wiped them out at Dunkirk, but he held off his Panzers so they could escape. An army without equipment is no army," chimed in Hopkins, "and the British Army was neutralized at Dunkirk, at least for now. Let's hope Herr Hitler underestimates the power of Lend-Lease to restore their equipment."

"What about our Pacific territories? We must…"

"Let's just see what the prime minister of England does first, shall we, Cordell? This is nothing more than a confirmation of what we expected all along. Just make sure the Brits get everything they need, short of a few divisions," Roosevelt said, retrieving his fork and pushing it into the peas on his plate.

0100 Hours, April 1, 1941
London

Mae Seghesio went back to work. The American Embassy offered her a job in the newly established Lend-Lease office. It helped get her mind off Cedric. Lisa worked there as well, but more to steal her emotions with a sense of purpose. She refused to go back to the States. If America had been involved, perhaps Cedric wouldn't have died. She'd said as much to Andy, who tried to explain the circumstance from a different perspective. It was to no avail. He feared his sister would never love again.

In the same office was Yvette Popov, who seemed genuinely interested in the comings and goings of each of the embassy's staff. Yuri appeared at least twice a week to check this or that. Andy had grown to like him. He was a fine officer, obviously dedicated to his mission, and very efficient. He got things done that men with more rank never could, and he could do it in a few hours, to the absolute surprise of others. Yuri was now arranging a trade of code machines between the two countries. The American devices were being transported to England in the solid armored bulk of the new British battleship *King George V.*

"Those are a lovely pearls, Mae. Where did you get them?" Yvette asked.

"Andy bought them for me in New York last year. It was a sort of a pre-engagement present."

"You're blushing like a schoolgirl," Yvette said sweetly.

"We've been married a year, and he still makes me blush. Our meeting was kismet, Yvette. He's absolutely wonderful. How did you meet Yuri?" she asked, tucking a folder away in a gray cabinet.

The question took Yvette by surprise. She was no good at this syrupy stuff. To her, men had meant only a few moments of pleasure and a good living. "Oh! We've known each other for a time. It was Admiral Shears who properly brought us together."

"Do you plan to have children?"

This second unanticipated question made Yvette shudder. She had never really thought of herself as worthy of that gift. "We'll see when the war is over."

"I'd like to start a family right now, but Andy is unsure about it. We'll see, too," Mae said as her pretty mouth curled into a smile, and her hazel eyes gave Yvette a wink.

Jack Burns crashed through the embassy's large oak doors followed by Andy with Yuri Popov right behind him.

"Son of a bitch! We had a fucking deal!" he bellowed, oblivious to the women's presence.

"Commander, if you'll let me explain, I..." Popov said, with a look that matched his apologetic tone.

"Forget the explanations! Where I come from, if two people promise something they deliver. They damn well better!" Burns yelled, pointing his finger directly at Yuri Popov's slender nose.

Popov was taken aback by the tirade, but his anger grew as Burns' index finger jabbed the air just inches away from his nose. "Commander, please calm down," he entreated. "It's just a misunderstanding." Popov thought the more he supplicated, the more his own temper might subside. No doubt Burns was ready to take a healthy swipe at him, and he didn't want to retaliate; that would mean causing Burns great harm. He knew no other way.

"Jack," Andy said, grabbing him by the arm. "Calm yourself, for Christ's sake! We're not in the BOQ! You call me a maniac! Jesus, look at yourself!" He flung the smaller Burns in front of the full-length mirror in the embassy's foyer.

Burns was shocked. It showed a wild man, totally out of character for a high ranking officer of in the United States Navy by the name of John Paul Burns. His hair was a mess, his tie and jacket askew, and the brass buttons of his jacket undone. When he saw the expression on Mae's face, he was totally ashamed of himself. "I'm sorry," he said with true embarrassment. "Major Seghesio, is there somewhere we can talk?"

"Right this way, Commander Burns," Yvette said, opening the door to an office behind the reception desk. As the two Americans left, Popov's face registered triumph. The look was not lost on Mae.

"What went wrong, Jack?" Andy asked. "You've done nothing but scream since we left the Admiralty building."

"The Limey bastards double-crossed us, that's what," Burns said, pouring a glass of water.

"How? I'm still not following you, sir," Andy added.

"We were supposed to get a few ENIGMA machines for the PURPLE machines that just came over on the *King George V*. After we handed them over along with the cipher books, our allies, if you want to use the word, tell us they have no Enigmas to spare."

"Couldn't that just be temporary? I don't know what the hell all this code stuff is about, but if it's important to us, they won't let us down. These people have been great to me. Why do you think they're double-crossing us?" Andy asked.

"Those PURPLE machines were supposed to go to the cipher stations in Hawaii and Manila, but Washington thought they could wait to have direct access to the Jap diplomatic code, if it meant the ENIGMAs would help in detecting U-boats in that undeclared war we're fighting in the Atlantic. Washington would keep sending the PURPLE stuff along in diplomatic pouches until we could replace those machines. It's not very efficient because the information gets old very quickly. Time is of the essence when you're talking about fast-moving aircraft carrier task forces and three-hundred-mile-an-hour airplanes. Nonetheless, we gave a priority to our so-called allies to appease those in Washington who want us to do more without angering those who want us to do less. That way we help the British and save American Merchant Marine seamen's lives. Nobody is shooting at anybody in the Pacific yet. That's their logic."

"But they've shared everything up to now, haven't they? How about that magnitron to help develop our radar. They even transported a few banged up Me-109s and Heinkels over to Dayton for us to dissect. Christ, they even let Tommy and me throw around brand new Spitfires."

Burns shook his head. "So they gave you and Hamilton a Spitfire ride.

Yeah, the magnitron was helpful, and you even shot down four Nazi planes. Taranto was a blast. But all that stuff is a front, Andy."

Seghesio couldn't believe his ears. He wanted to be angry, but this was Jack Burns. "You've got me there, pal. I'm lost," he said, turning away, seething.

"Joe Rochefort taught me one thing," Burns said, rising and starting to pace, talking one thought but trying to develop another, the pain of it clear on his face. "Knowing the enemy's code is worth a battle line full of battleships. I think the British know it, too."

"I can understand that. It takes ten times as many men to perform an offensive action as a defensive one. If you know the enemy's plans, your defense gains great advantage; you can concentrate force. If you know what the enemy is doing, and how he's set up to meet you, you can outmaneuver him. We learned that at the Academy."

"How do you think we'll get into this war, Marine?" Burns said, rubbing his chin.

"Like you said, nobody's bleeding in the Pacific yet. Bombs are falling on London. Mae's childhood home was destroyed a week ago. We'll come to England's aid to stop the Nazis."

"Andy, you're a dumb asshole Leatherneck," Burns said, cupping his hands and burying his face in them. "Can't you see what's up? One. The British bastards know we're not going to war in Europe again, no matter how many bombs that fat cocksucker Goering drops on them. Congress won't let it happen. Two. The Nazis have them by the balls. Three. How do you get the United States in the war to save their asses? By having the Japs attack us as we concentrate on Hitler. Four. Because of their pact with the Japs, the Germans will declare war on us. Get it?"

"Jack. The Nazis are Lucifer personified. We really don't have a choice."

"You'll get no argument from me about that. If it was up to me, I'd lead the first air strike against Berlin right after lunch. However, the people back home have trouble understanding why we have to help the British again, only twenty-two years since we did it the last time. The Brits know that and are using it as a halfback fake. If the outposts closest to the enemy, our real enemy, can't accurately predict their actions because we've denied them direct access to the necessary information, we'll spill a lot of blood needlessly."

"You're talking about the Philippines?" Andy asked.

"I'm talking about Hawaii, Seghesio."

"Pearl Harbor?" Andy was incredulous. "The Japs wouldn't dare…"

"Jesus H. Christ, I wish I had a dollar for every time somebody said the Japs wouldn't dare! Have you forgotten that mission we flew off *Lexington* and

Saratoga? Guess what, Marine? Everybody's forgotten about it, and nothing's changed."

"But we had intelligence. We knew…"

"Do you think the Japanese are as stupid as you are? What the hell will they do with the six fleet carriers they'll have when their *Shokaku* and *Zuikaku* join the navy this summer? Attack the Philippines without securing their eastern flank? Your British friends know. They're scared shitless of an attack on Singapore and Hong Kong, two places that the Japs want along with the Dutch possessions the Fuhrer will give them as soon as they get into the fray with us and Britain. They know damn well those two colonies are goners the minute the Japs…" Burns' expression suddenly changed, as if to acknowledge a profound discovery. "I'd bet my whole year's salary that they're reading the Jap's fleet code, too!"

Andy was astounded. "I've had no indication of that."

"Oh, Christ! Of course they are! It makes perfects sense. If the Japs attack us, we're in the war. The Japanese military acts independently of the diplomatic corps. They always open with a sneak attack. Giving us ENIGMA only preserves our neutrality with the Germans. Another halfback fake! Now they've got PURPLE, and they already have JN-25. They know it all! Everything! They realize Singapore and Hong Kong are pawns in the bigger picture," Burns said. He ran his fingers through his thick hair. "It's a waiting game they're playing, and they hold all the Japanese trump cards. Son of a bitch!"

Andy tried to puzzle out Burns' reasoning. He was one of the brightest men he had ever known. Like most successful commanders, Burns thought a problem through inside-out before plotting tactics or overall strategy. That he stumbled across this line of reasoning didn't surprise Seghesio, who remained skeptical; it wasn't so much the leaps of logic, but rather why an ally would go to such great pains to outlandishly betray the only friend it had left in the world. War would undoubtedly come to the United States. How Burns deduced the Japan-Purple-Enigma connection flabbergasted him.

Yvette Popov heard Jack's profound discovery on the specially coded telephone in the Lend-Lease office she inhabited down the hall. In her anger, she broke a pencil in two. She kept an eye on Mae feigning attentiveness, while listening to the two Americans. Jack Burns had to be sent back to America, along with that snooping diplomat with whom she would have a decisive engagement that night.

"I'll be going now. Have a lovely evening," Yvette said.

"You too, Yvette. See you in the morning."

"Watch that Commander Burns, Mae. He's in an awful state," she said in parting.

"He's Andy's oldest friend. I'm sure he'll take care of him."

So will I, Yvette thought. *So will I.*

2200 Hours, April 1, 1941
London

Frederick Morris began his career with the diplomatic corps straight out of Harvard in 1925. He remained a bachelor because he "really hadn't found the right woman," but in truth his sexual preferences were undecided. At times he leaned toward men, yet he frequented high-end prostitutes; only they somehow allowed him to enjoy the charms of women. His wealthy family, New York blue-bloods who traced their lineage to the Revolutionary War, had major interests in the very conservative world of banking and high finance.

He had just broken off an arrangement with a Swiss diplomat before it became serious. His passion for the man was undeniable, but shame overpowered his emotions. He was regularly seeing a woman who had been recommended to him by a friend. She only worked by referral, and she was always most anxious to meet him. She might be the one who would confirm his sexuality once and for all. The phone call came at two in the afternoon, and the next eight hours were an eternity. He made his way to her flat in an upscale neighborhood, and stood waiting outside the door at precisely 11:00 p.m.

Morris was an aide to Averell Harriman, who worked diligently at the Lend-Lease office in London for his dear friend Franklin Roosevelt. As a result, he was privy to much secret information, including British intelligence estimates that seemed overly ambitious in some areas and contradictory in others, as if the data had been manipulated for the purpose of deception. The threat of the Japanese Navy to Singapore and Hong Kong had been played down in some documents while others requested the presence of a strong naval force in Singapore. Some reports had the Germans about to cross the English Channel; others had them reversing course and attacking Russia. Harriman questioned Churchill's aides, especially Admiral Shears, but was more or less put off, or the reports themselves dismissed as nothing more than conjecture. Morris found it hard to understand how any nation that cried for help so long and hard could afford to have intelligence consistently out of line. A report he gave to Harriman that he in turn passed on to Shears said just that.

But it was of no importance to him now. His knock was answered by the most gorgeous blonde in the most alluring black satin dressing gown. She smelled wonderfully, and the warmth of her lips on his face as she kissed his cheek in greeting aroused a host of now familiar feelings. She poured him a glass of champagne and sat close to him on the couch. An inviting fireplace provided the only light in the room. When she crossed her legs the dressing gown parted to her thighs. Her legs were sheathed in dark stockings held in place by a black lace garter belt.

She finished the champagne, and threw the glass into the fire. Putting both arms around his neck allowed the top of the dressing gown to open, revealing her ample breasts. "Shall we?" was all she said.

Amid their throes of passion, the front door burst open. The woman screamed at the top of her lungs only to be slapped down by one of the six men who rushed into the room.

"Frederick Morris, you are under arrest for suspicion of espionage against the British Crown."

"Who the hell are you?" he yelled, as another agent threw his topcoat over his naked body. The woman, barely conscious, was handcuffed.

"British Intelligence. This woman is a German spy. We believe you've passed on information of a sensitive nature to her."

Morris' eyes were wild with fear. "That's bullshit!" he yelled. "I came over here to…"

"To tell her about your Swiss boyfriend?" an agent asked. "Take him away!" he ordered.

Morris spent the next few days in Scotland Yard. Information about his crimes was confused and contradictory. Harriman was told it was espionage, evidenced by photographs of the German spy he engaged in sex. She gave a detailed explanation of their "long-term relationship" and the one he had with the Swiss diplomat, and how she exploited his deviance. Despite his protestations, and those of the State Department, he was not released. Churchill promised Harriman that Morris would receive a fair trial, but with the courts so backed up, it might be a year before it came up. Morris told his parents to stay away. Three attempts at suicide failed.

Yvette arrived home at two in the morning. The bastard who slapped her overdid it, and she had a mouse under her eye, to which she applied an ice bag. It was Friday, so she had two days to heal before work. Still, she wanted to put an ice pick into the ear of that heavy-handed bastard who probably fancied himself as a quite a righteous man.

Yuri came in an hour later. He saw the bag on her eye and a puzzled look crossed his face.

"What's the matter, Popov? Never saw a shiner before? I'll probably get a bleedin' DSO for this from His Majesty himself."

"Yvette, I'm sorry," he said, grimacing as he saw the ugly bruise.

Yvette was taken aback by such a show of concern from a man whose compassion was not usually in evidence. "I'll be fine, really. In my business it's nothing."

"Don't talk about your business. I...don't want to hear about it." He touched the bruise tenderly and saw her wince. "I'll fix us a couple of scotches. It'll help you relax."

"There's no need to coddle me. I've been through hell and back more than once, and I..." she found her breath short and her eyes welled with tears. "Yuri!" she blurted, "the bastard treated me like a common whore, and I couldn't do a damned thing about it! It wasn't supposed to go like that. I did it for England! He wasn't supposed to hit me! He didn't have the right to..."

Yuri held her close and tenderly kissed her cheek, her lips, and the bruise under her eye. "There now. It's over. I'll take care of you. Don't worry," he said, suddenly envisioning his mother's face, frozen in the shock of death.

He carried her to the couch, handed her the scotch, and cuddled her close until she fell asleep in his arms. And there they spent the night. Steaming in anger, Yuri did not sleep.

The next day, an M1 agent started out to work but never got there. A shadowy figure jumped from the dark of the foyer of his flat, and dragged him behind the stairwell and beat him to a pulp. "I'm such a fine actor. They say I'm going to be in the pictures someday because I'm so good in scenes where I slap whores around," the assailant said. He lit a cigarette, took a few drags, then extinguished it in the middle of his victim's forehead. To cover his purpose, he took his victim's wallet.

1800 Hours, April 5, 1941
Hiroshima Bay

News of the great victory at Taranto wasn't lost on Minoru Genda, who requested as much data as his spies and reporters could give him.

"They caught the Italian battleships at anchor in a shallow harbor and destroyed the fleet with torpedoes and bombs. The concept has been proven, and we've not launched an airplane yet!" he said with great delight to another aviator by the name of Mitsuo Fuchida, who held the rank of commander.

"And, with obsolescent aircraft, flying under the cover of darkness. But your plan calls for a launch at dawn, arriving over Pearl Harbor in broad daylight." Fuchida's tone had a sarcastic tinge.

"My intelligence says the American Pacific fleet sleeps late on Sunday. Our timing will be worth the cover of darkness. Don't forget we attack with over 350 aircraft, not twelve puny old kites."

"I hope your intelligence is on target, Genda, and the Americans behave the way you intend them to," Fuchida said, looking at a scale model of Pearl Harbor. "It's dangerous to make your enemy's assumptions for him."

"You had better hold those same hopes, too, my friend. You'll be leading the strike," Genda said, moving the *Arizona* around the diorama.

Fuchida was speechless as a wave of heat flushed his face.

"That is right, my friend. I'm sure you have much to do in the interim." Genda laughed.

Chapter 11

"Remember to keep your eyes open, and don't take anything for granted, Andy."

"You're getting more and more neurotic. Rochefort's made you paranoid."

"Is that so? Well just because you're paranoid doesn't mean they're really not out to get you," Burns shot back.

Andy laughed. The PBY's engines started turning over. "You'd better get aboard before they leave without you. We wouldn't want you to cause an international incident," Andy said.

He handed his bags to a waiting sailor. He then shook Andy's hand and gave him a warm hug. "Keep your guard up, Marine. When this all gets sorted out, we'll be needing you around."

"I'll take care."

"Hey, by the way. Where did you get Mae's string of pearls? I was admiring them last night over that bon voyage dinner you insisted on, but the mere presence of that Russian-British asshole and his bitch of a wife kept on interfering with my thoughts and genteel manners." Burns was like a bulldog with a bone when it came to the Popov's.

"I got it at Tiffany's in New York. When you drop off my parents' Christmas presents and they feed you until you explode, remember to ask them where it is."

"I owe Julie a bauble for putting up with my crap. I really miss her."

"Send us some Hawaiian sunshine," Andy said, yelling to overcome the roar of the PBY's engines.

"Take care, amigo!" Burns entered the PBY through the waist gunner's blister. The flying boat taxied into the Channel, turned upwind, and was off.

Burns thoroughly spooked Andy. His mind raced as he drove from Portsmouth back to London. Did Burns really have it all figured out? He was an affable Scot with a usually more-than-even temper who loved everyone. Why did his face turn as red as his hair every time he saw Yuri or Yvette Popov? What the hell was going on in Hawaii with Joe Rochefort to make him so...so...weird?

Tommy Hamilton greeted Andy back at the flat. Mae had just returned from the grocer's, and he was helping pack away the contents of her canvas bags.

"Hey, Andy!" Tommy proclaimed, shaking his fellow Marine's hand.

"And where have you been hanging out lately?" Andy asked.

"I did meet this young lady in the underground during last night's air raid, and we shared a pint of single malt scotch. When we awoke together this morning, alas, we decided it wouldn't work out."

"Did you give her a chance to decide or did you manage to leave without waking her?" Mae asked.

"You hurt me; I'm not like that," Hamilton said with a devilish smile.

"Yeah, sure. And these aren't breasts!" Mae said, cupping her hands beneath her bosoms. "Wait till I see your Miss O'Neil. I'll tell her a thing or two!"

"Mae! What's got into you?" Andy said, somewhat embarrassed.

"Only you, and that's slackened off lately, my dear husband," Mae said with a laugh. "But if you insist on getting your beauty sleep, I may not be able to speak of monogamy. I'm closing in on thirty, and I'll be the only woman of my age in London who's without a child. I'm sure even Yvette and Yuri are up to something. Have you seen how close they are? Even more so now than when we first met them."

Andy kissed his wife's forehead and put his arms around her. Mae almost disappeared in his embrace, and her smile warmed Tommy's heart, making him homesick for Patty. "She wants a baby, Tommy, and unless we go at it every night, Blitz or no Blitz, she's unhappy."

"Oh. Well then, I'd better get going, and let you two get on with perpetuating the species. I'll leave today's *Daily Mail* for you to read when the passion ebbs," he said, tossing the paper on the table. "You'll note the banner headline reads that our Japanese friends have made a special overture for peace."

0900 Hours, April 10, 1941

Winston Churchill and Admiral Shears reviewed the information that had just came over the wire services and in the diplomatic pouch from Washington.

"It's a feint. They want to keep the Americans off balance," Shears said.

"This fellow Nomura is the perfect envoy. He's a retired admiral who can interpret the Americans' policies from the standpoint of naval strategy. During the coming negotiations, he will surely get a feel for their preparedness. That will only help the yellow bastards in their planning," Churchill said. "When's he due back in Washington?"

"Sometime in May."

Churchill paced the room, puffing furiously on the ever-present cigar. "If war comes between the United States and Japan, I'm convinced their target will be Pearl Harbor."

"Not the Philippines? Our American friends are stripping the Pearl Harbor garrison. They're sending B-17s to MacArthur that should have gone to Hawaii. Their commanders are screaming bloody murder. Production of those precious planes hasn't reached the capacity to supply both garrisons. They're flying into Hawaii's Hickam airfield only long enough to be refueled and serviced." Shears glanced at the wall map to check his references.

"Those planes are of major concern to the Japanese Navy. They could intercept and sink their carriers long before they can launch their aircraft to their target, be it Pearl Harbor or Manila. But why don't the Americans think Hawaii will be the target?" Churchill muttered. "The Japs have to secure their eastern flank. Hawaii is that flank!"

"Perhaps the thinking is that neutralizing Manila is more important. They're after Singapore, Hong Kong, and Sumatra," Shears offered. "Maybe they feel they can take on the United States Pacific fleet at their leisure, after they've secured the raw materials they're really after, especially the Dutch oil fields," Shears offered.

"You never let the enemy gain an upper hand, especially when you can neutralize him in his own backyard by taking advantage of his good nature. That's what we did at Taranto," Churchill countered.

"I think you overestimate the ability of the B-17 Flying Fortress. Against fast moving ships at sea, it's effectiveness will be minimal," Shears said, looking again at the prime minister.

"I just hope the Japanese overestimate it, too!" Churchill responded. "That's why they must attack Pearl Harbor. And, that is why they must succeed. If they don't the Americans will decimate them after their Manila attack because they would have left the U.S. Pacific Fleet and its major Pacific support base unscathed. They will make quick work of the Japs and leave us to the mercy of the Germans."

"The minute a U-boat sinks an American man-of-war, the United States…"

"Still won't do a goddamn thing!" Churchill said. "I'm sure Hitler will do everything he can to be sure that state of affairs continues. American destroyers are attacking U-boats or leading our ships to German ships so we can sink them, and nothing happens! I bet that Goering himself could be shot down in cold blood by an American agent in a suit made of stars and stripes, in the middle of Berlin in broad daylight, and Hitler will declare it a tragic misunderstanding!" He walked to his desk and thought for a minute, rubbing his chin, and glancing back to the map. "And there's the Russian factor. I just know Hitler wants to defeat them before the United States can enter the war. Not having the Russian bear looking over their western shoulder will only enhance Japan's Pacific strategy."

Churchill looked up. "Let's see if Roosevelt will meet with us. By August I want a secret operations center set up in Singapore. It's time we started playing more aggressively. In the meantime, make sure we keep abreast of the Japanese fleet's every move."

"They can't make a move without us knowing," Shears smiled triumphantly.

Churchill's mind silently raced as he stared at Shears, still gloating because of his covert edge.

1100 Hours, April 10, 1941
Northern Ireland

Popov and Eversole taped the timer and the hypergolic tanks to the fourteen-inch naval shell sitting in the middle of a sandbagged pit. They set the timer and ran like hell for the slit trench two hundred yards away. The younger Popov made it easily, but Eversole was blown through the air for the last ten yards into the trench.

"That worked well," Popov said with a laugh.

"So it did. Now let's try it with the black powder and see what happens," Eversole said, wiping the dirt from his eyes.

"Why don't we try it on the gunpowder directly?" Popov asked.

"The stuff may not go up. It's really very stable until it's confined in a gun barrel, where the pressure of confinement causes more rapid combustion."

"This shit is so powerful that only a small amount produces an unbelievable amount of heat energy."

"Let's try it then, my boy," Eversole said, seeing Yuri's face light with pride.

The two walked back to the pit where they noted that the big shell hadn't exploded, and that the two sets of twin tanks had been the cause of the pit's eruption.

"Hmmm...this is a unforeseen development," Eversole said, his face twisting in disappointment.

"The damned thing is too thick. Remember, it has to pierce armor a foot thick before it erupts," Popov counseled.

"Let's try it with the powder. Yuri, tell no one of these results, please."

"Of course not, Chad."

Popov attached the twin tanks and timer to several powder bags in the group of forty set in a trench, about a hundred yards opposite the site of the first explosion. Eversole thought better of sprinting again, and waited in the trench. Popov set the timers, and again ran like hell. When the explosion went off, even the slit trench couldn't protect them from the concussion. It caved in and buried them up to their waists. As the two men crawled from beneath the dirt, they were pelted with a gray and yellow granular substance.

"What the hell is this shit?" Popov said, scooping the material up in his hands.

"Unexploded powder," said the incredulous Eversole. "I think, my friend, you've hit on something. The initial energy is so intense on the host that it cannot sustain a reaction. It would be hell in a closed space."

"Chad," Yuri asked, squinting through the man-made sleet, "what the hell are we up to?"

"I'm afraid to think about it, Yuri," Eversole said, examining the grains in his hand. "Only Admiral Shears and one other person know. That's why we hedge our report." Eversole looked up at the sky with an ominous feeling chilling his bones as the fallout rained down.

1000 Hours, April 16, 1941
Pearl Harbor

Admiral Husband E. Kimmel was nearly apoplectic. He crushed the orders in his hand. Admiral Bill Halsey, commander of the *Enterprise*'s task group, had never seen his friend and commander behave in such a manner. The rest of his staff sat in quiet rage, realizing all their battle plans, offensive and defensive, needed to be reworked.

"How the hell can 'Betty' Stark do this to me? Sweet Jesus! Three of our newer battleships—*Idaho, New Mexico, Mississippi*—four cruisers, two squadrons of destroyers! And the *Yorktown*! Taking her decreases our offensive striking ability by a hundred aircraft." He threw the ball of paper on his desk, more in despair than in anger. "We're on the defensive. The Japs will be licking their chops because we cannot project strength anymore."

"Their carrier strength is now double ours," Halsey offered. "What the hell is going on is Washington?"

"I'll tell you what," Burns said. "They're being courted by Churchill, plain and simple, and he's forcing the Japs into us. We weaken the force here, invite the Japs to attack us so we declare war on them and Germany can declare war on us, just like their Tri-Partite pact says. And we have to depend on Washington to let us know what the Japs are up to, because the PURPLE machine we should have here is sitting in the fucking Admiralty building or on its way to Singapore or Hong Kong."

"Commander Burns. This is profound. How do you figure…"

"Admiral Halsey, sir, begging your pardon. I think the Brits are reading JN-25. All their major fleet units are in the Atlantic or the Mediterranean. They are relying on us to defend their empire but we can't unless we're at war. What better way to do it than by luring us to challenge the petulant Hitler, and give the Japs a chance to stab us in the back?"

"That's seditious," Halsey interrupted Jack, "and you goddamn well know it!"

"They're so desperate that they'll do anything to get us into the fray, including keeping the Japanese fleet movements hidden from us. I'd even bet the president's men…never mind."

Kimmel stared sternly at Burns, who had almost uttered the unthinkable, the intolerable, for an officer in the United States Navy. "Sir, what the hell is the *New Mexico* going to do against a U-Boat? Do they intend to have the *Idaho* shell Wilhelmshaven's U-Boat pens? The former is a job for fleet-footed destroyers, the latter for aircraft. The German Navy has only four or five battleships. They're beautiful ships but they're dogmeat without air cover. And, they have only one inoperative carrier. How are they going to fare against the Royal Navy's battleships covered by Royal Navy carriers? Then why do they need *Yorktown* and our BBs?"

Kimmel listened to Burns' arguments, his eyes opening wider with each statement. "I think I should write a memo to Betty Stark. I'll tell him what I think and ask what he wants me to do. Any policy is only as good as the force available to support it. We can't back into a war with the people of the United States misinformed—that's courting disaster. Nor can we keep threatening the Japanese and be unprepared and under strength when they attack us."

Kimmel walked to the window and looked beyond the submarine base to the vast harbor and magnificent ships that awaited his every order. "Look at us. We're sitting ducks. If Washington takes a few oilers like they've hinted at in the past, the fleet will be tethered here even more so. With one less carrier, fleet air support is gone, so that makes the tether even shorter. The harbor's congested and our repair facilities are crammed together. One lousy bomb on the oil tank farm over there will destroy our ability to operate for months to come." He picked up the crumpled orders and stared at them ominously. "This is the kiss of death."

1000 Hours, April 16, 1941
Pearl Harbor

Tomi Zai was angered by the repetitious questions in Genda's letters about the disposition of the Pacific fleet's ships, but when he tempered it with what was at stake, he remembered what a special kind of hell Genda must be frying in. He put on his jacket and took a cab to the huge naval base. Again, he was freely given the boat tour of the fleet anchorage. There was no doubt about it—*Yorktown, Idaho, New Mexico, Mississippi*—all gone.

Again, Zai took the aerial tour of the harbor and Lahaina Roads, an alternate fleet anchorage. There too, the ships were gone.

When Genda received Zai's reply, it confirmed the sightings by diplomats at the Panama Canal Zone consulate of three mighty battleships, a number of heavy cruisers, twelve destroyers, and a monster carrier negotiating the locks. He really hadn't expected the United States to dismantle its own Pacific fleet before he got the chance to sink it and neutralize their anchorage. But he'd would take all the help he could get.

1200 Hours, April 16, 1941
San Pedro, California

Captain Franklin B. Van Valkenburgh saluted the flag and the officer of the deck as he was piped aboard *Arizona*, swinging around her anchor off San Pedro.

"Chief Jones! I thought for sure you'd be playing nursemaid on one of the new battleships. How did you manage to wiggle your way out of that? I bet you've got pictures of Betty Stark and his secretary engaged in an unnatural act." Van Valkenburgh couldn't have been happier. His job would be a good deal easier.

"Sir, please!" Jones feigned shock.

"Get ready for a surprise. We're going to be a flagship, and Admiral Isaac Kidd will fly his pennant from our mast."

"Sir, this is a banner day indeed!"

Arizona seemed to demonstrate her approval as well by normalizing the pressure in her Number 2 boiler. For weeks, it had given the engineering crew and the yardmen from Bremerton fits. The sudden roaring emission of steam from her funnel startled everyone, even Jones, who muttered, "You know I love you, but you sure can be one little bitch when you want to be."

Josh Friar went to work assembling the ingredients for Admiral Kidd's favorite supper. He was happier than any man deserved to be. He had been recently been promoted to chief mess steward, and gotten his second petty officer's stripe. He insisted that Chief Jones conduct the presentation.

Chapter 12

Andy opened the long-awaited sealed orders, anxious about what fate held for him. He was growing tired of the Lend-Lease administrivia and craved to fly again. Mae eagerly peered over his shoulder. She, too, was looking forward to leaving London, even though it had been her childhood home. The city was becoming dreary under the Blitz and the endless stream of bad news that traced the war's path. Even the coming of spring didn't cheer. Anyway, she looked forward to the baby she had been carrying for three months.

"That seals it!" he said, trying to sound disheartened as he studied her face.

"What's it say?"

"You can't trust the Marine Corps."

"Where are they sending us?" she asked, her patience running thin at her husband's teasing.

"To Iceland," he said.

"Good Lord! How can they do that to you? After all your good work you deserve something better."

"For two weeks—then we're going to Hawaii!"

Mae almost jumped out of her skin. "Hawaii! That's wonderful! We'll be with Jack and Julie Burns!" Andy was smiling with trepidation, and Mae saw it. "What's wrong?."

"It's a wonderful assignment, Mae, that's true. But I'm going over to help form a Marine fighter squadron." He looked at her almost sternly, saying, "That means someone's anticipating trouble with our Japanese friends."

"We'll be okay, Andy. Don't fret about me or the baby. I knew going into this it wouldn't be a bed of roses. Cedric taught me that."

A knock on the door announced the arrival of Tommy Hamilton and Lisa Seghesio. Lisa was looking much better, and her bitterness over Cedric was dissolving. Her smile was back, and her beautiful brown almond-shaped eyes had a sparkle that was not lost on Tommy Hamilton.

"What did your orders say?" Tommy asked, half-afraid to hear the answer, should it be bad news.

Andy repeated his deadpan act, but this time quickly added, "To be followed by Hawaii."

"Son of a gun! Me too!" They shook hands and slapped each other on the back. "My only question is, what the hell is in Iceland?" Tommy asked.

"For tourists? Not much. Strategically, it's the Atlantic mid-point in providing convoy protection, sort of like an unsinkable carrier. The problem is, we have to get there before the Germans do."

"But why us? We're not mud-Marines."

"We know airfields, airplanes, and aerial warfare. I think that's the crux of it. We'll see. Come on, Tommy, it's time we begin to work on our tans."

"Where are you off to?" Mae asked, with Lisa just as interested.

"To the embassy. I want to make the transition for my successor as easy as possible, and there's plenty of work to get done."

"Hey, can we stop in New York and eat at your parents' place again?" Tommy asked. "I've had that veal rollatini on my mind ever since your engagement party."

"New York is on the way to Hawaii," Andy said, closing the door behind him.

Mae placed the orders on Andy's desk in the tiny spare room that served as a study. She saw by Lisa's far-away look that she desperately wanted to say something. She had been carrying the burden much too long. Mae sat down beside her and put her hand on Lisa's as they lay folded in her lap. "Is there something you want to tell me? Come on, it's okay. I know your heart was shattered when Ced died, but you can love again. He wouldn't have it any other way, you know." She reached over to hug her sister-in-law. "Everyone deserves someone. Cedric knew you loved him unconditionally."

"Oh, Mae. I feel like a harlot! Tommy's always there with that wonderful smile and his good humor. He's so strong and I need that now," she whimpered. "I'm not nearly as tough as I thought."

"It's not about tough, nor about strength. In matters of the heart, there are few words that can describe its pain or pleasure."

"I love Cedric so, Mae. I really do. He is so much like you. Giving, caring, funny. I…"

"There, you see? You're still talking as if he were alive. How can anyone doubt your affection? It's time to move on, dear. That's all. And if Tommy is the one you choose to move on with, so be it."

"Thank you, Mae; thank you so much."

"I have a question, though," Mae said, after thinking for a moment. "Isn't he already spoken for?"

"I'm not that way!"

"I didn't say you were, Lisa. I'm just remembering a young woman named Patty James he was quite fond of."

"You didn't know?"

"Know what?"

"She's married. She wrote him a long letter about a man she met at work who swept her off her feet. She mentioned security, a permanent home, all the things that military wives seldom have. I think Cedric's death precipitated it. Tommy wrote her all about it. He was looking for understanding, and was turned away instead."

"He never mentioned it to me or Andy." Mae was totally shocked.

"He doesn't hurt very well. It's all inside when it comes to his feelings."

0600 Hours, April 25, 1941
San Pedro

Chief Gwyeth Jones went below deck to see how work was progressing on the Number 1 turbine that wouldn't engage to turn its propeller shaft. It started acting up about the time Captain Van Valkenburgh announced they were rejoining the fleet at Pearl Harbor. It had already caused a delay of thirty-six hours with little hope of being fixed anytime soon. The engineering crews were sweating rivers of water in the 110 degree heat. Jones ordered them above for a breath of fresh air. He then sat down on a stool and talked to his ship.

"You have to go. You have no choice; I have no choice. We're a part of a bigger whole. We're not alone in this. It's our job."

He listened to the creaking steel, the steam pressuring turbines, and the minute vibrations as the *Arizona* spoke to him.

"You're the best warship that ever sailed the seas, manned by the best crew. Both of us were born to go in harm's way. It's Japan that threatens us."

The ship rumbled again, ever so slightly.

"Yes, you will. I will. I promise you that," he answered.

In the company of Chief Jones, Joshua Friar went to see Captain Van Valkenburgh and Admiral Kidd.

"To what do I owe the pleasure," Kidd jested.

"Well, sir, this October brings the Silver Anniversary of the *Arizona*'s commissioning. I was thinking that we give our lady a party and invite the fleet to attend. I'd be happy to cook up a dinner for you and the other brass...er, officers of the fleet. We could sponsor something to get the other ships' crews over here and have a wing-ding, on board and ashore. Sir."

"That's a splendid idea!" Van Valkenburgh said, noting that Kidd was smiling as widely as Friar. "Josh, I'll work on it as soon as we get the old girl over to her berth at Pearl. We'll have a party to remember. Well done!"

"Thank you, sir. I'd better get going on your supper."

"Keep it light, Josh. The missus tells me that the shadow of my ass weighs ten pounds!"

1500 Hours, April 25, 1941
Washington, D.C.

Sumner Welles was engrossed in his work as an undersecretary of state for Russian affairs. He was quite taken with his importance, as the Lend-Lease program was now quietly being sought by the U.S.S.R. as a means to build against the Nazi invasion everyone knew was sure to come. He was given MAGIC decrypts. The Kamchatka peninsula or possibly the port of Okhotsk might be targets of a coordinated German-Japanese attack that would catch the Red Army in a two-front war. The last decrypt he received was alarming, and he contacted Constantin Oumansky, Russia's ambassador to Washington.

"I've brought some Russian caviar for you, my friend. It is from the Caspian Sea, the best in the Soviet Republics."

"Many thanks. May I offer you a bit of refreshment—perhaps this fine Finnish vodka I've been able to requisition?"

"Ah, Sumner. You know my answer!"

As Welles poured a healthy glass of the clear but potent spirits, he decided there was no call to play games. The Russians had to know about the danger from the Germans, despite their thin-skinned non-aggression pact. That no one in history had invaded Russia without suffering a bitter defeat was axiomatic. That Hitler would try it had been predicted, and now Welles had it documented. An invasion meant the Fuhrer taking both men and machines away from the blitz on Britain, and making France, Italy, and Africa more vulnerable to "future offensive operations." The Russian sipped his vodka, then closed his eyes as the fiery liquid passed down his throat. "Sumner, it is heaven. Thank you!"

Welles smiled at his guest. He really liked this man, who was always forthright and plain-spoken. It was refreshing when compared to the British and Free French diplomats he had been forced to deal with. With them, it was always *if*. With the Soviets, it was always *when*. "My friend, I have information I'd like to share with you."

Oumansky became fully alert. He trusted Welles as a man of his word, who saw what lay behind the pacts and headlines. He drained the glass, gave a loud sigh, and set it on the table.

"What is that, my friend?"

"I have it on good account that the Germans will turn their armies on the Motherland in June."

The Russian's eyebrows raised. He took the bottle of vodka and poured another round.

"Who's account might that be?" he asked. He downed the vodka in a gulp.

"The Japanese ambassador in Berlin, Hiroshi Oshima, told his superiors to be prepared for it."

"Do you think the Japanese will threaten us from the east, Sumner?"

"I don't think so, at least not right away. They have other priorities just now."

Oumansky rose and walked to the window. "The cherry trees their emperor bestowed on your government in happier times are lovely in full bloom. Have you appreciated their beauty, Sumner?"

"Spring is the season for rebirth, and those trees have marked it for years."

"I fear the blossoms will fall, and with them all hope for reason from the Nazis. Our hope of defeating them rests on the blossoms."

Welles looked curiously at this friend. "I'm afraid I don't follow you."

Oumansky let the spring sun warm his face, taking him back to the Steppes, and the little village at the base of the Ural Mountains where he grew to manhood.

"How did you come by this information? I know you may not be able to tell me the truth, but my superiors will ask; so, I need an answer."

"We intercepted a message from Oshima, and decrypted it. We can read some of the Japanese code, and that's the truth."

"Do you think the United States will declare war on Germany when this happens?"

"I sincerely doubt it. The pact you signed with Germany precludes that action."

Constantin smiled. "Your government must support us. You must get into this war before the Japanese smell your weakness. You and I both know the Pacific Fleet is not nearly up to the task of defending the American Pacific, let alone the European Pacific, what is left of it. And they will come, just like they came to Tsushima and helped to bring Nicholas down. Actually, when you think about it in those terms, those little yellow bastards did us a favor." He turned and smiled to Welles. "Beat them to the punch, Sumner. Attack them where they least expect it. Go after their fleet while it lies in sublime anchor off the Kuriles."

"We don't work that way, Constantin. You know that."

"Ah, yes. Your sense of fair play. The American Indians know of it well."

Welles chuckled at the slur. "Do you think you can fend off a German invasion?" Welles asked, trying to get the Russian on task.

"The blossoms will tell it all," Constantin said, pointing to the window. "Will the summer be long, and the fall be filled with unusual warmth? If the blossoms remain the Germans will be in Moscow by your Thanksgiving, and Russia will fall. In any event, I will schedule a meeting with my German 'ally,'" he chuckled. "I hope Hans Thomsen has an opening in his schedule in the next few days."

"I hope so, too."

"Sumner, if war comes to Russia the blood of millions will be shed as your country decides on the obvious. Do not wait too long, my friend. The contagion becomes stronger with time."

Ambassador Kichisaburo Nomura reviewed the evidence before him showing the Americans were able to read the low-grade code in use between Berlin and Tokyo. The chief diplomatic code was secure, he reasoned, because they weren't acting on the vital information it transmitted.

He was mistaken. All information to or from Tokyo was read by OP-20-G as soon as Nomura sent it or received it by the PURPLE machine that decrypted Nomura's high-level code. Doing nothing was a ruse that allowed the Japanese to think their code was secure. However, the user list needed to be curtailed, just to be sure that Nomura's errant assumption remained fact. As a result, Sumner Welles was taken off the MAGIC distribution list, along with Admiral Kimmel in Hawaii, and his Army counterpart, General Walker C. Short. Now, they not only had to rely on Washington for their decrypts, but also on the analysis as well. The "feeling" behind the messages couldn't be extrapolated from the summaries they received. The last smidgen of real-time communications was squashed.

1200 Hours, April 26, 1941
London

Chad Eversole duly reported to Admiral Shears.

"You got this through the new PURPLE machines we received ?"

"That is correct, sir."

"Are you sure the American commanders are off the list?"

"Their call signs were eliminated and we didn't detect any radio transmissions going to Hawaii."

Shears lit his pipe and sat back in his chair. "They are doing our work for us.

Speaking of work," he said, "our Norwegian underground friends in the Baltic have done a magnificent job. They tell us the *Bismarck* is on the loose. It was confirmed with a sighting by a Swedish cruiser. She's sailing with a cruiser we believe to be the *Prinz Eugen*."

"She'll wreak havoc if she gets to open water." Eversole knew the battleship was the most powerful in the world, sleekly designed, armored to near impregnability, and much too fast for a ship with a 50,000 ton displacement. She also carried the biggest guns afloat.

"We're putting together a plan now to intercept and sink her. I've got a number of units in on the chase. Take a look at the map."

Eversole noted that a number of ships, marked by different colored pins for each type, were converging to form several task forces. Among them were the *Hood* and the brand new *Prince of Wales*. He looked at the picture of the young man sitting on the admiral's desk, and remembered young William Shears was manning the communications shack on the *Hood*.

As Chad Eversole left the office, Shears picked up the phone.

"*Bismarck*'s at sea," Shears said. "The prime minister wants her on the bottom. What do you have, John?"

"*Bismarck*! The name itself is terrifying," Admiral Sir John Tovey responded. Commander of the Home Fleet, he flew his flag from *King George V*, which rode the high tide at anchor in Scotland's Scapa Flow.

"It's vitally important to the war effort to sink her, not only from a military standpoint, but for the morale of our people," Shears said.

"*Bismarck* can outgun anything we have nearby and she can outrun anything we have that can punch holes in her. I've got to slow her, and that means attacking from the air. I'll call up *Ark Royal* from Gibraltar to have her planes make an intercept from the south, and I'll assign *Victorious* and her air group to cut her off to the north. She'll be ducking in and out of fjords to avoid detection, so we'll have to conduct a thorough search by air."

"I'm getting that done now."

"Very good. Is the cruiser the only one with her?"

"As far as we know, John."

"Then range will be a factor. *Bismarck* cannot outdistance the cruiser."

"John, will you put *Hood* into the search?"

"Of course. Her guns are a match for *Bismarck*'s, although her armor isn't. Being less hefty and more lightly armored should give *Hood* an advantage in maneuver."

"I guess that's so. Which ship will *Hood* sail with?"

"The brand new *Prince of Wales*. They should give an excellent account of themselves against the German."

"Yes, I think so."

Tovey noted the hesitancy in Shears' voice. "Is there something else, Admiral?"

"No, not at all. Carry on. Keep me informed."

"That I will."

———————

"Why do they need me to fly the PBY? I'm due to leave here in a few days." Jack Burns' parting words were echoed in Andy's ears.

"It's got American insignia on it and the Royal Navy pilots need to be brought up to a higher level of proficiency on the aircraft," Averell Harriman said.

"I have only ten hours on the aircraft, sir. How high do you think mine is?" Andy saw Harriman's eyes narrow as his brow furrowed. He was caught in a lie, and now was forced to tell the whole story. "Sir, what's the scoop? I don't mind doing a job, but I've got to know what's going on."

"Okay, Andy, here it is. The British are short of pilots, and they need all their best flying fighters and bombers. They consider patrol aircraft an auxiliary, because they can't blow up anything or shoot anything down. The few pilots they've put in PBYs weren't fit to fly combat aircraft. They've lost or damaged a number of them already."

"Why not use the Spitfires or the big Wellingtons and their carrier airplanes for recon?"

"Because they're stretched so thin, and the Germans have given them cause to be alarmed. Ever hear of the *Bismarck*?"

"Who hasn't? It's the biggest, nastiest battleship afloat, but it's been jammed up the Elbe by a sunken freighter, and…"

"She's back at sea. She's joined up with a cruiser, the *Prinz Eugen*, we think."

"That means hell for the convoys."

"Churchill wants it sunk. He's asking us to help find it."

Andy had no choice. With Roosevelt's best friend approaching him, the "request" had to come directly from the President of the United States. But once he was up there, no one could tell him what to do.

"Okay, sir. Can Tommy Hamilton fly the right seat?"

"Whatever you wish, but remember, you're not to attack it. Leave that to the Brits. Understood?" Harriman asked.

"Yes sir. Understood."

———————

0200 Hours, May 1, 1941
Battleship *Bismarck*

Admiral Gunther Lutjens was generally acknowledged as one of the finest officers in the Kriegsmarine. He had grave misgivings about his mission. The *Bismarck* on its maiden voyage would be sailing against the convoys of merchantmen the Royal Navy was now defending with American battleships. They would fire on the German ships if they were attacked, neutrality be damned. He had wanted a true task force to sail boldly into the Atlantic; *Bismarck,* her soon-to-be-completed sister *Tirpitz,* and the very deadly heavy cruisers *Gneisenau, Scharnhorst,* and *Prinz Eugen. Bismarck*'s skipper was Captain Ernst Lindeman, a forty-five-year-old graduate of the German Annapolis at Murwick, a classmate of *Prinz Eugen*'s commander, Helmuth Brinkmann. Both they and their crews had yet to be battle-tested, but the ships' complements were well-trained volunteers who worshiped their ships and their officers.

Hitler, too, had misgivings about the mission, and expressed them to Lutjens when he visited *Bismarck* just prior to her sortie.

"Can she survive against the Royal Navy?" he asked.

"None of theirs is a match for the *Bismarck.* What we cannot outrun, we can outfight," Lutjens answered.

"What about the British carrier planes? Look at what they did at Taranto," Hitler said almost in a whisper, lest other ears should hear the Fuhrer express fear.

"The Royal Navy's carriers are in the Mediterranean or enroute. By the time they respond, we will be in Brest, our battle pennant bloodied. Besides, we will be on the high seas, wheeling and maneuvering, not sitting ducks in a harbor. And *Bismarck* is German, Fuhrer, not Italian."

As Hitler laughed, Lutjens caught the look in Lindemann's eyes. Both men feared aerial torpedoes more than battleships. Though they denied it openly, they realized their ships were in grave danger if the Swordfish and their deadly torpedoes entered the impending fray. The Royal Navy would never let them near a convoy. Their fight would be against ships-of-the-line, not some thin-skinned, popgun-armed merchantmen.

0700 Hours, May 26, 1941
Scapa Flow

"I hate these damn things! How the hell can anybody miss this monster?"

"My sentiments exactly. I want my fighter back!" Andy said, seeing a smile cross Hamilton's face.

"Do you remember how to make this house fly?" Hamilton asked, running down the checklist.

"I'm just going to aim this fat bitch down the middle of the channel, gun the engines, and wait until she lifts her nose," Andy responded, as he turned over the PBY Catalina's twin engines. "Have you got the radio channels keyed to the Royal Navy's frequencies?"

"That's a roger."

"Okay, then, hold on to your balls. Pilot to crew, prepare for takeoff...I think."

Ian Stokes, the waist gunner, was nervous. It was his and radio operator Trevor McIntosh's first combat mission. The nineteen-year-olds had just graduated from aerial gunnery school.

For two days, Andy and his crew continued the tedious job of searching the vast sectors of the North Atlantic assigned to them. Then, on May 21, a pilot astride a reconnaissance-equipped Spitfire flying at 25,000 feet thought he saw two massive ships, each in fjords separated by an arete. He turned hard, and put his cameras in action. Upon returning to his base in North Scotland, the film contained the unmistakable photographic images of *Bismarck* and *Prinz Eugen*. Tovey summoned the *Prince of Wales* and the *Hood* to give chase, and both ships left Scapa Flow, steaming at full speed for the Denmark Strait. The weather worsened, enveloping the German ships in heavy rain that limited visibility to less than a quarter mile. They literally disappeared.

Tovey ordered the *King George V* and *Repulse* to join the hunt. The cruisers *Norfolk* and *Suffolk*, anticipating the German battle force's escape from the narrows of the Denmark Strait, patrolled off Iceland. The clouds lifted on May 23, and their new powerful searching radars hit paydirt. Lutjens ordered the cruisers engaged, and for the first time *Bismarck*'s eight fifteen-inch rifles roared in anger, belching huge tongues of flame and halos of brown smoke. The compressive effect rippled the sea, and actually moved the 50,000-ton ship several yards off course. *Norfolk* was rattled to her bilges by the one-ton shells as they erupted the gray-green sea abeam in white geysers over two hundred feet high. The British ships settled back into a squall, fourteen miles behind, but kept in radar contact. The ten fourteen-inch rifles of the *Prince of Wales* and the eight fifteen-inch rifles of the *Hood* were now only three hundred miles away.

Lutjens ordered a reverse course to engage the cruisers again, aware that they were broadcasting his position to the entire Royal Navy. But Lutjens realized his luck had run out; he would have to fight his way back to protective air cover, and that meant making for the French port of Brest or St. Nazaire. The British had no doubt already closed off the North Sea and the safety of the fjords. He ran at flank speed all night.

"Contact! Bearing 320 degrees northwest. Two large ships!" *Hood's* radar officer announced. Billy Shears radioed the information back to Tovey on *King George V*. He could hardly keep his voice from cracking. The battle clock above his console read 0500 hours.

"Engage targets," was Tovey's succinct response.

Billy Shears passed the word on to the *Hood's* captain, who ordered his big guns aimed at the enemy.

The *Prinz Eugen's* port hydrophones picked up the sound of the propellers of heavy ships, sending the bridge officers scrambling for their binoculars. No radar contact was made as yet, but it was known that the radar's range was shorter than that of the hydrophones'. Smoke appeared on the southwest horizon, and the tall masts of two warships appeared and were immediately identified as a *King George V*-class battleship, and the HMS *Hood*. Lutjens reflected on the *Hood*. He knew she was one of the world's most famous ships, in part due to a series of world cruises she conducted in the 20's and 30's. Lutjens long admired the ship's clean, modern lines, and her impressive armament. *Hood* was thirty feet longer than *Bismarck*, but was six thousand tons lighter—all in the sacrifice of armor for speed.

Lutjens caught the flash of the *Hood's* guns, followed immediately by a similar eruption on the accompanying *KG V*-class battleship. He gave the order to the awaiting guns, trained and elevated, their breeches loaded with armor-piercing, one-ton ordnance. *Bismarck* fired a broadside every forty seconds, her well-trained gunnery crews working feverishly.

Bismarck was struck by several shells from the *Prince of Wales*, one of which caused her bow to flood, while another opened a fuel tank to the sea. The damage slowed her slightly, but she was still effective. Lutjens' attention was brought back to the gunfight by his chief gunnery officer.

"Look! That one tore into him!"

Billy Shears' eyes were wide with fear, as the *Hood* shook and rattled from the hammerblows of the shells falling on each side. She healed from side to side as she maneuvered, but the ship surged with power and defiance, her bow heaving as it parted the heavy seas. The battle cries of his mates stirred him, the smell of cordite from the roaring rifles replacing fear with a lust for victory. This was what his father talked about when he described the heat of battle he'd felt as a young lieutenant at Jutland. He was further emboldened by the determination on the faces of the other six men in the communications shed. His earphones came alive with a message from *Prince of Wales*. Just then, something terrible began to happen.

Shears heard a thunderclap aft of his position, followed by a shudder from deep in the bowels of the ship. He heard what sounded like steel being struck by an immense hammer. Cracks began to appear in the bulkhead in front of his console. The ship shook violently as the lights flickered out. As he rose in fear, he was stunned by the ear-shattering rumble of the deck buckling beneath him. He and the others ran for the hatch. They were met by a purplish wave of concussive flame that blew them backwards and incinerated them.

To the men on the *Prince of Wales*, the unbelievable was happening before their eyes—the pride of the Royal Navy was blown to bits, disappearing beneath the waves in seconds, taking all but three of a fourteen hundred man crew with her. The gunners gritted their teeth and fired off their fourteen-inchers, attempting to finish the work they had started. Their vengeance was cut short, however, as another of *Bismarck*'s salvoes struck, killing everyone on the bridge except her captain and his signalmen. The compass station evaporated in flame, a gun director tore from its mounts, and a radar station collapsed. Fragments from another salvo holed the stern, and peppered the superstructure with shell splinters. The *Prince of Wales*, so new her builders were still aboard making final touches and calibrating equipment, turned and escaped in a smoke screen.

Shears received the news directly from Tovey, with his "most sincere sympathy." Telling his wife would be harder than taking his own life. At home he sat with her briefly until Mrs. Tovey arrived, but she really wanted none of his uniform; he went to his library. He sat and wept for the first time in his adult life. He poured himself more scotch than he took note of, and puffed on a huge cigar he was saving for the day of Germany's defeat. It was irrelevant now. Perhaps he, too, was irrelevant now.

He almost fell out of his chair as he opened the third drawer of his desk and reached for the Remington .44 he kept there. It was a gift from the American Admiral Chester Nimitz, whom he had become quite fond of during his tour as a naval attache in the United States. He even spent some time on several American battleships—the *Pennsylvania*, the *Oklahoma*, and the *Arizona*. The alcohol-induced fog was becoming difficult to see through. Why didn't Nimitz send the *Arizona* to help young Billy? He noted the cigar's ashes had fallen on his deep blue slacks. Was he on fire? He felt so very hot. Had William died in fire? The thought made him retch.

He put the pistol to his temple, pulled the trigger, but the mechanical click that meant he was still alive enraged him. The revolver's magazine held no ammunition. He fumbled in the drawer again and found one round, which he quickly loaded into one of the pistol's six chambers. He put the pistol to his head again and pulled the trigger. Nothing. Again, and again—nothing.

His chances were now one in two that he would be dead in an instant. He again put the pistol to his head and a faint smile of relief crossed his face. Then the phone rang.

He put the pistol down, and fumbled with the receiver.

"I wanted you to know I feel absolutely horrible about your son, Edgar. I truly mean that."

"Thank you Prime Minister. We appreciate your condolences."

"There will be a memorial service for the crew as soon as we sink that monster born in the kilns of hell. And we will sink her, I promise you."

Tears were flowing again, and he saw that revenge would mean nothing if he weren't alive to witness it. He put the Remington back in the drawer. "It will avenge my son's death to see her heading for the bottom, taking all her demons with her."

"The Americans are aiding us in locating the ship, Edgar. I've asked..."

"If the Americans really want to help, they would have a battle force ready to sink that Kraut killer on sight. I need no one to hold my coat when I fight, sir. I need someone willing to bleed with me!" he raged.

"I guess you are right, Edgar. I shall see you tomorrow, if I may stop by your home."

"You'll be welcome, Mr. Churchill."

Churchill resolved he would never allow Shears to forget the feelings he voiced that night. Grief and vengeance were good manipulators. They might come in handy one day. Battleships...their pride and passion captured the souls of nations. Sink one, and a nation would sacrifice itself for revenge. Nothing had changed since 1898, he thought, sipping the remaining brandy in his glass.

Admiral Shears would need no reminding. As he left the library, Mrs. Tovey ran to him saying his wife was having trouble breathing.

0900 Hours, May 26, 1941

"How much longer, and why in the hell are we searching this area? I thought the *Bismarck* would run back to Norway."

"She's banged up, Tommy. The *Hood* and *Prince of Wales* must have gotten off a few good shots. The German commander's battle reports were intercepted and his position was triangulated. *Victorious*'s Swordfish attacked and got a hit, but the damned ship is so well-armored she shook it off. The shadowing cruisers lost contact, but her calls for help from U-boats and the Luftwaffe will be her undoing, because they keep her position updated."

"Hey, I've got something," Ian Stokes reported. "I'll pipe it to your headset, sir."

"It's in code. Raise Portsmouth and see if they're getting it."

"Roger, that, sir," Stokes responded.

A few tense minutes passed. Then Andy's headset came alive again. "Gull one, this is Nest. Request you search area 6, south southwest, heading 200. Do you confirm?"

"Roger that," Andy replied.

"Contact *Modoc* on frequency 110, over. She'll bring you up to task."

"*Modoc*?" Tommy Hamilton said. "That's our Coast Guard cutter we saw tied up in Portsmouth. She's supposed to be collecting weather data. That battleship'll crush her. What the hell is she doing out there?"

"Trying to get us into the war, I'd say," Andy replied. "I've got the course laid in." He pushed the throttles forward and pulled the big Catalina around to the heading Hamilton plotted.

An hour later, the big flying boat broke out of the clouds at ten thousand feet, all eyes searching the green sea for any hint of the German behemoth. Trevor McIntosh spotted the first tell-tale signs.

"Oil slick! I see an oil slick just south of us. Do you see it, sir?"

"Roger that. Nice going, McIntosh. All right, everyone, listen up. We'll follow the slick eastward. Keep your eyes peeled for the Luftwaffe. We're getting close to the limit of their range. They might try one-way flights to save the ship for all we know, so be sharp."

"One-way flights? That isn't characteristic of the Germans," Tommy said.

"There's a big propaganda war to be won here. They've been screaming about sinking the *Hood* and scuffing up the *Prince of Wales*. Churchill has been demanding the *Bismarck* be sunk. Wouldn't it be worth a few Me-109's and 110's if it meant the ship makes port? They could even have U-boats pick up the pilots after they ditch. Hell, I'd order it."

"I guess I would, too. Shit! We might start the war. I'd make a lousy martyr."

"You and me both."

It didn't take long to spot the wounded *Bismarck*. Her secondary 5.9 inch turrets and 4.1 inch antiaircraft batteries opened up, the black puffs of their exploding shells falling far short of the lumbering Catalina.

"Send your contact report, Stokes. I'm getting the hell outta here," Andy said.

"Look at her! She's immense," Stokes said.

"Did you hear me? Send the report!" Andy snapped.

"That bleedin' son of a bitch sank the *Hood*!" he yelled to McIntosh. Ian Stokes began to fire his .50 calibre machine gun at the massive warship. McIntosh joined in.

"Tommy, send the fucking position report!" Andy said in frustration. "As soon as it's confirmed, go back there and slap the shit out of those two bean heads!" He applied power, and turned away from the antiaircraft bursts that were coming uncomfortably close.

"This is Gull One. Contact. One battleship bearing 240 degrees, five miles, course 150 degrees. My position 49.33 north, 21.47 west. Time of origin, 1030 hours."

Pilots aboard the carrier *Ark Royal* copied the latest position report and scrambled to their Swordfish torpedo planes. They headed directly to the position Andy had posted, and followed the blood spoor of the wounded *Bismarck*. They attacked boldly, pitting their canvas and wood against the wall of antiaircraft fire and even the big fifteen-inch guns that fired into the sea directly in their path, hoping the huge geysers would throw them off their attack runs. The ungainly Swordfish managed to put two torpedoes into her. One exploded on the amidships armor belt, causing little damage. The second hit her stern, and jammed the rudder leaving *Bismarck* to circle helplessly. The next day she was put under by Tovey's battleships *King George V, Rodney*, the cruisers *Doretshire,* and the ghostly *Norfolk*.

Andy returned home exhausted. He opened the door to see Lisa standing there in tears.

"Where's Mae?" he asked, knowing something must be terribly wrong by the look on his sister's face.

"Uh, she's had a problem."

"Lisa, what kind of problem? Out with it." He tried to remain calm, but his chest tightened.

"The baby, Andy. Yesterday. She's had a miscarriage," she blurted, wringing her hands nervously, her chin quivering as she tried to fight back the tears.

Andy rushed to his sister and hugged her. "Where is she, Lisa?"

"In St. Andrew's hospital. Yvette Popov took her there when she started complaining of pain. We were all just playing cards, suddenly she started writhing in pain. I feel terrible for her."

"Let's go."

She lay there with Yvette clutching her hand and stroking her auburn hair. "Wake up, dear. It's Andy." Yvette hugged him and left the room.

"Mae, can you hear me?"

Her hazel eyes fluttered open.

"I'm glad you're here, Andy. I don't know what happened. I just couldn't take the pain. I still feel so weak."

"Rest easy, sweetheart. You'll be okay." Mae drifted off to sleep.

A man in a white coat entered the room with a clipboard in his hand. "I'm Doctor Lynde. From what we could determine, she was in her fourth month. Am I correct?" he said, shaking Andy's outstretched hand.

"Yes. She looks so weak, Doctor," he said.

"She lost quite a bit of blood. This is supposed to happen only in the first trimester."

"Are you sure she'll be all right?"

"Absolutely. We'll keep her with us for a while, though. We don't want the bleeding to start again. You can try to have another child in a few months," he said, reassuringly.

"Thank you, Doctor." He kissed Mae's forehead. She blinked, but didn't waken. He looked to the doctor, who said, "She's heavily sedated. We've got to keep her still for awhile."

Outside in the waiting area, Yvette Popov cried in sobs, Yuri trying vainly to console her. "She's going to be fine, Yvette. The doctor told me the worst is over."

"Dear God, I hope so." Yvette hugged Andy, then said, "Yuri, perhaps you had better take me home. I'm sorry, Andy, but I just can't take anymore of this. I really love her so, and I can't stand to see her so hurt."

"She's been here for twenty hours waiting for you to come. She hasn't had a thing to eat," Lisa said.

"I won't forget this, Yvette. Thanks," Andy said.

Back at their flat, Yuri couldn't break loose from Yvette's clinging hold. The crying had started again. "Tell me about it," was all he said.

"There's something about her that makes me want to be a better person," she sniffed. "When I'm around her, I want to be like her. Did you see she was still wearing her string of pearls? She wouldn't let the hospital people touch them." Yvette sat down and blew her red nose and wiped her swollen eyes. "When she lost the life she carried, it reminded me of how much we're both victims, even to the point where the life we create is snatched from us, through fate, or purpose," she said standing. "And I realize now you can't earn respectability by deceit." Her body straightened, her toughness emerging.

"I'm not following you, Yvette." Yuri looked into her eyes and cocked his head, waiting to hear what she desperately needed to say.

"I had an abortion, just before I met you." His expression told her then and there that Yuri Popov truly loved her. "Go ahead and ask," she said. "You're entitled."

"I don't need to know," he said, moving to hug her.

"Yes, you do. Now that I love you and you love me, you have to. I cannot continue living this lie. Today I learned it's a rotten thing to do."

Yuri took a deep breath. "All right then. Who's child was it?"

"Billy Shears'. And now there's nothing left of him. Nothing."

Chapter 13

Yuri Popov tossed and turned in a cold sweat. Little Nina called to him with outstretched arms, her face showing confusion and fear at the carnage around her. The beautiful face of his mother was fraught with anguish as she reached out to him. Papa kept his eyes on the ground as the faceless horseman cut him down with his saber and laughingly taunted Yuri while cutting his baby sister in two. Mama's face remained frozen in horror.

"Mama!" he screamed, sitting upright. "I can't help you! I can't move, Mama!" he yelled in Russian.

"Yuri! Wake up!" Yvette grabbed his big shoulders, slippery with perspiration. He wriggled away from her, headed for their bedroom door. Yvette took the pitcher of water from the nightstand and followed him. She managed to turn him around, ducking as he flailed with his fists, his eyes wide open, exposing the terror within. Yvette saw her chance and heaved the water directly into his face.

Choking and spitting, he lost his footing on the damp floor and fell. Yvette ran to him and pulled him close. He stared at her, climbing from the abyss.

"I can't stop them, Yvette. They keep coming and coming. Every time I close my eyes, I'm back on that frozen lake and those bastards are cutting up my family."

"It's the invasion, Yuri. You saw soldiers kill your family before your eyes. It's all related in your mind, I'm sure," she said, holding him closely.

"I feel so helpless, so totally useless. I know children are experiencing the same things I did. Admiral Shears said it would be far worse than anything we can imagine, that the Germans will kill every Russian they can, Jew or not. They hope terrorism will cave in the nation. He curses the Americans for not intervening, yet I don't see how he expects them to declare war when they haven't been attacked. The Germans have tried to avoid that at all costs. I want to go in, but Shears prohibits it. I speak Russian! I don't know what…"

"They want you to be so angry you'll do anything to get even. Don't be so quick to bite the bait. A whore knows that men who are desperate will pay or do almost anything for their desired reward. That bastard Shears will…"

He angrily pushed her away at that, and immediately regretted it. He looked directly into her eyes, held her shoulders, and whispered, "Yvette, he's still our superior officer. We can't allow personal animosities to get into this."

"You're already involved, or are you sitting on the floor stark naked and soaking wet because it's how you like to spend your evenings?"

He glanced at the moon peering in through the window, just as it had through the trees around the frozen lake so long ago, yesterday. He was so confused. A warrior kept from war usually becomes desperate, he thought, and it was desperation that marked his behavior.

0800 Hours, June 6, 1941
Pearl Harbor

General Walker C. Short, commander of the United States Army in Hawaii, pensively stroked his chin and re-read the message again.

"It doesn't make sense, Kim. The Japs have no interest in Russia. What they want is to the south, along the rim of the Pacific."

"Militarily, don't you think it makes sense for them to join the Nazis in attacking Russia? Fighting a two-front war would be near impossible for the Red Army," Admiral Kimmel offered.

"The Imperial Japanese Navy and Army are geared for an island-hopping offense. They don't have the heavy weapons or the raw materials to sustain a protracted land campaign. They don't train for it. Defense in depth and lightening bolt-quick light offense is their trademark."

"I agree. Still, the concept is intriguing."

"Look at the trouble the Japs are having with China. It's a feudal state already torn apart by Mao and Chiang, and they still can't mount an offensive worth a good goddamn," Short responded, rising from his desk and walking to his window. A B-17 stood poised for takeoff at the edge of Hickam Field's runway. "The only thing the yellow bastards can do well is kill innocent civilians. The Red Army, on the other hand, needs only to attack, retreat, burn, and do it all over again, and wait for the Russian winter to set in. After that, they only have to bury the frozen Nazi corpses. Why that asshole Hitler decided to attack Russia and take the pressure off England will remain a mystery forever."

As the B-17 became airborne, Short turned to his friend and said, "There goes another pacifier to Doug MacArthur. You'd think the Japanese fleet is already in his backyard and the Imperial Marines were chasing his ass down Manila's main drag with bayonets."

"We needed those planes for deterrence and long range recon. I guess Doug has them convinced the Philippines will be target number one when Japan attacks," Kimmel said, as he looked away in disgust.

"I bet every fucking Jap spy on these islands counts each one that comes and goes. If Hawaii is neutralized, Doug's ass is in a sling. How the hell can we reenforce him?"

"We can't, even if we were completely untouched. We wouldn't have the transport, the battle line, or air cover to do a damned thing about it. My best ships are in the Atlantic chasing U-boats or making a statement."

"No B-17 is going to stop a well-equipped and trained carrier task force from doing what it intends to do," Short offered, "unless you constantly attack to upset carrier operations. You know, have them reeling and maneuvering so they can't launch or recover an airplane. Anyway, I just don't think the Japs are that good."

Kimmel turned to him, his face showing the trepidation caused by Short's last comment.

"General," Kimmel said, almost in supplication, "I can't emphasize enough how important it is to keep your fighter force alerted. My ships are tied to the harbor because I can't get enough air power up to protect them if they sortie. Without it, they're sitting ducks. I need those fighters."

"I fully, understand Kim," Short replied, "and I've got you covered. The Army Signal Corps is going to set up a radar site on the heights at Opana, north and west of here. From what I'm told, that should give us plenty of warning of any attack."

Kimmel's face lit up. "That's great!"

"That furrowed brow of yours tells me you needed to hear that. I'm still worried about those reports of sabotage operations the Japanese nationals who inhabit these islands might try at the outbreak of hostilities. I'm spacing the aircraft out in the open so blowing up one plane in a hangar doesn't mean a dozen are lost."

Short turned to the window again, watching yet another B-17 take off and head westward. "I wish to high hell we could get those PURPLE messages decrypted here. I don't know what the hell we're losing in the translation. Any progress with the Jap fleet code?" he asked.

"Very little. Joe Rochefort tells me it's a bitch."

0800 Hours, July 4, 1941
Bletchlely Park

Chad Eversole felt uncomfortable facing Churchill and Shears together.

"I want you to do everything in your power to promulgate the thinking that sabotage will be rampant in the Hawaiian Islands," Churchill said, as he gazed out the window to the gardens surrounding Bletchley Park.

Eversole was totally confused.

"Sir," he said to Admiral Shears, "am I mistaken in thinking that you want to confuse the Americans so they take their attention away from an attack on the Philippines? Or, perhaps, Hawaii? We have it on good account that the Japanese are running naval exercises that strongly suggest carrier operations against those two targets. The rotational transfer of personnel in the Imperial Japanese fleet scheduled for August has been put off until February. This would indicate the admirals and captains want to keep their staffs and crews intact for an operation. The lads here have told me there's been a lot of Japanese interest particularly about the American base at Pearl Harbor."

Churchill turned at that last statement and stared directly at him. *It is Hawaii that holds Churchill's interest,* Eversole thought, and he realized the prime minister had no intention of telling the Americans that the Japanese were training their carrier air groups and gathering intelligence for a more than probable attack on Pearl Harbor. He choked back his alarm and cleared his throat. He looked Admiral Shears directly in the eyes. His stomach tightened, and beads of sweat formed at his brow.

"The Americans will no doubt declare war on Japan the minute any ship of theirs is threatened, let alone sunk. If they knew in advance about it, they'd…"

"Damn you to hell, Eversole!" Shears was besides himself. He paced the office in a rage, flailing his arms about. "The fucking Germans sank an American merchant ship in the Gulf of Suez. They did nothing! A U-boat torpedoed a destroyer and killed eleven American sailors. Nothing again!" Shears swept the papers from his desk in a furious swipe. "What makes you believe they'll take reprisals on the Japanese, even if the attack does not succeed? They want to hold our coats while our men die fighting their war as they become rich selling us weapons that we spend our blood to use! The *Hood* carried American shells. Did Americans die? Don't you see what…"

"Edgar. That's quite enough!" Churchill said. He put his arm around the admiral and guided him to a chair by the fireplace. Shears' eyes were swollen with tears, and it shook Eversole to the bottom of his soul. How do you recompense the loss of a son? But would treachery help? He decided to remain logical. "Prime Minister, do you actually believe the Germans have a chance of defeating the Soviet Union?"

"Their chances are excellent. Joe Stalin killed off the Red Army's leadership in his purges. They're a gangly lot of ill-educated and ill-trained barbarians with no battle discipline. How can they stand up to the Wehrmacht? They'll be at the gates of the Kremlin in no time. Then, with Russian resources and slave labor, they'll bowl Britain over by the end of next year. We'll be lost,

Chad, and America will not come to our aid. They will seek a separate peace with Hitler, to give them time to build up their weaponry and manpower. But that will be too late for us."

"Roosevelt cut off the supplies of aviation gasoline from the Japanese. He just froze their assets. They will surely...."

"Roosevelt just called for the creation of a neutral Indochina to placate the Japanese, Chad. Did you know that?" He looked at Eversole's pained expression, and said, "Hmmph. I thought as much. The Japanese cannot successfully carry out an offensive operation. How do they dare think they can take on the Pacific fleet? We need to almost guarantee the success of a Japanese initiative if we are to survive the Germans. I need you to continue feeding them this information. I need leverage when I meet with Roosevelt next month."

"Here in London, or are you going to Washington?" Eversole was flabbergasted.

"You'll know soon enough, Chad. You're going with me."

Eversole smiled proudly.

"Eversole," Shears said, calm and in control again. "Send Yvette and Yuri to Singapore. We're setting up an operation there, and it's important that they be in the Pacific as soon as possible. Their supplies will follow. You will join them in September after the conference with Roosevelt. Have them on their way by the end of the week."

"Yes, sir."

"Tell them they'll also spend some time in Hawaii—as sort of a goodwill gesture around the American Thanksgiving holiday. They can see their old friends. You know, Seghesio, and Burns."

"Jack Burns is no friend of anyone British, Admiral," Eversole offered.

"By the way, Chad," Churchill said, pouring himself a whiskey, "where do we stand with those new explosives you and Yuri have been playing with?"

Eversole measured each word as he gave a brief report.

1700 Hours, July 4, 1941
Lahaina Roads

Tomi Zai, tourist, soared high above the fleet anchorage at Lahaina Roads in a little Piper Cub. He prayed he would someday send this piece of crap and its walrus-like pilot down in flames. It was his fourth flight this month. He prayed the American fleet would use this anchorage. The water was deep, meaning any hope of salvaging a sunken ship was short-lived. They would avoid the risk of torpedoes by running shallow and burying themselves in the harbor bottom. There was plenty of water beneath the keels here, not the forty-foot shallows of Pearl Harbor.

Genda requested that he check on Kaneohe, too. It was wider than Pearl, giving torpedo planes more maneuvering room, but during a chartered fishing trip he had treated the consulate's staff to yesterday, he'd seen that the crystal clear water was much too shallow.

Smiling so hard his face hurt, he asked the pilot to make a pass over Pearl Harbor. Genda wanted to know how many warships were tied up side by side. With the fleet out on an exercise, it was impossible to determine, but he snapped away with his Nikon anyway. He also photographed the oil tank farm that held the lifeblood of Kimmel's fleet.

Flying along in the little plane brought on a surge of nostalgia. He missed his Zero fighter and the comradeship of the carrier ready room. He missed leaping from the flight deck and soaring above the wave tops. He wanted to thunder through the clouds with Yamamoto's Wild Eagles again.

Tomi Zai went to the Royal Hawaiian Hotel for a few drinks before going back to 1742 Nuuanu Street, where the consulate stood. He had developed quite an affinity for single-malt scotch and kept several bottles under his bed, ready to go after the attack that meant expulsion from Hawaii. He sipped at his third drink, growing more mellow with each, taking in the beauty of the purple and gold shades the setting sun cast on Diamond Head. His view was suddenly blocked by a massive Marine in the company of a beautiful woman, the same one who had been with him at the World's Fair in New York. He would never forget that Marine as long as he lived. He rose to tempt the Marine with insult, but remembered just in time he was an agent of espionage. His entire mission would be compromised, perhaps the whole coming attack, should the Marine recognize him.

He quickly placed several dollar bills next to his near-empty glass, bowed ceremoniously to the white pig behind the bar, and left. He cursed Genda for putting him in this position. With his face mostly hidden by his straw panama hat, he slipped past the unsuspecting American. Someday, Yankee, I'll face you as fate intended, and I'll send you to a fiery death, splattering your bloodied carcass in your colleagues' faces.

1900 Hours, August 1, 1941
The White House

President Roosevelt met with Stimson, Hull, and Hopkins as he reviewed his agenda for his meeting with Winston Churchill. "I don't think anything will come of it. He wants a declaration of war, but it won't be forthcoming."

"I think he knows that Mr. President. He's looking for a preparatory agenda to our eventual entrance into the war against Germany and, no doubt, the Japanese," Stimson answered.

"War precipitated by Germans becomes more remote. He won the Battle of Britain the minute the Fuhrer turned his legions on Russia."

"And if he beats the Russians?" Hull asked.

"He won't. Two things of historical significance have come into play here. First, no one has launched a successful attack across the English Channel since William the Conqueror. Second, no one has ever conquered the Russian winter. The German supply lines will close with the first snows. What Winston wants us to do is to make sure his Pacific empire is intact after Germany falls to the Russians. I wouldn't be surprised at all if he wants the French possessions as well."

"Your leaps of faith are inspiring, Franklin," Hopkins guffawed.

"Thank you," he said, with a broad smile, "but don't misunderstand me." Roosevelt wheeled himself to the Oval Office's windows. "I know Hitler must be stopped, but that's only going to happen when our country feels imminently threatened. The American people are angry at the ship sinkings, but not nearly angry enough to go to war. However, dislodging the Japanese from the territories they currently hold and will conquer in the war's first few months will be an immense undertaking."

"It will be a horrible, bloody affair, worse than war with Germany. We'll practically have to kill them to the last man to win a war," General Marshall interjected. "The tenets of their religions and traditions have death in combat as most honorable."

"Shouldn't we get into the fray as soon as possible then?" Stimson asked.

"What concerns the prime minister is a fray that lasts a few months, with us sinking the Jap fleet, isolating the Japanese Islands, and forcing a truce, whereby we get the colonies he covets. He's also concerned that Russia will fall, and we will do nothing when Hitler turns his legions on England again. I'd stake my ass on that one!" he laughed. "Now that's a leap of faith!" Hopkins said.

Roosevelt turned his chair and faced Hopkins. "If Japan wins a great victory at the onset of war, Germany will declare war on us to live up to their tripartite obligations. That keeps Russia off-balance because they will expect a Japanese invasion from the east to balance Hitler's invasion from the west. That means Churchill wins. We have to prevent a great Japanese victory, but by doing so we wave off Germany's declaration of war. Therefore, Churchill needs to have us hit hard by the Japanese. That's my fear. That's why I have to meet with him."

"I gather you don't trust the prime minister," Hopkins said.

"Quite the contrary—I trust him to do whatever he can to save England. If I were he, I'd do the same damned thing."

"By the way, Mr. President, Ambassador Nomura sends his thanks for not closing the Japanese consulates as you did the German ones. He sees it as a sign of hope despite the latest embargo."

"Tell the ambassador he's welcome, Cordell. But don't tell him that if we close the Japanese consulates down, how would we ever be able to intercept their PURPLE messages? I didn't come to that conclusion by magic!"

All four men had a hearty laugh at the pun.

0900 Hours, August 10, 1941
Argentia Bay, Newfoundland

Churchill climbed into the launch, which immediately left the towering side of the HMS *Prince of Wales* and headed across Argentia bay to the heavy cruiser USS *Augusta*. He eyed the American ship keenly, taking in the beauty of her sleek lines and gauging her armament. While the Royal Navy's ships-of-the-line were staid, solid-looking, and austere, the American ships resembled racing yachts.

The launch slowed and he could clearly see Eversole on deck, waiting for him with a broad smile on his face. Shears stayed aboard the *Prince of Wales*. His self-control was frail, and he claimed his stomach had been troubling him throughout the voyage. Though he laughingly attributed it to spending too much time ashore, Shears told no one that his bowel movements contained fearful amounts of blood.

The President of the United States waited near the gangway, his left arm firmly held by an Army officer. His right hand held a cane. This surprised Churchill, as his agents had told him that Roosevelt could only maneuver in a wheelchair or with the aid of crutches and braces. In fact, the King himself said that during his visit to the United States just last year, the president was practically wheelchair bound.

When he reached the top of the stairs he said, "Good morning, Mr. President! On behalf of His Majesty King George VI, I present you a letter of greetings."

Churchill watched the smiling Roosevelt closely as he put out his hand to accept the letter. The man's legs must have been killing him. Churchill realized the man he hoped to out-negotiate for a deeper commitment to the end of fascism and Imperial Japan was much stronger than he realized. It made Churchill feel more secure.

"Good morning to you prime minister!" Roosevelt responded. "Please convey to your Sovereign that I accept this letter in the interest of securing peace and an end to tyranny."

"I was admiring *Augusta* as we came across the bay. She is a beautiful warship."

"And I've been admiring *Prince of Wales* through my binoculars. I was eager to study one of the *Bismarck*'s killers. I eagerly anticipate walking her decks tomorrow. I find it interesting as to how her guns are positioned. Four rifles to a turret make a deadly combination."

"Did you know, Mr. President, that the configuration was initially flawed? When she fired her fore and aft quad turrets at that late Nazi monster, the recoil actually bent the hull stringers. The guns had to be realigned and the stringers reenforced. She's just been released from the yard for this trip."

"But the *Bismarck* is on the bottom. That's what counts."

"And may I thank you for your help, Mr. President," Churchill was quick to say. "It was a Lend-Lease PBY flown by an American Marine who found her. With such cooperation, Hitler's days are numbered, and the Jap menace will see his rising sun set."

"And so we begin our discourse, prime minister."

Eversole witnessed the exchange with great interest. He saw that Churchill clearly admired the president. Perhaps the cooperation he sought could be overtly arranged, rather than accomplished by a plan that held back vital intelligence—the plan that Chad Eversole officially knew nothing about. That he had been taken off the user list of JN-25 decrypts seemed to confirm his most troubling suspicions.

The two men sat in *Augusta*'s ward room and began talking about the world situation. Churchill came to the present after an hour and a half's oration that Roosevelt found intriguing.

"Your delay to decisive action causes the German to be bolder and your own people to cower, thinking that the Hun is unstoppable. When Hitler conquers Russia…"

"I don't agree, prime minister. Hitler will not conquer Russia. He's made a fatal strategic error."

"You say that because England is 3000 miles more at risk than your country. Once Hitler reaches Moscow…"

"He will be defeated at the gates, just like Napoleon."

Roosevelt reached across the table with his gold Zippo lighter and held it for the Prime Minister's cigar.

"Let's talk about some new weaponry my scientists are working on, supporting the Russians, and dealing with the Japanese. I think that's what this is all about, don't you agree?"

0800 Hours, August 12, 1941
Hippotaku Bay, The Inland Sea

Minoru Genda and Mitsuo Fuchida watched the torpedo planes making their attack runs on targets in a harbor formed by high cliffs, and had a tiny island at it center. The new shallow-running torpedoes were working quite well. The planes had to drop down swiftly to launch their weapons with enough accuracy and altitude to avoid slamming into the island or the escarpment. It was so much like the topography of Pearl Harbor that Genda and Fuchida found confidence in the aerial expertise being demonstrated. Seven of eight torpedoes hit their targets. The lone miss came from a torpedo that broke in two when it hit the water's surface.

"I say we switch to torpedoes only," suggested Fuchida.

"If the ships are anchored side by side, how do we strike the ones between the outer ships and the island?"

"If we do enough damage to the outer ships, the inner ships will be trapped."

"But for how long? We only have six months to a year to work with. A trapped ship is not as impotent as one sunk or heavily damaged."

"I guess that means we need the horizontal bombers. Their crews are much improved. You're right, you're always right, my friend."

"Me? You are mistaken. It is Yamamoto who is always right."

Chapter 14

Mae Seghesio was breathless at the sights slipping beneath the wings of the Lockheed Ventura. The rolling mountains of Oahu seemed to be an endless, lush, verdant mosaic composed of striking greens and browns. Waterfalls foamed titanium white. The seas surrounding the island varied from deepest cobalt blues to the brightest of aquas. No artist could have painted a more beautiful portrait.

"I understand why Gauguin thought this was paradise," she said.

"Yeah," Andy added, "but he left it for Tahiti. Can you imagine what that place is like?" He looked over at Jack Burns, who sat at the controls of the twin-engined plane. "How're you doing?" Andy asked, already knowing the answer he would receive.

"Better than ever. God, I love this! I thought I'd never get back to it."

"Does the guy who lent you this plane know about your...ah...misfortunes with things with wings?"

"He's an ex-Navy pilot. He flew off the *Saratoga* when it was first commissioned. He's planning to run the first interisland air service, and he knows me well. I took a trip to Maui last month, and he checked me out. I think I'm ready to challenge the flight surgeon and get back on flight status."

"Well, good luck. God knows, you've earned it."

"Oh, Andy! Look! They're so...beautiful!" The warships passing below the Ventura's left wing were bathed in the sun's first rays, giving their pale gray hulls and sparkling white canvas deck coverings a magnificent radiance. The early morning due glistened on their mooring lines, completing a perfect contrast with the clear blue-green harbor's surface.

"That's Battleship Row," Andy told her.

"What are their names?" Mae asked.

"Yeah, Marine, or have you spent too much time ashore to remember?" Burns teased.

"Piece of cake. Let's see...the first one is the *California*. Those two astern of her are the *Maryland* and *Oklahoma*. *Tennessee* and *West Virginia* come next. Then there's the *Arizona* and the *Pennsylvania*. That last one is the *Nevada*."

"What about the aircraft carriers there on the other side of the island?" Mae asked.

"Perhaps Jack would like to answer that. He used to fly from them when he was a young man."

Julie Burns shot a look at Seghesio that would melt a witch's heart. "Very funny, Seghesio. Don't listen to him, honey!" Julie advised.

"No one listens to Marines. Mae, they're the *Enterprise* and the *Lexington*. I helped design *Enterprise* and flew the first SBD from her deck." He couldn't help chuckling. "And a few days later, I lost the first SBD that flew from her deck."

"You've always loved *Enterprise,* haven't you? Andy's told me about the special bond you have with her."

"I saw her conceived, born, and baptized. I was there when she took her first steps. Yeah, I really love her."

"You see why I don't have to worry about other women? He's fixated on that one," Julie said, pointing to the orange-tinted deck below.

"The way they glimmer all in a row on the velvet sea reminds me of my pearls when I first saw them in Tiffany's," Mae said, holding the strand up and kissing it. "Don't you agree, Yvette."

"Oh, yes! I only wish Yuri was here to enjoy this with me. Admiral Shears runs him rampant."

"I never have thanked you for telling Jack about Tiffany's, Andy," Julie said, waving her hand so the new diamond ring became plainly evident.

"It scored a lot of points," Jack said, looking at her in adoration. "Hey, we're getting low on gas. Tour's over. Let's go to the Royal Hawaiian for some breakfast." With that, Burns headed south for Honolulu's airport.

Andy noted that the Ford Island Naval Air Station was quiet. It's fighters sat neatly parked in rows, but a little tour-guide's Piper Cub circled the base incessantly. The seaplane base was empty, indicating the long-legged PBYs were out on patrol, but the absence of fighters in the sky heightened his sense of bewilderment as did the neat rows of Army fighters at Hickam. How easy it would be for enemy fighters to strafe and destroy them.

Furthermore, none of the ships, the thin-skinned carriers or the thick-shelled battleships, had torpedo nets around them. A torpedo pilot probably would've noticed it sooner, but Marine pilots weren't inclined to love ships the way their Navy counterparts did. Burns was too enamored with his piloting to notice. Remembering the heavy-gauge submarine net at the harbor's bottleneck entrance, Andy almost dismissed his concern; a sub couldn't operate in the shallows of the harbor. But there had been the British air attack at Taranto that used torpedo planes so effectively against battleships in a confined harbor without protective torpedo nets. He made a mental note to speak to someone about this, thinking that this first-hand information would have an immediate impact. He had just scanned a report from an Admiral Ingersoll that stated a new generation of aerial-launched torpedoes were more than likely to sink to a depth of seventy-five feet. He credited his information to "informed sources." Andy was proud! It was he and Jack who had done the full write-up of the Taranto mission, had it labeled "Top Secret," and sent it to the Naval Bureau of Ordnance.

He turned to Mae and kissed her on the cheek, happy to see she was her old self with the blush of health. He stole a glance back at Battleship Row. Yes, they did look like pearls.

1200 Hours, September 7, 1941
The Inland Sea, Japan

"I wonder why they don't deploy the torpedo nets around their ships. Surely the lessons of Taranto have…"

"They think we cower at the mention of the words 'United States Navy.' They are too egotistical and too racist to think we can do them any harm, we funny-looking, little yellow men," Genda said, poking at the torpedo before him.

"The design is brilliant. We must thank our Italian friends for this find," Fuchida said.

"This one's from the first of the two British Swordfish planes that were shot down during the attack. It wasn't released. See here? It never armed itself," Genda said, pointing with a pencil to the unengaged arming mechanism. "The British pilots pressed their attacks to point-blank range. It was quite a feat of flying," Genda replied.

"Slow and vulnerable as it is, the old Swordfish is quite maneuverable. That's what makes them so effective. Had they attacked in daylight, they probably wouldn't have been as successful."

"They attacked the *Bismarck* in full daylight." Genda's eyes never left the weapon before him. "The design is much like ours. See how the fins are shaped so the torpedo doesn't sink too deep? If it worked for the British, it should work for us," Genda commented.

"That, and one thing more. The British were totally committed to their task—just like our Wild Eagles."

"I needed to hear that, Mitsuo." Genda turned to Fuchida with tears in his eyes. "I'm so full of fear. Their defenses are formidable. So much relies on catching them unaware. I stay awake at night going over details. How will I react if a fourth of the strike force is lost, as we are projecting? I know these men. I've known them forever."

"What you should be worrying about is getting the third wave off our decks after the first two have cowered the Yankees in their holes," Fuchida said, bent at the waist and turning the little propellers on the rear of the torpedo. "From what Tomi Zai tells us, they are pompous pigs awaiting slaughter. Their careless attitude and lax preparations will render all their defenses useless. They will learn to dread the Rising Sun the day we begin taking what is legitimately ours as yellow men, and kicking the white devils out of the Pacific. We will succeed, my friend. I will not come back alive if my death ensures success. I swear to you."

About to enter the room to examine the British torpedo, Yamamoto stopped to listen. He wiped tears that started to flow when Genda gave Fuchida a bearhug. Some invincible force we are...an admiral who cries like an old woman, and two warriors who hug like young girls.

Admiral Isoruku Yamamoto realized he was one of the luckiest men ever to live. If war had to come so very soon—a war he must win in less than a year—surely the gods had smiled upon him by giving him such men.

1100 Hours, September 25, 1941
The White House

"He never mentioned Hawaii. Not once," Roosevelt said, as he glanced through the decrypt.

"Are you sure, Mr. President?" Hull looked at him curiously.

"I'd remember. Churchill and this Eversole fellow mentioned the Philippines and Malaya or the Kra Isthmus, at least a dozen times, but never Hawaii. It's troubling."

"Tokyo is asking its consulate in Honolulu for the exact moorings of our ships, torpedo defenses, whether they're tied up side by side...all of this indicates a military interest in Pearl Harbor. I would assume Churchill would share any intelligence with us regarding this matter."

"I would think that if the Japs were about to pounce, they would want to know the disposition of the fleet to determine when they could sortie and launch as devastating an attack as possible," General Marshall said.

"Don't you think that information of this specificity would be more useful to a strike leader bound for Pearl Harbor than a general or admiral about to bomb Manila or Singapore?" Secretary of the Navy Frank Knox said.

"It would certainly help to know what their carriers are up to. If Kimmel were to read this, I'm sure his alarms would go off."

"Can Kimmel and Short defend themselves against a determined carrier assault?" the president asked.

"Hawaii's the most formidable base we have, either stateside or abroad," Marshall said. "I'd like to send Short a few squadrons of the new P-38s fighters, but we don't have them in any numbers. However, he's got plenty of AA, P-36s and P-40s, and his troops on the ground are well-trained and well-equipped. Remember, the Jap carriers are limited as to how many planes they can throw into an attack. Even if the new Jap Zero is as fantastic as we've heard, we've still got them outnumbered."

"What about the fleet?" Roosevelt asked, giving a scrap of bread to his dog Falla. "What can we expect from it?"

"Its only at half-strength, whether we consider it a deterrent, or a real offensive, power-projecting force. The *Yorktown* is escorting convoys with the newest battleships in the Atlantic. The battleships at Pearl need better communications gear, AAA, and radar. They're approaching the end of their service lives. I got an invitation on my desk sent to me by Admiral Kidd to come and celebrate the *Arizona*'s twenty-fifth birthday party," said CNO Stark.

"But isn't their presence a deterrent?" Marshall asked.

"It might not be viewed that way by the Japanese. They might consider it a target," Stark responded. Then he added, "I hope Short and Kimmel aren't making a similar assumption."

Roosevelt steered his wheelchair to the window, a copy of the New York *Herald Tribune* on his lap. This was getting maddingly complicated. He had just read the headline telling of a recent polio outbreak in New York. It always seemed to come each fall, he thought.

"Where is the *Enterprise*?" Roosevelt asked.

"At Pearl, with *Lexington*," Stark responded.

"And *Saratoga*?"

"Tied up at San Diego, finishing a refit."

The leaves were turning their brilliant fall hues late this September, and sunlight seemed increasingly precious. That world events mirrored the season seemed quite appropriate. Had nature always timed human events to solstices and equinoxes? Now that was a question for the philosophers.

"I want the carriers running all over the Pacific with their escorts to keep the Japanese off-balance as to their location and mission. Send *Saratoga* to Pearl when she's ready. Same orders."

"What about the battleships?" Stark asked.

"If we send the battleships along, the Japanese might just be prompted to do something we're not prepared for. Anyway, they'll slow the carrier forces down, won't they?" Knox asked.

"We're still thinking of the battleship as our offensive punch." Stark sat shaking his head. "A carrier has never fought in a naval engagement yet. Everyone knows what a battleship can do."

"Just make sure the carriers aren't in the harbor more than a day," Roosevelt said. "It was explained to me a long time ago that mobility is the carrier's biggest offensive threat and defensive safeguard. Make sure they stay mobile."

"Should we inform Kimmel of the bomb plot message?" Marshall asked.

"Hell, no!" Stark yelped. "He'll use it to beat me up for more stuff I don't have to send him!"

"Betty's right," Knox commented. "We give him enough data to tell him to keep on his toes. He's an experienced commander. He'll do his job."

"So is General Short," Marshall added.

Roosevelt turned back to the window, watching the first leaves fall with a rustle of wind. "Has that new radar been set up in Hawaii yet?" Roosevelt asked.

"It's in transit. The crews have been fully trained. It should be operational by the middle of November."

When his men left him, Roosevelt went back to the *Herald Tribune*. He had just started reading when Eleanor called on his private line. "Ed Murrow is reporting that the Nazi offensive is stalling with the first snows, and the Red Army is counterattacking. Why don't you tune in, dear?"

Roosevelt reached for his radio. Murrow was a dear friend and confidant. "Thanks; I'll be up shortly for dinner," he replied, turning on the RCA radio on his credenza. His grin was widening with each of Murrow's sentences.

0800 Hours, September 30, 1941
USS *Arizona*

"Are you sure you can get all this stuff, Chief? I don't want to promise anything I can't deliver."

"How can you say that, Josh?" Jones feigned a look of hurt. "Have I ever let you down, sailor?"

Friar bought it. "Gosh, no, Chief. I mean...I just want to be sure..."

"Do you think I'd embarrass my ship? My ship?" he repeated for emphasis.

"Well, she's my ship, too! Don't you forget that, Chief!" Friar shot back, with an unaccustomed bellow.

"Ha!" Jones sneered, putting on his cap and stomping away.

"You heard me, Chief! And that stuff you promised better be there! You here me?" Friar said, anger on his face. "Don't you go walking away from me! Hey Chief!"

Jones looked angry from Friar's angle, but he was broadly smiling. He had done his job. That Friar claimed outright ownership of the *Arizona* confirmed what he needed to hear. Everyone under Friar would think the same way. It was what they called team-building, and it made for a happy and effective ship. Perhaps it really was time to move on to one of the new battlewagons gestating in the birthing yards back home.

0800 Hours, September 30, 1941
Headquarters, Commander-in-Chief Pacific Fleet (CINCPAC)
Pearl Harbor

Admiral Kimmel looked again with disbelief at the last dispatch from Stark. It asked him to be prepared for a possible mission to have one of his carriers deliver aircraft to a Russian port, probably Vladivostok. This meant plying the Sea of Japan with a carrier task force to deliver instruments of war to Japan's traditional enemy, the Soviet Union. His carriers were equipped for the South Seas, not the cold Northern Pacific. If he's inviting war, Kimmel thought, why does he want to have a precious carrier sunk in Japan's home islands?

What exactly do I prepare for? Kimmel put his face into his hands and exhaled in exasperation.

1400 Hours. September 30, 1941
British Consulate, Singapore

Yuri Popov glistened with sweat, his hips driving hard against Yvette's. She moaned in ecstasy with every thrust, unable to think of anything but the exquisite pleasure welling from her loins as he penetrated ever deeper.

At last, he fell next to her, totally spent, and in absolute happiness. They lay for a while, in loving silence.

"I thought I could never love anyone, Yuri, but my feelings for you spring from the heart I thought I didn't have. Thank you, my precious one." She kissed him passionately, and felt him rise again.

Their arrival in Singapore had brought their passion to yet another stage. Yuri could not live without her next to him.

The phone broke in on their reverie.

"Ah, I see you've arrived. How's the flat?" Shears said.

"Just fine, Admiral."

"It has a lovely view of Keppel Harbor, doesn't it?"

He began again after a short, disturbing pause, "You and Eversole need to bring me up to speed on the experiments with the new explosives. The information is vital to my plan. May we meet on Tuesday morning at eight?"

"Very well, sir."

"Oh, by the way, we are going on a goodwill tour to the American naval base in Hawaii. I'm sure you and Yvette will be happy to see your old friends, the Seghesio's."

Yuri put down the receiver to the phone, and faced Yvette. "Why does that man give me the creeps of late?"

"Because he knows our relationship has gone beyond professional, and he hates me." Yuri's nightmares had ceased soon after their arrival in Singapore a few days ago and she wasn't about to let them start again. "Come, we have some unfinished business," she said, laying most alluringly.

Yuri awoke early on Tuesday, and quietly donned his white Royal Navy uniform. He kissed Yvette's cheek and she reached up to him. Shortly after he left, she felt a rising queasiness. Minutes later, after unsuccessfully trying to fall back asleep, she raced to the bathroom. The last time she experienced such distress she was carrying the child of Billy Shears. This time joy bubbled.

Across Keppel Harbor, Admiral Shears was also sick, vomiting up all but the blandest of foods. Last evening he dined with General Percival, the British Army's Commander of Malaya, and the hot, spicy local food had kept him up all night, despite the medications he had illegally obtained before leaving England. His stools were blackened with blood again. He steeled his resolve and got back to the business at hand.

He would ask Churchill to dispatch British warships to Singapore to elevate the spirits of the local colonials, who felt increasingly vulnerable as Japan rattled her saber. The United States Navy would not dare pay a visit. Their fleet was spending more time tethered to Pearl Harbor and its Army Air Force cover. The two carriers left in the Pacific Fleet were running helter-skelter around the Pacific in the company of fast cruisers and destroyers. If they only knew, Shears mused.

He opened his safe and took out the plans and encrypted radio codes for Operation XYZ-41 and reviewed them thoroughly. Using a magnifying glass, he next pored over the aerial photos again. Except for *California* and *Nevada*, few of the battleships were moored singly with any regularity. The upcoming visit to Pearl Harbor would answer questions needed to complete the last details of his grandiose scheme. For now, he would instruct the Singapore listening station JN-25 decrypters to monitor every movement of the Japanese fleet, and the American Fleet, especially their carriers. Having Eversole insured the success of his venture. A good soldier, that one, a very good soldier.

He read the MAGIC decrypts Percival had given him last evening. As he expected, things were heating up. Tokyo's ship-position request for Pearl Harbor was most disturbing. Surely, the Americans now knew what was coming. Chances were good that the lucky bastards were in the process of laying a superb trap for the incompetent Japanese, especially if they were reading JN-25, which they still claimed they could not do. It made the success of his mission all the more imperative to Great Britain. If America defeated Japan in just one fateful day...

The pressure actually calmed his aching belly.

Chapter 15

The *Taiyo Maru* yawed and rolled against the swells the northern Pacific threw against her. Her bow smashed through waves that threatened to engulf her, spewing rivers of green water over the neat teak decks and plumes of green spray against her bridge. Though the passengers were seasick and shaken by the wild ride, her crew were absolutely unaffected. They ate heartily, joked with each other, and took precise readings of wind and temperature. On the bridge, their eyes were glued to their ever-present binoculars, scanning the ocean and sky.

Jacob Fleischmann was returning to his home on Oahu from Japan after completing a business trip that started in Australia, passed through Singapore and Hong Kong, Bangkok, the Philippines, and Tokyo. He had made the trip for each of the twenty years since becoming a fabric buyer who specialized in fine oriental silks and cotton. This was the first time it had been such an ordeal. At fifty-seven, he was sure he was on death's door. He never left his cabin and clung for dear life to the commode. He hadn't eaten in two days.

He set out on a valiant attempt to reach the promenade deck to gain a sense of the horizon and fresh air. Someone had told him years ago that this would help cure the illness. A Japanese officer in a starched white uniform met him as he wobbled down the passageway and caught him just as he lost his balance.

"Are you okay, sir?"

"As well as can be expected," Fleischmann replied. "Thank you for your assistance."

"You look quite ill. Have you seen the ship's doctor?"

"There's nothing he can do, young man. I'm just seasick. If anything, I should have taken the Dramamine he gave me before we left Hiroshima. I've never experienced anything like this before."

"The Pacific is unpredictable this time of year, sir. We should be out of the rough weather in twelve hours or so. Then it's a day's sail to Honolulu. You'll feel better soon."

Fleischmann tried to stand up, still aided by the Japanese. "You speak wonderful English. Have you spent time in the United States?"

"My father was a diplomat, and I lived my early years in Washington and New York. Then Dad got into the import-export business, and we visited America regularly. We went back to stay again when I was in my teens. I graduated from U.S.C. in 1934. See?" he said, holding up his class ring. "I still have many friends in the States."

"Well I'll be damned! It's a lousy shame what seems to be happening between our two countries, isn't it?"

"It certainly is. I think we can work it out, though. Cooler heads will prevail," the Japanese said, still smiling warmly.

"I hope so. More people need to be like you and me who spend time in each other's homes. We'd appreciate each other much more. Ah, well," Fleischmann sighed. "Anyway, thanks for helping me out, Mr..."

"It's Ito. Ito Fujita. My American friends call me Izzy."

"Thank you, Izzy. You think you might help me up to the promenade deck? By the way, the name is Jake. Jake Fleischmann," he said, extending his hand.

"It would be a pleasure, Mr. Fleischmann."

Fujita fondly recalled his years at Southern Cal. He had made a lot of good friends through those years, a number of whom were commissioned officers in the United States Navy and Army, thanks to the ROTC program. Some would be stationed in Pearl Harbor. If peace was unattainable, a few might even rise to meet him in the coming attack. That Fleischmann was as sick as a dog was not attributable to the time of year. Unbeknownst to her passengers, the *Taiyo Maru* was pursuing a course through the northern Pacific far from the regular shipping lanes where few save the occasional Russian freighters bound for Vladivostok ever ventured. He, himself, was to report back to Genda on the drawbacks of taking off and landing from a carrier plying this route. The same course would be plotted for the *Kido Butai* should war be decided upon, and with each passing day, the options seemed to narrow.

Fujita couldn't wait to see the magnificent American base and its warships when they docked in Honolulu. He, too, planned an aerial tour of the harbor, just as Tomi Zai had done on numerous occasions. He looked forward to destroying the *Lexington*. He had visited that ship as a young man during Navy Day in 1931, while he was still at U.S.C. He harbored no hate for the ship or its crew. He was a bomber pilot trained to the point of delirium to deliver a massive bomb. The professional pilot relished nothing more than hitting a carrier square in the center of the flight deck, having his bomb penetrating to the hangar deck to explode among the parked and gassed aircraft residing there, and blowing her sides out. If any of the Americans he knew should rise to challenge him, so be it. He expected them to be as professional as he, fighting to the death. It's the way they played football, a sport he became quite a fan of. It was winner take all, and Genda had convinced him he was a winner in the grandest sense.

2000 Hours, November 5, 1941
Pearl Harbor

The party was turning out to be a grand affair. Admiral Kidd and Captain Van Valkenburgh were having a good time exchanging stories with others who had been in command of the battleship. Even *Arizona* seemed content with all the attention, according to Gwyeth Jones. She gleamed from bow to stern, from bilge to mast, from beam to beam. Friar worked his mess crews hard, but he and his men were smiling. Jones had orders, this time written in stone, separating him from *Arizona* on December 5, 1941. Back in the United States he would add his perfectionist's touch to the fitting out of the USS *Iowa*, the first of a class of monster battleships designed to be the most lethal afloat.

Mae Seghesio was thrilled with Yvette's good news. "I'm so happy for you," she said. "I knew you felt so unsure about handling motherhood, but you're absolutely glowing!"

"Yuri tells me that all the time." Yvette tucked back her long blonde hair. "I don't know why. I can't keep anything down and I feel just awful. Have you and Andy...started trying..."

"We will, shortly," Mae said, the smile waning from her face. "I'm just getting my strength back. Andy's under a lot of pressure forming a fighter squadron. He doesn't know if he is shipping out with them, or staying here at Pearl Harbor to train another. The men have only minimum training in their Wildcat fighters when they arrive, and Andy says it's like starting from scratch. He'd like to get back into the ranks, as he puts it. He thinks his career will be short-circuited if he stays here."

"Yuri said the same thing. He had grown tired of...Lend-Lease duty, and he was hoping they would assign him to a ship when we got to Singapore, but he's buried in paper again."

Mae noted her change of expression, and was about to probe a bit, but they were interrupted by Admiral Shears.

"Good evening." He nodded to both women.

"It certainly is, Admiral. Have you lost some weight?" Mae said, looking at Shears with a critical eye.

"I've had a bout with an intestinal disorder, and it had me fairly starved. The doctors tell me it's caused by an amoeba in the water at Singapore. But, I'm on the mend."

"I'm sorry to hear that, sir," Mae said, not believing him.

"Yvette, may I congratulate you on your blessed event," he said, taking her hand. His touch chilled her and she saw the bleakness of his face, though his lips held a smile.

The band began playing *String of Pearls*, and Mae saw Andy making his way toward her through the sea of brass and their glittering wives. "May I have this dance, miss?"

"I'd be delighted, Marine," she said.

As they danced beneath the massive guns of *Arizona*'s aft turret, Mae marveled at the impressive array of ships in the harbor with lights strung from bow to mast to stern and reflected in the mirrored glass of the harbor's surface. "Look, Andy. More pearls!" she exclaimed.

"Indeed there are, Mae," Yvette Popov said, gliding past in the arms of her husband, who nodded to Mae and patted Andy's shoulders.

"Don't talk to Englishmen. They can't be trusted," said Jack Burns, looking resplendent in his dress whites as he went gliding past with Julie in his arms.

"Hush up, you old Scottish tyrant!" she said, slapping Burns' hand.

Lisa Seghesio had just arrived in Hawaii two days before and wore Tommy Hamilton's beautiful engagement ring. Andy was thrilled for them both. John Munroe and Nancy Herbst had been married in San Diego, but he couldn't attend this party; he was somewhere in the vast Pacific serving as assistant squadron commander of VF-6, *Enterprise*'s fighter squadron. She expected him back soon.

Yvette suddenly squealed. Several couples looked around just in time to see Yuri putting a sapphire encrusted necklace around her elegant neck. Hugging him, she encountered the Colt Automatic he had taken to carrying everywhere again, tucked into his pants at the back.

As Jack Burns stared stone-faced at Popov, his peripheral vision caught a figure standing near him and Shears. The face brought a surge of energy to his memory. Then, he had it. It was Chad Eversole. A little older, a little stouter, but still showing that classic British profile David Niven was making famous. Ah, the good times they had working with Yardley to break the Japanese code way back in the Washington Naval Treaty days. Burns began picking his way over to him, but an alarm went off in his head freezing him in his tracks. Eversole worked for British Intelligence! The pleasant vision of the past disappeared behind a veil of suspicion. Why the hell was he here tonight? With war maybe hours away, it would seem he'd have better things to do. But Burns didn't have the temperament to hide. He saw Julie talking with Yvette, and used her for cover.

"There you are, darling. What's all this fuss?" he said, most genially.

"Oh, Jack. Look at the necklace Yuri gave to Yvette. Aren't they just beautiful?" she gushed.

"They certainly are!" Burns said. "Are you trying to make all us husbands look bad, Yuri?" He smiled so hard his eyebrows hurt.

"Jack, old man! A pleasure to see you again! I figured you wouldn't be far behind your beautiful wife. Still angry?" Yuri said, a teasing expression on his handsome face.

"I was way out of line back in England." *The fuck I was,* he thought.

"No apologies necessary," Yuri said, taking Jack's outstretched hand.

"Jack," Julie began, "Yvette's expecting a child. Isn't that wonderful?"

"It certainly is! Congratulations!"

"Thank you, Commander Burns," Yvette said, turning her cheek for his kiss.

"Correction! It's soon to be Captain Burns," said Joe Rochefort. "I have it on good account that this sailor man will be promoted, effective 8 December 1941, 0001 hours. Congrats, Jack!"

Burns' mouth tightened momentarily. Only Julie and Andy Seghesio noticed it and knew the reason. Lieutenant commanders led fighter and dive-bomber squadrons, and commanders were CAGs. Captains did ships.

The crowd gathered around Burns to slap his back and shake his hand, but in spite of his returning elation, he looked again for Eversole. Shears was still there, but Eversole had vanished.

0900 Hours, November 10, 1941
Washington, D.C.

Constantine Oumansky sat patiently waiting for Sumner Welles to receive him. He had come unannounced, but told Welles' pretty brunette secretary the business he needed to discuss was "urgent." He stopped fidgeting with his fedora and settled back on the comfortable sofa in the outer office and stared at the brunette's bosom as she typed—until she shot a very unfriendly expression at him. He cleared his throat and picked up the *Washington Post*. The banner headline's article on the stalled German offensive due to Mother Russia's worst winter of the century brought a grin to his full face—the blossoms last spring told him all he needed to know about the outcome. Continuing to scan the newspaper, he smiled openly at the remark that "Americans have nothing to fear. Their Navy is strong and ready." Secretary Frank Knox must not know what he knew.

"Constantine, my friend, come in!" Welles said. "I'm sorry to keep you waiting so long. I was on the phone with the secretary of state. Mr. Hull is very busy just now." He winked.

"Thank you for receiving me, Sumner."

"Receiving you?" Welles closed the door to his office. "Am I to assume this is an official visit?" He offered Oumansky a cigarette from a gold case on his desk.

"No. Not at all," the Russian said quickly, "but I have some information for you. Perhaps you may view it as a return for the favor you did for me and the Russian people last spring. Perhaps it's what you call…'yesterday's news,' but I think it's important enough for me to risk reprisal by telling you, as you did for me."

"Vodka, Constantine?" Welles said, motioning the Russian to a chair by the fire.

"No, thank you."

This must be serious, Welles thought. "Okay, my friend. What do you have?"

"Our agents in Tokyo report talk about a massive attack to come very shortly in the Pacific." Welles knew Russian agents in various guises had access to the highest levels of the Japanese government.

"Then I should tell you that if our negotiations fail, we expect the Japanese to attack either the Kra Isthmus, Singapore, Hong Kong, or the Philippines."

"My intelligence is so reliable that we are moving the two million men of the Siberian Army to the west to fight the Germans because the Japanese have decided to strike southward. I assume we've reached some sort of accommodation with them. Specifically they have decided that the oil and metal ores they need can be had more easily in the South Pacific than in the freezer of Siberia."

Speechless, Welles stared at the Russian ambassador. "That's a huge leap of faith, Constantine. Are you sure…"

"Positive. And you have pushed them to the point where they are totally committed to defending their honor. Despite your negotiations, war is imminent. What should concern you the most is the target they have chosen; and like our Port Arthur, it will be hit in a surprise attack."

"We're prepared for that eventuality. General MacArthur…"

The Russian shook his head. "It will be Pearl Harbor, then the Philippines after your Pacific Fleet is neutralized."

Welles was incredulous. He sat back in relief with a grin on his face, one that scoffed at the Russian's information. "They wouldn't dare, Constantine. The fleet is…"

"There. And they accept the gamble. They feel you are strangling them economically, and they would rather risk dying with honor than be subservient to white men. I must stress that all this comes from the highest levels of the Japanese power structure." He tried his best to be convincing, but he saw that Welles refused to accept it.

"We're strong there. The Japanese..."

"I don't wish to belabor the point, Sumner. Do with this information what you will," Oumansky said with a wave of his hand. Why were these Americans so damned hardheaded?

"When will the attack come?"

"Exactly? That I truly do not know. I would watch their aircraft carriers. When they disappear, expect them to reappear within striking distance of Hawaii."

"A carrier attack!"

"By the way, Hawaii has become a favorite item of discussion among the British as well. Some of their top-secret codings mention it as often as Singapore and Hong Kong. There is something called XYZ-41 which we keep hearing about in their fleet and diplomatic codes. Is there some joint exercise between the Royal Navy and your fleet afoot?"

"I don't know of any. You're reading the British fleet code as well?" Welles asked, cocking his head. The cavalier grin suddenly disappeared, much to the obvious delight of his Russian friend.

"Son of a bitch."

"No, Sumner, my mother was an honorable woman. A bit of a flirt, but true to my father."

"Does anyone else know what you can do?"

"I'm returning a favor, remember? You did not get this from me," Oumansky said, crushing out the cigarette, "but war will come to Hawaii. I'm just trying to repay the Russian lives you may have saved with some American lives. The Japanese are treacherous, and we owe them for Port Arthur."

"Anything else?" Welles was shaken. In the time it took to smoke a Chesterfield, his world had turned upside down.

"One other thing. Do not underestimate those little yellow men."

Welles saw Oumansky to the door and hurried back to his desk to call Hull.

0900 Hours, November 16, 1941
Pearl Harbor

Andy Seghesio kept his wingman tucked in tight. "Stay right there, Murphy. Don't deviate a degree no matter what I do."

"Yes sir," came the nervous voice response.

Seghesio looked over to the fledgling's Wildcat. "You're doing fine, Murph. Just fine."

"Thank you, sir," the young Marine said sheepishly. Then, more authoritatively, "Sir, take a look down at your five. Should he be up here?"

A yellow Piper Cub circled the anchorage in wide turns, giving its occupants a spectacular view of the heart of the Pacific Fleet.

"We can't chase him away. It's not restricted airspace," Andy said. He hesitated but a moment. "However, there's nothing that says we can't screw with him a bit."

Andy nosed the Wildcat over with Murphy glued to his left wing. He came up in a rush next to the Piper, and barrel-rolled as he flashed past. The turbulence from the Wildcat's pass buffeted the little plane, as did Murphy's a second later.

Andy came around and flew not twenty yards behind the little plane, bobbing and weaving menacingly. Murphy pulled along side and positioned his wing tip not five feet from that of the tourists.

"Hey, Major! There are two Japs in that plane shaking their fists at me. Hey! Who're you flashing the bird at?"

"They obviously have no sense of humor. We're in enough trouble already. Let's get back to Ewa." He looked over the battle line below; the torpedo nets still weren't in place, despite the report he made weeks ago. It was almost Thanksgiving now. Rumors had it that the carriers were about to sortie again on an extended mission, and the fighter squadron he hoped to lead would depart with one of them. The carriers seemed quite able to take care of themselves, but the battleships looked pathetically vulnerable. Perhaps, he mused, it was the aviator in him talking.

The two Wildcat pilots were laughing into their oxygen masks as they headed for home, leaving the Piper's pilot trembling like a leaf, and Tomi Zai and Ito Fujita as angry as bees in a broken hive.

0600 Hours, November 21, 1941
San Francisco, California

Captain Vladimir Gagarin leaned on the rail of his ship as he watched the last crated and wrapped Panzer-busting P-39 Airacobra fighters loaded and tied down on the deck. A hefty ship, the *Uritsky* carried a dozen of them, a dozen Sherman tanks, ten two-and-a-half-ton trucks, spare parts, and ten tons of small arms ammunition in her hold. She would depart San Francisco this afternoon for the long voyage across the Pacific to Vladivostok. Her Lend-Lease cargo was desperately needed by the Red Army, and he meant to get it to them. A crusty old salt who had been the last man off a Russian cruiser as it sank from Japanese torpedo and shell hits, he had actually fired his pistol at the bridge of a Japanese destroyer that raced by his splintered lifeboat. Too old to command a ship of the line, Gagarin would do all he could to save Mother Russia. It wasn't a naval war out here in the Pacific, anyway, he would say to his junior officers, more to comfort himself. It wouldn't be unless the Japanese became involved, and only the Americans had a fleet that could fight them off. The Japs were tough, he told his men, but he personally claimed responsibility for taking Yamamoto's fingers at Port Arthur—and that the Japanese admiral would never forget it.

The journey through the northern Pacific this time of year would surely prove to be arduous. He insured his ship was in tip-top shape for the journey and that the crew was well-rested and ready to deal with whatever treachery the sea threw at them. The constellations had disappeared. He scanned the dawning sky that painted the bay's surface a brilliant gold. The sun's newest rays danced off the Golden Gate Bridge, a structure that awed him on every journey to this beautiful American city. It was time to go to sea. After all the years of weighing anchor and feeling the throb of the engines, he still became excited as to what adventures were in store for him.

Two figures, one clad in a dark overcoat and fedora, the other in a khaki field coat and peaked cap, arrived at the wharf and started up his gangway just as he was about to order it stowed. No one was on deck to challenge the intruders. The ship's crew was at a minimum; healthy men were needed for the infantry. Gagarin, still agile for a man of sixty years, rushed down from his bridge, his right hand drawing the pistol from his coat pocket. Rounding a bulkhead, he faced the trespassers.

"Captain Gagarin?" inquired the man in the overcoat. "Please put the pistol away. We mean you no harm. I'm Ivan Filitov, KGB. This is Miles Cooper of British Intelligence. I will produce identification if you allow me." Filitov went to his pocket, but Gagarin waved the pistol menacingly. "Captain, please. You are wasting valuable time. If I wanted you dead, Titov behind you would have killed you already."

Gagarin felt something at his right shoulder, and an instant later saw the long barrel of a .44 pistol. He lowered his gun.

"That's good. Do you suppose we could get out of this chill and perhaps have a cup of tea in your quarters? Should the crew ask, say we're customs agents."

"Fine." Now what would the KGB and British Intelligence want with him and his ship? Gagarin found himself confused, angry, and helpless.

0700, November 21, 1941

Opana Heights, Oahu

Privates Joseph Lockard and George Elliot had labored in the hot sun on the Opana heights for several hours, setting antennae, taking temperature and barometric readings, and aligning their vehicles. It was only nine in the morning, yet the temperature had already risen to 90 degrees. They were about to power up their equipment when the field phone rang.

"Elliot, are you set up to search yet?" asked Lieutenant Robert Breslowe, commander of the Signal Corps unit they were attached to a mere two weeks ago.

"Almost, sir. We have to check the circuits, and we have to warm up the system before we start scanning."

"Okay. Some Limey officers might be up to take a look at the radar. They're big brass. An admiral named Shears, and a commander named Popov. They're dressed in khaki uniforms. Tell them everything they need to know. Don't hold back anything from them. They're allies. Got it?"

"Popov? That one sounds Russian. Are you sure they're Brits?"

"Elliot, I'm an officer; you're a slob. I'm sure. Got it?" The line went dead.

"If he's such a smart-ass, he should come up and run this stuff, like he knew how it worked anyway," said Elliot.

"What's up?" asked Lockard.

"Breslowe said we're to expect some company. A few British Navy officers who want to see the radar in action."

"Well, we're ready to go. Hey, I got a blip here, bearing north by northwest, at 280 degrees. It's outbound," Lockard reported.

"Must be one of the *Big E*'s squadrons. She sailed today. I met some of her guys at the Royal Hawaiian last night. Shit, can those Navy guys drink. They usually go off in that direction to recover their air groups, before heading to wherever the hell they go."

"I saw her at her berth last night. No steam in her funnel. Anyway, this blip is too big to be a fighter and too small to be an air group."

"Maybe it's one of those Catalina search planes. They rotate search areas every few days."

"Should I call the other four stations to see if they're up yet?"

"Fuck 'em. It's too early to bother anybody, and it's Thanksgiving."

"I hope we're relieved soon. I got a Japanese woman in Honolulu who's absolutely crazy about me."

"As long as you have money."

Shears and Popov decided to postpone the radar visit. Admiral Kimmel invited them on a night gunnery exercise aboard *Arizona*, which was about to sail off with several other battleships. That radar was operational in five sites strategically set around Oahu and told them all they needed to know. Shears realized his mission had became all-important now, as the Americans had another ace in the hole to beat off the Japanese. Now the date of the attack became an obsession; he had to predict it accurately, or England was doomed.

He looked at Popov, whose value to him had lessened the instant he fathered Yvette's child. An agent with other priorities was of little use. A contented man was one who wouldn't take chances. That whore had compromised the best agent he ever had. Maybe it was her way of getting back at him for Billy, he thought. Well, he'd see about that.

1000 Hours, November 20, 1941
Hiroshima Bay

"Tell me, Ito. You've seen the belly of the beast. What is it like?" Genda greeted Fujita with a warm hug.

"They are strong and well-armed, but they lack preparedness, certain no ill will come their way. I think we can achieve total surprise."

"How is Tomi Zai?"

"He cried when I departed. He longs to be with us, sir, yet his work is selfless."

"He will have his day. I swear it."

"He also sends his best wishes to you." Ito hesitated when he saw Genda's furrowed brow. "He means it, sir. He knows your time of crisis is near, and he prays for you every night," he added.

Genda turned away, his eyes momentarily blurred. He cleared his tightened throat and said, "So, Ito. Can we fly off carriers on the northern route?"

"We can do anything we damn well please. Nothing on this earth can stop the *Kido Butai*. We will prevail. Do not doubt it a second."

2000 Hours, November 22, 1941
10 Downing Street, London

Winston Churchill reviewed the latest transmissions from Shears and Eversole as he sat in the library of the house on Downing Street. The presence of radar convinced him the Americans knew something was up—yet, radar was defensive. That meant they were still willing to let the Japanese make the first move, that the United States would not be the aggressor, that they hoped to catch the Japs red-handed and deal them a crushing blow in return with their huge B-17 and overwhelming air force. Barely a week past, Charles Lindbergh had made yet another inflammatory anti-British speech that attracted nationwide attention and stoked isolationist fervor. The United States remained divided, even after the American destroyer *Reuben James* had been sunk by a U-boat that same week. How long could England hold out after the Nazi field marshalls rallied their troops and defeated the Red Army?

What disturbed him as much as the radar was the newest American initiatives to obtain a last-minute "modus vivendi" with the Japanese; buying time to prepare for war. Their own Office of Strategic Services estimated that for every month the United States delayed entry, the war would last another year.

Desperate times called for desperate measures. It was now or never, he thought.

0900 Hours, November 22, 1941
CINCPAC, Pearl Harbor

Kimmel re-read the cable just received from Washington. He looked to the fleet intelligence officer, and said, "Ed, what the hell is this all about?" He was trying to stay calm, but was losing patience with every tick of the clock.

Lieutenant Commander Edwin Layton read the document, then looked up at Kimmel in confusion. "It can't mean a goddamned thing. With all due respect, I can't figure out what the hell Admiral Stark is trying to say."

Kimmel went to his window and watched the *Arizona* and *Oklahoma* sortie. "Read the damned thing out loud. Maybe somebody else in this room can tell me what the hell the Chief of Naval Operations is trying to tell me. Everyone, listen up!" he barked.

"I won't go into the pros or cons of what the United States may do. I will be damned if I know. I wish I did. The only thing I do know is that we may do most anything and that's the only thing I know to be prepared for; or, we may do nothing—I think it is more like to be anything."

Kimmel started to laugh. "We're doomed!" he guffawed. The others in the room joined his nervous laughter.

0800 Hours, November 22, 1941
Washington, D.C.

Cordell Hull sat with Roosevelt and outlined the reasoning behind his last-ditch effort at negotiating the Japanese out of the war.

"Mr. President, if we wish to delay hostilities, or in the best case avert them entirely, we have to give the Japanese a bone to chew on."

"Appeasement? I think not," the president answered caustically.

"It's not appeasement. What I propose is diplomatic denial; we deny the Japanese the possibility of war until we're ready, while we build our forces to engage Germany. We need to pursue an agreement with the Russians to land, refuel and rearm our Philippine-based B-17s for the strategic bombing initiative against Japan. The threat should keep them off balance. The fact the Russians have moved their troops out of Siberia is indicative that they have already reached an accommodation with the Japanese, which no doubt includes denying us the Siberian Russian bases. We can buy time by giving them some oil, rice, and the idea we don't want to fight over issues we can overcome. In return, I will ask them to limit their forces in Indochina, so as to not pose a threat to the British and Dutch possessions."

"How does this help with Germany?" Roosevelt asked.

"We ask the Japanese to renounce their Tripartite agreement. Then we're free to pursue Hitler's end."

"All of this in three months, bought for some rice and oil?"

"That will be what we'll need to build up MacArthur's B-17 wings into a creditable deterrent to the Japanese. Perhaps in that time, we'll both be able to cool to the point of a real accommodation. We can then negotiate from a position of strength."

"But you said we weren't going to get Joe Stalin's airfields," Roosevelt said. "Are we going off in another policy direction?"

"In essence, yes. The 200 B-17s we plan for the Philippines can command the area. It's all we need to contain the Japanese. We can defeat them later."

Roosevelt half-smiled. "It'll never work, Cordell, but for the sake of world opinion and for a few more days of peace, give it a try. Hell, I'll even write Emperor Hirohito. You never know."

On Saturday, November 22, 1941 Ambassadors Kurusu and Nomura had dumbfounded the secretary of state by saying, "Any agreement with the United States would outshine the Tripartite Pact." Hull responded he would have a concrete proposal by Tuesday, November 25. He shook with nervousness. Perhaps, just perhaps, he had achieved peace.

0800 Hours, November 22, 1941
The Kurile Islands

Admiral Yamamoto read the cable indicating the diplomats would be given four more days to reach an agreement. The ships of *Kido Butai* would sail on November 26. If peace were to break out by then…well, that would be fine. However, the old sailor knew better. He looked to the northeast where his striking force awaited the orders to sail. He thought of Genda, Fuchida, and that crazy young Fujita aboard the *Akagi*. Fujita had made it back from Hawaii just in time to fly back there again, but this time with the portents of death on his wings. He had talked to Fujita about the United States upon his return. They agreed it was their favorite country, next to Japan, but that the Americans needed to be taught a lesson in humility. What Yamamoto silently feared was that the lesson would climax horrifically for Japan.

While he was surrounded by men who would answer his every call, Yamamoto felt so alone. He wished he was on the *Akagi*. He found himself rubbing the amulet of Tsushima, bringing a smile to his face. He sent up a prayer and went off to bed.

Minoru Genda tried his best to buoy the spirits of Admiral Chuichi Nagumo, Yamamoto's choice to lead the strike force. The diminutive admiral was a worrier by nature. He strode *Akagi*'s decks with Genda in tow, checking every detail, and reading the operations orders again and again.

"Remember, it's the ships and the airfields we are after. No other targets. I don't want any news reports of hospitals or houses being strafed or bombs falling on civilians."

"Of course, Admiral."

"If one American ship or plane should find us, it might be prelude to disaster. I fear we will not bring all six carriers home."

"Admiral, surprise will be achieved. Our two-wave attack will be successful. Quite frankly I would prepare a third wave to destroy their fleet's fuel supply and dry docks and further cripple the ships moored adjacent to Ford Island."

Nagumo turned so quickly his neck hurt. "There will be a third-wave attack only if the American carriers are knocked out in the harbor, losses are minimal, and each American battleship is neutralized. If the carriers are not in the harbor, we will recover the second wave as we head westward."

Nagumo did not care so much about causing damage as he did about avoiding harm to his ships. He saw his mission as one of demoralizing the Americans as well as destroying their fleet. If he incapacitated them for a year, he would have accomplished his objectives. That was what Yamamoto wanted. "These six flight decks and the aircraft they carry are needed to conquer the Pacific territories. The very unglamourous task of supporting the ground campaigns and isolating Australia are more pressing. Do you understand?" the little man said, quite sternly.

"Yes, sir." Perhaps the fever of battle might infect Nagumo, and change his mind but, after seeing his nervousness, Genda doubted it.

2300 Hours, November 23, 1941
10 Downing Street, London

Another set of eyes read Yamamoto's operations order, impressed with its thoroughness. The mightiest armada in the history of mankind would soon be putting to sea. It might very well succeed. Overwhelming concentration of force was their strategy. Churchill wished he would have written it himself, yet he harbored doubts of its success. Did the admiral leading that pack of sharks feel the same way? Hell, it was the United States Navy, not some backward Chinese fishing fleet or a few stray gunboats, which was all the Imperial Japanese Navy had heretofore dealt with. If the Americans caught them early...

He had ordered *Prince of Wales* and the battle cruiser *Repulse* to Singapore to deter Japanese invasion. When he considered what the orders before him indicated, he wondered if he had made a major miscalculation.

He removed his glasses and rubbed his eyes. The hour was late, but the next few days were crucial to England's future. He picked up the phone and dialed Bletchley Park. "Make sure I get any decrypts regarding Japanese fleet movements, and any traffic sent by Tokyo to its Washington embassy," he said.

"Yes, Prime Minister," came the reply. The female voice then cleared itself. "As a matter of fact, something just came in. It concerns..."

"Send it to me by courier at once," he ordered.

Churchill paced nervously until the pouch arrived. As he read, his blood boiled. "Confound them!" he shouted to no one. "Those bastards! What the living hell is the matter with them?" he thundered, throwing the offending document into the air.

Several aides rushed in upon hearing the outburst, but stopped short when they saw Churchill's shredded message floating down all around him. "I need to phone the consulate in Hawaii, and right this bloody minute!" he roared.

The phone had rung only once. "Eversole here."

Churchill couldn't believe his string of bad luck. He wanted Shears. He owned Shears. Eversole thought too much. "Eversole, this is the Prime Minister. Is Shears available?"

"No, sir. He and Commander Popov are on a sortie with several American battleships. May I help you?"

"Eversole, make sure all your equipment is ready. You will have a job to do in the next two weeks. How familiar are you with the American battleships?"

Chapter 16

Tingling with excitement, Andy Seghesio opened his orders. He was expecting command of the fighter squadron he'd been training, and thus fulfilling a life-long dream. Looking on in suspense Tommy Hamilton saw Andy's expression turn sour.

Andy was shattered. They had no right to rob him of his destiny. How could they? He threw his leather flying helmet and goggles to the tarmac.

"Uh, what's it say?"

"Here! See for your goddamn self!" He thrust the paper at Hamilton. "Sons of bitches!" he bellowed, as he started his jeep, and made his way to the headquarters building.

Hamilton watched him tear away before beginning to read the special orders. He started to laugh, quietly at first, but then with such gusto that other pilots in the ready room came out to find what was so funny.

"It's Seghesio! He's crazy!"

"Why is that, sir?" Murphy asked.

"They just promoted him to lieutenant colonel, that's why," he replied.

"I would think the major would be pleased."

"Uh-uh. Majors lead fighter squadrons, not lieutenant colonels. It means you're not going to Wake with him as your C.O. Obviously, the Marine Corps has bigger things in mind for him."

"I betcha it has something to do with the four krauts he nailed during the Blitz," Murphy said.

Hamilton glared at the young pilot. "That might very well be classified information you're spewing, Lieutenant."

"Horseshit! The whole Marine Corps knows about it, sir. It was the talk of our basic aviation class at Quantico."

Joe Rochefort and Jack Burns watched from the Ford Island pier as the *Arizona* eased into her berth with the help of three hard-working tugs. Her starboard side bore a large scrape amidships, and oil oozed from below her waterline.

"So it's true," Burns said.

"It sure as hell seems to be," Rochefort replied.

Chief Jones was the first ashore to greet the men from the navy yard. Burns and Rochefort approached him, and Jones came to rigid attention and saluted them.

"What's the story, chief?"

"We scraped *Oklahoma*'s bow. No major damage. The torpedo blister was punctured, and we're losing a little of its oil. We only need a couple of days in the yard, sir. We'll be fine."

"You said 'we'. I guess it was *Arizona*'s fault, then?"

"If you mean the ship's fault when you say *Arizona*, and not Captain Van Valkenberg's fault, you'd be dead on."

"I'm not following you," Rochefort said.

"She didn't answer the helm. Her steering gear froze up in the middle of a zig-zag maneuver last night just as we were heading back to Pearl after a superb gunnery drill. As soon as we glanced off Oklahoma, every thing was fine again."

"Will everyone swear to it?"

"I don't know what anyone will swear to, but I tell you one thing—you mention Pearl Harbor on that ship, and something always goes wrong. She hates it."

The two officers looked at him quizzically. "Beg your pardon, Chief?" Rochefort said.

"I can't explain it. I just know. Excuse me, I have some work to see to."

"Of course, Chief. Good luck."

"That's the real Navy, Joe," Burns said, as they watched him walk off.

"By the way, where do you stand with that other navy—the one with the ships that have those funny names."

"We still can't crack their code. They keep changing their keys."

"Do you know where their carriers are?" Burns asked.

"It's funny that you bring that up. Kimmel's intelligence officer told me this morning that all their merchant ships have been called back to Japan, and he asked me the same thing about their carriers."

"And?"

"We lost them. I hope they're just trying to leverage the negotiations in Washington by showing their strength."

"Shit, they'd better do it now before the battleship *Iowa* or the new carrier *Essex* gets here," Burns said.

Taking his foot off the pier piling, Rochefort turned to him, and stared with a worried bend to his brow. "Exactly."

———

"Mae? I'm home," Andy Seghesio yelled.

"I'm in the bathroom. I didn't expect you so early."

"Me either," he said, taking off his coat, and pouring a jigger of scotch, which he wasted no time in downing.

She'd heard it before—that "I'm-so-angry-and-hurt-and-no-one gives-a-shit" tone. She stepped out of the bathroom and hugged him. "What's wrong?" she asked.

"The sons of bitches promoted me, that's what's wrong!"

Mae stared at him, confused. "Help me with that, dear. What's wrong with being a...uh..."

"Fucking lieutenant colonel."

"Does a fucking lieutenant colonel outrank a regular lieutenant colonel? Who gives who the orders?"

"Oh, you're something, you know that?" he said, bursting into a laugh and hugging her.

"Yes, I am. And you're lucky to have me. But why the long puss?"

"It means I'll never command a fighter squadron, dammit!"

"Trust the Marine Corps," she said, kissing his cheek. "Remember when you didn't want to go to the World's Fair, but the Marines made you? If you hadn't been there, I'd probably be a harlot in London. Granted, I'd have more fun, but..."

"Very funny. Burns is right. I shouldn't talk to Brits."

"All Scots are terribly constipated. It comes from screwing their sheep."

He had to laugh again. "I love you, Mae," he said, cupping her breasts in his hands.

"And besides, if you went to Wake Island, whose tits would you fondle?" she said, kissing him again.

"Are you in the mood, Mrs. Seghesio?"

"Always for you, Fucking Lieutenant Colonel."

———

Shears and Popov left the *Arizona* as soon as she entered the navy yard's dry dock. The shipwrights confirmed Chief Jones' opinion that her hull was perforated too far below the waterline to repair by unloading and dumping ballast. That wouldn't raise her far enough to reach the cut in the blister. Both *Oklahoma* and *Arizona* had bows reminiscent of triremes, where they extended outward from the ship's rail to keel, more for aesthetic effect—they weren't designed to ram anything.

Popov and Shears motored off in an embassy car to the apartment the British kept in Honolulu for visiting dignitaries and embassy personnel wanting to be discreet with the island's natives.

"They're incredible!" Shears said.

"I can't believe how they perceive their situation. They spend all their time thinking of what they can't do and ignore what they can do. It makes them sitting ducks. I cannot even begin to think how they would fare in an all-out battle. They train hard, and their equipment is excellent, if a bit dated. The gunnery exercise last night was magnificently executed, but their fighting spirit is weak. They are the perfect victims. It must come from the top."

"No doubt about it. Our operatives tell us that Kimmel and Short literally pace the floor like caged lions, frustrated at what they don't have and what they can't do. As is, they could make a considerable defense against the Japanese. I'm sure not having direct access to PURPLE exasperates them. They see only what Washington wants them to, or interprets for them. I think they're about to get the worst beating in the history of warfare."

"A Japanese attack? Maybe you aren't revealing a state secret, sir, but you sound as if it was fait accompli," Popov countered. "That they aren't reading JN-25 is another story," he added with an evil grin.

"There is a good chance that the Japanese won't succeed. They're leaving a sloppy trail and the Americans have their new radar to alert them."

"I don't know if I agree, Admiral," Yuri said, downshifting to make a right turn. "I have much higher esteem for the Japanese Navy than is fashionable."

"Yuri, the Americans are still trying desperately to reach an accommodation with the Japanese, and the Japanese are buying into it."

Arriving at Shears' apartment, they found Eversole hard at work putting together the tanks of explosives he and Yuri had perfected in England. "Ah, there you are!" he said with genuine happiness.

"Chad, what the hell are you doing?" Yuri asked, his expression laced with surprise and fear. "Why did you bring those along?"

"It's as simple as ABC," Shears answered, "or is that XYZ?" He gave a malicious laugh. He suddenly clutched his stomach.

"What we have to do is gruesome, but there's no choice. They can't be trusted, these Americans. And, we cannot do without them." Eversole's face bore a twist of pain.

"What is it you need me to do?" Popov asked.

0500 Hours, November 25, 1941
Carrier *Akagi*

Akagi led the procession of warships from Hitokappu Bay into the angry

Pacific. A fine rain was falling, and mist shrouded the ships in an eerie white light. The brand new sister carriers *Zuikaku* and *Shokaku* were in line behind. To port were *Kaga*, and the sisters *Hiryu* and *Soryu*. The carriers were accompanied by two battleships, two heavy cruisers, a light cruiser, nine destroyers, and fleet auxiliaries. It was the most powerful task force ever to take to sea in the history of warfare. The ships surged to the mission, shaking off the turbulent sea as no more than a common nuisance. Pilots laughed and joked, eagerly awaiting the action they had trained so hard for. Mechanics affectionately worked over the 493 fighters, bombers, and torpedo planes carried by the six flattops. Even the cooks seemed ready for action.

He couldn't have had it better. Genda opened his diary and wrote November 25, 1941, about to chronicle the greatest military undertaking his country had ever launched from the moment *Akagi*'s propellers thrust the ship into history. The words didn't come. He rose from his desk and went to the bridge for air. His mind stuck on what Yamamoto told him—that the attack would follow a declaration of war by a few hours. Yamamoto felt they would still catch the Americans unaware. Genda didn't dispute this, but he held reservations.

He decided to seek out the comical Fuchida, finding him on the hangar deck, pulling a large, detailed map of Pearl Harbor beneath the fuselage of Ito Fujita's bomber. Fujita kept his eyes on the bombsight and screamed when he hit the bomb release.

"I got her!" Fujita yelled. "Commander, bring the *Lexington* under my sights again!" he laughed.

"My back is killing me with this stupid game. If you want the *Lexington*, you will have to wait until a week from Sunday! If you don't hit her then, you'd better not return to *Akagi*. Better to go to *Shokaku* or *Zuikaku*. The young fools on those two virgins don't know how inept you are. You can lie and get away with it over there!"

"You shouldn't tease him so much, Mitsuo."

"Fuck him. He'll get over it!" Fuchida laughed.

"Do you think the green pilots on *Shokaku* and *Zuikaku* will wilt in the heat of battle? I know you jest, but I'm concerned that…"

"Brawls will break out when pilots are ordered to remain to guard the fleet against American air strikes or a wayward task force. Everyone wants to go Pearl Harbor so badly they're not beyond killing each other for a place on the mission." He placed his hands on his friend's shoulders. "Genda, if they have to crash into an American ship to guarantee a hit, they will. They may be young and untried, but do not doubt their will."

0900 Hours, November 26, 1941
The White House

Roosevelt looked pale and detached as members of the cabinet and chiefs of staff entered the Oval Office. Cordell Hull was already talking with him in muted tones. A tray of cold breakfast sat before Roosevelt, barely picked over. His steward poured him a cup of coffee, and chanced a smile at his boss. The president smiled back, but the steward knew that something of grave consequence was on his mind. He quickly excused himself, closing the door behind him.

Roosevelt felt the eyes around the table focus on him. He lit a Camel cigarette, then said, "Gentlemen, I have it on good account that the Japanese will attack us within two weeks, while simultaneously attacking the British at Singapore, Hong Kong, and the Kra Isthmus. Expect hostilities anytime after December 1."

"Mr. President, how is that you came by this information?" Stimson asked.

"British intelligence indicates the Japanese fleet, including its six largest carriers, is at sea. Our own intelligence confirms this by stating they've lost track of them. It seems they're not broadcasting. The Japs are explaining this off as a port call, but the British are sure their fleet is under radio silence lurking somewhere. And a convoy of troop transports is heading south."

"That means the Philippines are in grave danger as well. The Japs can't leave that flank open," Stark said.

"What about the modus vivendi?" General Marshall shot out. "We need time—at least until the second week in December. We've got B-17s in the final stages of production that will double MacArthur's air power. Can't we stall..."

"It's not our decision," Hull interrupted. "The Japanese are bent on war."

"But Kurusu's renouncement of the Tripartite Pact. What..."

"A sham, nothing but a cover for treachery," Roosevelt said. "We cannot appease them. It would turn all the lands in the Far East and the South Pacific into a bunch of Czechoslovakias."

"We should send a war warning to Hawaii and the Philippines," General Marshall suggested.

"Certainly," Admiral Stark added. "However, alerting the population by unusual activity might not be wise. Let's emphasize reconnaissance and defensive measures. We must be sure that no commander seizes the initiative and fires the first shot."

"Indeed," Stimson added. "That must be done by the Japanese. We cannot have any of the isolationists in Congress labeling us warmongers."

"See to it. And see how fast you can get those B-17s from Seattle to Manila," Roosevelt said.

"Not nearly as quickly as I can throw those two Japanese pissants out of my office today," Hull said, shaking with anger. "I'll give them something they can't possibly accept. Maybe they'll get the message that we are ready, willing, and able to take them on."

Marshall looked at Stark, whose forlorn expression was a mirror of his own.

_____

2000 Hours, November 27, 1941
10 Downing Street

Churchill read the American dispatch, highly pleased with himself. It appeared he had succeeded grandly. Now he had to insure the Americans were on full war alert in the Philippines. He judged that the Japanese fleet could reach the Philippines in four or five days. The Americans would figure that if the Philippines were the target, the Jap fleet should be spotted in that time. Hawaii, on the other hand, was a longer voyage, at least eight days, and required a mid-ocean refueling. If the Jap Fleet wasn't spotted in four days, eyes would focus on Hawaii, and the base would probably be fully alerted and on a war footing.

So what? Churchill thought. Let the Japs attack in the fully alerted face of the Americans. From what Shears reported, the attack would be an unqualified success, anyway. Add all the miscues he had created, and you had the makings of a real disaster. If the Atlantic experience was a barometer of American tolerance, demolished airplanes, broken destroyers and sunken freighters didn't count. The Japanese needed to sink one American capital ship. Just one.

"Remember the Maine!" he muttered, lighting a Corona, and sipping his whiskey and water. He finished dressing for the reception at the United States Embassy, where Averell Harriman was eagerly awaiting his arrival.

_____

0800 Hours, November 29, 1941
Pearl Harbor

Burns, Seghesio, and Rochefort sat on a bench at the end of the West Channel, watching as the *Enterprise* pointed her graceful bow to the harbor entrance. Although her destination was unannounced, they knew by the twelve Marine F4F-3 Wildcat fighters on her flight deck that they were bound for Wake Island, to provide escort for the B-17s being rushed to MacArthur. Burns and Seghesio still felt betrayed, which was not lost on the irascible

Rochefort.

"Well, guys, there she goes," Rochefort said. "What a ship! Magnificent, isn't she? I'd bet her crew is tickled to death to be leaving this hole to run in the open sea in the finest ship in the United States Navy. She seems to have a real bone in her teeth, doesn't she? Imagine…wheeling around at flank speed, churning up a huge rooster wake, her bow aglow with white water as she heels in to the wind to launch and recover those falcons on her deck…God, I love this Navy!"

"And I think you'd better shut your mouth before I shove your head up your ass," Seghesio said.

"By the way, Andy. Do you want to be called Lieutenant Colonel Seghesio, or just Colonel Seghesio?" Rochefort rubbed the oak leaves on his collar. "Wait a minute! You've got a Ph.D., right? I guess it's Doctor Colonel…or, is it Lieutenant Doctor Colonel? I'm confused."

"You're flirting with death, you little spook," Burns said.

"Sorry, Captain Burns. I meant no disrespect. Hey, did you hear that John Munroe was just appointed the assistant CAG of *Enterprise*? There's a real fighter pilot. I'd bet he's the best pilot in the whole Navy. Don't you think so, Captain?"

"I think you're going to turn up missing tomorrow. And speaking of missing, you useless piece of crap, have you found the Jap carriers yet?"

"No. Which brings up a question for you. I mean, you being a captain and all, perhaps you might be able to help. Here." Rochefort reached into his pocket and pulled out a cable. "This came in yesterday from the Office of Naval Intelligence with a bunch of other stuff. Are we conducting any exercises with the Royal Navy?"

"Not that I know of. Why?"

"It's funny. The intercept came from Moscow through a Russian listening station in Vladivostok. See? There's the routing."

"So the Russians are spying on the British? Interesting," Seghesio commented, his voice wry.

"Oh, shit, Andy. It happens all the time," Rochefort answered. "We all spy on each other."

"XYZ-41," Burns said, reading the listing out loud. "I don't know anything about it, but I'm getting a very uncomfortable feeling."

"That's because you hate the British," Andy said.

"You know that British admiral from Singapore who came with Yuri Popov to the *Arizona*'s birthday bash?"

"Shears?" replied Andy.

Rochefort felt they were on to something. His years as a spook/codebreaker had developed a sixth sense about the way pieces of information fell in line, and it intensified as Burns put together his thoughts.

"You know, Joe, I could have sworn I saw this British guy Eversole with them on the *Arizona* during the birthday party."

"Who's he?" Rochefort asked.

"Way back when I was recovering from an airplane wreck…"

"Which one was that?" Rochefort interrupted.

"Very funny. I was reading Japanese decrypts during the Washington Naval Treaty meetings, working with a British officer named Chad Eversole. It was twenty years ago, but the guy hadn't changed all that much. When I tried to find him again, he had disappeared."

"What does this Eversole fellow do now?" Seghesio asked.

"I think he still works for British Intelligence. He kept his commission, but basically does spook work. He wasn't wearing a uniform that night."

"What could XYZ-41 signify?" Burns asked.

"It could be a hundred different reasons. Who knows why they name anything the way they do?"

"It must have some significance. I just…"

"Don't strain yourself, Jack. You might get a hernia and be even more miserable."

"I have all weekend to rest up, Joe," Burns said as he watched the *Big E*'s wake begin to boil. His ship had sailed without him.

Rochefort saw Burns' bright blue eyes mist over. He knew better than to barb him again. "How about a round of golf tomorrow? My treat. We'll celebrate your promotions."

"I don't want to celebrate my promotion," Seghesio said.

"Then, we can celebrate 'It's the-last-Saturday-in-November-and-we ain't-at-war-yet.'"

"You've been working too hard, Joe."

"Not hard enough," he answered. "I still don't know where the hell the Jap carriers are, and it's starting to scare the bejesus out of me. I've got a funny feeling that tomorrow's round may be the last for a long time."

This time, he wasn't smiling.

———————

Yvette was feeling ill again. It was late in the evening, and she was bitterly amused that her "morning sickness" afflicted her around the clock. That was fine, especially if "Yuri junior" was born as handsome and strong as his father. It had to be a boy. A girl would never put her through so much agony. She decided to take a walk in the gardens of the exclusive little apartment complex. They terraced just below, overlooking the ocean, and she thought the salt air and tropical fragrances would ease the queasiness.

When she saw the embassy Chevrolet pull up, she wanted Yuri to join her. The gentle trade winds and brilliant stars made for a perfect tropical evening, and they should share it.

Yuri promised her that when they returned to Singapore, the first thing he'd do was officially make her Mrs. Popov. She'd miss Julie and Mae and Lisa, but there had never been a time when she was happier than right now.

Upstairs, she heard Eversole whistling in his flat, and saw Shears' apartment door standing open.

She went in thinking that Yuri might be there with the admiral, who was still feeling ill; she heard Shears moaning in the bathroom. She was just about to call out when she saw the tanks and timers. Curiosity led her closer to the wooden boxes of evil-looking things. The coffee table held several maps of…Pearl Harbor? There were ships' positions labeled with their names—the *Arizona*, *Nevada*, *California* and *Utah* had been circled in red. There was also some kind of notation referring to 7/12/41, and a military time designation of 0715. Several other diagrams on the table looked like the floor plans of… battleships? Renderings of the huge guns that sat in those massive turrets gave it away. Which ships were they?

She gasped, suddenly arriving at a dreadful conclusion. It had to be. Much as she tried to think otherwise, it had to be.

She ran back to her own apartment, only to meet Yuri, dismayed at the fear on her pretty face.

She never saw Chad Eversole following her.

"Shears," he said, into the phone.

"This is Eversole. Burns was at the consulate today."

"What did he want?"

"Information about a joint exercise called XYZ-41."

Shears was silent as anxiety gripped him. He exhaled slowly. "I think it's time to put Yuri to work, Chad."

"Right away," Eversole replied.

Chapter 17

Admiral Husband E. Kimmel held a staff meeting aboard the battleship *California* to discuss the crisis. "What do you think of sortieing the fleet for a week-long exercise east of Hawaii?" he asked.

"In view of your orders not to alarm the populace or to further antagonize the Japanese, I would caution you not to sortie the fleet, Kim," said Admiral Pye, who commanded the battle force from *California*'s bridge.

"What if I told you I didn't give a damn about the populace or what the fucking Japanese thought?" Kimmel retorted.

Captain William Smith, his chief of staff, spoke up. "The fuel reserves we would consume in such an operation would hinder a long-range operation against the Marshalls, if war breaks out. We can certainly have the fleet ready to sail upon the outbreak of hostilities, Admiral. You might want to exercise the option to sortie a few ships, say to greet the *Lexington* and *Enterprise*. *Enterprise* is due back on December 7. It's a half-way measure to be sure, but perhaps it would serve without getting Washington in a snit should negotiations go sour."

Kimmel pondered, still convinced the best way to secure his fleet was to keep it east of Hawaii. However, if war did break out, and his oil reserves were not what his reports led Washington to expect, he'd be derelict. The Marines now on Wake and Guam might need the battle line's support in case of attack.

"Sir, the Japanese won't attack us. We're too strong," Pye said confidently puffing on a huge pipe, as the others around the table nodded in agreement.

Kimmel was dumbfounded. Had Bill Halsey been here, he might have given further credence to his argument. As it was, it sounded irrational in light of pre-established operational plans.

He gave up the idea reluctantly, hoping General Short fully realized how important his air force was to the fleet.

"Why, Yuri?" she whispered, tears streaming down her face. "They are good friends. They are good people," she sobbed, trying to keep her voice down. "What if Jack or Andy is killed in this treachery? Or Mae, God forbid, or Julie? Why don't you just tell them?"

"Because we can't trust them. We have no choice. The American political bastards are oxymoronic belligerent pacifists who would sell us down the river if they could defeat the Japanese quickly. We cannot let them off so easily, Yvette." Looking angrily at her, he loaded a clip in the Colt .45.

"What will you do with the explosives?"

"I...don't know," he stammered. "They're for a contingency operation to insure the Japanese are successful. Shears hasn't told me the details."

"You're lying to me. I can tell because I've never seen that look on your face. You've never lied to me before, Yuri."

"Stop it! I cannot go on like..."

"Then don't!" She calmed herself and blew her nose. His face was angry, his eyes confused.

She looked at him forlornly. "Are you going to help the Japanese kill Americans by not telling them, or will you help them by killing Americans yourself?"

He was stunned, taken aback by the quiver in her chin that betrayed unbridled anger.

"You'll do well to remember why we're here...to save the Crown. That's what we're all about. Your mission hasn't changed, Yvette. Our playing house may have gotten out of hand, but..."

The breath left her body in a gust. She rose and went to the door.

"Get out of here, you dirty bastard!"

If she knew what he would do that day, she would kill him. The door slammed shut behind him. "I'll always love you. Forgive me," he whispered.

A child played near the entrance with a nanny watching her. She was the daughter of an embassy worker, and Yuri stopped to play with her on occasion. She turned to him: it was suddenly little Nina's face he saw! He closed his eyes as chills coursed through him. When he looked again, the child was herself, but the nanny smiling at him was Mother! You fool! He ran to the Chevrolet and took off with a screech of tortured rubber.

0700 Hours, December 1, 1941
Kido Butai

Akagi heaved in the rough seas, wave after wave crashing over her bow and drenching the flight deck. All flight operations were canceled, even the protective combat air patrol. A plane couldn't be launched or recovered in this weather. As the weather inhibited the Japanese, the low cloud cover and drizzle also protected them. They were too far from Hawaii to be seriously concerned about search planes, but a B-17 might just happen by.

At the hum of powerful aircraft engines, all chatter on the bridge ceased.

Every eye searched the overcast skies for the shape of a plane. Even the hum of machinery seemed to fall off, as if *Akagi* herself were desperately trying to go undiscovered.

The sound dissipated, and everyone breathed a sigh of relief. Genda managed a smile. He leaned against a bulkhead and breathed deeply. Admiral Nagumo wiped his brow and sent up a quick Shinto prayer.

"See, Admiral? We are charmed. *Kido Butai* is invincible, like ghosts who can only strike and never be stricken!"

"Genda, if you are still politicking for that third wave, forget it. I'm more convinced than ever that our foray will not go unchallenged as we planned." He turned away in a huff, walked the short distance to his day cabin, and slammed the door.

Genda looked out over the fleet, the carriers and battleships pushing aside the Pacific's ire as they pointed their bows eastward. Nothing could stop *Kido Butai*, not even a petulant commander.

A runner flashed by Genda and knocked on Nagumo's door with a radio message. The admiral read the message and turned to Genda.

"Here. It's what you've been waiting for," he said. "I pray for your strength."

Genda read in turn: "Climb Mount Niitakayama—1208, repeat 1208." It was Yamamoto's order setting the commencement of hostilities for December 8 this side of the dateline.

0700 Hours, December 3, 1941
USS *Enterprise*

Commander John Munroe gave Major Paul Putnam a hearty handshake in the fighter ready room. "The Wildcat will do okay. Just don't abuse her because Wake Island can't fix anything. I don't think there's a screwdriver on that island, let alone a fighter maintenance facility."

"We'll be okay. It's short duty. Why we have to escort B-17s, I'll never know. Who the hell would attack them out here?"

"They think the Japanese might interdict with fighters from the Marshall's," Munroe answered.

"That would be a hell of feat. I bet you'll be back here in less than a month to pick us up."

"I hope so. Anyway, I gave that kid, Murphy, the manuals for the gun solenoid system. They jam with full loads of ammo in the cans. We haven't figured out why, but they're easy to fix once you're on the ground."

"Pilots, man your planes!" came the order from the PA.

"I guess I gotta go."

"Happy trails!"

Munroe went up to the carrier's island to watch the Marines launch off the flight deck and head southwest. He couldn't shake the feeling that they would never be seen again.

He would be happy to get across the International Dateline to regain December 2, the day lost crossing from east to west. It would be again when that happened. For the first time in his life he was experiencing a sense of mortality, and it scared the hell out of him. He wanted that day back. He felt *Enterprise* heel over as she changed course, her escorts following suit, heading back to Pearl Harbor.

0700 Hours, December 3, 1941
Pearl Harbor

Jack Burns carefully placed his hat on his head, checking his appearance in the foyer's mirror. He couldn't help touching the eagles on his collar. Much as he'd prefer flying as a CAG, maybe the Navy did have something more in mind for him.

"Julie, honey. I'm going," he yelled out, picking up the leather briefcase. Just as he did, the phone rang.

"Jack?" she called out. "Honey, are you there?"

"Waiting for my goodbye kiss. What's cooking?"

"Andy's swinging by to pick you up. I need the car. We're going to lunch, then we're shopping for Mae's farewell supper for the Popov's tonight."

Popov again! I'll be glad when those Brit sons of bitches are gone! He tried hard to stay cool, knowing his scorn for them made Julie uncomfortable.

"Andy's car is giving him all kinds of trouble. He bought it without looking at it too carefully. He said the little old lady who sold it to him reminded him of his mother. There's a mechanic at the base who's going to look at it for him today, so I…"

"Never mind, Julie. I can see where this is going," he laughed. "See you. Be careful," he admonished as he kissed her.

"Always," she responded.

Hidden in the bushes a hundred meters up the street from Jack Burns' hilltop home, Yuri Popov saw Andy Seghesio arrive and honk the horn. Out came the chipper-as-usual Burns, who threw his briefcase into the back of the Dodge convertible and hopped over the door into the front seat. He slapped Andy on the back and the two were off. Popov cursed out loud. Why the hell was he going to work with Seghesio, today of all days? Damn them!

Not a minute later, Yvette, Mae, and Lisa climbed out of a taxicab and Julie Burns came out. He watched in horror as the four of them got in Burns' Mercury station wagon and headed off. He ran to the Ford he had stolen that morning, desperate to chase them down.

Julie downshifted as she rounded a curve and touched the brake pedal. It felt a bit mushy, but noticing the silence of the usually lively and loquacious Yvette distracted her.

"What's wrong, Yvette?" she asked. The words alone caused her to break into tears.

"Julie, something dreadful is about to happen," she sobbed. "Dear God, forgive me, but I must…"

"Uh oh!" Julie Burns shouted.

"What?" Mae asked.

"No brakes! Shit! Hang on!"

The Mercury picked up speed, despite her downshifting to second gear. Julie yanked the emergency brake, but it only made the rear end slew left and right. "Oh, dear God!" she screamed. She had time to think how fortunate it was that the children were with the next door neighbor and not in the car.

"Lock the transmission! Jam it into first gear!" Mae yelled.

Even with Yvette's help, the transmission only emitted a loud grinding noise. The speedometer read thirty-five miles per hour. Julie turned the wheel to negotiate a curve bordered by a long wall of volcanic rock. At its end was the little beach Navy families frequented. If she could just get onto the beach, the sand would bring them to a safe stop. She wrenched the wheel back to the right, and she almost made it, but the laws of physics were working against her.

The Mercury's right front wheel hit the end of the wall and launched the car into the air. It flew fifty feet before landing on its left side. It skidded and flipped, its doors flying open, shedding its engine hood and tailgate as it went. It tumbled onto its roof, skidding to a stop.

The dazed and battered women scrambled out. Despite the agonizing pain of a broken arm, Julie saw that Yvette was missing. Horrified, they found her pinned beneath the car. The Navy Shore Patrol jeep ran up the beach and four burly sailors pushed the car upright. Yvette did not move.

Yuri stopped short and pulled the Ford out of sight when he saw the SPs at the scene. He counted three women; Mae, Lisa, and Julie Burns. Shocked, he watched them carry Yvette's limp and bloody body into a waiting ambulance. "Mama, I'm so sorry," he cried.

Lying in the tall grass on a bluff a quarter mile away, Chad Eversole witnessed the whole affair. He saw Yvette's body being taken away. With grim sadness, he speculated that even if the primary target had gotten away, perhaps this had worked out for the best.

––––––

With her wounds healed, *Arizona* was "resting comfortably," as Chief Jones put it. The repair ship *Vestal* had tied up to *Arizona's* port side to facilitate finishing repairs. She was bound for the Bremerton Navy Yard on December 13 for a general overhaul and to be equipped with that scientific wonder called radar. The post for the gizmo's antenna had been installed on the foremast while she lay in dry dock.

Jones listened to the ship's band for the last time. It was quite an ensemble, probably the best in the fleet. Though not a music lover, he always put aside his tasks to listen to the band's rehearsals and performances. Their music seemed to be at the heart of what her young men were all about, and Jones always gave the heart and brain equal time. There was to be a fleet band competition on Saturday, but he'd miss it. After leaving *Arizona's* deck for the last time to embrace the fetal *Iowa* on Friday, he tried to resolve that he would not return. He wanted a clean break. The *Pennsylvania's* band was the odds on favorite to win, anyway, he told himself.

Josh Friar saw Jones pause on the quarterdeck, just about to leave the ship. "Hey, Chief, what are you up to?"

"Listening to my favorite band. Where are you going?"

"I'm practicing with the ship's softball team. We've integrated," he said with a wink. That had been Jones' idea. "We're scheduled to play those fags from the *Enterprise*, whenever she gets her fancy ass back here. Sunday morning maybe."

"Rumor has it she reenforced Wake Island with a Marine fighter squadron."

"So I've heard," Friar said. "Hey chief. I've got a few minutes before batting practice. How about I make you a real country breakfast?"

"I know what you're trying to do, and I appreciate it. You've been nicer to me than I deserve. I don't need the breakfast, but I'll treasure the memories."

"Come on. Let's go to the galley. You're worse off than I thought," he said with a shake of his head.

"What do you mean?"

"You sound like Miss Scarlett talkin', for Chrissake. Maybe if you eat something, you'll come to your senses."

––––––

Shears read the JN-25 transmission with disgust. "Climb Mount Niita-kayama 1208." The fucking Japs might as well announce their arrival with a brass band! Surely, the Americans must be alerted. He drove to Pearl Harbor, expecting to see the fleet on the move, the skies filled with planes and barrage balloons, and the gates closed to all nonmilitary personnel. But he saw nothing out of the ordinary. If a base could be laid back, Pearl Harbor was. He was coming to think Yuri might be right, that the Japanese didn't need their help. Yet if the Americans had decrypted JN-25, and were now inconspicuously deciding how to react...

Shears surveyed the fleet one last time. The carriers *Lexington and Enterprise* were still out at sea. *Nevada* and *California* were moored off by themselves, but the *Vestal*'s position to *Arizona*'s port side gave him pause; the *Vestal* saved him a lot of speculation and planning. This one was handed to him, a needed gift.

The pain in his stomach was a continuing agony. He couldn't last another week. His strength was ebbing by the day, and the opiates he took at mealtimes further weakened him. He fed on hatred, vengeance for Billy, England's loss of glory, and her subjection to the whims of America. It was better that it end now. Billy's death took his mental facilities; the demon in his gut took his physical stamina. There wasn't much left to give. He hoped the prime minister appreciated his agony.

He got back in the car and glanced at the rear view mirror, which happened to be positioned so his reflection was full in it. He trembled at what he saw. He ripped it from its mount and tossed it into the harbor, glaring at *Arizona*.

Shears drove home, where he found Yuri shaking like a leaf, his head in his hands, and Eversole holding his shoulder.

"We must talk," Eversole said.

"Where's Yvette?" Shears asked.

"In the hospital," Eversole responded.

Yuri moaned and rocked, fingers pulling on his hair in a frightening display of grief.

––––––––––

Yvette Popov lay with an intravenous needle in each arm, drifting in and out of consciousness. Her condition was complicated by the miscarriage. Mae and Julie left her side only to have Julie's arm set, and their minor wounds bandaged. Lisa, who escaped with only a bruised thigh, went off to call Tommy, Andy, and Jack. No one answered the phone at Popov's apartment.

Andy and Jack rushed in fifteen minutes after the call reached them. With tears in their eyes, they embraced their wives.

"Oh, Andy, what a horrible thing. Poor Yvette," Mae sobbed. "She's so pale. The doctor doesn't think she'll...she lost her baby." She shuddered in her husband's arms.

Julie Burns couldn't catch her breath. Her tears soaked into Jack's khaki shirt, as she held him so tightly it hurt. "The brakes—brakes didn't work," she said.

Yvette gave out a groan that sent Tommy and Lisa running for the doctor.

"Mae," she said, recognizing her for the first time. "I'm…dying," she gasped.

"No, you're not. You're hurt, but…"

"Can't feel my legs, can't breathe," she wheezed. "Yuri…?"

"We're trying to find him. Rest now," Mae said, gently stroking her bruised face.

"My baby. Is the baby…?"

"The baby's fine," Julie lied.

Yvette's eyes opened wide. "Yuri!" she yelled. "You must stop Yuri!"

"Yvette, honey, I don't understand you."

Yvette's eyes rolled back in her head. A doctor and nurse hurried in, stethoscope at the ready. "Everyone out of here."

"No!" Yvette screamed hysterically. "No! Mae, come here. Pearls, Mae!" she managed, as her breathing became labored and irregular. Mae pushed aside a nurse and ran to her friend's side.

"Save…pearls!" Yvette said, but the words she needed wouldn't come, and Mae's image was dimming. She made a desperate grab for Mae's necklace, and tugged at it, breaking the string.

The last image her eyes transmitted to her brain was Mae's face, haloed in brilliant light. It made her smile, and her body relaxed. The pearls clattered onto the tile floor. With her beautiful blue eyes still focused on Mae Seghesio, Yvette died.

Jack and Andy had seen death before, but nothing prepared them for this. They were numb. Only the tears coursing down their faces betrayed what they felt.

"Someone has to tell Yuri," Tommy Hamilton muttered.

0600 Hours, December 4, 1941
The Northwest Pacific

Captain Gagarin stood on the bridge of *Uritsky*, his massive, gnarled hands gripping the binoculars he had purchased in San Francisco. At three o'clock in the afternoon, the foggy drizzle had dropped visibility to less than two miles at these high latitudes. He hadn't sighted a ship or plane in the last thirty-six hours as his good ship steamed along at ten knots making for Vladivostok.

Though he had just finished a bowl of borscht soup and loaf of bread not two hours ago, his hunger returned. It was the sea, he thought with a smile. While the swells and shear emptiness of the ocean would make others queasy, it brought a heartiness to certain types of men. He felt at ease on the rolling deck, the way a farmer did atop a tractor plowing a rolling meadow in the Ukraine. Miles of horizon on land or sea gave a man pause to reflect. Gagarin saw the two jobs as not all that different. If he couldn't sail, he would be a farmer. Both occupations united man with the forces of nature in a delicate balance, much like the thin line of fortune that separates the conqueror from the vanquished. The most successful farmers understood this basic axiom. So did successful captains.

"Mastheads twenty degrees off the port bow!" the lookout bellowed.

"What do you see, Victor?" he yelled, turning his binoculars to the bearing.

"Must be warships! Low silhouettes!"

Dammit! The KGB and the M1 man had it perfectly figured out!

"Can you determine nationality?" He held his breath.

"Pagoda superstructures. Dear God, they're Japanese!"

The worst had happened. He had to pray that the line of reasoning the fucking KGB man and that bastard Englander had advanced would hold water. In the wheelhouse the ship's helmsman anxiously stood by for the order to change course, but Gagarin already knew that if he had seen the Japanese battleships from his low-slung bridge, they had definitely seen *Uritsky*'s bulk from their towering masts.

"Two destroyers heading toward us! I see…I see a carrier now. Make that two…no, three carriers!"

"Easy, Victor. Stay on them!" Gagarin ran to the communications shack on rubbery legs. He hadn't been this scared since Tsushima. He pulled out the coded message he'd received in San Francisco, and addressed the young radio operator, "Nicholas, be calm. Set the radio to this frequency, and tap out these code numbers. This will tell the Japanese we mean them no harm."

"They're turning their guns on us! Captain!"

"Ignore him, Nicholas. Go ahead."

The radioman did what his captain instructed. Miraculously, the destroyers turned away, and minutes later, the Japanese force disappeared into the mist.

"Captain, why didn't they shoot at us?" Victor asked, warming himself in the radio room.

"Shooting at us might force the USSR to declare war on them."

"If they're up in these latitudes, they can only be up to no good," Victor said. Worry left his eyes, and astonishment took its place. "They're going to attack the Americans at Dutch Harbor in the Aleutians! Yes! That's it!"

"Who knows?" Nicholas said, "but shouldn't we warn the Americans?" He turned to the radio set, sure his captain would do something so plainly necessary. "After all, they..."

"Get away from there, Victor," Gagarin said calmly.

"Sir?"

"We were spared today. Let's leave it at that, shall we?" he said, reaching over to turn off the radio.

"What was that you had me send, Captain?" Nicholas asked.

"I have no idea, nor do I care, and neither should you two." He pointed a stubby finger directly at Nicholas' nose, and glared at Victor. "Forget it. Tell no one. Give thanks you are alive."

"I will obey, Captain, but I don't understand."

"I think we just helped to defeat Hitler," he answered as he stretched. At least that's what the KGB and M1 men had told him.

Victor looked at Nicholas totally confused. He put the radio in the "receive" mode, being careful not to touch the "send" key.

Captain Gagarin sailed the *Uritsky* into the night, and out of history.

0300 Hours, December 4, 1941
Pearl Harbor

It was three in the morning when they left the hospital. Andy volunteered to find Yuri. Jack couldn't go along; he was needed at home with the children—Julie's broken arm and jolted spirit required complete rest tonight. Tommy went to talk with the Shore Patrol who retrieved the Mercury. They had a few questions to ask about the condition of the car. They really wanted Jack Burns to come, but they understood his predicament. Andy drove Mae home, tucked her in bed, and headed for the British apartments in Honolulu.

Yuri had lost it. He sat in a corner rocking back and forth with a picture of Yvette in his arms. "Mama, I let you down again. Little Nina died because a huge horse rolled over on her, Mama!" he sobbed. "Papa couldn't save you. Mama, please speak to me!" he sobbed.

Andy Seghesio pulled into a parking space, and looked up at the dim light in Yuri and Yvette's apartment window. He turned off the ignition and took a deep breath as he put on his cap. This wasn't going to be easy. He climbed the stairs to the second floor, thinking the last time he had done this was to help Mae with Yvette's surprise baby shower.

Preoccupation with his morbid task led him to knock on the wrong door. Shears answered.

"I'm sorry to disturb you, but I'm looking for Yuri, and..."

"He's not home," the admiral wheezed. "He's out running errands for me. Is there anything I can do for you, Colonel Seghesio?"

Andy was embarrassed at his error at a time like this. He should let Shears know about Yvette, he quickly reasoned. After all, she did work for him. "Yvette was killed in an automobile accident this afternoon, and I…"

"My God! What will Yuri do when he finds out?" Shears said, feigning shock. "We're due back in Singapore in two days."

"I want to tell him myself. May I wait until he returns?"

Shears was caught off guard. He had to let the American honor his moral obligation. To do otherwise would raise suspicion. "Surely. Make yourself at home," he said, pointing to the couch.

"If I am imposing, sir, I can leave." It was then that Andy saw the bright red tanks and what he recognized as plastic explosive in an adjoining room. His discovery was not lost on Shears.

"I must make a phone call to our diplomatic representatives about this turn of events, Colonel Seghesio. Please excuse me." He looked unaccountably nervous.

"Of course." As he watched Shears dial the phone, Chad Eversole crept up and smashed a night stick on the back of Andy's head.

"Put him in his car and get rid of him," Shears directed. "We've got our work cut out for us. Sunday is coming."

"What about Yuri?" Eversole asked.

"Yuri must complete the job he bungled this morning. If Burns learns why his wife had the accident, our positions here will be compromised. I would think Yuri would be quite willing to give it all for Great Britain, don't you."

Eversole stared in numb agreement.

Chapter 18

Shears' and Popov's Chevrolet sedan hastily departed the Aiea apartment complex and disappeared into the night. Chad Eversole was left to cope with Andy Seghesio's inanimate body. Slightly built compared to the well-muscled Marine, he dragged him feet-first down the staircase after carefully wrapping the bloody head in several towels to avoid leaving a trail as Andy's head bounced off each steel step. He stuffed him in the trunk of his own Dodge convertible, which he planned to drive to a seedy area of Honolulu frequented by servicemen. King, River and Hotel streets were well-known for prostitution, raucous bars, opium dens, and interests that were generally categorized as the darker side of human activity. That a naked body would show up in a vehicle without a license plate in that den of iniquity was not unusual. It might be days before the car was examined and the trunk opened.

Out of breath, Eversole loaded his Beretta, screwed on the silencer, and stuffed it in his waistband. He jumped behind the wheel and started the Dodge.

The car bucked and backfired as Eversole guided it onto Honolulu Boulevard. Puffs of black smoke burst from the tailpipe when Eversole downshifted to merge with the traffic. The car's engine died with a gasp and a wheeze, and would not be resuscitated. With dimmed headlights, he guided its drift to the side of the four-lane road.

Eversole cursed his damned luck. It would upset his timetable considerably. When a moan arose from the trunk of the inert car, his anxiety reached new heights. Son of a bitch! That whack on the head should have killed anybody, but not that thick-headed wop-of-a-Marine in the trunk. He reached for the Beretta. He'd wait for a lull in the traffic, open the trunk, shoot him, and run off. He had seen enough Hollywood movies to assure himself that things like this happened all the time in an America, even in Hawaii. It would take three seconds, he estimated, as he grabbed the door handle and flung the door open, but things went badly again.

The bumper of a passing Dole Pineapple truck ripped the door off its hinges, and dislocated Eversole's left arm as he gripped the door handle. He lay on the concrete and howled in pain as the nervous driver screeched to a halt, and came on the run.

"Hey! Are you all right? Where are you hurt?" the Hawaiian native asked. Eversole turned quickly, pointing the Beretta directly at his head.

"Get in the car!" he ordered. The startled man jumped back in fear. "Get in the fucking car or I'll kill you right here, you fat bastard!" he yelled.

The cowering Hawaiian did as he was ordered. Eversole held the pistol three inches from the Hawaiian's temple and fired. He was about to move to the trunk to finish the job on Andy when a police car came to a halt across the street. The moaning from the trunk became louder and the pain in his shoulder intensified. He quickly returned the Beretta into his waist, then walked to the rear of the still-running Dole truck and waited there, his hand to his face.

"What happened?" the cop asked.

"I…don't really know," Eversole responded, with feigned anxiety. "I was driving behind that car. The driver pulled over and tried to get out, but he flung the door open so fast I couldn't avoid it. When I stopped, I see the guy in the passenger seat pull out a pistol and shoot the other one. Sweet Jesus! Look at the blood. Lord, he's got to be dead!" Eversole made himself gag for effectiveness. It had the desired effect.

"Easy, now. It's okay. Can you continue?"

"Yes," Eversole gasped. "Then he waves the pistol at me and screams I better forget everything I've seen. Then he ran off." He forced himself to vomit. "My pills! I need my pills! Heart…truck…glove compartment," he gasped. "Oh, the pain…getting worse!" he stammered, gripping his chest.

"Let's get your medicine," the cop said, gently moving Eversole closer to the passenger's side of the truck, away from the street. "You sound British or Australian," the policeman asked, in an effort to calm the panicked man.

When the cop reached out to help Eversole into the cab, he thrust his stiletto under the cop's sternum. The cop was dead before he hit the pavement.

Eversole took the cop's big flashlight and wrapped it in several rags he found in the truck. It would have to do. He stuck it under his left armpit, bit down hard on a rag, and wrenched the arm with his right hand. The pain was searing, but his arm popped back into its shoulder socket.

Across the street, pedestrians were gathering around the empty police car, and glancing at the truck and the car with a missing door and a dead man slumped behind the wheel. He couldn't shoot Seghesio without being caught, but no one would know him anyway; he was buck naked and had no ID. It would take at least twelve hours for someone to match him with a missing persons report. And Seghesio's concussion practically guaranteed he wouldn't remember how he got where he was.

Eversole dragged the cop up into the truck's passenger's seat, then ran around to the driver's side, jumped in, and headed off.

In the parking lot of a produce market at Pearl City across the harbor from the Ford Island naval base, he undressed the cop, and put his own clothes on him to further confuse the identification process. Every minute of delay, every false lead that had to be followed further guaranteed his ultimate success. He took the cop's gun belt and put on his pants. He then wrapped the officer's bloody shirt around a rock, tied the sleeves, and threw it into the harbor along with the truck's ignition key.

Eversole wondered how Yuri was making out with his end of the mission, as Yvette's death had had an unanticipated effect on him. The only other time he heard Yuri utter the name "Nina" was on the shore of that frozen lake over twenty years ago.

0400 December 4, 1941
Carrier *Akagi*, Pacific Ocean
800 Miles Northwest of Pearl Harbor

Genda and Fuchida had been listening to Radio Tokyo's programming for the better part of three hours on *Akagi*'s darkened bridge as she surged eastward into the predawn gloom. *Kido Butai* had just completed its mid-ocean refueling operation without a hitch, and the ships were tensed and primed for the high-speed run to Oahu. Fuchida kept his arms folded as he sat comfortably with his eyes closed near the operator's console. Genda paced furiously, smoking one cigarette after another.

"Damn them to hell! What are they waiting for?" Genda bellowed, thrusting his arms in the air.

"It is in the hands of the gods now," Fuchida said without stirring. "Relax. If it is meant to be, it…"

"*Higashi no kaze ame*," was the phrase that began and ended the weather report. Genda stood motionless, his body rigid. Fuchida opened his eyes and smiled.

"I guess that is it, then," Genda said, just above a whisper.

"Indeed it is! Tell our flight crews!" Fuchida said in jubilation.

"I think we first should inform Admiral Nagumo," Genda corrected.

"He already knows!" The diminutive Nagumo stood in the passageway. "I've been listening all afternoon." His face broke out in a huge smile. "Bring spears, enemy!" he blurted with fists raised in the air. It was an ancient Samurai expression that signified a wish to begin battle and end the agonizing prelude.

On the flag bridge of the *Nagato* at anchor in the Inland Sea, Yamamoto looked over the battleship's fourteen-inch guns to the bow pointing majestically eastward in salute to her sisters going into harm's way. He sent up a prayer as the sun began to rise. The next few days were critical to Japan's future. The flower of his country's youth, its resources, and the sacrifices of his countrymen to build such a mighty fleet that was about to stab at the heart of America's Pacific power lay in the hands of the Fates. One mistake in judgment, a freak chance of nature, an accident, one probing pair of eyes could cause a catastrophe from which Japan would not recover.

"The wind just blew!" announced a junior diplomat in the Honolulu consulate. Tomi Zai never felt such a surge of contradictory emotions. While the embassy staff nervously started burning code books and top secret documents, he climbed to the roof, and looked out to the enemy anchorage aglow in the dusk. He shook his fists high in the air as tears of rage and joy, disappointment and validation coursed down his cheeks.

2200 Hours, December 5, 1941
10 Downing Street

Winston Churchill was in a bathrobe and slippers when an aide delivered the Winds message to him. A smile of delight lit his face, yet his eyes moistened.

"Anything wrong, Prime Minister?" the aide said.

"Nothing could be more right, my good man! I would assume that things are going very well, actually. Be sure this gets to Honolulu."

1900 Hours, December 5, 1941
The White House

"East wind, rain. That's it, then, isn't it," Cordell Hull said. "Magic told us this would indicate hostilities are imminent."

"Where is 'it' going to happen? That's the sixty-four dollar question," Admiral Stark added. "I hope Doug MacArthur is ready."

"The two troop convoys are half-way there. The first of the forty-eight bombers are due to take off Saturday night. We need a few more weeks."

"I think the Japs will be in Manila by then," Roosevelt replied. He removed his glasses and rubbed his eyes. He wheeled over to the window, and looked at the land he knew in his heart to be living its last few days or hours of peace. His eyes unconsciously focused on the young men walking down Pennsylvania Avenue, and he thought of the new novel he was trying to find time to read. *Their Hearts Were Young and Gay*—how appropriate, he mused. "Nonetheless,

I'll take my appeal directly to Emperor Hirohito. Perhaps, just perhaps, it might make a difference."

"It might, Mr. President," Cordell Hull said.

"Maybe not. I recommend that you send an alert to our forces," General Marshall cautioned. Roosevelt nodded in agreement.

"Right away, sir." Stark went to send another war warning, again with no specific information, to all of the United States' Pacific outposts.

"Perhaps you should contact the Russian and British consulates, Mr. President." Sumner Welles said. "They might be in receipt of some up-to-date intelligence that…"

"I doubt that, Welles. Besides, what would they share with us that we didn't already know, or they haven't wanted us to know at all?" Hull sat heavily in a stuffed armchair.

Welles could only frown. It was impossible to be a prophet in your own land, he thought. It was playing out just as Oumansky said it would.

0800 Hours, December 5, 1941
CINCPAC, Pearl Harbor

Admiral Kimmel grimaced as he read Stark's war warning. Were the Japs still headed to the Kra Isthmus? Borneo? The Philippines? Hell, were they heading for Diamond Head? What about their transports off Formosa? Were there any units of the Royal Navy besides *Prince of Wales* and *Repulse* in the South Pacific? Should he order a sortie to the Marshalls? What could he possibly do now? He'd remind General Short about the air cover for the fleet when they played golf Sunday. There weren't many Army planes flying patrols. He had reduced his own search area to the south and west of Hawaii with a few patrols alternating on the northern approaches, because he didn't have the aircraft. He reasoned that any northern approach was the concern of the Aleutian command up at Dutch Harbor, but he knew better.

0900 December 4, 1941
Pearl Harbor

"Hey, Hamilton. This is Clement over at the JAG's office. I'm investigating the Burns' accident. Do you know where Captain Burns might be?"

"He and Rochefort are at the British consulate. He's been trying to get some information about some joint operation we're running with the Royal Navy. Can I help you, Jerry?"

"Does he or his wife have any enemies?"

"Everybody loves Julie. The few who don't like Jack respect the hell out of him. Why?"

"Does he owe anybody money?"

"Yeah, the mortgage bankers. What the hell is this all about?" Clement was stumped. His investigation of sexual hanky-panky turned up nothing thus far. Jack and Julie were closer than George and Gracie. He decided to confide in his old friend.

"Listen, Tommy, keep your big mouth shut about this, but Burns is in danger. I'll send some plainclothes guys to the consulate to nab them, and to pick you up, too. We've got SPs going to his house to pick up his wife and kids. You got a weapon there?"

"I'm a Marine," Hamilton replied, not trying at all to hide his indignation.

"Sorry about that."

"Shit. Hold on a minute, Jerry. The other line's ringing."

"Tommy? Is Andy there with you?" Mae asked.

"No, Mae, he isn't." Hamilton felt a chill.

"He didn't come home yesterday. I was so out of it I may have forgotten, but I know he wasn't here this morning. I don't know where he can be. I've tried…"

"Hold on. I'll be right back." He picked up the other phone. "Clement, have you got something I should know? And don't give me that confidential crap."

Clement hesitated but realized Hamilton must be on to something, too. "The SP's accident investigation found that Burns' station wagon didn't have just a mechanical failure. Some clever son of a bitch sabotaged the brake's master cylinder. He just plain jammed it up. No fluid leaks to leave a telltale sign. The person who did it knows his shit, Tommy."

"Good God! Jerry, hold on." He picked up the other phone. "Mae, you said you haven't seen Andy since he went to see Yuri?"

"I…don't know. I'm still so woozy, Tommy. The pain killers they gave me must have really put me under. I just woke up and found he hasn't been home. I called Yuri but got no answer. I thought he might've gone straight to work. He's been busy, I know, but he usually calls if…"

"Hang on, Mae. I'll be right back." Hamilton picked up the other phone again. "Jerry, I've got Andy's wife on the other phone. She hasn't seen him since he went to see the husband of the British woman killed in Burns' wreck. I think you'd better get your bloodhounds out hunting Seghesio as well." He hesitated a moment. "One more thing—find out if anyone's claimed the body of Mrs. Yvette Popov."

"Right." Clement hung up.

"Mae, I'm going to have Lisa come over right now. Don't answer the phone or open the door for anyone else."

"Has something happened to Andy?" she asked.

"No. Please do what I ask, okay?" He hung up the phone, then dialed Lisa. When she started to ask questions, he said, "Just trust me for now. I'll explain later." He hung up and went to the safe, where he retrieved a Colt .45 automatic and three clips. He slammed one home, and pulled back the bolt. He put the other two in his pockets.

As Hamilton ran to his car, he tried to figure out who the enemy was. All indications pointed to the most unlikely candidate; he must have thought or said "British" ten times in the last ninety seconds.

1000 Hours, December 5, 1941
USS *Arizona*

"We're gonna miss you, Chief. Good luck," the Officer of the Deck said, holding his salute. Fighting back his tears, Jones stood ramrod straight and returned the young JG's salute, and said, "I'll miss you, too." Jones walked down the gangway to a waiting launch for the last time.

Cheers erupted from *Arizona*'s decks, guntubs, and masts as hundreds of sailors and officers waved their caps. Jones stood dumbstruck. Following an impulse, he did a most unusual thing for a chief petty officer; he blew a kiss to his family.

"Now, sir?" Josh Friar asked Admiral Kidd.

"Now, Josh."

Friar pulled the foghorn line, and *Arizona* wailed her own goodbye. The foghorn's low voice held a hint of sadness that brought the tears to his eyes. He turned away and stepped into the waiting launch. He would soon be on his way to the birthing yard where *Iowa* awaited his guiding hand.

The big man, still unidentified, lay semiconscious in the Honolulu hospital, his feet shackled to the bedpost, his head swathed in bandages. A police guard sat outside his door, and another sat near the foot of his bed.

A radio tuned to WGMB softly played in the background. Christmas music alternated with big band jazz. At the notes of Glenn Miller's *String of Pearls*, the man's bloodshot eyes opened, and he winced with pain.

"Who are you, fellah?" the officer got up and asked.

"Oh, God, it hurts." The officer pulled the man's hand down, fearing he might disconnect the IV running into his arm.

"Who did this to you?" he asked, after telling the other guard to get a doctor.

No response. The sick man stared at the ceiling and blinked. The doctor shined a flashlight into his eyes and saw that the pupils reacted. "I think we're getting him back."

"Any leads from missing persons?" the first cop asked.

"There's something about a Marine Corps officer," the second cop answered. "The driver of the car was identified an hour ago. He was a driver for Dole Pineapple. No priors arrests. His truck is still missing. How the hell he got in the convertible is still a mystery. We still haven't found any leads on our guy, either."

"This guy could be the Marine. What's his name?"

"Andrew Seghesio. A lieutenant colonel."

The man in the bed opened his eyes and looked directly at the officer. "Mae?" he muttered before drifting back into semiconsciousness.

"Phone them," the doctor said.

"He looks awfully young to be a lieutenant colonel," the first cop said.

Yuri Popov waited with intense anticipation for Jack Burns to appear. Shears had convinced him Yvette would still be alive if it weren't for Jack Burns. The brake job was to kill him, not hurt innocent women…not Yvette, or Mama or little Nina. It was to kill a modern-day royalist who wanted to take his country from him. That was it, just as America let England bleed. He couldn't wait to put a bullet in that bastard's head. He had been waiting on the rooftop since last night, just as he waited in the trees by the lake for his chance. He grew further incensed and delusional. A gray-colored Navy car arrived at the consulate. When Rochefort got out, he lined up the crosshairs on him, thinking the next to emerge would be Burns. He wanted to kill Rochefort as well, but that might keep Burns from getting out. He could pepper the car with bullets, but that would only lead to capture or death, and he wanted to die at the end of the mission, not before. There he was!

Yuri took a deep breath, let out half of it, and his index finger pressured the trigger. "Come on, you bastard," he hissed. "I've got to do this right. Show me just a little more, you bloody fucker."

At that moment, another car, this one a very business-like black, roared around the corner, its blaring horn creating enough disturbance to make Yuri take his eye off the target. Popov saw Tommy Hamilton emerge, yelling at Rochefort, who shoved Burns back inside.

Yuri resighted the cross-hairs and fired…an instant too late. The bullet smashed into the concrete just beyond Burns' head. Suddenly men with drawn guns were pointing at Popov. Screaming a line of profanity. He pulled back the bolt, fired several rounds at the car, then started to take out the men running toward him. He killed two outright, and wounded another. A hail of bullets started to break up the concrete at the top of the roof. One grazed his arm, another his ear.

He looked at the Japanese tied up and gagged next to him. The man's eyes bulged from his head when Yuri placed the .38's barrel to his temple and pulled the trigger. He untied the body and put the pistol in the limp hand. Yuri stuffed the rope in his pockets and put the gag handkerchief in the man's pants. He dropped the rifle next him. Bleeding like a pig, he ran across several rooftops and down to the Buick he had hijacked last night with its driver.

He would finish this another way.

———

Jack Burns had a what-the-hell? expression on his face as a bullet tore through the roof of the car and imbedded itself in the seat not an inch from his thigh. Another pierced Rochefort's hat as it lay on the seat between them. People in the street scurried to safety. He saw three men fall; others put a hail of bullets into the roof of the building across the street. Tommy Hamilton yanked Rochefort and Burns out of the car, just as another shot shattered the driver's side window. "I said 'close the door and get down,' not 'get down and close the door,' you assholes! You're like fish in a barrel in there!"

"Who's fucking bullets are they anyway?" Burns asked, while Rochefort put his finger through the hole in his hat.

"I'll be damned if I know. Who told you to come here?"

"Shears did. He told me he had some information on that XYZ exercise."

"It wasn't Shears. I called the embassy—he and Popov left last night for Singapore with Yvette's body. The JAG's office confirmed that her body was claimed last night from the hospital morgue by one Yuri Popov."

Burns' mouth opened wide. "Then who the hell called me? I swear it was Shears' voice. And why didn't Andy phone to tell me? He went to..." Burns suddenly thought of Eversole.

"Don't swear, Jack. We've obviously been duped. This XYZ thing is getting more and more mysterious. Even if it's a feint, what's it supposed to take our attention from?" Rochefort said.

Clement appeared with two men, pistols drawn. "Are you guys all right?" he asked.

"They're fine, but I think you ought to tell the captain here about his car," Tommy said.

One of Clement's men viewed the body on the roof. He was glad the man was a Jap. When he rolled him over, he was mystified at what appeared to be rope burns on the man's wrists.

1800 Hours, December 5, 1941

Mae Seghesio sat by Andy's side through the afternoon. That he recognized her and hugged her was a great sign, the doctor said. He smiled at Lisa. The blow he had been dealt was so severe that it had blackened both eyes and put concentric hair line fractures in his skull. His nose would bleed occasionally, but the doctor said the evidence of brain swelling had subsided. Andy couldn't remember a thing about how he had sustained the injury. He vaguely remembered Yvette's death, but couldn't process any information after that.

"Did you go to Yuri's apartment, Andy?" Mae asked, with Clement close by.

"I…I don't know Mae." He hesitated when the red oxygen tanks with their twin dials caught his eye. His face twisted in pain.

"What is it, sweetheart?"

"That tank. I've seen it before somewhere; I know I have."

"You're a pilot, aren't you? Surely you've seen oxygen tanks," Clement suggested.

"Ours are blue. The dials, though. They remind me of…shit, I can't remember," Andy said in frustration, holding his aching head.

"Hey, Andy!" Jack Burns said, coming in with two no-nonsense looking men in civilian clothes. "Whoa! You don't look so good. I looked like that once."

"Hi, Jack. What's up?"

"You'd better get your ass up, or you'll miss the war," Burns whispered. "Rochefort told me that the Jap embassy's chimney started spewing smoke when a coded message encoded in a weather report was broadcast by Radio Tokyo. It's too hot in Hawaii to light your fireplace. Rochefort told me it was expected. Something is definitely up."

"So why don't they black out the harbor? Christ, the place is lit up like Macy's at Christmas!" Andy said, looking out the window at the glow in the distant harbor. "Mae, maybe you and Jack should visit Kimmel and tell him how the blackout in England made it difficult for planes to see ground targets."

"We're too far from Japan to be considered a target," Clement said.

"Haven't you heard of aircraft carriers, Jerry?"

"They wouldn't dare."

"Speaking of carriers, has Rochefort found any lately, Jack?"

"No. That's why Joe keeps insisting we go on full alert. Others on Kimmel's staff are sure the Jap carriers are in their home ports, and they outrank him."

"The operation with the British. Has anyone found out what we're doing?"

"It's odd you remember that, Andy. Was XYZ mentioned when you went to see Yuri about Yvette?" Clement asked.

Andy closed his eyes and rubbed his chin, trying to bring an image out of the fog. "There's something about the British that..." It wouldn't come, no matter how hard he tried. "Shit! This is driving me nuts!" he yelled, throwing a pitcher of water across the room.

"Andy!" Mae said, grabbing his massive arms.

"I know, pal. I know. I've been there." Burns put his hand on his friend's shoulder. He saw Andy's eyes had focused again on the red oxygen tank.

2100 Hours, December 5, 1941
Waikiki Beach

Chief Gwyeth Jones wanted to get drunk. Try as he might, it just didn't happen, and the effort at the Royal Hawaiian was costing him a fortune. A couple of the bar girls tried to entice him, but he decided to go back to the barracks and turn in. He had some things to square away in the morning. Then he'd have the rest of the day to catch the fleet band competition at the Bloch Recreation Center. First he'd walk to the beach, take his shoes off, and shuffle along the sand. It was snowing and bitter cold back east where *Iowa* awaited him, and it would be at least a year before he'd be back here again, if at all. Even if *Arizona* hated it here, he loved it. As he walked, he got the distinct feeling he was being followed. He turned quickly but saw nothing, except the shadows of the palm trees lining the beach. The pounding surf blocked all but the loudest noises. He shrugged and started walking.

"Hold it right there, mate." Something cold and metallic jabbed behind his ear.

"I've only got a few dollars in my wallet. It's in my pocket here. Take it." Jones slowly brought his hand to his waist, where a switchblade nestled in the waistband of his slacks.

"Easy, mate! Don't do anything stupid!" The metal pressed harder against his head. Jones had no choice. "Now that we're all calm, strip off that uniform."

"What the hell is this? Listen, I don't go that way, not that I judge, either. There's a place on Tenth and River where you can get all you want."

"Take it off! I can kill you and do it myself, if you'd rather!"

The accent was obviously Australian. "Okay, friend. You got me." Jones undid his shirt and pants.

"You want the underwear too?"

"No, but I do want the shoes and socks. Quickly!"

Jones complied. "Now what?" He spun around quickly and saw in the pale moonlight that the man was bloodied. Perhaps that's what slowed his reactions. He pushed the arm attached to the gun away, and pounded a fist into the man's jaw. The attacker fell, but still hung on to the pistol—a Colt .45 automatic with a silencer. The man started to bring the gun around, but the Chief scooped up a handful of sand and threw it into his eyes. Nevertheless, he got off two muffled shots, and Jones fell on top of him.

Yuri Popov pushed the body away and dragged himself to the water to wash his wounds. The cool water felt wonderfully refreshing, even on his sore jaw. That son of a bitch had one hell of a punch, he thought.

The swim gave him pause to think of alternatives to kill Rochefort and Burns. He had a fleeting thought that if the Americans didn't know anything now, they never would, and he should just rejoin Eversole to carry out the gist of the mission. He quickly concluded that was a rash assumption. The whole picture could change in twenty-four hours, especially with Burns' annoying penchant to probe. Had Yvette said anything before she, uh...? Probably not. He found himself wincing at the thought of her. Yes, Burns needed killing. He had to pay for Yvette, didn't he? And Billy. Shears wouldn't have it any other way.

It didn't take him long to arrive at a solution. He waded ashore, collected Jones' uniform, and was gone into the night.

—————

0300 Hours, December 6, 1941
Pearl Harbor

Shears and Eversole took the explosives into the shanty they had rented in Pearl City. The old battleship *Utah,* now used as a target ship, was moored directly in front of them across the narrow West Channel. Yuri was to meet them there when his part of the mission was completed, but he was uncustomarily late. Considering his mental state, Shears thought it might be better if he never arrived at all. Hopefully, the suspicious Burns and Rochefort were now neutralized.

The small boat they'd bought weeks earlier lay by the wharf, waiting for dawn. They aimed their binoculars southward across the flats of Ford Island to Battleship Row. Everything was as it should be.

"If intelligence has it right, tomorrow's the day," Shears said, looking at his watch.

"I should hope so," Eversole retorted.

"Indications are they are right on schedule. They should attack at seven in the morning. The yellow bastards will miss the carriers, though *Enterprise* might sail into the middle of the attack. *Lexington* left today to deliver a Marine fighter squadron to Guam," Shears said.

Eversole stood up and wiped his brow. He looked at the admiral who lived on hate and psychosis alone. It was frightening how a strong man could come to this. Killing and dying were all he had left. He hesitated a moment, but he had to speak. Too much depended on it. "Admiral, look out there. Is that a base ready for a fight? The Japs could come in a garbage barge and a zeppelin and destroy half the fleet. Why not reassess the situation? If we're caught, the results could be exactly what we've tried to avoid. We could be on our way to Singapore in…" Shears pulled a pistol on him.

"You bloody bastard! The only reason I keep you alive now is to help me get this shit to the target. Churchill said to watch you, that you'd lily-liver on me. He said England couldn't count on you."

Eversole's face turned hostile. "I killed two men for you tonight, and for your prime minister, you pitiful old bastard. I don't yet know what I did for England." He looked into Shears' tired, vicious eyes. "Don't dare preach to me about a sense of mission or purpose. I've cut the guts out of more men close up for England than you or that pompous red-headed bastard did with your ships or polo ponies."

The admiral nodded, and dropped the pistol away. "So you have. Then what will killing a few more mean, considering how good you are at it, especially these American sons-of-bitches?"

"Tomorrow they'll die anyway," Eversole said.

"The Japs have never attempted something on a scale as grand as this!" Shears screeched, his body riddled with tremors. "Look at the power these Americans take for granted, man! The Japanese could very well fail! How do you know that the fleet won't leave tonight? There are rumors that Kimmel wants to sortie at dawn on Sunday. How about if their *Enterprise, Saratoga,* and *Lexington* are really lying in ambush, baiting the Japs to attack those antiques out there?" he yelled, pointing to Battleship Row. "Tell me, Eversole. Tell me of your God-granted guarantee the Japs will succeed. Tell the people back home your beliefs after we've gone it alone for two years! Tell them the Americans won't make peace with the Germans after they've annihilated the Japs in six weeks! Tell the people in Singapore and Hong Kong they're now… Texans! Tell my wife. Tell my Billy…tell him…" he broke away shaking, in tears.

Eversole watched in despair as Shears collapsed to his knees. There was no way out. He'd have to kill friends to make sure they were allies. He, in fact, already had. How ironic that the first American deaths of the war in the Pacific came at the hands of the British.

"I'm taking the boat out to bury Yvette." At the shanty's door, he turned to

Shears and said, "What should I tell her when I drop her beneath the waves?"

0600 Hours, December 6, 1941

CINCPAC Headquarters

Under the watchful eye of two Shore Patrolmen, Joe Rochefort was talking to the executive officer of the SS *Lurline*. The liner had just arrived in Honolulu this morning from the West Coast. Rochefort was bone-tired, and tried hard to be professional and interested.

The officer was concerned about high-powered radio traffic coming from an area northwest of Hawaii, infrequently used by any ships, warships or otherwise. He gave approximate radio triangulation positions that were disturbing. Rochefort thanked the officer for his concern and casually said good night.

He broke into a near panic as soon as the man left. Had he found the Japanese carriers? He made several calls to Kimmel's staff, but it appeared he was the only one working as the rising sun shed its first rays on Diamond Head to officially annoint Saturday, December 6, 1941.

Chapter 19

"The clothes are of British origin, or maybe Australian," the Honolulu police detective said to Clement over the phone. "Witnesses saw a man on the scene last night who was wearing them. I don't know how the hell he came by them."

"Don't take it wrong, Lieutenant, but I've got to know. Was your guy a straight shooter?" Clement inserted a degree of hesitation in his voice.

"Malameula was a family guy, and a ten-year veteran of the force. He received several commendations for bravery and leadership. A good cop. More than that, a good man." The lieutenant choked up.

"Of course. Sorry. I had to ask."

"That's okay. I understand that more than anyone."

"What about that guy Oka we found on the roof? Anything there? "

"Not a thing. He was a devout Catholic, a family man, and one of our leading businessmen. Model citizen type. What the hell he was doing up on that roof with a rifle, I'll never know."

"We don't think he's the shooter, Lieutenant," Clement said. "He was a patsy used to throw us off, and it worked. That his car's still missing reenforces the theory. If you find out anything else, would you ring me up?"

"Do you have any idea what this is all about? If it's a security thing, I'd understand."

"Lieutenant, you know as much as I do. Someone is trying to kill United States military men, and we don't know why," Clement replied. "Good day."

"I know why," Tommy Hamilton said. "It's got something to do with the war warning and the XYZ thing. I swear the Brits are into it for some reason."

"Whoa! Don't let that get around," Clement replied.

"Frederick the Great said 'skepticism is the mother of security.' Do me a favor, Jerry. Go to the British and see if you can get anything on a Chad Eversole. I'd bet my last dollar he's here, and involved," Burns said.

He picked up an envelope from the flight surgeon. "Hey, here's some good news! I'm cleared for an evaluation flight. Finally! I've got to schedule it." He ran to the phone.

"Who are you calling?" Hamilton asked.

"Some guys who owe me at the flight line. I want to log in some air time this weekend. It might be my last chance to call back a chit."

The rising sun found Jones face-up on the beach unable to move. He was freezing, in shock from loss of blood, and his tongue was swollen from dehydration. He heard voices that grew panicky as they approached.

The bullet had hit him in his right arm at the biceps, then glanced off his side. It literally knocked the wind out of him as it broke two ribs. The pain made it difficult to breathe.

"Holy shit."

Jones' blurry eyes tried to focus on the two in khaki uniforms looking down at him.

"Shit, the guy's almost dead. How will we find out who he is?" the other man said.

Jones' eyes opened wide. He pointed to the tattoo on his arm.

"BB-39. Wait a minute! That's a battleship! You're a Navy guy?" Jones signified agreement.

"You wait right here with Eddie, sir. I'll be right back with some help!"

Sir? I'm a goddammed chief! I work for a living! Who were these guys anyway? Couldn't they tell a working man from a sissy-pants officer? If he lived, he'd give them hell about that.

Eddie elevated his feet on a bunker of sand, and built another beneath his neck to straighten out his wind passage. He then took off his neckerchief and pressed it into the gash in his side. Cool water from the canteen sprinkled on his lips tasted sweeter than candy.

A few minutes letter a doctor came running up the beach with the other man, who carried several blankets. The doctor injected morphine and dressed the wounds. Soon thereafter, he was loaded onto an ambulance.

"You two fellows did a fine job," the doctor said. "You might have saved his life."

"We Boy Scouts have a motto, sir. 'Be prepared.'"

0700 Hours, December 6, 1941
Carrier *Akagi*

"The carriers are not in port. *Lexington* left yesterday, her destination unknown. *Enterprise* may return in the afternoon," Fuchida reported.

Ito Fujita howled in protest. "Then postpone the attack!" he said, to the laughter of his mates.

"Perhaps, Fujita, we should send you out to find the mighty *Enterprise*, rather than sending you to Pearl Harbor."

"Or better yet, you should explain the postponement to Tomi Zai, who provided us this update. What say you?" chimed in Fuchida.

"I say, death to *Arizona!*" he blurted. The roars of his mates lifted Genda's heart.

"There are still plenty of targets. Our mission is too great to be one-dimensional," Genda lectured. "We'll get their carriers later. What a battle it will be!"

"Tomi Zai would praise you to the gods for that battle, Genda," Fuchida said.

Nagumo paced nervously on *Akagi*'s bridge. Although he promised himself to be more forthright, the doubts returned with intensity. What if *Enterprise* and *Lexington* were lying in ambush? No one had reported on *Saratoga* since November. What if she had sortied from California to take part in the trap? What if the new carrier *Hornet* was forgoing her sea trials and was making her way through the Panama Canal? These Americans were not only rich in material resources; they were known to be resourceful, too. Maybe scores of B-17s were massing for takeoff right now in Seattle to land at Hickam Air Field this night to refuel, and attack him at dawn?

Nagumo saw there was a chop to the sea. The whitecaps made perfect camouflage for a lurking periscope, or the wake of a torpedo. There were a lot of submarines in Pearl Harbor. And there was that Russian freighter he had been ordered to ignore. Would he be the victim of the greatest double-cross in history? He should have sunk that Russian piece of shit—screw his orders!

Nagumo reread the operational plan Genda had drawn up for tomorrow's launch and recovery. He looked forward more to recovering the greatest carrier-borne air strike in history at midday tomorrow than launching it at dawn.

He went to his cabin to take something for his nervous stomach; and to pray.

0700 Hours, December 6, 1941
USS *Enterprise*

John Munroe watched four more of the *Enterprise*'s Wildcats roll off her deck to strengthen her combat air patrol. The radar officer gave the planes vectors to follow as they intercepted the Devastator torpedo bombers in their mock attacks on the task force. The longer-legged SBD Dauntlesses were out at the limits of their search arcs. He thought it unusual that they were carrying 500-pound bombs, but thought little of it. He sipped at his coffee as he read the operations order Admiral Halsey had just issued, and signed by Captain

George Murray, *Enterprise*'s CO. He almost spit out the mouthful that he had just ingested. It read:

1. THE *ENTERPRISE* IS NOW OPERATING UNDER WAR CONDITIONS.

2. AT ANY TIME, DAY OR NIGHT, WE MUST BE READY FOR INSTANT ACTION.

3. HOSTILE SUBMARINES MAY BE ENCOUNTERED. STEADY NERVES AND STOUT HEARTS ARE NEEDED NOW.

GEORGE D. MURRAY

CAPTAIN, U.S. NAVY

COMMANDING

APPROVED:

WILLIAM F. HALSEY

VICE ADMIRAL, U.S. NAVY

COMMANDER AIRCRAFT, BATTLE FORCE

Murray wasn't on the bridge, but Halsey was on his "perch," a stool on the bridge from which the entire flight deck of the ship was clearly visible.

"Sir, may I have word?" Munroe asked.

"Sure, John. What's on your mind?" Halsey said, exhaling a blue cloud of smoke, and stubbing out his Chesterfield.

"Sir, it's this order. This gives the appearance that you're out to start a war. Begging your pardon, sir, but is this authorized?"

"By that little Nip bastard Hirohito himself," Halsey replied, with a loud guffaw.

Munroe stood wide-eyed. Halsey went on to the next order of business.

"John, the weather is getting lousy. The scouts report it's kicking up the same all over their search arcs. I think we ought to bring the boys in. What do you think?"

"I think they'd better get used to enemies other than weather, sir."

Halsey laughed out loud. "I guess you're right. We'll keep this up for another hour." Halsey strained to look at the front closing in on his ships. "It looks like we'll have to slow down to keep the destroyers from getting banged up in the swells. This storm looks like it'll be a good one. There'll be no breakfast at the Royal Hawaiian tomorrow. We might make it for lunch, though. By the way, what movie's playing tonight?"

A chief spoke up. "It's *Sergeant York,* Admiral."

How appropriate, Munroe thought. What better way to bring in a new war than to celebrate an old one?

0600 Hours, December 6, 1941
Pearl Harbor

Yuri Popov was weary and hurting. His arm ached, and his ear seeped blood if he so much as touched it. Wearing the stolen uniform and the ID card he found in a pocket, he risked entry into the chief's barrack. When he got to the address on the billet card, he just as casually walked up to Jones' room and entered, if he were in a hotel. No one asked for an ID—no one saw him. The place was practically empty. Yuri owed it to the weekend.

He scavenged Jones' shaving gear and towels, and had a long, hot shower, listening carefully for any intruders. A first-aid kit hung on the wall at the end of the corridor. He made good use of it dressing his arm and ear before taking a clean uniform out of the closet. God knew where Burns might be now, but he would show up at his office today—and there he would die, along with anyone else who might be there. Then for the mission's final phase. What would Shears be doing Sunday when the Japanese arrived? What about Eversole? Could they make it to the consulate before the attack?

As he drifted into a fitful sleep, he dreamed of Yvette holding a faceless child, crying over his fallen body. He awoke in a sweat, hardly able to breathe.

The sky was brightening as he quickly dressed. He put the other uniform in a duffle bag and left the room.

0900 Hours, December 6, 1941
Pearl Harbor

"There were definitely two guys up there," Clement reported. "The Honolulu PD says the dead Jap's blood was A positive, and the blood splattered around the edge of the roof was O positive."

"I told you that yesterday," Hamilton responded.

"Yeah, wise guy, I know. But I have to prove it, not bullshit about it. How's Seghesio?"

"Still in a fog," Burns reported.

"I was afraid of that. In any event, you guys stay holed up there on base. I don't want you leaving for anything."

"Any luck in finding Eversole? That bastard is on this island. I guarantee it."

"We're not getting any help from the British. Either they know nothing or were told to shut up or are as confused as we are. I'd bet it's a blend of all three."

"That would be Eversole." Burns turned to the window, watching the destroyer *Ward* sortie for picket duty at the harbor's entrance. "Any help from Washington on XYZ?"

"We might as well have made it up," Rochefort said. "I can't convince anyone on Kimmel's staff that the Japanese carriers are lost. I get sympathy only from Ed Layton, his intelligence guy. Everyone looks at us like we're sunstroked." He thumped down on a chair, ripped off his tie, and dejectedly threw it into a waste basket. "That's where we're all gonna be soon."

0900 December 6, 1941
Pearl Harbor Naval Hospital

Josh Friar heard about the wounded shipmate who was found on the beach, but didn't dwell on it. A sailor found on the beach in a drunken state who met with some sort of evil was also not unusual. It happened. But when he heard about the tattoo he suspected the worst. At the hospital his fears were confirmed. After hours of uncertainty, Gwyeth Jones had been identified.

The Chief was sedated, pierced by two IVs and a catheter. Through the half-light he recognized his friend.

"Who did this? I'll kill the motherfucker. I'll tear him a new asshole." Tears streamed down Friar's face. Admiral Kidd and Captain Van Valkenburg were more subdued, but their anger was no less intense. Kidd gently but firmly laid his hand on Friar's shoulder.

His eyes seemed more alert than before. Jones mumbled, "Uniform?"

Friar had heard the rumors about the state of undress in which the Chief was found. "Gone," he said.

"Aussie," Jones managed, seeming more animated with each passing second.

"An Aussie got your duds?" Friar said.

The effort took the last of his energy. He slipped into unconsciousness, leaving the three men dumbfounded.

"We ought to let the adjutant general's office know about this," Kidd said.

Clement reviewed the transcript of the statement given by Friar and Kidd, comparing it that to the Honolulu PD's identification of the clothing on the dead cop in the pineapple truck. Both said "Australian or British." Perhaps because it wasn't unusual to see an Australian or New Zealander sailor or soldier in Hawaii, Hawaiians assumed anyone with a hint of a British accent was from the Land Down Under. Clement, however, had heard the word "British" from Burns, Hamilton, and Seghesio in connection with this XYZ thing.

What if he set a trap? It would be hurried at best, but perhaps it might work. He needed more resources, but it was Saturday, and his crew was already stretched thin.

It was noon when the *Arizona* first felt the angry, alien vibrations on her keel that charged the water with a static only her metal body could feel. The unbridled fury coming to her was something she had never felt before. Though the harbor was calm as glass, it felt as angry as it did in any storm, except this wasn't anger that nature displayed when she sought an equilibrium of the wind, sea, earth and sky to settle some ethereal dispute, sometimes in a spectacularly horrific display. This anger seemed contrived, manufactured for the sole purpose of causing…death. The only other time the sea felt somewhat as charged was during gunnery exercises, when she and her sisters exploded their main batteries—but this was so much more intense.

It emanated from northwest, an acrimonious portion of the sea of which *Arizona* and her sisters despised because of its unpredictable nature. The pounding of propellers against the billowy brine became more truculent with each passing minute. She saw her sisters felt it, too. *California* wallowed ever so slightly. *Nevada* pulled on her bow hawser. It wasn't fear of battle that caused the ships to react as they did; they were born and bred to live and die as warriors. It was the sensation of helplessness.

1200 Hours, December 6, 1941
Pearl Harbor

Tokyo wanted one more report on the ships at Pearl Harbor and the disposition of aircraft at Hickam Air Field and Ford Island, especially B-17s. Kaneohe Naval Air Station was added as well. Genda wanted those carriers and Nagumo wanted to insure his getaway would be clean. So Tomi Zai left at noon to conduct his final reconaissance.

He had become quite a figure around the naval base. A few of the tour guides even recognized him and greeted him by his pseudo-name. He was pushing the envelope by going back yet again. He didn't fear being caught, or even death, as much as being denied the opportunity of fighting the Americans in the aerial arena.

Tomi Zai drove confidently to Honolulu Airport for his last aerial tour over the harbor. To his great relief, a new pilot had taken the fat walrus' place. Thankfully, there was no explaining to do. He just kept smiling and bowed his head a few times like this buffoon expected and took snapshots of the pretty ships below.

1200 Hours, December 6, 1941
Washington, D.C.

"This meeting with Nomura tomorrow is fruitless. We've backed the Japanese to a wall," Cordell Hull lamented, putting on his topcoat. "I don't think it's worth a Sunday afternoon."

"Perhaps the president's note to Hirohito will make a difference. Maybe we'll be able to forestall…"

"The inevitable? Hardly, Sumner. The Japanese aren't going to let us build up the Philippines while their offense remains static. It's now or never for them, their supreme precious moment in time."

1100 Hours, December 6, 1941
Pearl Harbor

Yuri Popov grew tired of waiting outside the office. He had been there for hours, only then realizing that Burns must have taken the day off. It was eleven o'clock, and the building's parking lot was near empty, except for a Ford sedan with government plates. Time was running out. If he never came in today, a large part of the mission would be left open to chance. He'd better go inside.

"Excuse me," he said. "I'm Petty Officer Jones. I'm looking for Captain Burns and Commander Rochefort."

The pretty Hawaiian receptionist seemed nervous at his inquiry.

"What a lovely accent," the secretary said. "Where are you from?"

"The U.S. Virgin Islands. St. Thomas to be precise. We're more British than you would think," he laughed.

"It's sounds delightful. My goodness, what happened to your ear?"

"An accident aboard ship. Is the captain…"

"I'm afraid not, Chief. He took the day off."

Her eyes flickered unnaturally. "Do you know where I can reach him?" he asked.

"I'm afraid he can't be reached," she said, still smiling.

"Pity. I…" Popov caught a surreptitious movement from the corner of his eye. He leaped behind the desk, knocking the woman out of her chair. He instinctively brought out the silenced Colt and fired at the figure charging him, and again through the wall at the figure whose shadow appeared on the floor. They dropped simultaneously, their guns clattering to the floor.

"All right, you bitch! Enough fucking games!" The woman didn't answer. He punched her face and squeezed her breast until she screamed. "Stop screaming!" he said, pulling her hair and shaking her head, and slapping her several times. "Where's Burns? Tell me or I'll kill you!" he yelled, pressing the barrel of the Colt into the woman's nose.

She couldn't take it. It wasn't supposed to go this way. "He's at the BOQ at the Kaneohe Naval Air Station."

He pushed the woman away. She cowered at his feet. "Thank you for the information," he said. Something prevented him from pulling the trigger. Was it Yvette's face he saw? "Get up, Yvette." he said, suddenly serene.

"Yvette? I'm not…"

"Just get up!" he yelled. "And take off your goddammed stockings!" With them, he tied her hands and feet, gagged her, and locked her in a steel closet.

Both dead men were FBI agents. He took one man's ID card. It would come in handy. He took the man's money and decided to make a quick trip to the base PX.

He looked out the window and noted that there was nothing unusual going on. There was the Ford sedan, that apparently belonged to someone now lying inanimate in the office.

Popov pulled out the phone line before he headed for the lone Ford, conveniently left with its key in the ignition. At the base's gate he pulled out onto Route 99 for Kaneohe.

————————

Tommy Hamilton had been unable to sleep for most of the night. His mind couldn't let go of yesterday's treachery. Even making love to Lisa didn't relax him. He got out of bed at six, and took a long, hot shower. He promised Jack Burns some pointers on the SNJ, and he was one of the privileged few who knew where Jack was hiding out.

He was about to leave when he saw the .45 automatic lying on the dresser. He picked up the sidearm and tucked it in his waistband, put on his jacket, and gave the sleeping Lisa a peck on the cheek. She was sleeping in this morning and planned to visit her brother at the hospital. Tommy would meet her there.

As he drove to Kaneohe, he decided he'd stop at the diner on the corner for a quick breakfast. Even though he had an invitation to sit at Julie's and Jack's morning table, he turned into the diner near his apartment. The Burns' had been through hell, and he didn't want to put Julie to any unnecessary trouble.

————————

1230 Hours, December 6, 1941
Kaneohe Naval Air Station

Upon Clement's advice, Jack Burns spent Saturday morning at home. Julie needed comfort, and he needed his family. They had a long, gloriously fattening breakfast, spiced with a great deal of laughter. Mae Seghesio came by with news that Andy was doing much better.

"You still have the look of a losing quarterback on Monday morning," Jack said, when Joe Rochefort and his wife stopped in.

"The trouble is, I don't know how to win this game. What the hell is with these Australians, and is there a connection to XYZ? And, if I could kill a few guys on Kimmel's staff…"

"Do you think they're Australians?" Burns jested.

"I think they're British agents."

Julie Burns and Mae Seghesio turned to face Jack Burns, whose smile vanished. When he saw his wife's stare, he said, "Julie, why don't you and the ladies take the kids and go to the PX. They're bored, and can use some ice cream, don't you think?"

"Sure," she replied, almost pleased about the out her husband gave her. "Let's go, Mae. I think there are some things we really don't want to know."

"We'll be visiting Andy later. Maybe you can join us?" Mae said.

"Absolutely. Call when you're ready. I'll get us reliable transportation," he said, with a wink at his wife.

Rochefort picked up where he had left off. "Clement called this morning. A chief from the *Arizona* got his clock cleaned by a guy with an Australian accent. When they checked his room at the chief's quarters, all the clean uniforms were missing. The bastards might be parading around with our uniforms and ID's now. Why the hell would Austrailians do these things? There's nothing for them to gain. The British, though, have plenty to worry about. Just think about it, Jack. What if they …"

Burns waved him off. "Oh, shit! This is getting too surreal for me to digest, and you know I'm not a Anglophile. Maybe my check-out flight tomorrow morning will clear my head."

"I wouldn't bet on that, Captain Burns." There at the door, malicious as Lucifer himself, stood Yuri Popov, his silencer-equipped Colt .45 pointing directly at Jack Burns' heart. "Why don't we all sit for a minute? It's amazing what one of these badges will do," he replied, flashing an FBI shield. "Its owner had no use further use for it, so I borrowed it, so to speak."

"So you're not a chief petty officer anymore?" Burns asked.

"No. Your PX had a wonderful selection of casual wear. Don't you agree?" Popov said, opening his arms as a model would.

———

1230 Hours, December 6, 1941
Pearl Harbor

Jerry Clement felt a sense of dread when the base operator told him the phone was inoperative, the one he had used to call Burns this morning. He called the FBI to meet him at the office.

The little river of blood flowing down to the pool at his feet showed the worst had happened. Banging erupted from the steel cabinet. The door was locked shut. He ran out to the waiting car full of FBI men and took the tire iron from the trunk. He raced back in the building, two agents in tow, and forced open the steel door. There, lay the hysterical Linda Yamashita, a Nisei who worked in the special operations division of the FBI.

"Oh, Christ! Are you okay?" he said cutting her bonds.

"You'd better worry a lot more about that British son of a bitch than the Japanese. He is one mean bastard!"

Clement pulled several photos from his pocket and gave Linda a hankerchief for her cut lip. "Who was it?" he asked.

"This blond fuck!" she said without hesitation. "He's just plain crazy. He called me Yvette. Anyway, he's on the way to the Burns' apartment."

Clement looked at her in horror and ran out the door.

1235 Hours, December 6, 1941
Kanehoe Naval Air Station

Yuri Popov was like a cat who had waited patiently to catch a mouse and needed to torment it before finally ending the cruel game. "You pried too far into XYZ, Captain. Why couldn't you just let it go? You were a pain in the ass back in England with your damned code machines and your presumptions. You haven't changed an iota," he said, sitting down opposite the two men. "Then you decided to kill my wife. Why? I could have killed all your wives, and your children a minute ago, but I spared them. I even spared the whore who tried to play me for a fool at your office this morning."

"I didn't kill anyone, Popov. I don't know that much about automobile brake systems. Do you?"

"It was meant to kill you, you bastard, not my Yvette. Not my child. You knew, didn't you?"

"I didn't know shit!"

"Oh, sure. That's what XYZ is all about, to shove your country's two-faced cowardly denials up your asses! We won't bleed for you anymore, Burns!" he yelled jumping up.

"You're crazy, Popov," Rochefort managed.

"Crazy? I guess I am. Who else would enjoy this…"

"Drop it, Yuri!" Tommy Hamilton had his .45 pointed right at Popov's head from a window across the room.

"I…don't think so," he said, putting the gun into his mouth. He couldn't let it end this way.

"Don't Popov! You'll die for nothing!"

"Oh, no, I won't." Looking aghast at what Popov was about to do, Hamilton had let his pistol droop ever so slightly. It gave Popov just enough time to take the gun out of his mouth and empty it at Hamilton. Hamilton managed to duck, but was cut by the shattering glass, and a round actually took the hat from his head. A round broke apart upon hitting the radiator directly in front of his face. The fragments ripped into his cheek.

Popov crashed through the window, landing right on top of Hamilton, who struggled to his feet to meet his adversary. Popov scissored his legs and knocked Hamilton down again. When he went for Hamilton's pistol, Tommy punched him in the face, and tried himself to reach it. Popov kicked him in the testicles.

Hamilton writhed in pain, but if he didn't overcome it, he would be killed in a few seconds. He tripped Popov just as he was about to scoop up the weapon. Hamilton seized the .45 and threw it in through the broken window; before he could point and shoot it, Popov would have bested him. Popov saw Rochefort and Burns coming to the shattered window with the pistol. The FBI men and SPs were scrambling in his direction. He couldn't dare let himself be captured, not now, not after all this. Once again, Burns would live.

He ran for the road, with Burns and Rochefort the FBI not more than fifty yards behind them, guns drawn, but they dare not fire in the crowded barracks area.

Popov ran directly in front of a car coming down the road; a woman was behind the wheel. She screeched to a halt as Popov threw himself across the hood, rolled against the windshield, and fell off to the side. When she got out of the car, Popov pushed her away and jumped in. He gunned the engine and tore off down the road.

One of the agents finally had a clear shot. He aimed the .357 Magnum carefully and fired all six rounds hoping to hit a tire of the fast-diminishing Packard. They badly wanted him alive. There had to be some logic to the mayhem he had caused.

1400 Hours, December 6, 1941
Carrier *Akagi*

The sky was darkening and the ocean was developing and ugly churn. "It will get worse before it gets better," the weatherman said.

"How will conditions be at launch tomorrow?" Genda asked.

"I would say that if this was a peacetime exercise, we would cancel it."

1900 Hours, December 6, 1941
The White House

Roosevelt sent his telegram to Hirohito, beseeching him for Japan's moderation. At a dinner party that evening, he leaned over to Mrs. Roosevelt and said, "This son of man has just sent his final message to the son of God."

1400 Hours, December 6, 1941
Route 83, Oahu

The fuel gauge of the Packard was falling off rapidly. He had heard bullets perforate the trunk lid, and one had shattered the rear window, and had gone on through the windshield. Now it was obvious another had pierced the gas tank. A few miles later, the engine quit. It wouldn't be long before his pursuers caught up with him. He needed another car, and one was coming from the direction of the harbor.

For the second time that day, he stepped in front of an onrushing vehicle, his empty pistol pointed directly at the driver's head.

Tomi Zai had completed his airborne reconnoiter of the harbor. The only thing left to check on was Kaneohe Naval Air Station. The field was big enough to handle B-17 bombers, and he reasoned that Nagumo wanted to be sure the planes weren't secretly sequestered there, rather than at Hickam Air Field.

At a bend in the road where Routes 83 and 61 intersected, he saw the man standing in the middle of the pavement pointing a pistol at him. His first impulse was to step on the brakes; then he remembered he was a warrior, and was being threatened with a weapon. It was time to go to war.

"Son of a bitch! You expect me to cower again, you white demon!" he yelled. "Fuck you, Yankee!" He downshifted the Pontiac to second gear, slowing slightly, then stomped on the accelerator. He expected gunshots, but the man merely tried to jump out of the way. The fender caught his hip and flung him like a rag doll up and over the roof. He lay motionless on the pavement behind the car.

Zai backed up next to the body. He didn't need a pain-in-the-ass survivor to identify him. He picked up the .45 and noted it was empty and, oddly, equipped with a silencer. He stuffed it in his waist. He searched the man's pockets, finding the FBI shield, and the ID card of Chief Petty Officer Gwyeth Jones of the USS *Arizona*. This puzzled him. How could he be two people? The silencer and the double identity squashed any fleeting thought of humanity. This fellow was up to no good.

Popov regained consciousness. He must rescue what he could of the bungled scheme before the Americans caught up to him. Unable to move, he saw the Japanese looking down on him, and somehow he knew what he was dealing with. Zai's face might as well have been a mirror of his own. "You couldn't even do this right you Nip bastard. How the hell are you going to pull off that party you've got planned for tomorrow?"

Zai was stunned. "What do you know about tomorrow, Yankee? Tell me, or I'll kill you!" Zai screamed, picking Popov up by his shirt.

"Yankee?" Popov replied, coughing up blood. "You fucking slopeheads are even dumber than they say."

Zai looked with contempt on the white man as he took out the knife strapped to his calf, and cut his throat. He hauled Popov off the road and heaved him clumsily into the brush. Zai left the scene with a mind full of questions. Best tell no one of this encounter. He didn't need to be caught, not when he was so close to achieving an end to this ignominy. They were in no way near alert status and he felt confident *Kido Butai* and the Wild Eagles would make quick work of this place tomorrow. It wouldn't be much of a contest. In any event, Zai took great pride in the idea that he had killed the first American of the war before a bomb or bullet had been loosed against them. It was odd for an American to have a distinctly British accent. The thought was quickly forgotten, however, as Kaneohe Naval Air Station came into sight.

As Popov lay near death, he saw his mother and Nina reaching for him. Was that Yvette, too? Who was the faceless child she carried? He uttered "Yvette" as the light overcame him.

1900 Hours, December 6, 1941
Pearl Harbor

Afternoon shadows worked their magic on the hills surrounding Pearl Harbor. A confused and confounded Kimmel wanted to do so much, but could do nothing. What was the threat?

He noted on his calendar that the fleet's musical groups gathered in the auditorium at the Bloch Recreation Center to begin their warm-ups. The *Pennsylvania*'s group was the odds-on favorite to take it all. Maybe the music would provide relief to the angst building in his chest.

Andy Seghesio lay resting in his Honolulu Hospital bed, with Mae and Lisa by his side. Tommy Hamilton had been released a bit earlier in the day, his face stitched and bandaged after the fragments from Popov's bullets were removed. Burns and Rochefort stopped by with their wives for a visit, and told the Seghesio's the incredible story of Yuri Popov.

"I...I don't believe it. Do you think it was he who did me in like this?"

"Could be," Rochefort said. "This guy was no ordinary naval officer. He was an intelligence agent, for sure. If he weren't an ally, I'd call him a spy. We'll see what their consulate says."

"Not only do I call him a spy, I call him a son of a bitch. I'd just like to shake the hand of the fellow who cut his throat," Burns said, with not the slightest hint of remorse in his voice.

"Hey!" he said, turning to Mae. "I see the way you've been skulking around."

"Jack! Quick! Cut her throat!" Andy said, his sense of humor back.

"Oh, hush! Don't give that mad Scot any ideas!"

An orderly came in with a cart, and started to lift the red oxygen tanks onto it. "You won't be needing these, Colonel," the orderly said.

"You leave them right there!" Andy snapped.

"But the doctor said that..."

"I don't care what he said!" Andy saw the confused look on the young man's face, and instantly felt remorse. "I'm sorry. I didn't mean to yell at you. Please, leave them there."

"Have you started some sort of long-term relationship with these things? If I'm in the way, I'll just leave," Mae said, as the others laughed nervously.

Andy did not laugh. "They mean something. I don't know what, Mae, but they do. I stare at them hoping it will come to me."

"Andy, do you still think that Shears is..." Hamilton said.

"I don't know what I think. I just need to have them here for awhile. After what you told me about Popov, I think it's more important than ever."

"Popov? Who's Popov? The British Consulate swears he's in Singapore with Admiral Shears." Jerry Clement had announced his presence.

"You're kidding me!" Burns couldn't believe it.

"I kid you not. He's supposedly on the *Prince of Wales* as we speak. Chief Gunnery Officer, in fact. Are we impressed?"

2200 Hours, December 6, 1941
Pearl Harbor

Shears and Eversole dressed in the uniforms of a United States Captain and Commander respectively. They got into the powerboat and made their way over to the Navy dock in Pearl City just before midnight. They decided not to wait any longer; Yuri was an hour overdue, and they presumed the worst.

The two-man crew of a thirty foot Navy launch were just leaving their craft when they were approached by two officers.

"Are you men through for the evening?" the captain asked.

"Yes, sir, we are," answered the seaman.

"Fine then. We need your boat."

"Sir?" He looked at his crew mate in confusion. "We were told to be back here at 0600 to begin bringing shore parties back to their ships. If we..."

"Oh? Well, don't worry about them. We'll take care of that, for sure." With that Eversole shot the two men dead, his silenced pistol firing two shots to each of their chests.

Eversole quickly loaded the bodies in the powerboat and tied them to the seats. He then tied a line from the boat to the newly-acquired Navy launch. Shears skillfully backed the launch away from the wharf, and then steered into the harbor. Two hundred yards out, Eversole loaded the eight detonators and plastic explosive from the powerboat into the launch. He jumped into the launch, and then fired eight rounds into the bottom of the other boat. It quickly sank, taking the two seaman with it.

"Nice job," Shears complimented.

"It's what I do best," he said without expression.

"It's off to the *Vestal*. Now we can only hope our Japanese friends are on time."

"I hope they're successful," Eversole said, matter-of-factly.

"They don't have to be. That's why we're here. Remember?"

2200 Hours, December 6, 1941
USS *Hoga*

Chief Boatswain's Mate Joe B. McManus and Quartermaster Bob Brown had decided to forego their regular Saturday evening pilgrimage to Honolulu, deciding to play a rather blistering series of rummy hands. They wanted to be sharp and alert when the *Enterprise* sailed into port the next morning. It had been a grueling week for their Yard Tug, the *Hoga*. Ever since coming to Pearl Harbor in January right after her commissioning, the tug was kept busy by the rush of ships in and out of the place at all hours and at all tides.

"I've got you again! Three fours and four kings! Ha!"

"You cheating bastard! How'd you get those kings!" McManus yelled.

"You gave them to me! I had two, you threw down two going for that straight."

"Ah, bullshit! You got another deck up your sleeve," he accused.

"And you've got your head up your ass," Brown retorted.

"I'm tired anyway," McManus said, looking at his watch. "It's almost midnight. The *Big E* will be pulling in about 0800."

"She's been delayed by a storm, remember?"

"Oh, that's right," McManus said, yawing and checking his watch again. "Well, I'm still tired. Tomorrow's going to be another busy day, and the crew's going to have to work pretty damn hard. The replacements we're supposed to be getting haven't arrived, and I hear they won't be here for another week. It's double-duty again."

"How about one more hand?" Brown shuffled the cards as McManus watched. Every time he manipulated the deck, he always managed to pull up the ace of clubs.

McManus stared open-mouthed. He then looked directly at Brown and said, "You double-dealing dirty bastard. If this was Dodge City, I could shoot you and get away with it."

"Tell you what I'm gonna do," Brown said. "Instead of giving me the ten you owe me, make it five. I enjoyed this."

"Not half as much as I'm going to enjoy tearing your tongue out of your mouth!"

"What do you say we go into town. I'll buy you a drink," Brown countered.

"Okay, but I know it won't only be *one* drink."

Hoga was too young to understand the powerful, undefined forces charging her hull; she was barely a year old. She was more uneasy about the battleships. They pulled ever so slightly against their mooring lines, imperceptibly shuddered, and rose and fell fractions of an inch. They never reacted this way before, and it was unsettling.

Chief Jones was rustled from his sleep by the emanations coming from the ships; actually, one ship in particular. It begged for him to come and keep his promise, but he was too weak to move, as much as he tried. A doctor came to examine him and he tried his best to explain what he needed to do. He uttered, "*Arizona*. Must go!"

"Rest easy," the doctor said. "It's about all you can do right now. The ship will be fine without you." The doctor moved to the window. "As a matter of fact, she's all lit up, pretty as can be. I can see her plain as day. She's fine. You're much too weak. Nurse," he said, still staring at the illuminated battle line, "give me a hypo. Standard morphine dose, please." He injected the syringe into the tube connected to the glucose solution dripping into Jones' arm. Soon the Chief was off to sleep.

The doctor couldn't quite understand the connection some of these old salts had with the metal monsters. He wished he could, because the relationship seemed so special. He looked to Battleship Row once more, then he flipped the light switch on his way out of Jones' room.

Chapter 20

Shortly before 0500 Shears and Eversole brought their launch abeam to board the *Vestal* as she lay moored to *Arizona*'s port side. They arrived in the khaki uniforms of American naval officers. Launches were busy all through the night, bringing the crew back from shore leave or ferrying navy yard workers and their equipment to complete various tasks to make the ship ready for her upcoming yard period at Bremerton. With so much equipment coming and going, the explosives didn't seem anything unusual. They wasted no time in bringing them forward across the *Vestal* to the hatch in *Arizona*'s bow that gained entry to the forward fourteen-inch turret and its accompanying magazine, three armored decks down. Its access was protected by yet another watertight door. Their presence wasn't questioned. With each passing minute, though, Shears seemed to weaken more.

"The shell magazines are a bit forward," he said, grimacing in pain. "We can reach them through..."

"Where's the black powder magazine?" Eversole asked.

"What are you talking about? We need the fourteen-inch shell locker," Shears said, looking annoyed.

"We can't set off a fourteen-inch shell with our stuff. The damned thing's too thickly built to penetrate. The shell needs to be traveling nearly at the speed of sound and make impact before it goes off. That's why they're able to survive the blast from the gun barrels, right?" Eversole said, his face expressionless.

"The *Hood*'s magazines went up when *Bismarck*'s shells..."

"Were traveling with tremendous energy at the speed of sound and detonated after piercing the ship, about a fifth of a second after impact. A direct hit of that type, shell-on-shell, would have done it. More than that, the powder would've gone up. We can't create that kind of energy here. It's easier to set off the black powder the ship uses for ceremony. It's nasty, volatile stuff and will generate sufficient heat to set off the gunpowder bags. That magazine is located amidst the smokeless powder store for her forward fourteen-inch batteries. That should do the trick, with a little help from the plastique we brought."

Shears felt side-stepped, cheated. He had been removed from the heart of the mission's brain-trust. "The prime minister said you had tested…"

"To hell with him! Do you think that troll of a man knows anything about what we need to do here? If we, or more likely, you, told him about this inconsistency, he would have done something even more irrational than this insanity. I work for England, not Winston Churchill. He would only have risked angering the United States by doing something more obvious and immoral than what we're doing now."

"Who is 'we,' Eversole?" Shears' expression never changed.

"Yuri and I—before I let you drive him mad. We were father and son, much like you and your Billy. The difference is, your son died with dignity. Mine… well, I'm sure that wasn't considered by you, or your fucking prime minister."

"Don't you speak of my son! Don't…"

Eversole slapped Shears full force with the back of his hand. "Shut up, you pathetic bastard! You can have me arrested, should we survive. But right now, I need you to lead me to the black powder magazine, or I'll put you out of your misery right here and now!"

0500 Hours, December 7, 1941
Opana Heights

Privates Joe Lockard and George Elliot powered up the radar set as the eastern sky showed the first faint trace of daylight around Opana. It was four in the morning and they still had "sack tracks" on their faces.

"Tell me, Joe. Who gets up this early? Does anybody attack this hour of the morning?"

"It's the northeast sector they're worried about. I understand there ain't enough search planes to patrol it, so here we are."

"Did you bring anything to eat?"

"I got some muffins and coffee in there," Joe answered, pointing to the little supply trailer that sat next to the radar trailer. "It's only a four-hour shift; we'll be back in time for breakfast."

"As long as they remember to pick us up."

The sweeping green lines of the set showed nothing unusual. It would be a long four hours. It was an absolutely difficult task just to stay awake. Elliot turned on the radio, hoping a radio station might be found to aid in the task. Surprisingly, WGBM came to life. "Hey, how about that! I wonder why they're broadcasting so early?"

"It's to give a heading to an incoming flight of B-17s flying in from the States. They should be here in time for breakfast, too."

0430 Hours, December 7, 1941

Kido Butai

Aboard the carriers of *Kido Butai*, Genda's and Fuchida's airmen were eating a ceremonial breakfast of *sekihan*, rice boiled with small red beans. It was a welcome change from the daily regimen of salted fish, rice, and barley. Aboard *Akagi*, Ito Fujita was as a happy as a lark.

"So, Fujita, are you ready to meet with destiny?" Fuchida asked.

"My heart never felt so light and free, Commander. I even prayed for the enemy to give full battle and not disgrace himself. It will make victory all the more glorious."

"That is so. Good luck to you! May your bomb find its mark!"

"Do not harbor any doubt of that, Commander," he replied. Fuchida pulled him full to his chest and hugged him.

Akagi's meteorologist intently studied his instruments. The sky remained dark, with dense clouds at three thousand feet. The sea was rough, creating a crescendo of white water with each wave that met the ship's bow.

"My advice would be to cancel the raid," the meteorologist said with a grin.

"Ha! What's the weather over the target?" Genda asked.

"Sunny and mild with unlimited visibility."

"On to Pearl Harbor!" he exulted.

Genda turned to see Admiral Nagumo just behind him, looking confident and eager in a neatly pressed uniform to begin the day's work. Genda saluted him smartly, and he returned it with a snap. "Signal the force to turn into the wind and prepare to launch the first wave," Nagumo ordered Admiral Kusaka, his chief of staff. "Order *Tone* to launch the reconnaissance aircraft."

"Order pilots to their aircraft!" *Akagi*'s Captain Aoki, growled to the officer of the deck.

As men of descending rank scrambled to obey the orders of their superiors, Genda saw *Kaga, Hiryu, Soryu, Shokaku,* and *Zuikaku* turn their bows in unison with *Akagi*, their escorting battleships, cruisers, and destroyers following suit. The pilots clambered up to the flight deck carrying updated target maps, courtesy of Tomi Zai, and rations of rice balls and chocolate for the long flight. Squadron leaders carefully positioned their samurai swords upon settling into cockpits, as their mechanics strapped them in. One by one, the powerful engines roared to life. Blue flame shooting from their exhausts created an eerie electric light that was refracted by the seamist and blown back by the spinning propellers to envelope the carriers' flight decks in a translucent sapphire cocoon. The sea seemed to calm, almost as if intimidated by the power of *Kido Butai*'s main battery.

The moment for which he had planned for years was upon him. Genda could not stop the tears coursing down his cheeks, silently asking the gods to grace Admiral Yamamoto. He raced to the flight deck to embrace Fuchida as he made his way to his bomber and to wish him good luck.

"Also wish me good hunting!" Fuchida said, his face aglow with confidence and passion.

A deck officer offered Fuchida a *hachimaki,* a white scarf carrying the Rising Sun emblem. "The crew wishes you to wear this for them, Commander," the man said.

Fuchida tied the scarf around his helmet, then saluted the man, who was overcome with emotion. Fuchida realized Japan would never again have a day so glorious as this.

At precisely 6:15 a.m., Fuchida rolled his Nakajima B5N2 with an 800 kilogram bomb attached to its belly off *Akagi's* bow, followed immediately by Ito Fujita and 180 other bombers, fighters, and torpedo planes. He was 230 miles north of Oahu. Climbing through the low-hanging cloud cover, he tuned his radio to WGBM, which had mysteriously played all through the night. It gave the weather over Hawaii as perfect, with a slight north wind. Fuchida corrected his course accordingly.

Aboard *Nagato*, Yamamoto rose at 1:00 a.m. Tokyo time, where it was already December 8, because of the Dateline, and ate a hearty breakfast, the same as his Wild Eagles were eating now. He cordially greeted his staff and sat down for the long wait until he would hear Fuchida's message regarding the status of the American defenses. "*Tora, Tora, Tora,*" would indicate the Americans had been caught by complete surprise. His midget submarines must be crossing the harbor entrance about now. He sent up a silent prayer for their brave crews.

0600 Hours, December 7, 1941
USS *Arizona*

CPO Zachariah Foster began his Sunday inspection tour a bit earlier than usual. He wanted to spend some time ashore with his old friend Gwyeth Jones again today. If he was lucky, he might even be in time for the breakfast he knew that Friar kid would whip him up.

Foster started with the rearmost turret today, whose crew had been getting a bit sloppy in keeping the turret as pristine as he demanded. The old hands taking advantage of a new ensign. While those slimy bastards might think they could fuck with a ninety-day wonder ensign right out of Harvard, they'd be suicidal to fuck with him.

0630 Hours, December 7, 1941
Ford Island Naval Air Station

Jack Burns kissed Julie goodbye and headed for Ford Island. Today's check-out flight would be short, but he relished the opportunity. He drove mechanically, pondering the Popov affair, troubled by Yvette's…murder. Yes, it was murder. And, he was further troubled by her dying plea to "stop Yuri!" And he was troubled by her dying act of ripping Mae's pearl necklace. He hurt for Andy, as he knew the pain of being earthbound.

Beyond all that, he realized he harbored tremendous anger. He wanted so badly to get a hold of Shears and that bastard Eversole. The more he thought about XYZ, whatever the hell it was, the more he was convinced that Eversole had something to do with it. That was no ghost he had seen that night on the *Arizona* a few months ago.

Burns looked at the brightening sky that heralded a beautiful day for flying. The SNJ was no Dauntless dive bomber, but he'd take things one step at a time. A captain now, he had to display patience. He pulled into the parking lot and was greeted by the check-out pilot, Commander Louis Zimmerman. "Zims" was an old friend from *Saratoga* days and had flown his wing when they had "attacked" Pearl Harbor a lifetime ago.

"Glad to have you back, Skipper!" Zimmerman said, shaking his hand. "I'm glad it's me that will get you through this. Why don't you ground-check the bird? We shouldn't waste any time getting up there to see the rising sun."

"I've been looking forward to this for a lifetime, it seems." He felt odd at Zims' metaphor for dawn, for a reason he could not nail down. The excitement of his coming adventure took precedence in his mind.

Jack was almost as nervous as a fledgling about to solo for the first time, but the name "Zimmerman" stirred yet another uneasiness that he couldn't put his finger on. He chalked it up to anxiety as he smiled at Zim and got into the J's front seat.

0630 Hours, December 7, 1941
USS *Enterprise*

The *Big E* was 215 miles directly west of Pearl Harbor at 0600 as John Munroe launched from her deck into the rising sun. He was accompanied by seventeen other SBD Dauntlesses of Scouting Squadron Six. Each carried full magazines of ammunition for their guns and a five hundred-pound bomb. It was their mission to scout for submarines as they flew on to Pearl Harbor, a day before the ship. The storm had slowed the carrier's progress considerably. One escorting destroyer, the *Dunlap*, developed engine trouble that slowed Task Force 8's progress even more. The *Big E* wouldn't arrive until Monday. Admiral Halsey had watched the takeoff, and was now enjoying a leisurely breakfast with his flag assistant.

0630 Hours, December 7, 1941
USS *Ward*

The supply ship *Antares* was heading into the harbor at 6:15 a.m. when her captain was astounded to see a small submarine porposing in his wake. He alerted the destroyer *Ward*'s skipper, Lieutenant William Outerbridge, who had already chased a ghost reported to him not three hours before. He again ordered his crew to general quarters, but this time he had a sighting. The old destroyer's four-inch guns opened fire on the sub, and several hits rolled it over. To be sure of a kill, he dropped depth charges. A minute later, an oil slick rose with a mound of white water. He sent a report to Headquarters, 14th Naval District. The duty officer there dismissed it, thinking that the skipper had killed a whale.

Two other midget submarines had entered the protected channel. Both were having difficulty with their gyroscopes and depth regulation. Their crews contemplated suicide, knowing their mission to torpedo an American battleship would be a failure.

0630 Hours, December 7, 1941
Pearl Harbor Naval Hospital

Andy Seghesio awoke in a sweat. His sleep had been full of red objects with black eyes staring at him. His subconscious interpretation told him they would cause harm. Fully awake, he focused immediately on the red oxygen tanks and gritted his teeth.

In a flash it was there! He rose too quickly, and his head pounded in protest; but he had to get to a phone. He staggered down the hall. Now he couldn't remember Rochefort's or Burns' number. A nurse tried in vain to stop him, and he kept going to the exit in his pajamas and navy blue bathrobe.

"Take me to the Pearl Harbor submarine base and step on it," he told the cab driver. When he noticed the driver staring at him through the rear view mirror, he simply said, "I had to get up and walk around. I've been having these nightmares."

0630 Hours, December 7, 1941
USS *Hoga*

Onboard the yard tug, *Hoga*'s Chief Joe B. McManus got up early and brewed a pot of coffee. Bob Brown was still asleep. With no big ships due in today, he decided to let the crew sleep a little later. He looked out over the harbor, and his eyes settled on Battleship Row. He blinked twice at the *Arizona*. He could have sworn the ship rose out of the water and settled with an unusual yet subtle motion. *Nevada*, moored just astern, seemed to do the same. McManus shook his head and headed below, thinking that he'd better give up hard liquor and leave the Saturday night whore-chasing and boozing to the younger men.

0630 Hours, December 7, 1941
USS *Arizona*

Josh Friar dressed quickly. He wanted to spend some time with Chief Jones before the ship departed for her stateside yard period.

"Mornin', Josh," Admiral Kidd said.

Friar turned in surprise. "Sir. I didn't expect you to be up yet."

"I couldn't sleep. I don't know why, but something about the ship doesn't seem right. I thought I'd nose around. So, where are you off to so bright and early on a Sunday?" Kidd asked, his faced creased with a smile.

"I'm taking breakfast to Chief Jones, sir. How about I whip up the same for you, sir?"

"I won't keep you, Friar. You're not on duty, anyway. One of the others will…"

"Beggin' the Admiral's pardon, sir, but that's my job."

Kidd smiled in amusement. There was no way that Friar would let him be handled by anyone else. "Very well, Josh. But let's make it quick. I don't want the Chief waiting because of me."

"How would you like your eggs, sir?"

Arizona rose ever so slightly under their feet. Kidd looked curiously at Friar. "Did you feel that?"

"Feel what, sir?"

0700, December 30, 1941
USS *Ward*

It was almost 7:00 a.m. when the *Ward* closed in on yet another sonar contact. Outerbridge ordered another depth charge run. Crew members thought they saw a cap of oil and debris rise at the top of a geyser of water. His report raised no eyebrows at headquarters.

_____

0700, December 7, 1941
Opana Heights

A little after 7:00 a.m. a lone blip coming in from almost due north had appeared on Lockard's screen, then disappeared. When he focused on the screen again, the blip returned, now much bigger. "Hey, come take a look a this!"

Elliot looked on in astonishment; then his professionalism took over. "I make it 3 degrees north, about…137 miles."

"I agree," Lockard answered, fascinated at the size of whatever was approaching. "You'd better call Fort Shafter."

Fascinated, Lockard stared at the blip that was closing rapidly on their position, steady in its approach and shape.

"They say its the flight of B-17s coming in from the States," Elliot said, hanging up the field phone.

"How can that be? The bombers should be coming in from the east."

"Let's just keep watching and see what happens."

"We're supposed to be off-duty."

"Yeah, but no one's come to pick us up anyway"

"Why am I not surprised? Hey, look!" Lockard said, pointing to the scope, "We're gaining on 'em!"

_____

0700, December 7, 1941
Pearl Harbor Naval Hospital

Chief Jones awoke with a familiar voice in his ears. "They are here! More are coming!"

He staggered over to the window. His eyes widened with each second. His ship had never been wrong before, and he had never heard her in such distress. His own clothes gone, he left his room and found a hospital linen closet a few doors down the hall. He quickly dressed in a white surgical uniform and made his way down the stairs. No one stopped him. He ignored the tightness in his side and his arm.

_____

0700 Hours, December 7, 1941
Japanese Attack Force

The report from the *Tone*'s scout plane was a delight to Fuchida's ears. The huge American base lay quietly asleep. He estimated the distance to target to be less than 140 miles, less than an hour's time to glory. He ate a piece of chocolate and drank green tea. He had never felt such exhilaration!

0715 Hours, December 7, 1941
Pearl Harbor

Tommy Hamilton hadn't slept a wink. He got up and headed over to the headquarters building at the sub base to see if Rochefort was having any luck with XYZ.

Lisa stretched as he kissed her, revealing the pretty satin nightgown that had set the tone for the previous evening's passion, which seemed especially good. If Yuri Popov's pistol was aimed a fraction of an inch higher, the bullet that splintered against the radiator would have gone through his head.

"Be careful," she said.

"Why's that? Is there a war on?" he laughed.

The phone rang as he was about to leave. Tommy listened intently, and his face tightened. "He did what?" he exclaimed.

"Who's on the phone?" Lisa asked.

"It's Mae. I think your brother has lost his mind," he said. He turned back to the receiver. "We'll be by to pick you up in a few minutes. Don't worry." He hung up and looked at Lisa. "You'd better get dressed and come with me."

0730 Hours, December 7, 1941
USS *Arizona*

Chad Eversole finished setting and arming the last of the explosive tanks at 7:35 a.m. He had worked feverishly for the past two hours to complete the task. He sat exhausted on the deck, breathing deeply for several minutes. Shears hadn't been the least bit helpful, too weak to move, too sullen to care.

"What time have you set them for?" Shears asked.

"They're to go off in about forty minutes. That'll give the Japs time to get their attack underway, if the Americans haven't already discovered them and put them under. We'd better be going."

"Does the ship have a full crew aboard?" Shears asked.

"It's none of our concern."

"I don't want anyone to die the way my Billy died."

Eversole was taken aback. "What? Don't you realize that the more men die, the more the outrage and reaction? Nobody will really care if an empty ship sinks, Admiral."

"Churchill didn't really care about Billy, did he Eversole?" Shears said, gasping weakly.

"I've told you time and again that Winston Churchill cares only about what Winston Churchill thinks. He can't help himself. Don't take it personally."

Shears straightened up and dug deeply for his last bit of dignity. "Disarm the explosives," he ordered, raising his chin with resolution.

"What the hell are you talking about, you bloody fool? I will not!"

"Get out of here, Eversole." Shears produced a pistol and pointed it in Eversole's face.

"What, again? Bastard! Just last night I pleaded for you to reconsider, and now you turn to jelly? You told me of your hatred for Americans and the craving you had to kill them all! Yuri and Yvette gave their lives for this, and you want to end it right before the payoff? I think not, you crazy son of a bitch! Now get up and let's get out of here before the fireworks start!"

"So now Americans die, is that all there is to it?" Shears said weakly.

"I want to follow my orders, which are to insure the United States gets into the war."

"I think not, Eversole. You're enjoying this too much."

"It's my job. I do it so well your god-like prime minister holds me in high esteem. Do you really think it was me he didn't trust, you idiot? Would he leave this to a man who can't focus? He gave you the illusion of command only to use your knowledge of the American battleships and your thirst for revenge, Shears."

The admiral trembled violently. "Then why only a few hours ago did you want to end this game?"

"It was my call. It was always my call. The harbor is asleep. Why risk being discovered? When Yuri didn't show up, though, I reconsidered." He glared menacingly at Shears. "This one's for *my* son, Admiral."

"I wonder if the Germans had the same attitude when they killed Billy?"

"If they were professionals, they did."

Shears' eyes lit up in anger. "You bloody devil! You deserve to die!" With the pistol pointing at Eversole's heart, he began ripping the wires from the timers and disabling the explosives. Eversole had to move quickly. The Japanese should be overhead any time now. He charged Shears, who turned and squeezed the trigger.

————————

0745, December 7, 1941
Opana Heights

"This thing is getting bigger. Are you sure they're B-17s?"

"What's their range now?" Elliot asked.

"Seventy miles and closing. And there's that other little blip again. See it here? Looks like it's turning west," Lockard said, pointing with a pencil.

"I'll contact Fort Shafter again."

0745, December 7, 1941
Pearl Harbor

Jack Burns felt like a schoolboy on the first day of summer vacation. The little SNJ soared like a falcon, and he relished every minute of it. The tug of gravity against his legs and arms as he performed rudimentary aerobatics was a sensation he had been craving.

"Good stuff. Let's take a crack at Battleship Row, shall we?" Lou suggested.

"Great. I'll shoot a few attack runs on them." Burns skipped over Diamond Head and saw a destroyer circling a debris slick. "I wonder what that's all about?" he asked Zimmerman.

"I dunno. Maybe somebody had an accident."

Jack climbed as he approached Battleship Row, wanting enough altitude to conduct a mock attack on the line of behemoths. Glancing at them as he turned tightly, he remembered Mae's artistically expressed comparison of the moored couplets of battleships to a string of pearls. As he focused on *Arizona* and *Nevada* his smile turned to a look of horror. "Zimmerman!" he shouted.

"What's up? Why are we skidding? How about a little less rudder, Jack!"

"Your name. It's Zimmerman! Dear God, why didn't I see it before?"

"What the hell is up with you? All of a sudden I'm a stranger?" The little SNJ slewed violently from side to side. "Hey, Burns!" the alarmed Zimmerman said, "You'd better get your head back into this or I'm taking over the stick! What's wrong?"

"XYZ. The infamous telegram...*Nevada* and *Arizona*, the western territories," he stammered. "The British knew then, and they know now! It makes sense. Oh, shit! Hang on, Lou! We're going in, and fast!" He scanned the northern horizon for the planes he just knew would be on the way. He saw nothing. "It's coming off today," he said almost in a whisper, "and it's been insured by Lloyds of London!"

Burns took one last look at *Arizona* and *Nevada* and knew they were the targets of double jeopardy.

"What the hell are you mumbling? What's Lloyds of London?" The little SNJ trembled, perched on the edge of a stall, as Burns made a tight turn to Ford Island, and headed for the runway, putting Zimmerman's heart in his throat. He took glum tribute in all but certifying his idea that the British had been reading JN-25 for years. Was there still time to do something? Anything? He looked at the Hamilton Chronometer on his wrist. It was almost 7:30 a.m.

1400 Hours, December 7, 1941
The White House

Roosevelt's conference with Stimson and Hull was breaking for lunch. The MAGIC intercepts Hull had received had him convinced something would happen today.

"The Japanese ambassadors have just requested a meeting this morning," Sumner Welles said upon entering the room.

"Probably to deliver the very ultimatum I'm holding," he replied. "The bastards are up to some deviltry for certain."

"But where?" Roosevelt asked.

"I bet our British friends might tell us that," Welles said.

"And why haven't they?" Stimson asked.

"Because it would ruin the plans they've had since 1939," Welles said.

Everyone in the room glared at him with silent malice. He couldn't have cared less. Being a prophet in your own land was fraught with condemnation. He'd seen it when Oumansky was ignored. Nevertheless, he tried to do his part. Perhaps someone in Pearl Harbor would be smart enough to catch on to the meaning XYZ. To be more direct in his cryptic warning would be considered just short of treason by many. After all, the British were our allies. Oumansky said the same thing, but the wry smile on his face implied the double meaning of that phrase.

0745 Hours, December 7, 1941
Pearl Harbor

Tommy Hamilton pulled up with Mae and Lisa a minute after the cabdriver had dropped Seghesio off, and cursed him for not having any money.

"I don't think you should go out in your pajamas," Andy heard someone say, "unless it's really important." He turned to see Tommy, Lisa, and Mae.

"I've got it figured," he said, pounding on the door to Rochefort's office. There was no answer.

"What might that be, dear?" Mae asked.

"Those red tanks in Shears' apartment. I know what they are," Andy said, smiling weakly.

"I'm listening." Lisa was trying hard not to laugh at the crazy man in pajamas whose head was swathed in bandages.

"They're explosives—for a big job. I should have known it because each of the tanks was marked with two different chemical formulas that when mixed make an explosive agent. I recognized the formulas in a dream I had last night.

I learned them somewhere, either at Annapolis or Stanford. I don't remember exactly. The gauges must control the flow and ignition. It's pretty sophisticated stuff. That son of a bitch Shears is about to blow something up. He must be a German agent, or maybe he's working for the Japs."

"Was it Shears who whacked you on the head?" Tommy asked.

"No. I remember looking right at him. It's the last thing I remember."

"Yuri?" Mae asked.

"I don't know, but Jack's right about the Brits. The bastards should've shot me," he said, seeing Mae grimace at the thought.

"That would have made too much noise," Lisa said.

"Unless they used a silencer, ala Yuri," Tommy suggested.

"But someone's finding me with a hole in the head in Shears' apartment or in the trunk of my own car could've been too risky, especially if I had been identified. Guns and bullets cause too much concern. It had to look like a regular mugging. Look at the trouble they went to in setting up that poor pineapple truck driver. He was shot to make it look like some kind of gangland violence. The cop was stabbed, but taken away from the scene to cause more confusion. Yeah, a whack on the head is much easier to explain. More people have baseball bats than guns anyway. This operation's got it all—deceit, trickery, double-crosses. We're still spinning in circles. Yeah, professionals did this."

"Remember the name that Jack keeps on bringing up? You know, the British agent he thought he saw on *Arizona*?" Tommy said.

"Eversole," Andy said, almost in a whisper.

———————

0745, December 7, 1941
Ford Island Naval Air Station

Jack Burns hit the runway hard. It wasn't that his technique was bad; he was just going to damned fast. He rolled the SNJ out, headed for the taxiway, and parked in a revetment.

"Lou, get to your headquarters, and see if you can get these fighter planes aloft and all the others dispersed. We're about to be attacked by the Japs," he said, scrambling out of the cockpit.

"What? For chrissake, it's Sunday. Nobody's here. What do you expect me to do?"

Burns stopped and turned to face Zimmerman. "Pray. I've got to find Joe Rochefort." He sprinted off, dropping his parachute harness, but not bothering to shed his leather helmet, goggles, or Mae West.

0750, December 7, 1941
CINCPAC

The night hadn't been generous in granting Joe Rochefort with any sleep. He had tossed and turned, finally getting out of bed at 5:00 a.m. to drive to the Headquarters building near the submarine base. There he had met with Ed Layton, Kimmel's intelligence officer, a fellow insomniac of late who met with him at 6:00 a.m. Both concluded that they would be at war by close of Monday. The Japanese carriers remained ghosts, but Layton was convinced they were off to support the invasion of Thailand or Malaya. "Where else could they be?"

Rochefort responded with a shrug of his shoulders. "Ed, I don't know where I am. I can't believe the whole scenario. We'll be at war in twenty-four hours, and we don't know where the party will start."

"Do you think that officer from the *Lurline* was onto something with those transmissions he heard?" Layton asked.

"I do, no one else does. They say a force heading in for an attack would maintain complete radio silence. They attributed it to some kind of wacky interference caused by a temperature inversion and the chatter from ships thousands of miles away. Ah, well." He saw it was 7:45 a.m. "The Officers Club is open. How about breakfast. I'll buy." Then he added, "Wouldn't it be more fitting if it were twelve hours from now?" A bitter smile crossing his face.

"Why's that?"

"Then we could call it 'the last supper.'"

They got into Rochefort's car and drove the short distance to the O Club. At 7:50 a.m. Jack Burns pulled into the club's parking lot the instant he recognized Rochefort's car. He stormed into the club, and stomped over to table, catching his quarry with a full forkful of egg in midflight.

"Let's go," he said. "And you, Layton, go wake up Kimmel. Tell him we found the Jap carriers, and the ceiling's about to come down on us."

0755, December 7, 1941
Pearl Harbor

Flying the *Tone*'s scouting float plane, Lieutenant Haruo Takeda loped among the puffy cumulus clouds surrounding the American base beneath him. Not one aircraft came to challenge him. It was like a sightseeing tour. He radioed Fuchida that no carriers were in port, though the old battleship *Utah* might be mistaken for one with her heavily timbered sides, a modification to protect her from shell splinters in her current role as a target-tow ship. She was occupying *Enterprise*'s berth, and she would surely be blasted by the eager Wild Eagles through mistaken identity. He made his last report to Fuchida and Nagumo, saluted the Rising Sun to the east, then headed due west. Perhaps, with a little luck, he might intercept *Enterprise* on her way into port. Then the aircrew's planes held in reserve could attack her, and that would certainly make him a hero.

He peered northward, and saw a myriad of tiny specks on the horizon.

0755, December 7, 1941
USS *Arizona*

Shears' bullet creased Eversole's shoulder, spinning him around. Shears was so weak that the recoil of the pistol made it difficult for him to re-sight the weapon on the target that still staggered at him relentlessly. Eversole punched him full in the face and pounded his ribs and abdomen, literally beating the breath of life out of him. When Shears fell in a heap, Eversole rushed to check the explosives. Only three were still functioning, but that should be enough.

"What the hell do you think you're doing?" Eversole's guts turned to lead.

"That son of a bitch is trying to blow up the ship!" He turned slowly to the huge man pointing Shears' pistol at his head. "Look at these! They're explosives! See the timers?" He pointed, looking as indignant as he could.

Chief Zachariah Foster eyed the officer before him with skepticism. He wasn't part of the ship's crew, and last night Jones told him about being shanghaied for his uniform. And those red tanks looked like big trouble.

"What are you doing down here?" Foster's stern face didn't crack an iota. His eyes glared at the violators.

"I was sent down by the *Vestal*'s skipper to see if we might weld a few plates to the deck above without the heat setting anything off down here. I found this guy busy at work, and the son of a bitch shot me!"

"Nobody told me about it," Foster said, ignoring Eversole's outstretched bloody hands. "These are my guns, sir. I rule this roost. Nobody does anything here without my say-so, not even the skipper." It was bending the truth, but he had to flush this man out, especially since he was trying to hide what had to be an Australian accent.

0758, December 7, 1941
Pearl Harbor

Andy Seghesio scrambled into Hamilton's car just as Burns and Rochefort pulled up, followed by Jerry Clement, unshaven and barely dressed.

"What's going on?" he asked.

"You'd better get some men off to the *Arizona* and *Nevada*. The British are coming and so are the Japs!"

"The British again? And Japs?" Clement's eyes opened wide. "Jack, you're confusing the hell out of me."

"Remember XYZ? It refers to the arrangement Germany's Zimmerman proposed to Mexico that got us into the World War. If The Germans won, they would reward Mexico with the territories she lost to us in the Mexican War, among them the states of *Arizona* and *Nevada*."

"The two battleships!"

"Very good, Jerry. And it was the British codebreakers who tipped us off on that one in 1917," Rochefort added.

"I saw the explosives in Shears' apartment. I know they're for one of them," Andy said, pointing across the harbor to Battleship Row.

"What's this got to do with the Japs?"

"Insurance, pure and simple. An ace in the hole. If their attack sputters, one or two ships would still be sunk for the outrage factor."

"How would the British know when the Japs are attacking?" Clement asked, struggling with the idea, but seeing black holes full of questions.

"The sons-of-bitches know to the second," Jack responded. "I'd bet they even know the Jap flight leaders' names. Everything that happened over the last week confirms it. They want to back us into this war, and they've done it. Look at us. We're confused and dead asleep! The perfect victims."

"So the British didn't tell Washington. But you said Popov mentioned XYZ to you, didn't he?"

Jack Burns spoke solemnly. "He picked up the name from our own coded messages and used it to further confuse us. There wasn't any official opperation Washington knew about. Someone back there was tipped off by somebody else, and in turn covertly tried to tip us off with the information, hoping that we could get to the bottom of it all. Washington persists in believing we can play this game of 'peaceful' war for a while longer to buy time. You can make up all kinds of wonderful stories if you ignore the facts, or worse, interpret them to fit your fantasy."

"What makes you so sure it's today?" Clement said.

Rochefort nearly exploded at the ignorant bliss around him. "It's got to be today! All of Yuri's and Shears' movements peaked for today. Dear God, there's not a plane in the sky! Not one gun on one ship is manned! What the hell can we do about it now?" Rochefort said angrily. He fervently hoped that Layton had reached Kimmel.

"I'll tell you what! We go to those two ships and alert their skippers! What time have you got?" Clement asked.

At 7:59 a.m. the drone of high-powered aircraft engines filled their ears. Several mottled-green aircraft with large red disks on their wings and fuselages appeared, screaming out of Kola Kola Pass to Battleship Row, each carrying ugly, long torpedoes beneath their bellies.

Andy Seghesio's eyes began to water; Jack Burns gritted his teeth.

"This whole operation was a masterstroke," Burns concluded.

———

Fuchida's body trembled with excitement. There below him just where the clouds had parted lay the heart of the United States Pacific Fleet. He counted the nine battleships in the harbor, including *Pennsylvania* in drydock and the target ship *Utah*. He quickly swept the anchorage for cruisers, destroyers, auxiliaries, all where Tomi Zai said they would be—and not one defending aircraft in the air! He fired his flare gun to signal complete surprise was achieved. The Wild Eagles split into their prearranged attack formations and dove upon their unsuspecting targets. The Pacific War had begun.

Admiral Nagumo wept at the words he yearned to hear. Three thousand miles away, Yamamoto roused himself from the meditative state he had entered and smiled at the sound of Fuchida's "*Tora! Tora! Tora!*" His plan to catch the Pacific Fleet with mooring lines secured was realized.

———

Eversole had to move fast or he would be a victim of the imminent maelstrom he created. He was desperately reviewing options for taking out the chief when the sound of several explosions reverberated against the hull. When Foster's concentration waned and glanced at the ceiling, Eversole reached behind his back, pulled out a snub-nosed revolver, and emptied all six shots into Foster's massive chest. He then looked at his watch—the Japs were a few minutes early.

Shears' body twitched. For a moment, Eversole considered moving him out of the turret, but more explosions made him think better of it. He turned Shears over and was startled to see his eyes focus on him.

"Leave," Shears gasped.

"I'm sorry, Admiral, but it has to be this way," Eversole said. He saluted.

Shears blinked in understanding. Eversole picked up his pistol and brought it in front of Shears' eyes. "Should I?" he asked.

Shears blinked slowly.

Eversole pressed the pistol's barrel against Shears' temple and pulled the trigger.

He was so unnerved by the sudden grasp on his ankle, he fell and painfully struck his head on the bulkhead. In a moment, Zachariah Foster was on him, beating him with a bloody fist, blow after blow against his head.

Foster was in agony from the bullets that had punctured a lung, tore through his abdomen, and shattered his ribs. Bleeding profusely, he staggered to the explosives and ripped at the detonator wires and tubing connecting them. How proud his friend Gwyeth Jones would be that *Arizona* had at last spoken to him.

As Foster was about to yank at the wires of the last pair of tanks, his neck was gripped by incredible pain. The world went dark as he fell to the deck. A bloody-faced Eversole withdrew the stiletto from Foster's throat, and wiped it off on the dead chief's pants. He cursed as he tried to piece together the dangling wires and tubing, but they were in too much of a shambles. An explosion rattled the ship—the Japanese had found *Arizona*. He packed plastique around the surviving detonator, and started his painful egress three decks up. His painful shoulder wound prevented closing the heavy hatch to cover the carnage in the deck below, but by the sounds of things, that might not matter.

The scene he emerged into shocked Eversole to the bone. *Oklahoma* was capsizing before his eyes. A huge waterspout erupted amidships of *West Virginia* immediately forward of *Arizona*. A near-miss bomb sent a shower of water and debris upward just to port of *Tennessee*'s stern. An instant later, a column of water rose beside *Nevada*. *California* was burning and listing. The attack was barely fifteen minutes old, and every battleship on the row had sustained damage; two were already sinking. A fire raged on *Arizona*'s starboard stern, and yet another bomb found its target striking the opposite side. The hangars at Hickam Field and Ford Island were afire. No antiaircraft fire of any significance met the attackers. All the fighters were in flames on the ground. The Japs needed no insurance—these ships were doomed anyway.

Eversole staggered across deck, taking bitter comfort in the fact that a bloodied man wouldn't be an unusual sight this morning. He made for the port side of the ship where the *Vestal* was still moored. The launch still parked to her port side meant freedom. A strafing Zero fighter tore up pieces of wood decking and sent steel splinters through flesh and bone. Sailors' dress whites displayed ugly red splotches, and all around men fell in the grotesque poses of death. Eversole felt a stabbing pain in his thigh. A piece of metal the size of his thumb protruded from it.

Jerry Clement and four of his best clambered aboard *Arizona* from the *Vestal*, and tried to make sense of the chaos. Unrecognized and unchallenged, Eversole limped passed them. Clement knew where to send his men. If you wanted to blow up a battleship, head for her magazines.

"The ship's magazines. Where are they?" he asked a terrified young sailor on the run.

"The hatches are forward and right here," he pointed nervously. "We gotta get off, man! Those fucking Japs mean business!" Bullets from a strafing Nakajima splattered against the number three turret above them.

The enraged Clement slapped the sailor with the back of his hand and pulled out his pistol, putting it against the man's cheek. "Listen to me, you son of a bitch! I need to know where those magazines are and I haven't got time to follow directions! Take me there and right goddamn now!"

The boy actually seemed to calm at this latest threat. It was much more immediate. A Jap plane might kill him, but the madman before him had much better odds. "Let's start with the forward hatch. There's a fire below in the passage to the stern magazines and it may be impassable."

"What's your name, son?"

"Cangemo. Giosue Cangemo, sir. Seaman Apprentice."

"All right, then, Jez. Let's get moving."

An Aichi dive bomber passed over Battleship Row after dropping its bomb on a hangar on Ford Island. He was so low Clement could see the pilot's goggled face. He emptied his .45 at the plane. Suddenly, it's engine caught fire. It spun on its wing and crashed into the harbor. Though his .45 slugs couldn't have brought down the plane, he liked to think they helped the cause, just a little.

———————

Because smoke had obscured their targets during the first pass, Ito Fujita's perfect arrowhead formation of five bombers came around for another run on Battleship Row. *Arizona* lay in the crosshairs of his bomb sight. Antiaircraft fire was now becoming more intense and his plane was jostled by the bursts of heavy-caliber shells. Nevertheless, he concentrated carefully on his target and dropped his bomb, hoping for a hit on the ship's bridge. He held the belief that the bomb's small load of explosive would do little damage to the battleship's armored decks. The best he could hope for would be to disable her for a long time. From the looks of things, the torpedo boys had done the real work. As the missile fell away from his plane, Fujita noted a flash on *Arizona's* port stern quarter. Someone else's bomb had scored a hit. The stern of the ship was burning.

A burst of flack sent shards of metal through his port wing. The Americans were getting the range. He applied power and climbed, then circled, not wanting to leave the scene until he saw his bomb explode.

Chief Gwyeth Jones commandeered the cab he was riding in when the driver refused to go any farther. Jones tossed the cabbie out, got behind the wheel, and roared off. At the gate of the pier by the Navy Yard he leapt from the taxi and ran to the waiting boats. Many of them were bringing oil-soaked, horribly burned sailors from the broken ships. A wounded officer who had just tied up a small launch staggered toward him.

"You've got to help me, doctor," he struggled to say. A large piece of shrapnel protruded from his leg, while a shoulder wound bled. His eyes were almost shut tight, each blackened. A strafing Zero sent both men flat on the concrete.

Jones quickly rose and helped the man to an onrushing ambulance. "Thanks, mate."

A suddenly insane Jones began to pummel the officer, his massive fists cracking ribs and tearing cartilage. When he fell, Jones kicked his head repeatedly, ignoring another strafing plane and stopping only when a corpsmen pulled him away.

"Arrest him!" Jones managed to scratch out.

"We don't tend to corpses, nor do we arrest them," the corpsman answered.

The shore patrol seized Jones, who stood there looking at his ship with horror-filled eyes. They had just cuffed him when they all were bowled over by the concussive wave that followed an enormous bang. It was prelude to a deafening, thunderous roll.

Jerry Clement had entered the forward magazine with the frightened sailor. He chanced a glance at his wristwatch; it read 8:09 a.m. Just before going below, he'd seen Admiral Kidd and Captain Van Valkenburg on the flag bridge, directing *Arizona*'s antiaircraft defense at the swarm of angry gnats tormenting her. The bomber's rear gunners fired at the men of the capsized *Oklahoma*. Floundering in the oil-coated water, some were roasted alive as the tracer rounds set it afire.

Three decks down, the sailor turned to Clement when he saw the heavy watertight hatch to the powder magazine wide open.

"That shouldn't be that way," Cangemo said.

"Why's that?" Clement asked.

"An explosion or fire can't be contained, that's why! Who the hell would…"

A tearing of metal was heard overhead while the deck beneath them quaked and buckled. An instant later Clement and his tour guide vaporized.

Ito Fujita watched the hands of the stopwatch. The bomb should hit in six seconds…five…four…Two seconds before estimated contact, his target erupted in a ball of flame followed by an explosion whose force rocked his plane at eight thousand feet. He stared incredulously at what he had wrought. Could that one bomb possibly have caused such destruction? Euphoria welled up his throat. He hadn't expected to succeed so grandly. The idea that he had single-handedly killed a thousand men in an instant was mind-boggling.

Tomi Zai stood on the roof of the embassy screaming his lungs out, cheering his Wild Eagles on. The harbor was a total shambles, and the second wave had not yet arrived. The explosion knocked his feet from under him and shattered the embassy's windows. He landed heavily on his rump, but immediately rose to see a fountain of brilliant yellow and orange flame erupt from the *Arizona*. Tears rolled down his cheeks, whether from joy or horror he didn't know. That his friends had caused such a beautiful structure to meet such a horrific fate brought simultaneous pride and shame. He watched the remainder of the attack in silence. But for the grace of the gods, that ship might have well been in his navy.

"I'm so sorry!" Gwyeth Jones whispered. He heard her scream at her mortal wounding, and her death wails split the harbor again and again. His tears flowed unabashedly. *Arizona*'s two fourteen-inch forward turrets fell into the caldera created by the explosion. Her foremast collapsed into the black hole as well, and as grains of her gunpowder pelted him like sleet, she began settling into her grave.

Josh Friar, picnic basket full of breakfast still in hand, rushed to the figure surrounded by SPs. He knew Jones anywhere, out of uniform or in dress blues. His tears told the story. "I'm sorry, Chief," was all he could say.

"So am I Josh. So am I." Arm in arm, the two men watched as their home and family perished.

Lieutenant Henry Williams was in tears. He watched stunned speechless from the bridge of a destroyer moored across the harbor. He thought back to the crisp March day in 1914 when he grasped President Roosevelt's finger and put the first bolts into the keel plates of the *"Arisinoma."*

The little *Hoga* worked feverishly and gallantly. She pulled *Vestal* away from the burning *Arizona*, then raced across the harbor to beach the terribly wounded *Nevada*, who had made a gallant effort to leave the harbor. Had she settled where she stalled, she would have blocked the narrow channel for months.

Ignoring the strafing planes, the bombs and torpedoes, McManus and Brown then directed *Hoga* back to *Arizona* to pour water into her gaping wounds.

"I know it was a useless gesture, but we had to do it," McManus said.

"Yes, we did. Now, let's get on with business," Brown answered.

They set about the grisly chore of plucking her dead from the harbor and rescuing any exhausted, oil-soaked swimmers.

John Munroe's flight arrived just as the second wave from *Kido Butai* did. He found himself in a nest of angry hornets. Several of the Dauntlesses sprouted plumes of flame as the Japanese Zeros' cannon shells found their mark.

"Get them off us, Barry!" he implored his young gunner.

"Goddamn! There's so many of the bastards, sir!"

Munroe dived for the runway at Ford Island while his rear-seat gunner valiantly tried to keep the attackers at bay with his twin .30 caliber machine guns. It was hopeless. The Zeros were too many in number and too aggressive in spirit. The Japanese fighter pilots had destroyed the Army Air Force on the ground, and when they actually had live, flying targets to attack, they went at them like wolves after deer. Munroe was sprayed with bits of flesh and splatters of blood marking his gunner's end. He was on the edge of panic, and on the brink of eternity. His left wing was chewed up, and the rudder pedals felt as if they were embedded in sponges.

Just as a Zero flashed by so close overhead he felt he could have reached up out of the cockpit and touched it, fire started licking at the cowling of his sputtering engine, but he coaxed it back to life. He withstood yet another pass by a Zero, but this one pulled around much too close and too tightly, trying to beat his mates for another attack on Munroe's rear. With grudging admiration to the Zero's fantastic maneuverability, Munroe slammed the left rudder pedal, and jammed the stick to the left, momentarily giving him a chance at a classic deflection shot. He squeezed the trigger and the twin .50 caliber cowl guns clattered to life. A second later, the deadly but lightly built Zero fireballed.

Rapidly losing oil pressure and pieces of wing, Munroe didn't have time to savor his victory. All the maneuvering put Ford Island's runway way behind him. He headed for the ocean off Diamond Point, smoking all the way, hugging the ground, and praying the Dauntless would hold together for a few more minutes.

It did. He made a rather good water landing, inflated his life raft, and jumped off the wing. As the battered plane slipped beneath the waves, he cringed at the sight of his shattered gunner, most of whose head was missing.

He broke out his paddle and made for shore. He wanted very much to get back into this fight. All he needed was a plane.

Seghesio, Rochefort, Burns, and Hamilton felt useless. They'd been skillfully manipulated out of the fight for which they had trained all their professional lives, but the scene around them was brutally frank in telling them their participation wouldn't have mattered an iota. And a sense of betrayal, the absolute stupidity of everyone from the White House to Kimmel, aggravated the pain. They found cover with Mae and Lisa at the submarine base the Japanese had obviously decided to ignore. The cacophony slowly died down, as the last Japanese airplane disappeared to the north.

"They'll be back," Rochefort said, "and soon."

"To paste the subs?" Seghesio offered.

"No. The oil tank farm behind us. If they can't get the *Enterprise, Saratoga,* or *Lexington,* they'll take the next best thing," he said lighting a cigarette, "and that's the oil to feed them."

Chapter 21

Mitsuo Fuchida landed aboard *Akagi* just before noon, the deck crew euphoric with the tales of victory brought back by the other pilots as they landed. He was overjoyed to see the first wave's aircraft, which had landed two hours earlier, being readied for a third assault.

"Will the American fleet be able to sail in less than six months?" Nagumo asked.

On Fuchida's answer hinged the third assault's fate. The truth was far more honorable than his wishes.

"No, it will not. But we did not hit the oil storage tanks, nor the repair facilities and submarine base, as we were ordered to concentrate on capital warships and the airfields to prevent a counterattack."

"Did you see any signs of carrier aircraft?"

"We saw perhaps a dozen Navy dive bombers. SBD types. They flew in during the height of the attack. We decimated them."

"What about B-17s?" Kusaka asked.

"We attacked several of them in aerial engagements, and destroyed several on the ground. The runways and maintenance facilities were destroyed, and…"

"So," Nagumo interrupted. "There may be B-17s as yet undamaged in Hawaii or enroute. The *Enterprise* and *Lexington* are still at large. We have won a major victory and our ships have survived without so much as a scratch. We lost only twenty-nine planes over the target, and a dozen more in landing accidents. I say we've pushed our luck as far as we can. Let's set course for home."

"I concur," Kusaka said firmly.

Genda saw the twisted look of imminent insubordination on Fuchida's face and spoke up before the strike leader could muster the words.

"Sir, I beg you to reconsider. The oil tanks and repair yards are intact. We own the sky over Pearl Harbor. We could send in a smaller force to hit those targets while we call our tankers to refuel the fleet, and arm the remaining aircraft to strike the American carriers should we find them. They have nothing left with which to strike us."

"What about their submarine force?" Nagumo asked. "They have survived, have they not?"

"They can be made to rest on the harbor mud in two hours."

Nagumo's mind raced between the poles of initiative and safety. Attacking again might buy long-term safety, but if the Americans sank two of his carriers by air strikes from their own carriers or attack by submarines, the vast advantage he had gained this morning would be nullified. His primary mission was to make the American fleet inoperable for six months. He did that.

"I'm sorry, Genda. It's time to withdraw. We're going home with our mission accomplished and our force intact."

Yamamoto pondered what he had wrought. The euphoria of absolute success was brief. Now, he had to conquer the Pacific in six months and prepare to defend it against the industrialized might and consummate hate of the United States of America. Hearing reports of how *Arizona* died could only hint at the vengeful enmity Americans had in their hearts for Japan.

Winston Churchill heard about the attack and did not so much as blink an eye. "We shall declare war immediately." He also had just received word from the Hawaiian consulate that none of the force he had sent there had survived. His remorse was brief. The ends justified the means, he thought. Who had said that? Was it Macchiavelli, or his own Savrola?

Franklin D. Roosevelt suppered with Edward R. Murrow when news of the attack on his fleet reached him. He was particularly distressed to learn of the horrible death of *Arizona*. That the fleet had been smashed, that he'd been taken by such utter surprise tore at his heart. Cordell Hull reported that Nomura claimed he had no knowledge of the attack.

"That pissant is a lying son of a bitch," he remarked to Roosevelt.

Sumner Welles knew better. That his position was vindicated was of small comfort to him. His country had been caught asleep, despite his best efforts. He looked forward to his luncheon with Oumansky tomorrow.

No one could identify the body of the wounded officer Gwyeth Jones beat to death. His fingerprints were unmatchable in the American military, active or covert. You couldn't accuse a man of murder when the victim didn't exist. Jones left the hospital a few weeks later, at last bound for the gestating USS *Iowa*, BB-61. He took with him one of the best stewards and cooks in the United States Navy.

Andy Seghesio was sent back to New York to recuperate. The Marines needed time to determine what to do with him. Mae was pregnant again, and the interlude would do them both good. Lisa Seghesio married Tommy Hamilton, who was sent to Quantico, Virginia to train a new Marine fighter squadron. Jack Burns, too, was called back to Virginia. Someone in the Navy thought highly enough of him to give him command of the brand new USS *Essex*, the first attack aircraft carrier of her class. Almost finished in the birthing yards at Newport News, she would be the biggest and fastest afloat.

John Munroe became the CAG of *Enterprise*'s Air Group Six. He was destined to have a very busy year keeping the Japanese at bay.

Joe Rochefort cracked JN-25 a few months later. Vindication for his humiliation on December 7, 1941 came on June 4, 1942, when his code-busting efforts led to the sinking of *Akagi, Kaga, Hiryu,* and *Soryu* at Midway.

Epilogue

The day dawned bright and sunny, with the Hawaiian trade winds blowing gently across the harbor's busy surface. The honor guard came to rigid attention as an elderly but spirited gentleman in an elegantly tailored navy blue suit made his way aboard. His close-cropped, salt-and-pepper hair and tortoise shell eyeglasses gave him a dignified and scholarly appearance. The gentleman was accompanied by his wife, two daughters, and his son, a smart young lieutenant (jg) with wings of gold on his chest and an Annapolis class ring on his finger. The five of them sat in chairs under an awning among former shipmates, who greeted him warmly.

Joshua Friar thought back to that long-ago Sunday. He looked to the pier where he and his friend had watched in tears as their ship died. Now, one of them was coming home for good, the other just on a visit.

"Chief, it's time. Come with me, please," the admiral in charge of the ceremony said.

His chest shuddered and his chin quivered.

"Are you okay, Joshua?" his wife asked.

"I'm fine, Ellie. Come on, Gwyeth," he said to his son.

"Yes, sir, Chief," the young lieutenant replied.

Josh Friar held the funerary urn firmly with both hands as the Navy chaplain recited the sailor's burial prayer. His son provided support by holding him firmly. With a tear coursing down his cheek, Josh handed the urn to a waiting diver with the Chaplain's concluding words, "We commit his body to the deep."

"Rest easy, my friend. And don't get into any fisticuffs with Chief Foster!" he admonished the urn. "Tell the Captain and the Admiral they're in my thoughts every day."

Seven rifles fired three rounds each while the bugler played Taps. Gwyeth Friar stood at rigid attention and saluted as his godfather rejoined his shipmates in the place where they died fifty years ago to the day. Thus did Josh Friar help Chief Jones to keep his promise to Arizona that they would be immortalized together.

"Is the president still planning on coming this morning?" he asked the admiral.

"Yes, he is, Chief. Mr. Bush is anxious to meet you."

"Well, you tell him *Arizona* is anxious to meet him, too."

More
Ben Baglio!

Please turn this page

for previews of

"I'LL BE SEEING YOU"

"AMERICAN PATROL"

and

"IT'S BEEN A LONG, LONG TIME"

the second, third and fourth books in

Ben Baglio's WWII Series

From Infamy to Victory

Ben Baglio's
From Infamy to Victory World War II Series
continues with *I'll Be Seeing You, American Patrol*
and the concluding book in the four-part series,
It's Been A Long, Long Time.

In *A String of Pearls*, we were just introduced to the intriguing events leading up to the Japanese "sneak" attack on Pearl Harbor. We met Chief Gwyeth Jones and Seaman Josh Friar, Marine Captain Andy Seghesio, Navy Lieutenant Commander Jack Burns, Squadron Commander John Munroe, Navy Lieutenant Joe Rochefort, Marine pilot Major Tommy Hamilton, their wives and children. We were also introduced to the discussions of Winston Churchill and Franklin Roosevelt on the eve of war, and got to know the Japanese who planned the Pearl Harbor attack, including the ferocious Tomi Zai, robbed of his life's ambition to fly in combat, but who nonetheless served Japan heroically in her brightest hour. We met and said goodbye to characters Yuri Popov, Yvette, Chad Eversole and Admiral Shears.

In *I'll Be Seeing You*, the second installment of this character-driven series, relationships are further developed, as are the first desperate battles of World War II. Roosevelt and Churchill's meeting during Christmas of 1941 tells of their broadening alliance. *Arizona* veterans Gwyeth Jones and Joshua Friar are assigned to guide the gestating battleship USS *Iowa*. Jack Burns' initial frustration at not being assigned a combat command is turned completely around, while Andy Seghesio helps get the marines on a war footing.

We are introduced to two torpedo plane pilots, Steven Amato and Danny Morello, who chronicle the Doolittle Raid and the climactic Battle of Midway. We meet Patsy Teresa and his best buddy Smitty, civilians turned Mud Marines, as they live the anguish of Guadalcanal.

We meet Sammy Stahlman, Larry LaMonica, and Joe Ruggiero who will define war on new personal terms. We are also introduced to two German subversives who come to the United States under incredible aliases to buy Adolph Hitler insurance for victory. And finally, we meet the Bedford Boys, whose fame will come to define the Normandy invasion.

In *American Patrol*, the third book in this series, the reader finds the United States fully engaged in war, and the tide of battle is turning further against her enemies. Her armed forces have taken the offensive against the Germans in North Africa and Italy, and defeated the Japanese on Guadalcanal. Andy Seghesio receives his first general's star, and Jack Burns captains his brand new carrier into battle in the Pacific.

Our well-known combatants pursue war on a personal level, and are asked to do the impossible regularly. The reader observes the battles of Kasserine, Sicily, Tarawa, the Marianas, and the Gilbert Islands through the eyes of Teresa, Smith, Stahlman, LaMonica and Ruggiero, who find the enemy entrenched in long-held territories and ordered to fight to the death. A marine pilot introduced in *A String of Pearls* returns, incredibly, against all odds, while German subversives make their desperate move to change the course of the war.

We are also introduced to scientists creating the ultimate weapon system, racing against their German counterparts who have already introduced super weapons into a fast-changing war. We follow the Bedford Boys as they prepare for the invasion of France at Normandy, and watch our old friends Steven Amato and Danny Morello as they are actively engaged in the war against the Japanese. And the reader knows that the worst is yet to come on the long road to victory.

It's Been a Long, Long Time is the fourth and final book in Ben Baglio's thrilling series. This book brings the reader to the climactic battles that bring World War II to a conclusion. The battles of Okinawa, Iwo Jima, Normandy, and the Bulge have ultimate consequences for our characters and their families.

Though the enemy knows he is on the brink of defeat, he fights more tenaciously than ever. Come ashore on Normandy with the Bedford Boys and Sammy Stahlman. Follow General George Patton through France and into Germany with Larry LaMonica and Joe Ruggiero. Listen in on strategy discussed in the Pentagon and Teheran. Stand on the bridge of a carrier with Andy Seghesio and Jack Burns when they come face-to-face with Tomi Zai. Meet Colonel Paul Warfield Tibbets, Jr. as he prepares his bomber *Enola Gay* for one of the last missions of the war.

The four-book set tells of the soldier's story through the lens of a changing America forged by world war. Societal changes are revealed by experiences on the battlefield, where we come to realize that nothing will ever be the same again, and that the sacrifice of thousands would demand it be that way. Indeed, the books chronicle the changes in the world driven by the evolution of Americans through the crucible of war.

About the Author

Ben Baglio has had a lifelong interest in history. His particular affection for the generation who fought World War II both on the homefront and on the farflung fields of Europe and the Pacific is personified by his first historical novel, *A String of Pearls*. The testaments to the desperate battles, from the *Arizona* resting at Pearl Harbor to the American cemetery at Normandy's Colleville Sur Mer overlooking Omaha Beach, speak to him of unimaginable valor and hope for better tomorrows.

Dr. Baglio has spent his career working as a public school educator and college professor. He is the author of the four-book World War II series *From Infamy to Victory*, as well as his nonfiction work *Kid's Are The Easy Part*, an insider's perspective on school reform. When not working as an educational consultant, he continues to write historical fiction. He lives with his wife on Long Island, New York.

Breinigsville, PA USA
23 July 2010
242296BV00001B/38/P